A BLAZE OF VALKYRIES

A Viking Dragonriders Adventure

DRAGONRIDERS OF SKALA
BOOK II

MELINDA R. CORDELL

Rosefiend Publishing.

Rosefiend Publishing.

A BLAZE OF VALKYRIES: A VIKING
DRAGONRIDER ADVENTURE

Copyright © 2022 by Melinda R. Cordell.

Ordering information: For details, contact the publisher at
hello@melindacordell.com

Cover design by We Got You Covered.

Amazon ISBN: 978-1-953196-56-9

Second Edition: May 30, 2022

Some parts of this book were originally published in the second one-third
of THE FLAME OF BATTLE, 2018 edition.

10 9 8 7 6 5 4 3 2 1 blast off!

❀ Created with Vellum

A DUBIOUS OPPORTUNITY

WHILE SINKR, HIS HEAD FULL OF PLUNDERED RICHES, had ordered Dyrfinna's ship to keep sailing, the rest of the Queen's fleet had taken shelter during the storm that had suddenly blown up.

Rjupa and Shriken had attempted to follow her ship in the wild winds, for now they were unable to lower their sail, and were racing wildly across the dangerous waves, the troughs between them growing deeper. The ship barely broke through the foam at the top of each wave.

"Try and fly closer!" she called to Shriken.

"Are you sure?" the silver dragon called back.

Rjupa understood what she meant, for the same gales that were sending the sea into a frenzy and rending the ship's sail was also making it almost impossible for Shriken to stay safely aloft. She and her dragon could survive being plummeted into the ocean from this height, but the icy water would quickly kill her dragon.

"I'm just trying to figure out how to save them," she called, trying to make her small voice heard over the screaming wind. "Maybe we could guide them to—"

Rain suddenly blasted down, so thick that Rjupa couldn't see. It was like suddenly standing under a water-fall. Everything vanished – ship, ocean, land.

Shriken shouted something that she couldn't hear, the dragon barely keeping her wings as the rain and the gusting winds pitched them to and fro.

Rjupa wanted with all her heart to keep pursuing Dyrfinna's ship – feared with all her heart losing her friends in a shipwreck, Skeggi in particular. Anguish tore at her, but she and Shriken were in great danger, and she would not let her silver dragon be killed in this storm.

She tapped on Shriken's neck the signal to return, and the dragon carefully wheeled around, fighting the blasts of wind that threatened to pitch her sideways, or blow her wings inside out, a very painful thing for a dragon to endure, though not as painful as the fall that ensued.

Rjupa frantically tried to clear the water from her face, but it was everywhere, blown in all directions by the cruel wind. She couldn't see anything, anyhow. In fact, in the growing darkness, flung in all directions, she could scarcely tell which way was up and which was down. This disorientation was even more dangerous, a common effect of storms and wind. Rjupa couldn't even tell if they were flying, moving forward or sideways – or straight down.

A dark shape loomed to their side. *The ocean!* Rjupa realized with a cold rush of horror. Somehow the wind had thrown them off so badly that they were now almost sideways in the air, the dragon's wings rowing frantically to get purchase and right themselves. And now she could feel gravity pulling at them.

Swiftly on her dragon's back she slid her palm from right to left to give Shriken her bearings while drumming with her other fist, which meant *Danger!*

Shriken fought her way to the level, Rjupa frantically turning her with the directional strokes of her palm, and the darkness of the ocean slowly swung below them, where it was supposed to be.

Now they were low enough for things to come into view again, despite the thick rain. Waves growing taller and taller, smashing over and swamping rocky islands that ordinarily rose clear of the ocean.

A faint bugling to their left. A flicker of flame, barely seen through the grey curtain of rain. Serja was calling them.

The relief that washed over her was so strong, there were few times in her life that she'd felt it so strongly. Shriken shook water from her face and bugled back as they banked toward the sound.

On the way back, they were struck by a downdraft that flung them toward the ocean as if they'd been swatted by a giant, but managed to recover, finally reaching the other dragons where they huddled on a great cliff overlooking a somewhat quiet bay. Below were the Queen's ships, and it appeared that most of them had made it to safety.

But Dyrfinna's ship was still out there – and Finna, and Gefjun, and Ostryg, and her dear Skeggi. She would have given anything to change places with him, to have some magic set him safely on Shriken's back while she took his place on the ship, wherever they were, whatever their fate.

The dragons moved aside as Shriken came flying in, trying to stabilize herself against the winds that crashed into the rocks, and she stumbled to a landing on the cliff under an overhang that kept the worst of the rain off.

Both dragon and rider collapsed, and the other drag-onriders and dragons gathered to help them limp to a more secure location against the back wall of the cliff, where they collapsed again, half-fainting. Rjupa had never felt so relieved to feel solid stone at her back and under her legs. Her body still felt as if it were pitching up and down in space.

The other dragonriders came over and, with their woolen saddle-blankets, roughly toweled Shriken down to dry her off and get her circulation going.

Her silver dragon draped a wing over Rjupa, keeping the rain off her, and she snuggled up close to Shriken's

3

side, the smooth silver scales warming her side and her cheek. The wind howled and blasted rain against the cliff, briefly whirled it away, then blasted the cliff again.

"Rjupa."

She realized somebody had said her name several times. She shook herself out of her dull thoughts and looked out from underneath her dragon's wing. "Sorry. I was in my own thoughts."

"Think nothing of it," said Egill, who crouched at her side with a steaming pottery cup of fruit wine. He was in charge of the dragons, the queen's second-in-command, as well as Dyrfinna's estranged father. Rjupa thought it funny that a man of such status would kneel at her side in his fine riding robes, offering her a humble cup of fruit wine. "Here, drink this. It will warm you."

It had been heated in dragon flame, so the cup smelled of that metallic tang of their fire. She drank and the fruit wine, a mild alcoholic drink, warmed her. The wine tasted just like the grapes that grew on the south slopes of Mount Pyrr, ripe and sweet in fall, and how she longed for that warm fall sunshine. But this was a very good alternative. She sipped, enjoying the taste – and thought of how she and Skeggi walked among the grapes earlier in fall, how he'd put a sweet grape in her mouth, and how, when they kissed, he tasted so sweet....

She clutched the warm cup to her chest. "I tried to follow Finna's ship," she said softly. "Please, as soon as this storm lightens up, I need to go back out there and find them."

Egill's face darkened at the mention of his daughter, but said, "If you are not needed for other duties when this storm passes, I can let you go. But it will only be for a short while, because we need you to carry messages back to the Queen to keep her apprised of our movements."

A gust of wind blasted rain over Shriken's wing, and cold mist drifted in around Egill for a moment before the blast subsided. Rjupa's heart went out to the fighters on the ships who were out in the cold rain, who didn't get to curl up against a dragon's warm side and wait it out in shelter. Once again she was struck by the incongruity of her station – a former thrall held by Iron Skull himself, who had lived under his cruelty, now friends with the Queen and her second-in-command and riding a dragon.

Now she was even more keenly aware of why she had been raised up and her friends had been blocked by Egill.

She looked him in the eyes now. "By rights, my friends should be here tonight with their dragons," she said. "Not just me alone. They rescued Thora that night when the Danes invaded."

Egill's eyes darkened. "A victory that would not have been possible if you had not killed Iron Skull and broken their command."

Shriken rumbled low in her throat. She knew what she meant. *Tread carefully, my dear.*

Rjupa lowered her eyes, out of respect to Egill, but also because she didn't like to talk about this decision of hers. "I, too, owe my lives to them. The Danes had found me, and I flaunted my victory to them, and was prepared to throw myself upon my dagger before they got to me. But your daughter and her friends rescued me, and they brought me here, where I could live a life that I never dreamed I could have."

Egill made some sputtering noises under his breath, but then said, "Give yourself some credit. Your work here has been exemplary, and you've risen on your own merits."

She wasn't so sure. Her friends all had their merits, too. But after Thora had died, Egill had immediately disbanded the Corae Guard and banished her friends from riding dragons – except for Rjupa, who suddenly became the most valuable rider in the stables, going on exclusive missions with Egill and the Queen.

Yes, he didn't suddenly choose to make her his personal favorite because of merit. Gefjun had told her how despondent Dyrfinna was after she'd heard the news. He had banned Dyrfinna from the stables altogether.

"I only ask that I may be released for a time to search for my friends," Rjupa said.

"You may, but we need you to return and deliver messages as we move closer to the field of battle," Egill said. "I'm sure they'll be fine."

Rjupa wasn't so sure. But she said nothing more, and when the next morning dawned clear, she and Shriken took off early and flew south, keeping the rising sun on their left side.

❧ 2 ❧
NONE SHALL GET
THROUGH ME

MANY LEAGUES AWAY, UPON THE WAVES OF THE NORTH Sea, the sun glared down from a cloudless sky upon six longships. One ship was facing the five incoming ships, and the gap between them was slowly closing.

This ship slipped through the waves like her namesake, the sea-flame – Saebringr. The crew had taken down her sail, and her decks were a bustle of commotion as Vikings hoisted their shields off the sides, prepared their weapons, and spoke to their comrades.

Sunlight flashed off the spears and swords in the five ships that glided through the waves toward the Saebringr like a pack of hungry wolves, the gilded dragon heads of the ships leering at the Saebringr and her crew.

Five ships against her, alone.

Dyrfinna, her dark hair braided out of her face stood at the prow of Saebringr, grimly watching the enemy come in. She wore a large wolf pelt around her shoulders, and her cloak was fastened with a silver dragon brooch, which matched the brooches her three friends wore.

A demoted dragonrider, Dyrfinna was commander of this ship and crew – though the higher-ups who had demoted her claimed otherwise. She stood with her bright sword in her hand like a Valkyrie, ready to plunge into battle.

On both sides of her stood her sword-friends, each wearing the silver dragon brooch: the Corae Guard. They had been the personal guard of the queen's daughter while she was alive. Now their mission was to revenge her.

Skeggi was just a little taller than Dyrfinna, with a crisp, brown beard that she missed running her fingers through, and wavy brown hair, and soulful brown eyes. He was singing a battle song to himself, under his breath, in a beautiful husky voice. She loved him. He did not love her back – Rjupa was his sweetheart, though she was elsewhere at the moment.

Gefjun, the healer and medic, rejoined them. She was all angles and sharp edges and sharp words, with fiery red hair. She was shouting insults at the incoming enemy in her cracked voice. "You barrel of drowned rats! You cracked pile of nut husks!"

Dyrfinna stood close to her friend. "Did you get the dragon eggs?"

Gefjun nodded. "Ostryg and I put them in here," she said, patting her medical case that she wore against her side. "It's reinforced leather so they won't be crushed, and I will stay well out of the fray when possible to tend to the wounded."

"We will do everything in our power to protect you," Dyrfinna said, gazing at her closest friend. "Those ruffians must not get their hands on these eggs. These are ours, a rare gift." *And they would rebuild my destiny,* she thought. *My whole life.*

"What happens if our ship is overpowered?" asked Ostryg. "What happens if these assholes board our ship?"

Dyrfinna didn't want to think about that. Still, she knew well that the battle didn't always go to the plucky underdog.

"Have the fisher boat ready to go," she told Ostryg. "Row Juni out of here with the eggs, if it comes to that."

"But one of those dragon eggs is yours," Ostryg reminded her. "Surely you don't intend to go down with the ship?"

No. I don't want to. Not anymore.

Dyrfinna could have counted on her fingers the times she'd succumbed to temptation – including just a few hours ago, when she nearly drowned in passion in Skeggi's arms for one glorious moment.

Now a new temptation assailed her.

Most any other time in her life, she would have been fine with sacrificing herself so her friends could be safe. But those dragon eggs ... she could sacrifice almost any other thing in the world, but not those eggs.

Just then, from the other ship, Nauma, apparently displeased with being ignored, tossed back her long, blonde hair. "With me is Illugi, the son of Gunnbjorn, wrecker of mead halls," she shouted, gesturing toward a man who scowled like an angry dwarf. "We have five warships, as you might have noticed."

"*We?*" somebody on one of King Varinn's ships asked, which struck Dyrfinna as odd.

Nauma thrust her spear into the air with a yodeling cry. Her crew behind her started chanting, "We whet our knives on your bones, for we are the child-killers! We are the child-killers!"

Dyrfinna's eyebrows went up. "Huh. Nice troops. Quality."

"You're telling me," snapped Gefjun.

Interestingly, it seemed that only Nauma's ship was cheering. The rest of the ships, with King Varinn's fighters, stood grimly silent, even looking disgusted.

Nauma shouted across the water to the other ships, "It seems fitting that my child-killers have met these scoundrels, for their Queen has killed a child as well – King Varinn's son. Isn't that right?" she cried to King Varinn's ships.

A roar from all of them, now, as they brandished

weapons at Dyrfinna's ship. "You are the child-killers!" they cried, as well as worse things.

"Yield to us, Dyrfinna Egilsdóttir, for your cruel queen has killed our prince, and now she must pay with the blood of her people."

Dyrfinna and her shipmates looked at each other in confusion.

"Are these people all out of their heads?" Gefjun said. "The king's son, a child? But the prince was a grown man."

Everybody shrugged. "Yeah. How do you consider a 25-year-old man a child?" somebody said.

"If he was a child, that would make us all little babies," Skeggi rumbled.

"Not to mention our queen killed him to get revenge on poor Thora, whom Varinn murdered."

"Aye," somebody said, and an angry mutter went around the ship.

Dyrfinna looked around, resolve growing in her. "Who are these people? This Nauma Nobodysdóttir?"

Skeggi was at her side, shaking his head. "I've heard rumors of these people. They call themselves the child-killers, for they show no mercy, not even to children. I didn't realize they worked for King Varinn. I thought he had standards."

"How can Varinn have standards?" Gefjun snapped. "He killed Thora, the best of all of us."

"*Had* standards, I said."

Dyrfinna went silent, thinking of how, after Thora came home from a visit to Varinn's keep, she so quickly became weak that she was soon unable to even lift her hand and turn a page of one of her precious books.

The tears had come trickling from her exhausted eyes. "I am too young to die," Thora had whispered. "How bitter it is to have no say in my fate. But Skuld has chosen to cut the thread of my life...but I only want to live."

That bitterness burned in Dyrfinna's heart, too –

because she was certain that Thora had been poisoned when at Varinn's house.

"Fighters, prepare for battle. Let Odin do with us what he wills." Her eyes grew steely. "We will make them pay dearly for meeting us, and their blood will flow like wine. May it be so."

A roar from her shipmates, making her heart glad, though she was still grim.

She had a sudden thought and turned to her friends. "The dragon eggs are safe?" she asked Gefjun in a low voice.

She lay a hand on her medical pouch. "I've got them wrapped and tucked safely away. I'll stay out of the fighting and tend to the wounded, but I'll do everything in my power to keep them safe. Upon her bones."

"Upon her bones," the sword-friends echoed, and Dyrfinna nodded.

Then she sprang to the bow and shouted across the water, "We are ready for you, Nauma and Illugi. And we will make you weep for daring to cross us."

From their enemy's lead ship, Nauma shouted, "So you will fight, little Dyrfinna? We are the child-killers, you know."

Ostryg climbed up on the mast, laughing. "Ha! Child-killers," he called, and laughed some more. "Just think about what a weak little shit you'd have to be, to go around bragging about killing children. Is it too hard for you to fight grown-ups? Are they too scary and mean?"

For all his faults, sometimes Ostryg really could say the right thing.

The cheers of Nauma's crew turned to angry mutters.

Dyrfinna raised a fist in the air and faced her crew and shouted, and they all roared approval for Ostryg's words.

Hakr shouted across the water. "I have never met you, Nauma – but I have crossed you before, foul Illugi, stinking rabble, wrecker of gambling houses, frequenter of brothels. You'll be killing no wee babies today. In fact, I have a gift for you."

He took two swift steps forward and flung a spear at the two adversaries. His aim was so true that he nearly ended the attack at once, but Nauma flung herself to the side barely in time. The spear hit a man directly behind her and pierced him through. He fell kicking onto the deck as black death came down over his eyes.

Nauma screamed in fury and spun back toward Dyrfinna's ship. "Forward! Forward!" she shrieked like a hawk. "Forward, and we will deal these sick wolves the death they so richly deserve!" Her voice traveled far over the water. "This is our fun. We want to shed your blood at close quarters, while looking into your eyes as you die."

"Oh, well, that sounds like great fun," Dyrfinna sneered. "Odin's eye! Are these excuses for humanity that depraved?"

Their oars struck the water, and the Vikings of King Varinn's ships roared. Dyrfinna's warriors rushed to the sides of her ship, eager to cut down as many of those so-called child killers as possible.

"Fighters, conserve your energy!" Dyrfinna cried. "Let these dogs come to us. Let them use up their strength in fighting us. We have a lengthy battle ahead, our ship against five, and there will be nobody to spell us."

But there on the ship, facing the Child-Killers, her heart sank.

A terrible grief came over her. But also a thrill of courage.

Dyrfinna drew her sword and she held it before her, the runes that said NONE SHALL GET THROUGH ME flashing before her eyes.

She thought of her mother giving her this sword. She thought of Mama standing here at her side, holding her own spear and shield, fierce, ready to cut down their enemies. Thought of her own grandmama, who had given her this ship, and how she'd fought so many battles as a pirate queen, despite the terrible odds stacked against her.

And she thought of the dragon eggs that these attackers absolutely must not get their hands on.

Dyrfinna lifted her sword high, and it flashed brilliant silver in the sun. Signe, her name was: The one who is victorious. Thinking of her mother and grandmother and their love for her, the flame of battle lit in her heart, burned through her veins. Her hand tightened on Signe's hilt.

She was ready.

Except just then, a man's harsh voice broke in.

"Stop right there, Dyerfinna!" a man shouted from behind the archers.

Dyrfinna's mouth set in a tight line. She did not bother to turn around.

"Nice of you to join us, *commander*," she said dryly.

❧ 3 ❧
BACKLASH

To the front of the ship came Sinkr, eyes still bleary, but he had at least washed his face, slicked back his hair, and was wearing his commander's cloak. He had a perfectly matched set of muscular arms. One gigantic bicep sported a blue tattoo of an eagle, wings outspread, and on the other, he wore a golden armband. Sinkr also wore a golden brooch with a beautiful stag on it.

Those golden gifts had been given by Dyrfinna's father – who said that Sinkr was like his own son. Egill had never given Dyrfinna any such golden gifts, even though she was his actual daughter.

Sinkr's long, blonde hair came down his broad shoulders like a waterfall, matching a long, neatly-trimmed beard. He was well-formed and muscular, wearing tight pants that clearly showed that he could crack a walnut with his butt cheeks.

But for all his golden gifts and gleaming muscles, he was still a little chickenshit commander.

And now Sinkr had finally awakened and had decided to take back his command. And he was *pissed*.

"I trust you've slept off your hangover," Dyrfinna said blandly without turning around.

Sinkr stalked up to Dyrfinna, then pulled himself up, flexing his muscles slightly as he posed. "I am the commander here, not you," he snarled.

"It's kind of late for you to be wandering in," she said, waving a hand at the five approaching warships.

Now Sinkr noticed, for the first time, the enemy ships arrayed against them. He looked for a moment as if he were going to weep – he even forgot to flex – but Ostryg thrust a spear into his hands. "Not the time, my friend. Defend this ship, if you want to have a prayer of continuing to command."

Sinkr let the spear fall with a clatter and turned away from Ostryg. "You should have had me awakened, Dyerfinna."

Her face flamed with anger. "You should have awakened when you heard the war horns sounding."

"Not good enough! Therefore, when we are finished with this battle, you, Dyerfinna, will take twenty lashes for your act of disobedience."

"Twenty lashes?" Gefjun cried. "Are you crazed from the heat?"

Dyrfinna felt a vein throb in her temple. "Twenty lashes? Why the fuck are you blaming me for your incompetence?"

"Do you want to make it twenty-five lashes?"

Dyrfinna stared at him, but said nothing.

Hakr, the old steersman with his white beard, came to join them. The seafarer had been around the world on many voyages in his long life, and this was why Dyrfinna had chosen him as steersman for her ship. She trusted him utterly, and treated him as her co-commander.

"This is not the time for discipline," Hakr said, his voice low. "As you can see, our enemies are watching."

"It doesn't matter," Sinkr said. "Some people need to learn their place. Now get out of my sight. I command this ship. Not her."

Dyrfinna didn't move.

"I said, get out of my sight," he added emphatically, staring straight at her.

She took an angry step back, then another, but then bumped against Gefjun, who was right there. And here was Skeggi and Ostryg. Her three sword-friends stood at her side, supporting her.

If Thora were still alive, he never would have spoken to me this way, Dyrfinna thought.

"That little turd can kiss my ass," Gefjun muttered.

Sinkr whirled, thinking Dyrfinna had said that, and shoved his muscular finger into her face. "Honey, you need to learn a hard truth about the world. There are no rewards for people like you, people who've had the Queen's daughter taking care of you and keeping you safe. And she put you in as her *guard*," he said dismissively, flicking a finger at Thora's dragon brooch that pinned her cloak, the silver brooch that Dyrfinna and her sword-friends wore. "Pff, that's just a toy to you," Sinkr added.

Dyrfinna's hand was on the hilt of her sword. She was instantly aware that Ostryg, Skeggi, and Gefjun had closed in to stand, shoulder to shoulder, with her.

"We are the Corae Guard," Dyrfinna said. "You know full well which dragon is on our brooches. She sacrificed herself to save our lives, and Thora's life. Take care of how you speak about her."

Ostryg's eyes were flat as he twirled a knife in his fingers, right in Sinkr's face. He didn't say anything, just stared at Sinkr until the young man looked away.

"That's right," Skeggi said in his musician's voice, which resonated all over the ship. "Take care about what you say about your betters."

Sinkr sneered and spun back to Dyrfinna. "My betters? How is that, may I add, when my betters raise their hand against their own family to cut them down where they stand. I don't care about your pretty dragon pins,

Dyerfinna. I don't care that you're a *demoted* dragon rider. Do you know what I care about? I can tell you for a fact that your brother didn't deserve to die at your hand. Even if you say it was an accident." Sinkr sneered the last word. "I was friends with your brother, you know."

"How were you his friend?" Dyrfinna asked. "I never saw you together."

"You don't know everything."

"No, I distinctly remember him saying that you were like a bantam rooster, attacking everybody in the ankles."

Several Vikings chuckled and Sinkr turned red. "You're young and inexperienced," he said, as if he wasn't even younger and more inexperienced. "And you're too cocky, acting like you know more than everybody else. Well, honey, that's going to bite you in the ass."

"I doubt that. I take care of my troops," she said.

"Yeah – in the same way you took care of your own brother."

Just then, a man on one of the incoming ships drew a meaty arm back to hurl a javelin.

"Watch out!" she cried. The javelin whistled in, narrowly missing Sinkr, and Dyrfinna struck it out of the air with her shield.

She truly, sincerely, wished it had struck Sinkr.

"Perhaps you should pay some attention to the enemy," Hakr scolded, standing alert with his shield up. "You see, they are almost here."

"Shield wall!" Dyrfinna called to her crew.

The shield-holders and shield-maidens that were ranged around the bulwarks now lowered their spears and locked their shields together with a shout. Behind them stood fighters with spears and swords, ready to repel any boarders.

Archers perched around the ship. The best shooters stood before the mast, where they could strike their targets without being blocked by rigging or cordage.

Just then, Nauma's archers let loose at Dyrfinna's ship. Black death rained from the sky. Those who could sing magic flung up a guard against the arrows to reinforce their armor and shield. Those who could not ducked beneath their shields. One man fell with a choking gasp.

"Steady," Dyrfinna called, for Nauma's ship had nearly reached them. Her child-killers leaned screaming over its sides, brandishing every kind of bloody weapon at them. "Let them come to us."

"I give the commands here – not you," Sinkr shouted. "I am the commander of this ship! Your daddy said so!"

But just then, Nauma brought her ship alongside Dyrfinna's, and they flung the first grappling hook into her ship.

"Throw it back out!" somebody cried, but at the same instant, somebody on Nauma's ship shouted "Heave!" and many fighters pulled on the rope, drawing it tight, and the hook caught. A second hook came clattering in, then a third. Then Nauma's warriors were pulling their ship to Dyrfinna's, the gap between ships growing smaller.

"Back away!" cried the old steersman. Quick as a wink, Hakr swung his great battle-axe and severed the ropes, which snapped, sizzling back into Nauma's ship. A space remained between the two ships. Spears and javelins and arrows flew across the gap as Hakr ducked behind his shield.

More grappling hooks came flying in. Some of them pulled tight, despite Dyrfinna's crew hacking at the ropes with swords and axes. Nauma's ships came crawling closer.

"Keep cutting the ropes so they can't board," Dyrfinna cried to her warriors. "And be ready."

Hakr nodded in approval. Despite the real peril she and her crew were facing, her heart warmed. He was like a father to her – more than that, since her own father had turned against her ...

With a great crash, the bows of two of Nauma's ships

met the front and sides of Dyrfinna's ship as the grappling hooks held and the ropes were pulled tight.

"Odin!" she whispered skyward. "Protect this ship and the dragon eggs on it!"

Battle was joined.

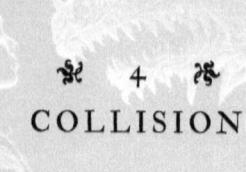

❦ 4 ❦
COLLISION

"YIELD TO US, BITCHES!" NAUMA CRIED, LEAPING TO the prow and brandishing her sword.

"Oh, you first," Dyrfinna said. "And you're going to give me that crown back if I have to take it off your corpse."

Dyrfinna stabbed with her spear, but Nauma flung up her shield, quick as a cat, and blocked it, laughing. "You talking about corpses," she said. "That's so funny."

One of Nauma's henchmen brought an axe down toward Dyrfinna like a sledgehammer, and she barely tumbled back in time. The axe sliced through where she'd been and cut a gigantic divot out of the ship's side.

Though Dyrfinna's main concern was to keep her crew alive against five ships full of the enemy, she couldn't help but focus on Thora's crown. She wanted, more than anything, to kill Nauma and rip that crown off her head.

She attacked again, but Nauma merely jumped back into her ship – much to Dyrfinna's frustration.

"Hold the ships steady!" one of the child-killers cried. "Attack!"

"Stand firm, crew!" Dyrfinna cried.

Metal clashed with metal, and the shock of arms on all sides of her ship rang out. Dyrfinna thrust and slashed at the Vikings that crowded to scramble aboard. Dyrfinna's crew lifted their shields to block the intruders, working their swords and spears around the edges against the enemy. Behind them, fighters with spears and pikes stabbed across the small spaces between the ships and took out anybody who tried to climb over.

Shield to shield, Dyrfinna's warriors defended their lives with the courage of despair. All along the edges of Dyrfinna's ship, there was no space between her fighters, who stood shoulder to shoulder to keep the rabble off their ship. The air was filled with arrows, flashing spears, and swords cutting into shields and fighters.

There was only the narrowest crossing point for each ship, but Nauma's Vikings were doing their best to come over, one at time.

"We need warriors with lances!" Dyrfinna called again. "Step up, quickly!"

"That's enough out of you, Dyerfinna," Sinkr's voice rang out. He was standing next to one of these crossing places, and now he turned from the fight. "Get it through your head. I am the commander of this ship, not you. I make the commands, not you."

"He's a commander!" somebody from Nauma's ship shouted. "Grab him!"

"I don't care who knows it!" Sinkr yelled defiantly at the enemy, flexing slightly to make his muscles pop out. "I'll tell you who makes the rules on this sh—"

A burly giant of a man leaned over from Nauma's ship and clubbed Sinkr in the back of the head with one great fist. Sinkr promptly collapsed.

Nauma's crew caught his limp body before it could fall into the sea and hauled it onto their ship – though they had a little trouble when his well-formed jutting buttcheeks got stuck on the sill of the ship, and they had to give Sinkr an extra yank to get him onto their deck.

"We have your commander!" they shouted, dancing

around Sinkr's prone form on their deck. "We have your exceptionally beautiful commander. Glory is ours!"

"You can keep him, thanks," somebody behind Dyrfinna shouted.

"Gladly," shouted one of the enemy shieldmaidens as she dragged the unconscious Sinkr toward the back of the ship. "He's our prisoner now."

Dyrfinna looked back at her friends and shrugged.

"That's just really sad," Skeggi said, not sad at all. "Well, I guess you're our commander now."

Dyrfinna grinned as she went back to directing the battle with Hakr's very capable assistance.

Most of Nauma's fighters were forced to be spectators further back on their ships, because there wasn't enough space at the front of the ship for all of them to fight. But the archers among them kept a deadly rain of arrows falling into Dyrfinna's ship.

The odds were about equal at first, but as Dyrfinna caught up spears and hurled them into the midst of her foes, she knew that fresh fighters would keep pouring in against her weary crew. Her fighters would be thinned while theirs would not.

Nauma, led by her strongest warriors, shrilled battle-cries and tried to fight their way aboard Dyrfinna's ship, and Dyrfinna herself raced over to block them. "No quarter!" she cried.

"You can't keep us back forever!" Nauma shouted, and she placed a foot on the edge of Dyrfinna's ship. Her sword cut through the shoulder of one of Dyrfinna's fighters, who crumpled to the deck.

"Come on!" Nauma shouted, and she leapt through the gap onto Dyrfinna's ship, followed by two of her fighters.

Dyrfinna leapt forward with her sword, seeing only Thora's crown. One of the attackers slammed their shield against hers with extraordinary force, throwing her back.

A cry of victory rose from Nauma's child-killers as she set foot on Dyrfinna's deck. "Forward!" shouted the child-killers, pushing to follow her. Nauma laughed, blonde braids flying, and thrust her sword through one of Dyrfinna's crew members –

A stone came flying in, smashing into Nauma's shield, and driving her back against the side of the ship, stunned.

"How do you like that, hah?" Hakr cried. The old steersman had seized that rock from out of the ballast and had flung it.

Roaring like a bull, Hakr followed his stone on the attack, slashing at Nauma as she fought to rise.

"Get her! Get her!" Dyrfinna smashed into the group of Nauma's warriors and buried her sword into another man's shoulder between the plates of armor. She kicked the dying man aside as she desperately fought to get at Nauma.

Skeggi lopped another one's head off, and down the enemy fell.

"Stop her before she gets away! She's wearing Thora's crown!" Dyrfinna cried.

Nauma's last warrior seized her, and carried back aboard her ship, reeling – the crown still on her head.

"After them! After them!" shouted Dyrfinna, her reso-nant voice carrying over the clash of arms and groans of men, as she leapt into the gap before Nauma's fighters could close it. She hacked at the enemy on all sides, cutting them down at close quarters as they strove to do the same to her. "Forward, for Thora's sake! Cut down every one of these foul creatures and get Thora's crown back!" Dyrfinna shrilled.

She hacked and slashed, hardly knowing what she was doing, as if a Valkyrie were driving her sword and shield.

Through the crush of fighters and shields, Dyrfinna glimpsed Nauma on the other end of her ship, trying to get to her feet.

Dyrfinna's eyes locked with hers. "Come here, Nauma! Is it too hard for you to fight adults? Would you rather kill helpless babies?"

But Skeggi seized her arm.

"You can't conquer her whole ship on your own," he said sternly. "Fall back now."

Dyrfinna groaned in despair, on fire to break through the crowd and kill Nauma.

Nauma just smirked at Dyrfinna and adjusted Thora's crown on her head.

"Bring that troublesome bitch to me alive," she called. "I can have some real fun with her."

"Gladly," one of the fighters said.

Spears and pikes suddenly sprang out at Dyrfinna more thickly than before, nearly impaling her. She was forced to leap back onto her ship, bitter and angry.

Already the child-killers who had fled Nauma's ship were climbing back on board from the other ships behind hers.

Dyrfinna knew that her fighters, stretched thin, were not going to hold their one ship against so many.

"We can't win against these odds," Skeggi said quietly as they climbed back into Dyrfinna's ship.

"Don't say that," she warned, taking her place by his side. "You need to fight so we can all see Rjupa again."

She thought of that kiss that she and Skeggi shared in the water. A flame of anguish lit inside her heart, and she spun away and savagely cut down an attacker.

That Viking spun and brought down his axe before she could twist out of its way. The axe's edge slammed against her leather armor and she found herself flung back against her comrades, throwing up her shield to defend herself against her attacker, who lunged after her, swinging his axe down hard into the edge of her shield. The blade stuck fast between the planking, and he yanked it back hard, nearly jerking her wounded shoulder out of its socket.

Her shoulder was on fire.

She turned on her attacker, and when her mouth opened, a bellow broke out of it ... a sound she hadn't

heard since the awful night that she had nearly trans-
formed into an undead draugr.

The world went red and her sword flew as if it had a
mind of its own. Though he tried to fight her off, her
sword kept getting past his as her fury worked through
her and her silver sword, inscribed with the runes NONE
SHALL GET PAST ME, fairly caught fire. She was faintly
aware of people getting out of their way as she drove him
back, but her white-hot focus was on killing that man.

He backed up against the side of the boat, still trying
to defend himself. Several of Nauma's men ran to his
rescue, but Dyrfinna whirled and cut through them, then
leapt back and buried her sword in the man's neck.

He collapsed before she could pull her sword free, and
she ducked as the other two men came on. She yanked the
sword out with a spurt of blood and charged the other
two with a scream, lunging for their legs.

She sliced up into one man's groin and he fell, blood
spurting with the rhythm of his heart.

The man next to him turned a florid face on her, as if
he were about to explode. "That was my brother! You
killed my brother!" he shouted as he raised his sword and
lunged. She barely dodged his blade, and felt the sharp
pain of its cut upon her cheek.

"I'm a brother-killer," Dyrfinna snarled as she blocked
his attack, their swords clashing. "It's part of my legacy."
While his furious eyes were full on hers, she stabbed him
deep in the side with her long dagger and yanked it
upward before she pulled loose and shoved him away to
bleed out.

She couldn't help but feel a pang of guilt as he crumpled in agony to the bottom of her ship. She couldn't help
but think of her own brother. If he'd lived – if she hadn't
killed him – he would have been on this deck with his
sword, fighting with her. And her father would approve
of her.

Ha. Even if she led armies and won battles, he'd still

look at her, and all he'd see was the person who killed his darling son.

She turned back to the next attackers—more attackers, an eternal series of attackers.

The day dragged by as the fight raged.

It's only a question of time, Dyrfinna realized as she worked her sword from behind the shield's protection. Her arm on fire, her body exhausted, longing for rest, longing for water, she knew that she and her soldiers faced only one fate.

But the whole time she held her little sister Aesa in mind and knew that she was going to fight until the last extremity. None of these bastards was ever going to hurt her little sister if she had any say in the matter. And if she was going to die, she was going to take as many of these people as she could with her.

"We can't die," she muttered as a fighter closed in on her. "We have to stay alive ... we have to keep Aesa safe. We have to revenge Thora."

And get her crown back, she thought. Not surprisingly, after that initial rush, Nauma had not rejoined the fight, but had vanished. So she was a coward, then.

Dyrfinna clashed against her attacker, but though she'd been trying to keep a tight grip on her sword in her blood-slick hand, it slipped. The attacker lunged past her guard. She tried to pull back, but it wasn't far enough – his sword cut into Dyrfinna's shoulder, the second time she'd been wounded. She yanked herself loose with a spray of blood. That was going to hurt later, but right now, in the initial shock, it was a numb pain, dulled.

Dyrfinna brought her sword around and struck his sword away, brought up her shield, and slammed it into his body. Her sword darted like a serpent to bite the man on the side of the neck. A bright spurt of blood leapt into the air with his heartbeat as he shrieked and fell.

She longed for a drink of water. Though they fought on the ocean, her throat was so dry that they might as well have been fighting on the desert sand. She tightened the buckler of her shield and turned to face the next attacker.

But a new sight made her heart drop into her stomach.

While the battle had been going on, one of King Varinn's ships, unable to get through the other ships that surrounded them, had been lurking at a distance, its fighters cooling their heels.

A gap had opened between Nauma's ships. Now this ship had all its oars out, and it was rowing at top speed toward her through this gap. The lion on the prow of this ship was made of iron, which extended down its bow and reinforced its front – making the ship an incredibly effective battering ram.

"Fighters, brace yourselves! An iron ship is going to ram us!" Dyrfinna cried.

The ship crashed into the side of her longship. Timber splintered and groaned, and the impact sent most everybody tumbling, including all the warriors who blocked boarders from Nauma's ships with their shield-wall.

The Vikings on this ship were fresh and vigorous, and had been waiting hours to enter the fray. As soon as the ship struck, they came over the side into Dyrfinna's ship with hot fury, shouting battle cries and swinging their axes and swords overhead.

By contrast, Dyrfinna's forces had been fighting all day under the hot sun without a break; they were exhausted, thirsty, wounded. Their barrel of fresh water was nearly empty.

5

BERSERKER

IN THE BACK OF THE SHIP, GEFJUN WAS OVERWHELMED with the wounded, but she worked quickly, binding up the warriors' wounds, quickly assessing how badly they were hurt and what she needed to do – or could do – to fix them.

And now these invaders were swarming onto the ship, right into the part of the deck where Gefjun had gathered her wounded. She'd been thrown off her feet by the impact and fought her way back up. Dyrfinna was fighting fiercely nearby, too engrossed in the battle to see what was happening to Gefjun.

One of the attackers picked Gefjun up by the back of her shirt and lifted her bodily off her feet.

"You stinking bastard cesspool!" Gefjun cried as her work knife fell from her fingers, clattering onto the deck. She tried to grab it even though she was dangling in the air.

The attacker shook her once like a misbehaving puppy, laughing. "Such a tongue on this one," he roared. "Do you bite, shrew?"

She tried to kick him in the groin, but he yanked her to one side in the air, and her kick went wide. He laughed again, and drew his sword.

Gefjun spit full in his face.

Hate blazed in his eyes as he shook her. "Apologize for that, or I'll make you apologize at the point of this sword."

Gefjun's eyes flashed. "I'm sorry that was such a feeble wad of spit. If I could drink a flagon of water right now, I would have been able to do a better job of it. Now give me a sword, so I can beat your sorry ass in battle."

He pulled her close so his stinking breath was full in her face, and the tip of the sword cut her cheek.

Gefjun stopped kicking and held very still, the sword hovering near her eyes.

The man laughed, low. "Finally quiet now, aren't you? It's so much more peaceful this way."

Still holding her in the air, he set the sword's point against her throat, smiling as she froze. "Will you wiggle and fight against me now?" he sneered. "I think not. Now, honey, the only way you're going to beat my ass is if you gaahwhhh."

"I'm sorry, what?" Gefjun asked.

His whole body shuddered as a spot of red suddenly spread out from his heart, turning his white linen red with blood.

His eyes rolled back and he collapsed, revealing a furious Ostryg behind him, yanking a sword out of his back.

Gefjun fell to the ground, choking. Ostryg was shaking, and his eyes were wide. "Did that bastard hurt you?" he demanded.

"You beat him to it," she coughed, picking up her work knife.

"He cut you," Ostryg immediately swooped down at her side, wiping the blood with his thumb.

"Not badly," Gefjun said, but Ostryg's eyes were wild. With his thumb, he wiped her blood across his forehead and eyes.

"That's unhygienic," she said under her breath, but

backed away. The spirit of the raging bear was entering his heart now – she recognized it, and was not going to say anything to bring him out of his trance. His eyes, meeting hers, blinked hard, and his body shuddered. Sweat popped out on his forehead and his veins bulged under the skin.

"Not a single one of these bastards is going to hurt you. Not one of them," he whispered.

Now Gefjun smiled. "Kill them all," she whispered.

Then Ostryg rose to his feet and whirled on the attackers with a roar, the cords standing out on his neck. "Odin, All-father, help me now!" he called.

He flung aside his shield, ripped the sword out of the hand of the man he'd just killed, and with a bearlike roar he went raging against the attackers that were clambering into the ship. Ostryg's swords flew and cut into the crowd.

Dyrfinna saw what was happening. "He's going berserk! Skalans, watch your backs, and push the attackers toward Ostryg. If you can't kill them, he will."

Ostryg tore through the attackers with both swords, his blades punching through leather armor, slicing through tendons and flesh. The attackers from the new ship fell back with a groan of dismay.

But one man came roaring out of the pack, a gigantic man in beautiful armor and gigantic muscles.

This man had the form of a god, for his arms were like tree trunks, and he wore the finest armor edged with gold.

The fighters all paused to see him, and for an instant, a reverent hush fell over the ship.

"I am Sigurd of the Bjarki, the king's champion," he announced to Dyrfinna's crew in a clear, resonant voice. "I slew more men than any of the great warriors of legend, and I have come to slay —"

Ostryg shrieked, the cords standing out on his neck, and flung his sword into Sigurd's face, still shrieking.

Sigurd of the Bjarki, finding himself with an unexpected faceful of sword, did what any man in his situation would do. He tottered, then fell over with an ignoble thud.

"I ... have not ... finished speaking ..." the great man said. Then he perished.

Thus came the end of the great Sigurd of the Bjarki, whose story was told by many poets thereafter, though probably not in the way he had imagined it.

Ostryg, who had been shrieking the whole time this had been going on, finally stopped. Then he spun to the left and attacked the next man.

With Ostryg raging through the fighters, the king's attackers dwindled until the last ones left simply ran back to their ship, out of Ostryg's reach.

Now Ostryg reached the prow of the ship that had crashed into Dyrfinna's ship. He slammed both hands against the iron lion that made up the prow of the attacking ship, which was jammed into the splintered back of Dyrfinna's ship. With a bellow, he heaved against the ship's prow, leaning hard against it, feet braced against the floor of the ship, trying to push it free until his muscles bulged and his eyes were fairly popping out.

"Help him!" several cried, and came running in to push the ship free.

"Stop them!" cried the king's attackers, and spears and pikes came stabbing from behind the iron lion's head.

But with a final grunt, Ostryg let loose with a great shove. There was a great snapping sound, the tearing of wood, and the prow of the enemy moved back, then sank slightly, returning to its normal level in the water, free of Dyrfinna's ship.

That done, Ostryg went staggering back, utterly spent. The spirit of the bear left him, the spirit of the berserker, and he turned now and walked, almost sleepwalking, to Gefjun. Here, he slumped down to the deck.

"I'm done," he said, soft as the whisper of a kitten, and he lay down at her side, and fell asleep at once, deeply exhausted. Gefjun immediately got to work patching up the wounds he'd gotten while he'd been raging.

"You don't even know when you get wounded," she snapped.

"Is he going to be all right?" Dyrfinna asked, casting a glance toward the lion ship, because something else was happening there, but she didn't know what it was.

"As far as I can tell," Gefjun snapped. But Dyrfinna knew she was angry only because her anger kept her from bursting into tears.

"Thank him for us when he comes to," Dyrfinna said. "For all of us."

At any rate, now a new roaring arose from the lion ship – fury and exultation. Dyrfinna faced it, sword at the ready.

6

THE EAGLE AND
THE WOLF

Battles raged around Dyrfinna. The warriors who had been tied up by the attacks in the back of the ship now returning to the sides to help their comrades fight off the enemy in the other ships. But she was watching the lion ship. There was a gap between ships, but not a large one – one that would be easy enough to jump.

Just then, a young Moorish man leapt onto her deck, a curved sword in hand. He wore a metal helmet and armor made of overlapping pieces of metal, and when he landed he looked around him with the piercing dark eyes of an eagle. A red cloak hung from his broad shoulders, and he carried a gigantic shield that nearly covered the length of his body, painted red and yellow, with a large metal boss in its middle shaped like a rose.

He shouted something in a language that sounded like Andalusian, and the men on the ship shouted and cheered.

His eyes met Dyrfinna's, and at once he drew up, regal as a prince, and stepped forward.

Dyrfinna did the same. The man wore the robes of a commander, a leader, and he had set foot on her ship.

Though she was weary in every limb, she went to meet

him, sword out. If only she still had that javelin she'd thrown a short time ago!

"Oh, you are going to regret this," Dyrfinna snarled.

"Am I?" the eagle-eyed man replied in accented Norse, in an extremely courtly manner that nettled Dyrfinna for some reason. "I am Ishaq ibn Maslama al-Andalusi. I believe that your ship is the one that is surrounded, and mine is one of the scores that have surrounded you. Perhaps it will be *you* who will look back upon this day and regret it."

Then he came upon the corpse of Sigurd of the Bjarki, the king's champion, and gazed down upon the wrecked man.

"Why am I not surprised," Ishaq said.

"Do you always talk this much before a fight?" Dyrfinna asked, exasperated.

Though Ishaq's face stayed stern, there was a dangerous sparkle in his dark-brown eyes. "Should we not speak? Are we not equal in leadership?"

"Hard to say," Dyrfinna said, eyeing him warily. "You're a bunch of child-killers being led by a bloodthirsty bitch. Your Sigurd of the Bjarki, the king's champion, was clearly fighting for the wrong cause. As are you."

He swiftly brought the shield around and set the spear against its side, then raised an eyebrow at her. "May I point out that your esteemed queen killed a five-year-old child and made our blessed king eat the child's heart. In light of that particular cruelty, I adjure you to think carefully about who you call a bloodthirsty bitch."

Dyrfinna set her shield before her and rolled her shoulders, her sword at the ready. "Your blessed king killed her daughter, my close friend," she said, grim. "We seek vengeance. We are going to make him pay the blood-price."

The eagle-eyed man made an exasperated hiss. "By the blessed souls of the dead, I have never heard a people lie so much between their teeth."

"We are not liars," Dyrfinna said.

"I disagree." With that, Ishaq lunged at her with his shield, bullying her backward through the crowd of fighters. She tried to catch him with her sword, but his gigantic, rose-decked shield covered him so thoroughly that she could not find an opening.

She leapt back. "We are not liars," she said again.

"Even in that, you lie." He struck his shield hard against hers hard enough to hit her in the chest, knocking her breath out. "Like the wolf whose totem you wear, you slink at the back of the crowd, waiting for your chance to strike, to bring down the innocent."

Her anger and annoyance at this man only grew as she choked, trying to suck in some air. "Like the eagle, you live on fish and carcasses," she said. "Like the rose, you grow in shit."

She struck Ishaq back on his right side, trying to throw him off his feet, but his black eyes narrowed, and he chuckled darkly. "How like you, how like your people, to insist upon your innocence even as you go on a warrior's voyage over a lie."

It was hard to concentrate fully on the fight, for she'd been wounded in the shoulder and then across her fingers from a javelin, and she was weary from the heat and the long battle. He was quick. If she had not been so exhausted, she would have been quicker. His blade was curved, like a scimitar, and she was astonished at the power that came down from that blade. She barely managed to parry his strikes in time, and one of them struck sparks, nearly knocking her sword out of her hands.

But she was not going to stand there and let him call her a liar, or her people dishonorable.

Dyrfinna stumbled backwards into a space where she could swing her sword without accidentally knocking some poor bastard down. Then, as her opponent sprang after her, she took the sword in both hands, shrilling like an angry hawk, and brought the brilliant silver blade down across the corner of his shield. The impact of the sword against the wood made her stagger, but it sheared off a corner of the shield and gouged the arm of the astonished Moor who held it.

He flung the shield aside and his sword leaped out, straight at her gut.

She flicked the blow aside as he came at her. Unable to bring her blade around to cut him, she punched him in the head with the hilt, a solid blow that sent him back two steps.

"Insolent," Ishaq growled, shaking his head. "You will not dare to lay a hand on me."

"Oh, I will," she said warily. "If you want me to keep my hands to myself, you can get your ass off my ship."

His dark eyes narrowed. "I will, but not until I sink your accursed heap of junk to the bottom of the seas."

Dyrfinna blazed. "This accursed heap of junk is my grandmama's ship, which carries her blessing, which saw her deeds of valor when she was a queen of the pirates!" She swiftly blocked his strike with her shield and stabbed at him. "You will not besmirch her with your feeble words."

"You dishonorable liar," he snarled. "Your words are lies. You have nothing to be proud of. Your so-called queen killed an innocent five-year-old boy while he slept and fed his heart to his papa."

"My grandmama?" Dyrfinna asked, completely confused.

Ishaq stopped dead and let out an exasperated huff. "No, not your pirate queen grandmama. Your *queen* queen. Queen Saehildr."

"Well, my queen queen didn't do that either."

"Every word that falls from your lips is a lie. I'll bet that your pirate queen grandmama is also a lie."

Dyrfinna's eyes went hard. "As if you could tell a lie from the truth."

Instantly they were engaged in a sharp hand-to-hand fight, swords clashing. He moved with such skill that she couldn't help but be impressed, even as she tried to find a way past his defense so she could plunge her sword into his cruel, child-killing heart.

"The Queen never would kill a child," she hissed, panting for breath. "And King Varinn killed Thora first!"

"King Varinn is an honorable man. Perhaps your Thora deserved to die," he taunted.

Red flashed into Dyrfinna's vision. Nobody, *nobody* talked about Thora like that. She targeted the corner of his shield that she'd hacked off, trying to add another hit to the one she'd already given him.

"Finna!" came Skeggi's voice, and her heart leapt. He came running, his blade at the ready, shoving an enemy combatant aside.

Skeggi leapt into the fray at her side, but in his eagerness to come to Dyrfinna's assistance, he tripped over his own feet and ended up crashing into the Moor – who in turn went staggering backwards, knocking down one of the enemy combatants who had followed him in. All three men fell in a heap, flailing and punching at each other.

"Hey, whatever works," she muttered, and she stepped in with her sword to finish him off.

One of the Moor's attendants flipped to her feet, whirling her pike skillfully and driving Dyrfinna back and keeping away any other attackers while Skeggi and the Moor tried to wrestle their swords away from each other. One of his defenders jumped in and stabbed Skeggi through the arm. He shook but hardly seemed to notice, so intent he was on his struggle.

Dyrfinna grabbed a spear that was lying under a nearby rowing bench, where it had fallen. She thrust her shield against the whirling pike, stopping it short, and swiped at the Moor's attendant, then stabbed at the attendant who had stabbed Skeggi.

Suddenly, a hook leaped out, grabbed the Moor's attendant, and yanked her overboard.

It was Hakr leaping into the fray. Ishaq saw the hook reaching to him, and in an instant whirled his sword around his head and brought it down like a sledgehammer on the hook. It fell to the deck with a clang.

Hakr merely grabbed his pike and spun it like a quarterstaff. "My girl, we need to retreat," he said as he attacked the Moor, the pike spinning so fast that Dyrfinna could hear it hum.

"Retreat? Never," she snarled, as Ishaq's eyes lit up at the word.

"Yes," Hakr said. "Because this miscreant rammed your ship hard enough to let the water into our lower deck. If we don't retreat now, we're going to sink."

7

A NEW STRATEGY

Ishaq's men were clamoring to get aboard. The fight was particularly hot in front of the ship, and Dyrfinna's fighters were hard-pressed to keep them back. The word *retreat* had brought new excitement into their enemies' hearts – and despair into Dyrfinna's crew.

"And I hope you do sink," said the Moor, fighting the old seafarer with renewed vigor. "As a matter of fact, allow me to call my men, and we'll set upon your ship and sink it and your infernal pack of liars to the bottom of the sea. Where you belong!"

Dyrfinna did not answer, because she was staring at his feet. Something strange was happening. Hakr's silver hook came creeping in from behind Ishaq as he spoke, floating about a handbreadth above the boards of the deck. It angled itself just in front of his ankles – and suddenly yanked back.

"Ill hap!" Ishaq said as his legs were pulled out from under him and he landed on his shield. His forehead struck the boards of the ship, a stunning blow that made Dyrfinna grimace. He struggled for a moment as if trying to pull his arms and legs under him to get up. Then he went limp.

A terrible roar of voices came from the lion's ship, and

a rain of arrows and pikes came flying in as the fighters on Ishaq's ship vented their rage on Dyrfinna's sinking ship.

Ostryg, who had hooked the Moor's legs, stood up and handed the hook back to Hakr. "I'd had enough of his talk." Ever the assassin, Ostryg pulled out a knife and put one knee on Ishaq's back.

"No. Wait," Dyrfinna said. "He'll be more valuable to us alive. That armor's got to be worth a fortune, and he's clearly one of their commanders."

"Maybe I don't want him alive," Ostryg grumbled as he found a coil of rope near the mast. "If he's alive, he's going to talk."

She tied her big handkerchief over his mouth. "Hopefully that will help you."

The men on Ishaq's ship were screaming, and arrows and lances came flying in, followed by several grappling hooks as they tried to pull their ship within boarding distance, but two shieldmaidens were pitching out the grappling hooks as quickly as they came in.

Ostryg began tying Ishaq up as Dyrfinna turned to Hakr. "What do you mean, retreat? Did you say what I thought you said?"

"I did," Hakr said. Holding his shield over his head to deflect the arrows, he went to the side of the ship and with a stroke of his axe, he severed a rope attached to a grappling hook, then a second one. One of the ships that had been pulled close to Dyrfinna's was now loose. He plunged through the battle to find other grappling hooks.

"Where are we retreating to? Into the ocean?" Dyrfinna said, following him with her shield up. An arrow punched her in the side, and she coughed, but it hadn't penetrated her armor.

"No. On this island, ahead." With a hand covered with blood, he pointed at an island upon which a low single-peaked mountain stood, with sheer, gray cliffs around which puffins and other seabirds flew. The island was all gray slope and gray cliff, gray scree and gray beach, upon which light brushes of green gathered here and there.

"We must go quickly, because our ship is taking on water," the old seafarer said. "If we sink, we've lost. But if we can get to that island, we can gain the heights and we can defend ourselves."

It would be a difficult climb to reach the heights, Dyrfinna could see that right away. But she could also see how their ship was getting lower in the water — and the prows of the attacking ships were getting higher and higher next to theirs, giving their attackers a better shot at them.

Like shooting fish in a barrel, she thought.

"Crew!" Hakr shouted to her crew. "Raise the sail! We must retreat to land."

There was a cry of disbelief and dismay from her crew.

"No!" Skeggi shouted, turning his bloody face to her. Head wound.

"Do it!" Dyrfinna cried, shoving back a suddenly jubilant enemy. "The ship is riding too low in the water as it is."

As they came down over the back of a wave, the bow dipped into the ocean and scooped up some freezing salt water, which splashed through the bottom of the ship as they climbed up the next wave. The ship had never done that before when the seas were calm.

All the same, her fighters were furious. "How could you take us from the fight?" they shouted, throwing down their arms in frustration. "We can't run away from this battle. Do you know how that looks? How dishonorable that is?"

"The ship is sinking," Dyrfinna pointed out as more salt water came roaring in over the bow.

"We can fight perfectly well on a submerged ship!" one of the Vikings cried.

"Why are we going to land, though?" Ostryg asked.

"We'll have a better chance of winning on that high

ground," the steersman said. "Especially if this is the island that I think it might be."

"What island is that?" Dyrfinna asked, but Hakr ducked suddenly to one side. A javelin that had been flung at him stood quivering in the wooden side of the ship where he'd just been standing.

"We can defend that ground with fewer men, and settle the odds in our favor," Hakr said as he yanked the javelin free from the wood. "Instead of dying on a ship, we can defend ourselves until the queen's troops, or her dragons, find us," he added with satisfaction. He whirled and flung the javelin back at the enemy. Somebody screamed.

Just then, king's berserker, roaring like a wild bull, clambered over the side of her ship, hewing his way through the throng of warriors with his axe, knocking fighters down like wheat before the scythe. Dyrfinna's warriors sprang to the ship's defense, but the berserker was a stout man, his face and neck bright red with exertion, and he swung the axe hard without stopping.

Hakr ran forward and met the berserker, his own battle axe swinging. He struck the berserker with such a blow on his helmet that he staggered back, stunned.

Then the berserker uttered a fearful roar and plunged forward. With one swing, his axe broke through the upper part of Hakr's shield and buried itself in his helmet with a sickening thud.

❧ 8 ❧

ALREADY AVENGED

HAKR FELL WITH A BRIGHT SPURT OF BLOOD.

Dyrfinna cried out. "No!"

Before the berserker could strike a second time, Dyrfinna ran full tilt into him, slamming her shield hard against his and shoving him back. As the berserker staggered, she flung her shield into his face, swiped up Hakr's axe, and used both hands to swing it in a swift arc around her head. She hummed energy through her arm into the axe to make her swing true and powerful. The axe slammed down like a sledgehammer, splitting the berserker's skull open.

The berserker sank to the ground in an awful pool of blood. It always stunned her how much blood one person could contain. Dyrfinna fell to her knees beside Hakr and set aside his battle axe, the bloody head of it sitting on the ground.

"Are you hurt badly?" she asked, raising the old captain's head onto her knee to get it out of the spreading pool of his enemy's hot blood.

Her fighters saw what had happened to the old captain. "At them! At King Varinn's horde!" They attacked fiercely, driving the enemy back from Dyrfinna and Hakr.

Hakr tried to speak, but for a while was not able to do

so. Dyrfinna raised her shield over them both to keep off the stones and arrows that fell around them. The cut in his helmet was very bad, and he was bleeding a lot, and his eyes rolled.

"I killed the berserker," she told him. "He is dead. You are already avenged."

Hakr tried to speak, tried again. "Thank you," he said, grasping her hand with his bloody hand. "Here. Take ... take this ring back ... back home to my wife. Tell her my last thoughts were of her. And take this brooch ... here."

"This one?" Dyrfinna asked, laying her hand on a silver brooch that fastened his armor.

"Yes. That goes to my daughter. It ... it belonged to my mother."

She put his ring on her finger, and fastened the brooch to her armor.

"And I give you this ring." He took a golden arm-band from his arm and placed it into her hand. "This was given to me by the previous Queen. Remember me, little Finna, as I go home."

Tears came to her eyes as she accepted his final gift. "How could I ever forget you, old friend?"

"And ... I will miss you," he said, squeezing her hand in his old rough hand. "Be strong, and a sure commander."

"I will." Tears blurred her vision.

The old sea-captain took a relieved breath and smiled at her. Then his face slackened, and his eyes wandered from hers into the sky, no longer seeing. His head rolled to the side with a sigh, and every muscle in his body slackened. He no longer moved.

Hakr was done with earth.

Dyrfinna could imagine him walking into Valhalla as if returning home.

She gently closed his eyes, sheathed her sword, and picked up his battle axe. She was weary, but she swung it around her head to test its weight and heft. The axe was very light, well-balanced, and made an easy yet powerful swing when handled the way he'd taught her, long ago.

"Farewell, my old friend."

One of the wounded fighters came over and dragged Hakr to the front of the ship, where his body would be out of the way of the fighting.

But now Dyrfinna quailed. How could she lead without him?

If she didn't fulfill his last request, the dragon eggs – and Dyrfinna's crew – would be good as dead.

She knew what honor meant: Staying in battle to the last stroke, to the last spurt of blood, standing firm and unafraid to the end.

But now that they had dragon eggs, there was no way that they'd fight to the last man or woman.

"Set course to that island," Dyrfinna shouted in command.

A shout of dismay. Her crew was furious. "We have to stay here and fight. It's wrong to leave."

"I don't want to leave this fight, either," she said. "But dying in mid-sea is no victory. What's the use of honor if you're dead? And besides, if we die, the enemy simply leaves our bodies to rot on the sea floor while they sail on to Skala to kill our people and our children. And we can't revenge Thora if we're all dead."

They grumbled.

"And there is this," she added, looking at where the eagle-eyed man was beginning to come to, groggy. "We have one of their commanders. So they'll have to give chase."

The Moor worked his mouth out from behind the cloth, slowly, as if his head hurt. "We have *your* commander," he reminded her.

"Eh," Dyrfinna said. "You can keep him. Just as we are keeping you."

❈ 9 ❈
RATS FLEEING A SINKING SHIP

THERE WASN'T ENOUGH ROOM TO PUT OUT OARS, clearly – the other ships were too close.

"All the ships are loose," called one of the shield-maidens who had been cutting the lines. Even though the ropes that had bound the attacking ships to them had been cut, the other ships still crowded close, and though they had drifted back slightly as they rose and fell on the waves, there was no way for Dyrfinna's crew to put the oars out without setting them directly on the decks of those ships.

Another grappling hook flew out but didn't gain purchase. Skeggi was already at the great sail untying the ropes. "Pull it up!" he cried. "The wind will carry us."

A command was a command, and the first crew swiftly took the ropes of the sail and began pulling up the enormous cloth. The wind, which was not quite coming from the right direction, was still enough to belly out the sail.

Skeggi swung the sail to catch the wind, and the ship began to slide away from the battle, bringing two of the child-killers with them in their ship. Dyrfinna's remaining crew shoved both of them over the side, letting them sink in their heavy armor.

Confusion and jubilation broke from the enemy's ships

46

around them. Dyrfinna could see the anger in her crew's faces as they raised the sail. She swung up her shield and deflected a spear that was flying in. With a great shout, she called, "Go! We need to stay alive to revenge Thora!"

"And to protect the dragon eggs," Ostryg said under his breath, but she shushed him. She didn't want anybody else to know about them – definitely not the enemy.

One of Nauma's ships tried to block their passage, trying to turn its sail enough to bring them forward. Dyrfinna's ship banged against their prow, a stroke that nearly knocked everybody off their feet. Yet another grappling hook came flying in, but it fell short of the target with a splash. Skeggi brought the sail around a little further to catch more wind, and Dyrfinna's ship leaned aft, squeaking past the prows that crowded in to block them.

"Crew One, to the oars, quickly!" Skeggi cried as their enemies leaned out of their ships with pikes, trying to catch their ship. "Get in position and prepare to row with all your might!"

Just then, their ship slid past the final prow, and they were free.

"Oars out!" Skeggi cried over the rattling of the oars as they slid out. "Now, row!"

The rowers pulled with all their strength, and the oars dug into the water with a will. A furious roar from the enemy ships behind them as Dyrfinna's ship began to fly across the ocean.

Now the enemy was jeering. They fought to turn their ships around and give chase, but there were too many in that small space, and they could not yet use their oars the way Dyrfinna's crew could.

"And we will make sure they follow us," Dyrfinna said. She ran to the back of the ship where Ishaq was sitting, his black eagle eyes especially baleful over his gag. "Stand up. I want them to see you so we can make sure your people give chase."

He glared at her coldly and said something through his gag that sounded like a curse upon her family for the next seven generations.

"Are you telling me that you do not want to stand up?" Dyrfinna asked.

"I'll help," said Ragnarok as he came over, much like a mountain coming to visit. He picked up Ishaq as if he were a puppy, despite his muffled protests, and set him on his feet, turning him to face Nauma's ships so they could see him clearly.

The cloth over Ishaq's mouth fell off while Ragnarok was picking him up. "I will have you know that this is very disrespectful," he informed them, shaking back his thick black hair. "You cannot treat one such as I in this manner. I curse your pirate queen grandmother, I curse your hair, which clearly has already been cursed; I curse your offspring..."

At that point, she swiftly stuck the cloth back in his mouth.

"Hello! We have your commander!" Dyrfinna shouted back, waving at the enemy's ships.

They were turning to follow her before, but now came shouting from the ships. Nauma screamed something, and the fighters on the ships moved with more haste than before. Her ships pulled around to give chase.

From one of the ships, Dyrfinna was fairly sure she could hear Sinkr yelling, "I'm the commander, not her!"

Dyrfinna's heart leapt. Ha. But Nauma's ships were beginning to pick up speed in pursuit. Her ship was dragging because it was sitting much lower in the waves, and from the extra weight of all the water it was taking on from the gap that the Moor's prow had left in their side. She prayed that Rán of the Seas would catch his sorry ass in her nets. Not today, though – later, when he was not in her sinking ship.

"You coward," taunted Ishaq, who had unfortunately spat out the cloth. "Running from a fight like a whipped dog. May an angry rooster get tangled in your hair every morning."

"We'd be perfectly happy to fight your people," Dyrfinna said, trying not to lose her temper. "Just in a place of our choosing, and not on a sinking ship. No thanks to you. And I accept your rooster curse because I will have a good chicken dinner every day."

"It's still not honorable."

"Don't talk to me about honor, you ... you commander person." She shouldn't have brought up the chicken dinner because now she realized she was starving. There had been no time to eat today.

"So what is your name, angry fighting woman?"

"My name is Go-To-Hel."

"Pleased to meet you, Gotohel," he said, not sounding pleased at all.

"I'm Dyrfinna. Just make yourself comfortable, because I have work to do. Ragnarok, if he acts up, feel free to drop him into the bilgewater, thank you." She rushed back to the middle of the ship.

Dyrfinna called out again to the rest of the crew. "Those of you who are not rowing – gather all the weapons and arrows lying on the floor of this ship, even if they're broken, and put them in this barrel next to me."

"Even broken arrows like this?" Ostryg held up several arrow shafts that had been broken into pieces.

"Yes, even those. Throw them in here. We will need every one of them."

"Why are we doing this?" one of the warriors asked.

"We will need supplies," Dyrfinna said as Skeggi turned the ship toward the far end of the island. "When we reach this island," he said, "we will be forced to abandon ship."

"What!" Ostryg cried.

"We will go up into the heights," Dyrfinna said, pointing to the low mountain that made up the bulk of the island, with long cliffs that plummeted down to the rocks at its feet. "We can defend ourselves there."

"Okay," said Ostryg dubiously.

"I appreciate that we'll have the high ground against our enemies, but it looks barren from here.

Now Dyrfinna pointed to where the island sloped down to a green, rocky meadow through which a large stream flowed into the ocean. "We are going to drive this ship into the stream. The draft of this ship is shallow enough to let us travel upstream, but from the looks of that mountain, we won't go far. We'll land our ship and head up to that peak yonder."

"What of the wounded?" Gefjun said from the back of the ship, where she was swiftly wrapping a badly sliced arm. "We have nine fighters who are in bad shape."

Ostryg, who was lying on the deck next to Gefjun, sat up a little, shaking his head. "I'm not in *bad* shape," he said.

"Juni, bind the wounds up and sing them better if you can. Have we anybody gravely wounded?"

"Yes," said Dyrfinna, looking down at two men who lay on the bottom of the ship, near where Hakr's body lay.

One of them half-opened an eye. He was a young man about her age, a rough character she'd known most of her life, but he loved his two boys. "Leave us behind, here in this ship," he said. "I am near to meeting the Allfather, and walking with the great warriors in Valhalla. There is nothing more that the enemy can do to me. Tell my sons how I died."

Dyrfinna prayed over him. "I will tell your family that you have brought them great honor in battle."

He coughed up some blood. "I never wanted to leave them," he said. "But I couldn't stay home and leave Thora unavenged."

"We'll carry on the fight for you," Dyrfinna promised.

"Hold those heights against those sons of hogs," he said, "and you will have done all of us a great service."

She placed an axe on his chest and wrapped his hand around it. "Here. Carry this into Valhalla," she said warmly. He nodded, and then his head rolled to the side as the last breath went out of his body.

Dyrfinna stepped back, her heart heavy, thinking of his two bright-haired sons and his wife.

All of Nauma's ships were starting to increase their speed in their chase, Dyrfinna noted. Exhaustion enveloped her, but she knew that all the rest of her crew felt the same. She could put the rowers in the back of the battle until they had recovered their strength, at least. She looked over her fighters, picking those who could hold five shiploads of Vikings at bay for the first attack.

"Hakr said we will have to abandon ship when we land," Dyrfinna said. "When we reach the shore, I need everybody to take all essential items off this ship. Carry what possessions you will need, and quickly. We need food, water, weapons most of all. Do you understand?"

Her troops nodded grimly. "Aye," a few of them said.

"Our enemy's ships are coming in fast. Anything that is still on the ship when they arrive is going to be abandoned and burned." The thought of burning Saebringr turned her stomach, but she would not allow the enemy to steal her ship for their own evil purposes. She swore it upon the deathless gods.

"Here comes the island!" somebody shouted.

"Aim the prow into the stream," Dyrfinna called. "Pull hard, rowers!"

They burst through the wall of foam that marked where the freshwater stream met the sea. Dyrfinna held on to the side of her ship as it rocked, and then they were flying into the island's interior. A few great trees towered over her for a moment, giving way suddenly to rocks that rose above the ship on the right side – the mountain that made up most of the island. The waters became shallower, rockier, and her ship struck one of the rocks with a hard shudder that nearly made Dyrfinna ill.

"Drive her aground here!" the steersman called, pointing to a narrow spit of sand at the foot of the mountain.

With a strong pull of the oars, the rowers made the ship leap forward, through the shallow water and up onto the sand, where the ship ground to a halt, the water in the lower deck sloshing loudly and making the ship rock.

"Take all the foodstuffs," Dyrfinna called. "Take everything of value that you can carry off this ship."

"We'll have to make multiple trips," somebody called back.

"Then make them. We'll make as many trips as we can before the enemy arrives," she said. "If we're going to make a stand at the top of this mountain, we need to have food and water and weapons. And everything that we take is one less thing that our enemies can use against us."

As exhausted as she and the others were, they all worked in haste, rolling the barrels of hardtack and other food off the ship. The water barrel was a challenge, and the thought of carrying or rolling all these things up the mountain's side made Dyrfinna's legs weak.

"What am I getting everybody into?" she asked Gefjun in a low voice as they helped the wounded fighters off the ship. "We don't even know what's at the top of that mountain — if we have any way to defend ourselves against the child-killers. What if I'm leading everybody into a trap?"

Gefjun snapped, "Finna, don't be stupid. Would you rather be surrounded by five ships as we slowly sink to the bottom of the ocean? At least we have a fighting chance here. Stop second-guessing yourself, and come on."

Skeggi came up beside them, dragging a gigantic piece of sailcloth behind him and carrying an armful of bows. "At least it's you in command, and not Sinkr," he added in his mild way.

Dyrfinna couldn't argue with that.

10

AN ASTONISHING RUIN

DYRFINNA SWUNG OVER THE SIDE OF THE SHIP AND onto the ground below. She staggered a little due to her sea-legs, but stayed a moment to help some of the wounded over the side.

One of the shieldmaidens hopped over the side with a small barrel of mead upon her shoulder.

"Aren't we supposed to save the essential items first?" Dyrfinna asked.

"Mead is essential," she was informed.

Well, then.

From here, through the trees they'd just passed, she could see Nauma's ships about two leagues back and closing in, their oars churning the water.

"Come on, then," she said quietly, then turned back to her crew.

"If she's carrying the mead barrel, I need to carry the ale barrel," Ostryg called back into the ship.

Her crew followed Dyrfinna up into the rocks, dragging or carrying or rolling everything they could. The fighters followed, some of the wounded leaning on their friends as they walked.

"Let's meet them here," somebody cried from next to the ship. "We can fight them off as they disembark."

"No," she said. "Climb up to the rocks. Let them fight their way up to us."

"I am not going into the rocks," Ishaq stated flatly. "I don't care if you throw me into the sea. Leave me here with your dead men."

Fury flashed through Dyrfinna, but she tightened her lips for a moment. "Ragnarok, please carry this encumbrance for us," she said.

"Oh, no, you will not," Ishaq said just as he was unceremoniously draped over Ragnarok's shoulder. "I said no, you stinking dogs!" Ragnarok just carried him up the mountain, swearing the whole way and cursing everybody within earshot with pustules, boils, arthritis, and bugs in their ears.

Dyrfinna climbed into the rocks, followed by her crew, all carrying their different burdens.

"You should have let me kill him," Ostryg said as they followed, with Ishaq's curses echoed off the rocks.

"Yes. I'm regretting my decision now."

"Just look at this ground," said Skeggi when they reached the top, satisfied, as she and the other fighters joined him. "And here we are to hold it."

As the top of the mountain rose into view, murmurs of amazement came from the warriors. Dyrfinna was struck quiet in wonder. Even Ishaq stopped swearing for a moment as he viewed the land, upside down over Ragnarok's shoulder.

The top of the low mountain was a flat plain, not large. Right in the center of the plain, elevated slightly, stood an old, abandoned mead hall with high stone walls.

On both sides of the great, battered doors of carved oak hung two enormous banners, now faded colorless by the sun and torn to pieces. The doors stood partly open. Some rubble lay around various parts of the walls, but otherwise the building was intact. Tangles of rugosa roses bloomed all along the walls in pink, dark purple, and white, having grown all these years without human attention.

"Amazing," Dyrfinna whispered.

The rest of her crew gazed in wonder. "What is this old hall doing here?" somebody asked. "Who would have lived in a place as lonely as this?"

The great roof had caved in at several places, and the windows made of translucent horn had been punched out to curl up on the ground. Despite the ravages of time, it was clear that this had been a fine hall once, many years ago. A stone wall that was about as tall as a full-grown man circled the parameter of the mountaintop, close to the cliffs. This wall, as far as Dyrfinna could tell, was still intact.

Skeggi shook his head sadly to see the old mead hall. "Look upon my works, ye Mighty, and despair!" he said.

Gefjun's eyes were wide as she looked around. "What was this place? Does anybody know?"

Skeggi gazed at it, eyes narrowed like a hawk's. "I've heard stories about a place like this. This is like the haunted mead hall where a secretive king, long ago, hid himself while he was fleeing his enemies. But they found him and killed him and the few remaining members of his court. It's possible that we stand on Púkifell."

"Demon Mountain?" Ostryg put his hands on his hips, looking around the ruined structure. "If this place isn't haunted, I'm going to be disappointed."

Several hisses came from the more superstitious Vikings.

"Don't say such things," one of the shieldmaidens warned as she walked back down the mountain for more supplies. "If it's true, may *you* be the one who suffers from it, not me."

"No king or queen or even jarl held this place in my memory, after the old king was murdered," Skeggi continued. "I've heard about this island – was told stories of its existence long ago – but I didn't think those stories were true."

"We can talk more about it after we bring the rest of our supplies up from the ship," Dyrfinna pointed out.

They all set off down the hill with most of the exhausted crew.

"This slope we just climbed must have been the old road to this hall," Skeggi said, looking back over his shoulder at where they'd left their ship, far down the slope, barely seen behind the great heaps of boulders that littered the mountainside.

"Probably." Dyrfinna, looking at the great hall, realized something. "I need to do some quick reconnaissance of this place. I will be back as quickly as possible."

She was already on the run along the edge of the cliffs, along the outside of the stone wall. She called over her shoulder, "That slope looks like it might have been the only way to reach these heights, too. But if there's another way for Nauma's fighters to reach the mead hall, I need to find about it *now*, and we need to find a way to defend it before Nauma's forces arrive." She'd heard of too many instances of a group of soldiers finding a great position in which they would fight off the enemy, only to be killed off by a small group of the enemy who'd sneaked up to them by some overlooked path.

"We need to find a defensive position for our fighters so we can be ready for the enemy!" Ostryg shouted from halfway up the slope.

"Supplies first," she called in reply. "Rescue all the supplies you can before the enemy gets their hands on them. I'll be back with you in a moment." With that, she began to circle the mead hall.

The old hall was set well back from the sheer cliffs that they'd sailed past only a brief time ago. As Dyrfinna ran past the front of the mead hall, she had a clear view of the rock-filled sea stretching out before them. Some magnificent mountains sat a long way off on the horizon, and flocks of puffins and skuas circled the cliffs. No trees grew here to block the ocean's view, though a few small cherry trees were clustered around the front of the mead hall. This time of year, the cherries still green and inedible.

This hall was very well placed, she realized, because any invaders from this direction could be clearly seen from far away – no chance of a surprise invasion – and the cliffs in front of it were sheer and unclimbable.

In fact, she had a clear view of the enemy ships sailing toward them. From this high, she could see the warriors that crowded the desks as the longboats came driving toward the land where they stood; the sun glimmered on their armor, swords, and battle axes.

For a fleeting moment, she watched as Nauma's first ship approached the entrance to the stream. The warriors that crowded the sides of the ship were chanting some kind of rude rhyme, but at this distance, she couldn't make out the words. Too bad.

But there was no time for idle gazing. If Nauma's first ship was here, then Dyrfinna's troops would not have much more time to prepare for their arrival.

ABANDON SHIP

SHE SHOUTED A WARNING TO HER PEOPLE – "THE FIRST ship is coming in!" – and continued her circuit around the small patch of mountaintop more quickly than before, ignoring the ache in her legs.

On the east side of the mead hall, opposite of where they'd climbed up, were more sheer cliffs. No way to climb up these cliffs without ropes and grappling hooks, she was pleased to notice. There was also a place for sacrifices at the edge of these cliffs, the holy stones now overgrown with grasses.

On the back side of the mead hall, she took note of an overgrown pasture that sloped downhill a long way, then turned into another steep, rocky fall that plummeted to the ocean. As far as she could tell, there was no way to get up those cliffs, though she wasn't entirely sure – she would send somebody to explore this place later.

Two wooden gates had been broken from their hinges and lay on the ground before the wall. Dyrfinna made a mental note to also send somebody to barricade this gap.

Old rugosa roses and berry bushes lined the inside of the wall, all of them overgrown, bristling with thorns and spilling over the top of the wall. The roses were blooming like mad, rose-purple blossoms and white blossoms, filling the air with a spicy fragrance she loved.

Just then, Skeggi came to join her, carrying a sea chest that was stuffed so full that it couldn't close. Her heart jumped to see his brown eyes, so serious. "We're almost ready," he said. "Oh, look at those roses." He set down the chest and plucked a blossom just below the swollen neck of the rose where the seeds would have burgeoned.

Dyrfinna felt her face warm, and shook her thoughts out of her head. "I wish I had more time to explore," she said, pointing at the back of the mead hall. Inside the wall was an old, overgrown orchard with rows of different fruit trees: some dead, some of them blooming. Closer to the hall were several outbuildings and an old stable that had tumbled in upon itself.

"Look at the old stables," she said. "There might be a forge and anvil in there."

Skeggi brightened. "There might be other useful items in this hall for us. I hope so. Come." He took her arm for a moment, but then remembered himself and his hand slid off. "If we're going to be surrounded by five shiploads of child-killers, we need to finish getting as many supplies as possible."

At that thought, Dyrfinna's heart failed briefly. "Great Allfather," she said quietly. "What have I done? What have I brought my people here to face?"

They began walking quickly toward the slope where the rest of her crew carried supplies up toward the mead hall to deposit them behind the stone wall. There, several of the wounded fighters that could walk were carrying supplies from the ship into an enclosure next to the mead hall – an old goathouse, perhaps, or a small stable.

"You didn't have a choice," Skeggi said in his warm voice. "And, you have to admit, this is much better than drowning in mid-ocean."

"I have to stop and take a hard look at our situation,"

Dyrfinna said, not stopping. "What are we against? What do we have to support us?"

She took a deep breath and took a clear look at their situation. "We're somewhere in the middle of the wide sea on a tiny island that, clearly, has not been lived upon for decades."

"But," Skeggi said, "we have a mead hall that we can take shelter in. Nauma's troops have to sleep outside if the weather turns to rain or snow. And what treasures that old hall might hold for us!" he added, looking over his shoulder at it.

"Spoken like a true bard."

"I don't mean the treasures of history, only," he added. "Maybe there's even an old armory inside that hall. Or a storage cellar with food in it."

"That food would be dust by now," Dyrfinna said.

"On the other hand," Skeggi said, warming to his topic, "if you have an old hall, then you'd also have a well or cistern – which means we'll have fresh water to drink. Those puffins and skuas on the southern cliff will provide meat. We've brought up nearly all the supplies we could carry. I know that we have hardtack for bread, because I carried that barrel up myself. So we won't starve."

"And there could be ways that we could signal for the Queen's troops, to make it easier to find us," Dyrfinna said. "A signal fire or something. But ... we'll have to pray that the King's dragons don't find us first."

Skeggi grimaced. "Always looking for the good in the situation, aren't you?"

"However, there's only one way to bring Nauma's troops up from the sea, so we only have to defend one approach. And it's easy to defend, too." As Dyrfinna walked in that direction, she made note of the great boulders and piles of rocks that stood at the top of the mountain along both sides of the slope. "Whoever lived here before was prepared for attack, clearly."

"There is that."

"But we have another problem," she reminded him. "The Queen's forces have no idea where my ship went after we'd been blown off course."

Skeggi shrugged as they joined the others. "Queen Saehildr has dragons. I'm sure they've already been looking for us. Old Red is probably worrying himself sick." he looked worried for his old dragon friend.

"But we have to abandon our ship," Dyrfinna said. "My ship. Because it looks like the enemy is already here," she added, judging by how fast the rest of her crew was hustling up the slope, carrying sea-chests stuffed full of items.

"The first ship is coming up the river," Gefjun called as if in confirmation, helping one of the wounded men limp to the mead hall. "Ostryg is back at your ship, trying to fire it before the stinking child-killers arrive."

Dyrfinna winced. "I know it's necessary," she said, "but that was grandmama's ship."

"It's okay. Your grandmama can get you another one. I'm taking the wounded inside that wall," Gefjun said. "Come on now, you're almost there," she added to the wounded warrior, coaxing him along.

Shouts from below. A burst of clear smoke billowed up from below, followed by a swirl of sparks.

"Hurry, everybody!" shouted Ostryg. "Draw your swords and honor your old captain and his allies! Show them honor as they leave for Valhalla!"

Dyrfinna drew her sword, Signe, and hurried down the slope.

The sail, though it had been drenched in seawater, was burning merrily, and flames raged across the entire deck. Even the bilgewater at the bottom of the ship was burning, incredibly enough.

Her crew members shouted and put their swords and spears into the air as Dyrfinna's ship, along with the bodies of Hakr and the two dead crewmen, went up in flames. The beautiful Saebringr, the Sea-Flame, which her grandmama had given her, was soon to be no more – and Hakr, her old friend, her guide, her mentor, was dead. *What happens to us without his guidance?* Dyrfinna couldn't help the lump that filled her throat.

Now Nauma's first ship was sliding onto the pebbly shore further downstream.

Ostryg was hurrying toward her as the first few arrows from the enemy came zinging in. "Move your asses! We have company!" he shouted at the rest of the crew as they carried the last few supplies they could grab. Ostryg grabbed a heap of grappling hooks that had been thrown off the ship's side earlier and rushed up the long slope, the iron hooks jangling and clanging around him.

"How'd you get the ship burning so quickly?" she asked in some amazement as they climbed the slope together, taking a sea-chest out of his arms.

The bearlike Ostryg hung his head like a sad child. "I sacrificed my barrel of ale to the gods of the ship."

"Your barrel of ale!" Skeggi cried in astonishment. "By the eternal gods! That is a sacrifice I would not have been able to make."

"I did it so we could have a chance to live," Ostryg said grandly, his grappling hooks clanging around him.

They all three had to stop for a moment in awe, looking back at the ship, now fiercely ablaze.

Another great billow of flames. Several of Nauma's crew, who were trying to jump aboard her ship in an attempt to pillage it, were repulsed by the flames. One of them caught on fire and rolled, screaming, across the ground.

Ostryg nodded with satisfaction. "Those bastards won't be able to help themselves to whatever supplies we had to leave behind."

"And Hakr and our shipmates will have the burial they deserve," Dyrfinna said, looking back at the raging fire of her ship.

"Yes. That too." Ostryg nodded with satisfaction. "I

made sure to give him an extra libation to speed his soul to Valhalla, and to make sure none of those bastards would take his axe out of his hands. Our enemy dead will also have an honorable burial, for they fought us and died with their hands on their weapons. Even that one that I stabbed in the face." Ostryg began hurrying up the hill with his grappling hooks, making a din like a hundred blacksmiths. "But now we are trapped on this island, with no way to escape."

The words chilled Dyrfinna.

A battle shriek burst from a second ship that flew up onto shore next to the first ship, followed by the booming of swords striking upon shields from the Vikings in the ship.

"Oh, we have a way to escape," Skeggi said ponderously. "The Queen arrives with her many ships and rescues us."

"And if she doesn't?" Ostryg asked. "What then?"

Skeggi frowned as they walked faster up the slope toward the mead hall and the rest of their fellow fighters.

The roar of the enemy as they arrived rang out from below.

"Well," he said, "death, too, is an escape."

12

A MESSY NEGOTIATION

DYRFINNA REJOINED THE REST OF HER GROUP BEHIND the wall at the top of the slope, and told them her preliminary observations about the area.

"They'll take some time in coming up," Ostryg said, looking down the side of the mountain toward Nauma's ships, where the fourth ship had pulled up onto the rocky beach. The fifth ship was still out in the ocean. "So we'll have a little time to get ready to kill them all."

Dyrfinna was placing her fighters among the rocks. "At least we have a chance to fight them, and defend ... ourselves." She was shocked that she'd nearly said "and defend our dragon eggs" out loud to everybody.

She knew the secret about the dragon eggs she'd captured wouldn't last for long – but the longer she could keep it quiet, the less chance there would be that the enemy would find out. That was a chance she didn't want to take.

Skeggi looked at her with his eyebrows raised. He knew what she'd been about to say. She shrugged, pulling a face.

She looked over the rocks. Some trees grew at the bottom, next to the rushing inlet. Brush and grasses grew thick on the hillside, making it possible, but difficult, for people to sneak up on them through it. The old road, however, was mostly clear, and from behind the rocks, Dyrfinna and her crew had an extremely clear view of Nauma's ships and her crew.

"We could shoot them from here if we wanted to," said an eager bowman.

"Wait for them to get close, when you can be absolutely sure of your shot," Dyrfinna said. "We must not waste a single arrow."

Dyrfinna put Ostryg in charge of several other fighters by the rock piles outside the walls. She explained their role, then left them prodding at the boulders and speaking excitedly as they went off in different directions.

Dyrfinna's ship was blazing. Skeggi went off by himself to singing a song to the gods for the dead warriors they'd left there. Some of Nauma's fighters shot arrows at him. He merely set his shield on top of the rocks to block their arrows and kept singing.

"That man is a good singer," said Ishaq, whom Ragnarok had dumped behind the nearby piles of rocks. "A respecter of the dead. He's not worthy to be a part of your bloodthirsty race."

Dyrfinna had been walking off to the opposite side of the wall to set her warriors into order there, but this crass statement brought her up short. "Does anybody have a moment to drag our prisoner the rest of the way up the hill to the mead hall?" she asked, exasperated.

"Your prisoner would also like a private moment to relieve himself," Ishaq added.

"Ugh. Where's Ragnarok?" she asked, but then saw him lugging boulders hither and yon at Ostryg's direction.

Skeggi finished singing, then sat silent for a moment before he arose. "I can walk him there," he said, dusting small rocks off his leggings.

"Oh, good." Dyrfinna was very much finished here. "Ostryg, do you need any help?"

"I've about got everybody in position," he said,

bustling past her. "It's going to set everybody back on their asses. It's going to be great."

"Do you ever not talk about asses?" Ishaq asked.

Ostryg stopped in his tracks and frowned at Ishaq, an effect exaggerated by his bloody arms and wild hair. He had lost his helmet along the way, probably while berserking. "Do I ever not...?" he began as if trying to puzzle out what Ishaq meant. Then he shook his head and went off to a different part of the rocks without another word.

A smile tugged at her mouth.

"I'll go with you," Dyrfinna told Skeggi. The worst moments were when she had to sit and wait for a battle to come to her. Better to do some small, useful thing to keep her mind off the carnage to come. She wanted to see how Gefjun was doing, too. "Let's get this prisoner secured."

She and Skeggi hauled the prisoner to his feet and walked the man between them to the mead hall.

Inside, Gefjun was getting the wounded settled on the west side of the great banquet room. She was stitching an axe wound on one man's shoulder as he grimaced in pain.

"I wish they'd made this damn wall higher," she began, busily stitching, but then she looked up from her work and noticed Ishaq, standing with his arms bound, between Dyrfinna and Skeggi.

"No," Gefjun said immediately, her eyes turning sharp as flint at the sight of the enemy. "I don't know who this is but I don't care. Absolutely not. I am not babysitting that damned prisoner of yours. Pitch him off a cliff. Just go."

"Yes, please pitch me off a cliff," Ishaq said, dramatically rolling his eyes.

"Watch your mouth. I'm half-inclined to do it," Dyrfinna muttered.

The wounded Viking, whose name was Arne, hissed as he looked at his shoulder. "You should know better, Finna, than to talk like that. Those regal types like this man would rather be martyred than to spend time with the likes of us." Arne gestured at Ishaq. "Look at him, standing straight as a rod in his fine robes and silver armor, while the rest of us are wearing rough linen and old leather armor. I don't care how much of an annoyance he is. Stow that man somewhere safe so we can trade him for ransom. If the enemy wants him back, let them pay a wagonload of gold. Make it worth our while."

The prisoner's eyes blazed. "You low, cunning, accursed animal," he snarled. "Setting a monetary value on human life."

The wounded warrior grinned. "What do you expect? We're Vikings. Besides, I could use some ransom money. I'm trying to build a fine ship for me and my sons," he told Dyrfinna. "Take them out into the wide watery world, all five of us. They haven't traveled far from home, and I want to fix that, but I can't until I build a boat, and that takes money."

Ishaq yawned loudly. "So do I just relieve myself anyplace? Since you *Vikings* live like dogs."

Arne got to his feet, Gefjun's needle and thread dangling from his unfinished stitches. Gefjun made an outraged squawk. "Arne! Sit back down!"

"Here in a moment," he said, turning to Ishaq. "I'll walk you around the corner. Just don't expect me to hold your pisser for you."

"You're an abomination," the prisoner said coldly.

"And you're not my type," the Viking said. "Now stop complaining and come on. Finna, get back on the front lines where you belong. That's where we need you the most."

"Wait. Her?" Ishaq said, but the burly Viking took his arm and led him away.

"Arne, get back here when you're finished!" Gefjun squawked. "If you tear out any of those stitches I swear I'll have your hide."

"Are you okay here?" Dyrfinna asked as Gefjun glared

after the man she'd been stitching up. "Do you have supplies enough for battle?"

"No, I don't," she said. "I brought all my medical goods that I had on board ship, but you know that I'll instantly run out of something, as soon as the battle begins."

Then Gefjun looked at Dyrfinna, saw her frown, and gentled. "Look, Finna," she added. "You've actually saved some of my men's lives by bringing us up here. Our water barrel was almost empty on board ship. I'm not washing wounds with sea water that's full of blood and seaweed and fish shit. Freyja brought us here to where we have a place to defend ourselves and a well with fresh water. I already sent somebody to pull up a bucket of water, and it's clear and tastes good. That alone is going to go a long way toward saving our fighters' lives, I'm telling you."

"Good," Dyrfinna said firmly.

Arne came back around the corner with Ishaq, who frowned again as soon as he saw Dyrfinna.

Arne sat back down in front of Gefjun and said, "I'm sorry if I ruined your work."

She fished the tiny needle out of his chest hair, still attached to its thread. "Don't tell me you're sorry when you walk away in the middle of my surgery work," she said. "It's a good thing my stitches held. I don't want to have to sew you up a second time." She began working on the rest of his open wound.

"Good luck, Juni. We'll try not to send too many wounded back to you," Dyrfinna told Gefjun as she and Skeggi left.

"Yeah, yeah. I'll believe it when I see it," Gefjun grumbled.

Arne lifted his chin slightly toward the prisoner. "I'll watch him for you," he told Dyrfinna.

"Thanks," she said, then leaned close to Gefjun to ask, "So, how are the eggs?"

"They're safe," she whispered, lightly patting the pouch around her waist.

Dyrfinna and Skeggi rejoined the rest of the fighters behind the rocks.

"I'll bet Arne wants some of the ransom money," Skeggi murmured.

"If he keeps the prisoner from escaping, I'd be happy to give him a fair share," she said. "If he wants to build a new boat for his sons, then he should be able to do it. His share of the ransom will be enough to let him hire some of the best craftsmen for the job."

It seemed strange to talk of home duties here, while their enemies were amassing down at the bottom of the slope. It seemed as if home were a long way off – as if it had never even existed.

At the bottom of the long slope before the ships, Nauma's troops milled around, beginning to get into a very loose formation so they could march up the hill behind their shields, shoulder to shoulder. Dyrfinna's ship was still ablaze, and burning so fiercely that the timbers of the closest enemy ships were beginning to smoke from their proximity to the burning vessel. Some of the fighters left their battle formations to douse their ships with water to keep them from burning, and now they were being forced to assemble a partial crew to move one of the ships away.

"That will slow them down," Dyrfinna said with satisfaction. She thought of Hakr there in the flames, and desperately wished he were still alive to guide her and give her council. Now she was doing this on her own.

What would Hakr have done in my place? she asked herself. *Think of how he would have handled all of these things.*

So she did.

"Remember that we are staying alive now so we can take revenge for our dear friend Thora," Dyrfinna told the first group of her fighters, who crouched in a nook of boulders at the top of the long slope. "We're going to stop these child-killers in their tracks, because we don't want these monsters to reach our home. And once that is done, we will meet with the rest of the Queen's forces as soon as we can, then and sail forth to revenge Thora."

Skeggi nodded, his curly beard glimmering in the sun. "I believe in fighting for honor, but I don't believe in dying for honor," he said, his dark eyes meeting Dyrfinna's.

She remembered their kiss in the water and looked down, a spike of longing in her heart. But this was not hers. Besides, his ladylove Rjupa was still out there some-place, flying around on her dragon.

She nodded toward the sun, which was slowly moving toward the horizon. "We still have a few hours of daylight," she said. "If our plan works, we can hold off the enemy until nightfall puts an end to fighting. Then we can reassess what we have and prepare for tomorrow."

A loud rabble of voices from below, growing louder. It slowly turned into a chant of some sort – or attempted to, as nobody was able to get into the right tempo.

Dyrfinna swiftly brought her shield down off her back, then carefully looked around the side of a great pile of stones, using a gap between the rocks to lower her chances of being struck by a lucky arrow.

A small group of burly warriors was coming up the hill with a white flag: two shieldmaidens, three Moors, and a berserker wearing a bearskin helm – Illugi, wrecker of mead halls, who was apparently Nauma's second-in-command. All looked angry and grim.

Dyrfinna whistled to her troops. "Hold your fire and let them come. Skeggi, Ostryg, Ragnarok, to me. We must meet them."

Dyrfinna warily came down the slope a little way, just far enough so that, when the enemy came close, they would not be able to see where her fighters were placed behind the rocks. Also, she was content to let them use up all their energy in climbing up to them.

"Who should speak, you or me?" she murmured to Ostryg as the enemy approached.

"I'd like to," Ostryg said, glowering at the emissaries from over his bear-faced shield. "I'll tell these sorry bitch babies to bite their—"

Dyrfinna cleared her throat. "I'll do the honors," she added mildly.

Now the envoy was close. "You may stop there," Dyrfinna said, sending her voice out the way that Hakr had taught, many years ago, so that most of the people on the battlefield could hear her. "Sir, I am Dyrfinna of Skala, and these are my associates, Skeggi, Ostryg, and Ragnarok, named Thorvald by his parents. Who are you and why have you come to us under the white flag of truce?"

One of the Moors inclined his head. "I am Mundir al-Qurtubi of King Varinn's army, a recent visitor to this *very* cold place," he said with a hint of humor. "We have come to discuss terms. We could easily leave you here on this island to die, with no ship to carry you home, but we are a generous people."

Ostryg grunted. Dyrfinna frowned but kept her eyes only on Mundir.

"You have taken one of our commanders, Ishaq ibn Maslama," he continued. "He is your prisoner. Tell us what his ransom will be. We will give you gold in exchange for our commander, and we will gladly go on our way."

"No!" Illugi, the henchman, blurted at the Moor. "That's not what we want."

Mundir's eyebrows went up while Skeggi's face turned down.

Illugi turned on Dyrfinna, baring his rotten teeth like an angry dwarf. "My ship is the ship of the child-killers," he said, spitting in his anger. "We don't need to be generous. We don't need to give you gold. You need to do as we say."

"I beg your pardon?" Dyrfinna asked.

"Don't act snooty, girl." Illugi turned his wild eyes on each person in Dyrfinna's group while he was speaking. "Now, you're going to give that man back to us. We're not going to pay you anything for him. Give him to us, or we will burn your tiny band down. You can't stand against us. And we're ready to prove it."

There was a strained silence for a moment. Mundir inhaled sharply, though his face remained impassive.

This is ridiculous. "Who is in charge of your party?" Dyrfinna said.

"I am," Illugi and Mundir said simultaneously. Illugi hissed, turning on his companion.

"These people fell in with our troops," Mundir said, gesturing at Illugi, "telling us that we have a common enemy in your people. That is why they are here with us now." This was said coolly enough, but Dyrfinna got the distinct impression that Mundir was ready for the child-killers to fall right back out again.

Skeggi, who was standing with his arms crossed, broke in. "Illugi, there is no threat you can give us that will frighten us. If you cannot speak to us like a civilized being, you might as well leave."

"*You* are the uncivilized people," Illugi blurted. "I'll say it again: Give us the commander, or we will burn you down." He stabbed at the ground with his pointing finger. "Without mercy."

"Huh," Dyrfinna said. "That sounds really bad. But we won't give you the commander. Sorry."

"Are you sassing me, girl?" Illugi said.

Dyrfinna kept her face impassive as she looked around at the rest of the enemy envoy. "I think we're finished here," she said to Mundir. "I'd be happy to talk with you, specifically, about terms later, but obviously not before a battle. Your commander can cool his heels behind our battle lines while we fight."

Illugi broke in. "I already told you to give us the

commander. You should be grateful I don't kill you where you stand, you little *bitch*."

A shocked silence at Illugi's words. Ostryg's hand dropped to his knife. Dyrfinna felt her face and neck go red, but she bit back her anger and reminded herself where the power lay.

"Do you think your emotional outburst is going to change my mind? I already said no," she said coolly.

Illugi's face blotched with anger – and, seeing this, she smiled. "Nice knowing you. Come on, gentlemen. We're leaving now." She turned and walked away. Her back itched, certain that Illugi was going to sink a knife in her spine, and she had to fight herself to not look over her shoulder at him.

"But what about *your* commander that we captured?" asked Mundir. "I have been wondering if you would mention him. Surely you want him back?"

He said the last question with such a plaintive tone that Dyrfinna couldn't help but bark out a laugh. She turned back. "Sir, I apologize for my laughter. My only response is that I'd recommend that you keep Sinkr far, far back from the rest of your men so you don't have to listen to his yammering. Enjoy."

They went up the hill. Illugi was muttering something nasty, but now the Moors were walking away as well. Illugi, now standing alone, pulled out his axe, but only brandished it at Dyrfinna before he turned and followed King Varinn's men.

"That child-killer is a piece of work," Ostryg said.

"I haven't seen anything like that before," Skeggi said quietly. "Our enemies are definitely at odds. What do you think happened?"

Dyrfinna, whose mind was now filled with all kinds of sharp rejoinders to Illugi's words, shook her head. "I think that the child-killers simply joined King Varinn's men for sport – and now Varinn's men are starting to have second thoughts. And who can blame them?"

"That Moor was pissed," Ostryg said. "I should have offered to kill Illugi. Maybe they would have taken me up on the offer."

"To be honest, I'd almost pay a ransom so they'd *keep* Sinkr," Dyrfinna muttered as they reached the safety of the rocks.

13

THORA'S GOLD

"Get into position!" Dyrfinna called to their fighters among the rocks as her small group rejoined them. "The parley is over, and the enemy will be coming up to pay us a visit soon."

"Let's make everything hot for them when they arrive," Skeggi added.

The crowd noise from the bottom of the mountain was getting louder – and then a war horn blew, then more and more of them. The crowd noise turned into shouting and cheering.

"Here they come," Dyrfinna called, taking her position in the gap between the high piles of stones that sat at the top of the long slope. The sun, hanging above the western horizon, was full in her eyes. Far below, the lines of attackers tightened up as they raised spears and sword and shields.

"They have a long way uphill to walk to get to us," Dyrfinna told her troops. "Let them work to get to where you are."

At Dyrfinna's side, Ostryg leaned on his battle axe and calmly surveyed the foe as they began to clamber up the side of the mountain toward them at a leisurely pace.

But the foe kept coming, and kept coming, until the slope of the mountain was filled with them.

A lot of the foe. Hundreds of them.

Dyrfinna's heart sank. "How many are there?"

Squinting at them, Ostryg said, "Oh, I'd say there's couple fewer than before."

"No, I *really* want to know how many people are here."

Skeggi was looking over the crowd. "At this moment, I'd estimate about three hundred. I don't know if they plan to hold any fighters in reserve back at the ships, but if their commanders have any sense, they probably have."

Dyrfinna had about fifty people in her crew, not counting the several wounded and Gefjun.

"Well," she said, rolling her shoulders. "This should be fun."

Skeggi scanned the crowd, his long fingers wrapped around his spear's handle. "Do you see that Nauma person anywhere? The girl who somehow stole Thora's crown?"

Now heat boiled up from Dyrfinna's heart into her face, and she glared at the oncoming army, looking for that telltale gleam of Thora's gold. "I don't see her. I'd expect she's in the back of the battle, keeping herself safe. How did she get that crown? Did she steal anything else from Thora's funeral ship?"

And suddenly Dyrfinna went cold. In her mind's eye she could see, clear as life, Thora walking to the holy mountain with no goods, all her valuables gone, everything that made her a queen-to-be stripped from her – arriving in the land of the dead in dishonor.

"Odin's *eye*," she whispered.

"But her ship was ablaze when we left it," Skeggi told her. "We saw to it – our dragons did – that every part was aflame. We saw the mast fall. Those flames were epic and beautiful." His face softened with sadness as if seeing them again.

"Look lively, children," Ostryg reminded them. "No time for dreaming now. You want to remember Thora?

Remember her standing at our side, cutting down the Danes with her blue magic."

Dyrfinna shook herself out of her thoughts, turning her anger toward the oncoming crowd of warriors, whose steps were slowing as they got closer, the high mountain already tiring them. *One thing at a time,* she told herself. *Hold off these fighters, and then we can find that Nauma and rip Thora's crown out of her oily hair.*

Ostryg rested his great axe on his shoulder. "I'll take that gargantuan fellow with the black beard," he said, pointing at one of the men who had pulled forward out of the group.

Dyrfinna drew her sword and glanced along its bright blade as she zeroed in on a thin man with a blonde beard clambering up the slope toward her. As tired as she was, her heart leapt. The man was compact and muscular, but he struggled with the rocks on the slope as he climbed toward her, fighting not to show how out of breath he was.

"Let them send their best to us," Skeggi said, twirling his spear. "We can tire them out just by waiting for them."

Dyrfinna set her shield at the ready, bouncing lightly on the balls of her feet, making some practice swings of her sword to warm up. When her adversary was finally within reach, he gasped for breath as he pulled his sword. Dyrfinna merely waited. He took a couple steps toward her, swinging his sword up, and she took a quick step forward and met the man with a clash of iron.

Now Nauma's fighters gave a loud shout—the yells of maddened men, the shrieks of warrior women. A swarm of fighters came running uphill toward them, the first to arrive.

There was one problem with this new position, Dyrfinna realized. Now that Nauma's forces were out of their ships, they could *all* fight—all three or four hundred of them.

"Fear not!" cried Dyrfinna, echoing one of Hakr's old phrases. "Left flank, now! Avalanche!"

At her cry, Dyrfinna immediately took several quick steps back uphill, closer to the safety of the piles of rocks behind which her troops worked.

From her left came the sudden groan of stone upon stone.

A huge boulder went tumbling from the heights of the rocky pass. Faster and faster it went, springing down the slope, breaking more rocks loose, which sprung many more rocks loose ... and the roar of rocks swallowed all the battle noise.

Dyrfinna and Ostryg had placed fighters here and there among the rocks. Now her fighters on the left had set off a rockslide that roared down the mountainside at the big groups of attackers.

Dyrfinna had seen rockslides before – had seen their destructive energy grow and grow as the rocks gathered speed down the side of a mountain, leaving almost other-worldly destruction in their path, as if one of the eternal gods had come down and in one fell swoop had smashed houses and trees into kindling.

This was the first time she'd seen a rockslide strike a group of warriors.

There was no time for Nauma's forces to get out of the way—just a sudden, panicked pushing into the crowd as the rocks overtook them, gigantic boulders spinning in the air as they crashed into the crowd. By now the rocks had gained so much momentum that the boulders bounced into the crowd and lopped off heads, arms, and turned flesh and bone into jelly.

A great plume of rock dust rose into the air, but the shrieks and howls of agony that followed the assault were truly painful to hear.

Dyrfinna backed away from her opponent that she was fighting, sickened by the sight and sound of what those rocks were doing. Her opponent looked down the mountain and instantly turned pale.

Screaming, the remaining army scattered to try and keep from being smashed into pulp by the flying boulders. Nauma's forces were flung into disarray by the surprise attack, shocked at the extent of damage the rock fall had caused.

The thunder of the rocks slowly died away, and the groans and heartrending cries from the rubble began.

Dyrfinna tried to steel her heart against the sound. "They would have killed us if they could," she told herself.

The blonde-bearded man she was fighting turned on her, furious. "You think you can make us turn tail and run away just because you got us with your big pile of rocks, your dirty little sneak attacks?" he sneered.

"Yeah, I think we can," Dyrfinna said.

He raced in at her, trying to bully her shield aside with his, his sword darting at her face and neck.

He was compact but extraordinarily strong, and she couldn't hold against him. Instead, she jumped aside, using his own momentum and strength against him, and he went stumbling past. As he passed, she gave him another shove, and then another so he couldn't regain his feet. Then he struck a patch of loose shale that slid out from under him. He lost his footing, falling on his rear. The rocks slid away under him, carrying him down the scree of the mountain, picking up momentum, his arms windmilling. His sword flew out of his hands into the crushed remains of Nauma's fighters. Somebody screamed.

"I got you with a *little* pile of rocks – does that suit you any better?" Dyrfinna called down after him.

By this time, the blood and mayhem caused by the rockslide was becoming clearer, now that the rock dust was settling out of the air. Now Dyrfinna could see the gory scene of dead, dying, and dismembered.

"That was sobering," Skeggi said, leaning heavily on his sword, looking as if he were about to be sick.

Ostryg shrugged, clearly pleased by the display. "Sobering, my ass," he said. "If they wiped out half our army with a rockslide, they'd be dancing around our broken bodies and singing shitty songs about how we died in agony."

Meanwhile, far below, by the ships, Nauma's henchmen and a group of Moors were having an intense argument.

After a while, somebody blew the horn to draw back the fighters that could still walk, and they slowly retreated back to the ships.

A while later, a single Moor came up the slope, carrying a white banner, and this time he came alone.

"Hold your fire," Dyrfinna told her troops, sheathing her sword. "I'm going to talk to him."

He wore a cloak and robes of simple black, and a dark maroon turban on his head, wrapped in the style of the Andalusians from Iberia.

"We request permission to find and bury the dead," he said, his robes blowing in the wind.

"Permission granted. It's almost nightfall anyway," Dyrfinna said, looking out at the sun, which was dipping toward the horizon, and the clouds of sunset were beginning to catch fire in oranges and reds. "We will cease hostilities until morning, unless your attackers try to force their way into our camp." She gestured at the piles of rocks heaped up at the top of the slope. "We will be quick to rain stones down upon your people if anybody from your camp tries anything funny."

"We are not a joking people," the Moor said.

"Well then," she said. "Take care of your dead and wounded. We will let you work in peace and will not harm you. We will resume our fight in the morning."

The Moor agreed, then carried the terms to his people while Dyrfinna returned to hers. Fighters from the enemy camps came up and began dragging aside the dead and tending to the wounded. In the meantime, Nauma blew the horn again and gathered her chiefs.

"Looks like a council of war," Dyrfinna said to Skeggi, who had joined her again. "We've got them over a barrel, I think."

"Works for me," Skeggi said, looking around at the rest of their army, who had settled among the stones and were watching the enemy's rescue efforts, gossiping as soldiers do, or merely watching with grave faces. "So does this mean we're done fighting for the day?"

She could see part of the enemy's army where people were beginning to set up a camp near the ships, building up fires to cook dinner and keep warm.

"Those bastards have the right idea," Ostryg grumbled as his stomach growled.

"No. We are not to that point yet," Dyrfinna said, sheathing her sword. "We need to build up these defenses against the enemy first."

Her friends were grim but cheerful as they worked, piling up rocks to make the barricades impossible for the enemy to breach. The only way the enemy could get at Dyrfinna's army was along the rise that they'd climbed, which led through a gap in the rock piles to the wall and the old mead hall beyond. Though the work was long and tiring, they went about it with a good will.

It was late when the fortifications were ready, and they drew straws to decide who'd keep watch while others rested. The guards were chosen for the evening and then for night watch, and were set among the rocks.

With that done, the rest of the army was at liberty, allowed to build their own fires for dinner and free to do what they liked for a little while. Many built their cook-fires near the wall, so they'd be ready in a heartbeat if the enemy tried to breach their defenses. Others walked out toward the cliffs, bows in hand, to shoot a puffin or a skua for supper.

Dyrfinna was gazing out across the ocean. "Do you see any sign of Queen Saehildr's fleet?" she asked her friends. "I was hoping we would have caught sight of them by now."

"I was too," Skeggi said, looking out over the sea and the small, rocky islands that cluttered the approach to the island. "I hope that the Queen's fleet haven't been whirled to the bottom of the sea, but I expect they simply were blown off course – just as we were."

Dyrfinna could only shrug. Their position was secure for the moment, but all the same, they needed relief. In the back of her mind, she winced every time she imagined watching her crew being killed, one by one, over many slow days and nights – imagining the Queen's fleet arriving too late, when only a few survivors remained of Dyrfinna's crew. And then living with that horrifying loss for the rest of her life. She, the one who had been responsible for all their deaths.

"At least the nights are very short," she muttered.

Less time to lie awake and think about all the things that might go wrong, she nearly said aloud, but squelched the words before they popped out.

Stop. She took a deep breath to calm herself. Then she took that fear and pushed it aside. The future had troubles of its own. There was no use in trying to guess which troubles it would bring. All she had was this moment, right now – and things were quiet now. And...

She turned and eyed the great mead hall there before her.

She pulled a hard ship biscuit out of the pouch at her side and began gnawing on that. Though she was starving and exhausted, she wanted so badly to explore the ruins and see what she could find.

"I'm going to see if Gefjun needs any help," she said to Skeggi.

Skeggi suddenly became as bright and alert as a dog

that has spotted a steak. "Uh-huh. You mean you're going to *explore* that old mead hall."

"And you're all ready to explore it with me," Dyrfinna said. "I can tell. You're not hard to read."

"*You* can explore the mead hall," Ostryg said. "I'm going to explore Gefjun."

Dyrfinna gagged.

"She'll probably just smack you," Skeggi said as they all started off in that direction. "And you will have deserved it."

Despite their banter, or whatever that was, Dyrfinna's mind was whirling. She wanted to figure out the battle strategy for the next morning, and was praying that there would be something inside the old mead hall or one of the outbuildings that would make it possible for them to hold on long enough for the Queen's fleet to find them.

What if the rest of the fleet had been lost – whirled by the gods to the bottom of the ocean? What then? Or, what if they didn't find her forces in time? How long would their rockfalls last before the enemy found some way to get around them?

"The worst thing," she said, "is that we're holding a position that we can't fight our way out of. There's no way off the island, outside of stealing one of Nauma's ships."

Skeggi shook his head. "It's incredible that the Queen's forces haven't found us yet," he muttered. "But if we don't get reinforcements, we're going to have the mother of all battles on our hands."

⚜ 14 ⚜
SIEGE PREPARATIONS

DYRFINNA WASN'T THE ONLY ONE WHO WAS EXCITED about the old mead hall ruins. Others from her ship were strolling around the grounds, or looking through the buildings out back. Somebody was calling for the black-smith, and judging from the conversation, it sounded as if there was indeed an old forge in the stables. Dyrfinna was delighted.

"Somebody bring the grappling hooks here!" some-body else called. "We can melt them down and make arrowheads and pikes."

"Not all of them!" Dyrfinna called. "Reserve two for later – just in case."

However, there were precious few trees around the top of the heights – which meant there was precious little firewood. Axes were ringing as they were laid to the five trees that grew along the rock piles.

Now, as Dyrfinna and Skeggi reached the hall, she heard somebody cutting down the old apple trees for fire-wood, which smote her heart.

She said to the woodsmen, "Don't be in too much of a hurry to use up that wood. Once it's gone, we can't get any more. Then we'll have to eat your food cold and uncooked, and fall asleep shivering on the ground around a dead cookfire pit."

"We can tear apart the old hall for wood," somebody called.

Skeggi grimaced. "Yes, but what happens when that wood is gone?"

"Ah, they'll have found us by then," somebody else said.

"Pray for the luck of the gods," Dyrfinna said to herself. "But never pin your hopes on them."

They found that Gefjun had moved the wounded into the great hall, along with the prisoner, so they went to find them.

Two great doors stood at the front and center of the hall, great oaken doors, beautifully carved with decorations, as thick as Dyrfinna's hand. They must have taken weeks, months of work. They'd held up against the sun and storms for decades. But one of the doors was hanging loose on one hinge, while the other had been torn from its place and was leaning against a wall.

"These were not knocked down by the wind," Ostryg said, inspecting the hinges.

The door leaning against the wall had large imprints, dents, in the wood. She pointed out the marks to Skeggi and Ostryg. "Looks like a battering ram did this."

"This is solid wood if it wasn't cracked by a battering ram," Ostryg said.

"Perhaps somebody faced a desperate last stand here, long before we arrived," Skeggi mused, touching the wood as if searching for answers. "Like the stories I've heard."

Dyrfinna sent for the ship carpenters, asking that the doors be set back on their hinges so they could be closed and barred – just in case things became desperate later. Then she stepped inside and looked with great satisfaction around the hall.

The sun was setting, the ocean and its sky all aglow in pearly pink and soft oranges, so the inside of the hall was dark. One torch burned in a bracket near the door, casting illumination into the depths of the main hall.

The old hall was certainly grand. It must have looked even grander during its heyday, when people had lived here. Its rafters stood high overhead, built with solid oaken beams – which Dyrfinna visualized as firewood for a brief, awful moment. The pillars that supported the hall were thick with decorative carvings. Dyrfinna ran her hand reverently over them, feeling how they'd been worn smooth by time and from the touch of many hands, now long gone.

The hearth stood on a raised platform in the middle of the floor, built up with black rocks, looking very stately. Far overhead in the roof was supposed to be an opening to let the smoke out, but this had been closed with a set of shutters. Somebody was carefully climbing around on the roof, trying to open them from the outside, while one of the walking wounded stood on top of a table with a pole, calling directions up to his friend on the roof.

The walls were built of solid stone, very thick. Viking-made longhouses and mead halls were wooden, but Dyrfinna doubted that the builder of this hall had been a Viking – somebody from Pictland or Anglica, or some country where they preferred building with stone.

High up, thin windows that could double as arrow slits let in a little light. A platform ran around the top of the hall that would allow archers to move from one window to another one, shooting at their enemies. Whoever had built this hall had clearly been prepared for an enemy onslaught.

So if we have to make a last stand in here, we can bar the doors and hold the enemy off for just a little longer, Dyrfinna thought.

But, looking around the place, she saw ancient arrows lying around the floor. A broken helmet against the wall. Piles of rags that might have been clothes at one time before the rodents and insects finished with them. Several gigantic tables and their benches stretched across the room, but five of them had been pushed against the back wall – today, by the marks in the dust of the floor. Benches lay overturned, and several of the tables were badly marred by axe and arrow strikes, as if they had been turned on their sides as a last defense against the enemy.

Dyrfinna felt a chill and turned away.

Gefjun was busily feeding a fire in the raised hearth at the center of the hall, saying her prayers to the gods of the hearth as she did. A third table, along with its benches, was being broken up into firewood by Arne, one of the wounded men, who was wielding an ax upon it, sweating profusely. A wounded shieldmaiden was neatly stacking the firewood next to Gefjun at the hearth.

"This is well-seasoned oak, so it should make a great fire," she said.

The worst of the wounded lay around the hearth where they could enjoy the heat of the fire. The dust had been swept off the floor here, revealing a lovely design wrought with neatly-cut black and grey stones. Dyrfinna crouched and brushed away more dust, rubbing her fingers over the gleaming stones, which were silky-smooth to the touch. She had not seen stones like these before. They must have been shipped in from far away.

Gefjun looked up from her work, and her face lit up when she saw Ostryg with Skeggi and Dyrfinna. "Where have you slackers been?"

"Oh, fighting off the enemy so we could keep the most beautiful woman in Midgard safe," Ostryg said, swooping her up into his arms and planting a big kiss on her lips.

Gefjun laughed. "Oh, stop."

"Never." He kissed her again.

"You smell terrible."

"It's part of my legendary appeal." Another kiss.

"Please, I beg you upon the beautiful feet of God, somebody tell the slackers to stop kissing," came the voice of Ishaq. Now Dyrfinna noticed him sitting at one of those gigantic tables, feet tied, and his hands on the table-top, also bound.

"Oh, but this slacker is just getting started," Ostryg said, kissing Gefjun all over the face and neck. She laughed, finally pushing him away, her face red.

Dyrfinna was busily looking all around the brazier, and leaned in toward Gefjun. "Where are the ... you know," she asked under her voice, tipping her head toward the fire.

"Oh, I don't know," she said conversationally, but her foot tapped an old bucket filled with fresh ashes, still radiating heat from the fire.

All four of the sword-friends gazed reverently at the bucket. Dyrfinna was studying the ashes, focused intently, hoping to see the tiniest movement from the dragon eggs that were buried in them.

"Anything new?" she asked Gefjun hopefully, still in a low voice.

"I'm afraid not. Nothing has changed."

"Ah, hurry up," Ostryg whispered, gazing at the bucket. "I want to see what they look like."

Ishaq's voice broke into the quiet. "Do you people ever feed your prisoners, by the way, like civilized people?"

Dyrfinna startled like a guilty person. The other sword-friends looked away from the bucket of ashes.

"If you keep up your complaining, I'm not going to feed you at all," Gefjun snapped, moving her hair out of her face and tucking it into her braid. "I've sent somebody out to see if he can shoot puffins. If you behave yourself, I'll share them with you."

Ostryg grinned, leaning up against the wall next to her. "Babe, why don't you do that little spell where you summon the puffins? Bring them all in here for supper."

Gefjun looked shocked. "I've told you a million times! I'm not going to call puffins to their deaths. They're too trusting. They fly in and land all around me with those cute little faces, and they offer me beakfuls of eels ..."

"They're sweeter after you roast them over a fire."

Gefjun gave him a little shove. "Ugh! Why are you like this?"

"Ostryg, stop asking your true love to summon help-less animals against her will," Dyrfinna said.

"But I'm *hungry*."

"Now come on, I want to explore this place. Do you want to come with us, Juni?"

Gefjun turned to Arne and the shieldmaiden, but they shooed her away. "You've worked hard all day, fussing over us like a mother hen. Go explore with your friends. We'll be fine for a little while."

They all walked away together.

"Do you think anybody suspects anything?" Dyrfinna asked in a low voice when they were out of earshot.

Skeggi pulled a face. "I hope not," he whispered.

15

EXPLORING THE
GREAT HALL

GEFJUN JOINED THE SWORD-FRIENDS. "I'VE ALREADY looked around this place to see what necessities it has. Come on, I'll show you."

She led them to the back corner of the hall behind several great chairs, where a small door was tucked into a recess in the wall. "This leads to the scullery," she said, leading them down a short, low-ceilinged hallway through which Ostryg had to stoop, to another door which opened into a well-lighted kitchen.

A gigantic hearth took up the central space, as well as a solid but beat-up table (*firewood*, Dyrfinna instantly thought) covered with old crocks and dishes and what looked like a solid inch of mouse poop.

Gefjun led them to an enclosed well sat in one corner. "I was so happy to find this," she said. "Look at this." A brand-new rope from the ship was attached to a bucket that looked about a hundred years old, though the inside was clean and watertight. Gefjun dropped the bucket into the well and drew it up, and everybody drank deeply of the fresh water.

Skeggi drank some more, then splashed his face to wash himself off. "This is the sweetest water I've ever tasted," he said. Gefjun smiled as if she'd dug the well herself.

Dyrfinna had to agree. She drank out of her cupped hands and couldn't get enough. After a long, thirsty day of fighting, she felt like a dry sponge absorbing the sweet water, each cell in her body plumping and expanding at the water's touch.

Finally, satiated at last, they washed their faces, arms, and hands with the rest of the water.

Dyrfinna dried her face on her sleeve. "I feel almost human again," she said. Newly invigorated, though still hungry, she nosed through the kitchen, pushing aside old broken crockery with her foot. Finding a barrel, she opened it to an earthy smell and a startled rat scrabbling out and launching itself into space. She scampered back while everybody else laughed.

Gefjun said, "We have water here, which is why I had everybody drag the wounded into the great hall. I also had Arne fill the water barrel from our ship and roll it out to the wall so our thirsty fighters can have water."

"I'll bet they've already drunk it dry," Ostryg said.

Dyrfinna dumped the dust and dead insects out of an old basin, filled it with fresh water from the refilled bucket, and washed four of the better-looking bowls left upside-down on one of the storage shelves. "At least we'll have something to eat out of, like those civilized people that our prisoner keeps nattering on about."

Ostryg started sexy dancing next to Gefjun. "I'm civilized, I'm civilized," he said, until she picked up an old platter and prepared to break it over his head, and he stopped.

"Juni, did our esteemed prisoner tell you anything else about himself?" Dyrfinna asked, making a face at Ostryg's dancing.

"No," Gefjun said, picking extra bowls and plates off the shelves. "He wouldn't say anything about who he was or what his occupation is, but I'll bet he's one of King Varinn's advisors. I'm almost certain I've seen him before, when the king was visiting Queen Saehildr's court." She looked inside a beautiful cup made of blue porcelain, but made a disgusted face at whatever was inside it and set it aside.

They brought the clean dishes into the great hall, where they found Arne cooking puffins in the great hearth in the middle of the floor, and several large loaves of bread that had just started cooking. "See?" he said. "I told you I had it all under control." Then Arne went back to talking with one of his wounded friends about the ship he wanted to build for his sons.

The sun had mostly set, though the sky in the west would stay bright for a while. By this light the sword-friends walked into the rest of the hall.

Here were the living quarters, with a hallway in the middle and rooms on each side. The hallway had a ceiling, for a second story. Dyrfinna went to the end of the hallway and opened the door to the outside. Here was the old barn, now roofless, where Gefjun had originally brought the wounded.

"I found some oil lanterns," Skeggi said, reaching up to where small sconces were set in the wall, each with a small lamp. He brought one down and lifted off its lid, peeked inside of it, then stuck it in his pocket. "Maybe I can render oil from a puffin for the lamp ... though, come to think of it, I guess there are about twenty puffins on the hearth right now, dripping fat into the fire," he added, returning to the great hall. "I'll be right back."

"He doesn't waste a thing," Ostryg said from inside one of the chambers, where he was looking over a small living space.

"A very useful attribute right now." Dyrfinna peered inside another room. There had been a bed here, once, but all the skins and the bed coverings had nearly rotted away into dust. The feather mattress had been pillaged by rodents, and the ropes that had supported the mattress were fraying in dusty threads. She sneezed vigorously.

"Here's a ladder to the second story," Gefjun said from

an alcove next to the open door, placing her hands on the rungs to see if they would hold. "I think." The ladder led up into a smaller alcove.

"Go up! I want to see," Dyrfinna said.

A light gleamed from the entrance of the hallway. Skeggi wandered back in, illuminating the hall with an oil lamp that burned with a brilliant flame.

"Oh, that's much better. Juni, do you need this light?" Dyrfinna asked as she climbed up.

"Wait a moment," Gefjun called down. "I want to make sure we don't have a bunch of thatch hanging down into the room. Unless you want to set the whole place ablaze." She climbed up and vanished through the hole.

"I'll bet it's storage," Ostryg said.

"Or hidden treasure," Skeggi replied, raising the lamp as Dyrfinna scampered up the ladder.

"Or snakes!" Ostryg shouted after Dyrfinna.

Some light gleamed in through a hole in the thatching. Dyrfinna sneezed five times in a row as soon as she climbed into the room and accidently banged her head on the sloping roof. She swore.

"Watch out for the roof," Ostryg called up.

"Thanks," Dyrfinna said sarcastically. Her eyes were watering, whether from the blow or from her allergies, she wasn't sure. "Juni?" she asked, trying to rub her eyes clear, grimacing at her aching head as she stepped off the ladder into the room.

Gefjun wasn't speaking. She was standing there, silent, staring at something in the darkness on the floor.

The loft was larger than Dyrfinna had expected, but the walls were blackened from years of smoke from the fire in the great hall, which had drifted through the cracks of the wall and thatching, so even with the light coming in, it was hard for Dyrfinna to make out anything through her watering eyes. It smelled strange up here. Old rooms had a smell like mice and paper wasps, which this one had, but there was another smell underlying it that she couldn't identify through her snot-filled nose. There were old trunks up here, all of which had been thrown open with the contents flung around the floor. In the far corner lay what looked like an old pallet with a large heap of rags thrown upon it. A cross hung on the wall, as if a monk had lived here at one time.

She took a few steps forward toward Gefjun to see what she was looking at – and was immediately arrested by her friend's bony, cold hand locking on her arm with a grip of iron.

"Not. Another. Step," she hissed. "Are you insane?"

Dyrfinna froze. With her free hand she rubbed her eyes clear – and now she saw what Gefjun was seeing.

Those were not rags on that old pallet.

Their skin had turned to paper, but now she could see the white of bone here and there, peeping out from the remains of somebody's sleeve, or the bottom of a jaw.

A number of people had been thrown into a heap at the corner of this loft, about five of them – it was hard to tell.

"Their last stand," said Dyrfinna, low, through her horror.

Skeggi's head popped up behind them. "Oh, hey, would you look at that? There are a few actual books over here!" He lifted several small volumes out of the litter around one of the overturned chests. "If only Thora could see me now."

❧ 16 ❧
MOVING THE DEAD

THE SWORD-FRIENDS SWIFTLY RETREATED TO THE GREAT hall.

"I'm all for burying the bodies immediately," Gefjun said, shivering from being on edge. "I don't care how you do it, just get them out of here. I liked this place before, but now I'm half-inclined to burn it to the ground."

Ostryg was hungrily eyeing the roast puffins on the fire. "How many years have those bones been up there? Another day or two isn't going to make a difference."

"I'd rather conserve our fighters' energy," Dyrfinna said. "We've gone through a lot today, and tomorrow we're going to be fighting for our survival. We can bury them with the rest of our dead."

"Bury who!" cried a very startled Arne, who had appeared at the doors, along with the ship's carpenters who had come to hang the doors. Both of the carpenters' eyes got huge, and one made the sign of the cross while the other made the sign of the hammer of Thor.

"There are maybe five bodies in the loft in the living quarters," Dyrfinna said, pointing in their general direction. "Very old bodies. We think this place was attacked long ago, and they were cornered and killed while trying to hide."

Skeggi's eyes lit for a moment, and he looked up from the book he'd found. "So the stories of the old king were true after all!"

"To be honest, I really was not interested in thinking about the whys and wherefores of their death," Gefjun said, throwing her hands wide.

"We will bury them," Dyrfinna said in a voice that brooked no argument, noting the fear in the eyes of Gefjun, the ship's carpenters, and Arne. "We can make a temporary cairn for them tonight to put them safely under rock and soil, and promise them a more suitable burial once our battle is over and won. We will placate their souls. I will have no hungry ghosts roaming here while we are trying to survive in the face of an enemy force much larger than ours."

Ostryg got up. "If you can find somebody to dig a shallow grave and more some stones, I can remove the bodies. I'm not afraid of some old bones."

Gefjun went pale. "No! Ostryg! Let somebody else do it. Not you."

"My superstitious darling!" he said with a laugh. "They're not going to hurt me. I'll be fine."

Gefjun's eyes flared and she got up quick. "You stay here," she said, low, a tremble in her voice.

"I'll help you move them," Dyrfinna said, getting up.

"No!" Gefjun half-shrieked, wild-eyed. "Finna, not you too! Don't you have any idea what the dead can do? Send one of your underlings to do the job."

Dyrfinna had always had a horror of sending somebody else to do a job she was perfectly capable of doing. If she could do it, she would. She caught Gefjun's arms. "It's okay," she said. "Juni, look. If they were walkers, or anything of the sort, they'd be up and walking already. Pray to the gods for their understanding and help."

She got to her feet to go with Ostryg, but then paused. "Wait," Dyrfinna added, looking around the hall. "Where did Skeggi go?"

To her surprise, Skeggi was sitting at the table next to the prisoner, Ishaq. The small oil lamp he'd taken out of the hallway was burning on the tabletop before them. Nearby was one of the bowls that Dyrfinna had rescued from the scullery, in which he'd caught the fat from the cooking puffins.

By the light of the small lamp they were both silent, reading the book that Skeggi had found lying on the floor in the loft. In silence, Skeggi carefully turned a translucent vellum page, and he and Ishaq leaned their heads together, continuing to read.

"...well, I guess that's fine," Dyrfinna said, bemused. "We'll let that be."

"Skeggi!" Ostryg shouted to see him startle and frown. "You like that book?"

Skeggi opened his mouth to speak, then looked down at the book for a moment. Then he went back to reading.

Ostryg huffed, hands on hips. "Fine. Come on, Dyrfinna."

"Wait a moment," she said. "We should have some light, too. That loft is dark as a cruel man's heart."

Dyrfinna left the great hall and took down one of the small oil lamps that lined the hall through the living quarters.

She filled the oil lamp from Skeggi's supply of puffin oil, just a spoonful, then rolled a wick from one of the old rags that had been kicked against the wall ages ago. She dipped it in the oil, fixed it in the wickholder, then wiped off her fingers and lit her lamp from his.

For a moment she watched the two men reading. She had never understood the allure books held for some people. It seemed strange to stare at a page all day instead of roaming the world and talking to dragons and having adventures.

Ishaq looked up at her gravely from the book. "Do you read?"

She looked at the densely-written pages with its

crabbed text that was not runic. It might have been one of those damnable Roman languages. No pictures, not even those illuminations that Thora's books always had, with the tiny illustrations of fighting snails and hapless people and rabbits and dragons that curled through the margins. "I can read a few runes, but not many. And not this language, either, whatever it is."

"A commander who does not read?" Ishaq said, shocked. "How is this possible?"

Before Dyrfinna could trounce him, Skeggi raised a hand to ward her off. "Book are rare in this part of the world," he told Ishaq. "I only read because Thora taught me how."

Ishaq's eyebrows went up. "This is incredible."

Skeggi shrugged and went back to reading, and Ishaq did too.

Seeing Skeggi reading reminded her of how Thora used to sit so quietly wherever she was, perfectly content to look at a book – though when she'd heard Dyrfinna sigh, Thora would put the book down, closing the book upon her pointer finger, and tell her the story that she'd been reading about, which Dyrfinna approved of. She was always of the opinion that stories should be shared, instead of being a secret conversation whispered to somebody through a bunch of black jots on a page.

Now, as she followed Ostryg through an unfamiliar longhouse on a deserted mountain, she missed Thora. She wished that she could talk to her. What would she have thought about her friends being surrounded by an enemy that they'd sworn vengeance against for her sake?

She and Ostryg climbed into the loft, the small oil lamp with its puffin oil making a very bright, clear light. She set it up on a shelf where the small flame could illuminate the room.

Though the bodies had lain there, for decades, they still smelled once they were moved. The dried skin cracked and shattered in a way that Dyrfinna was extremely uncomfortable with, and she regretted volunteering. Ostryg didn't seem to care – he just tied an old cloth around as many feet as he could find and dragged all of them at once off the place where they'd been left with a terrible clatter and hissed noises, and awful cracks.

"It's just bodies," he said, hauling the grisly corpses across the floor toward the ladder.

"Oh. That makes me feel better." She did not, in fact, feel better.

He shrugged. "I've seen worse. At least these people are all dried up. At least they're not still *alive*."

"Was this something you did often with your family?" she blurted out, trying to come up with some way to keep her mind off what they were doing. "Dragging bodies?"

One of the arms, or something – Dyrfinna was not particularly interested in finding out what it was – snagged on one of the overturned chests. Ostryg handed the towing cloth to Dyrfinna and kicked the bones free of the encumbrance. Something snapped, a brittle sound. Dyrfinna's knees turned to water.

"We were assassins," he said. "Body disposal goes with the territory. I was young at the time, so I didn't do as much work with this as the rest of my family did. Sometimes I'd come home from playing and everybody would be sharpening their knives, and I knew it was going to be a long night."

Ostryg never really liked talking about his assassin family, or what it was like growing up with them – he hated his father, Papa Ostryg, with the heat of ten thousand suns – but in the current context, as Dyrfinna dragged the remains of five dead people across the floor, it seemed to be the natural thing to talk about. Not to mention that she needed a topic of conversation that was interesting enough for her to focus on so she could keep from thinking about the desiccated skin on these people was crumbling and breaking as she dragged ... she burped sulfur, her stomach roiling.

"Did you ever have to help them kill anybody?" she blurted out as she neared the ladder.

Ostryg shrugged with one shoulder. "Not until I was eleven. Papa wanted me to start younger, but Mama wouldn't allow it." His voice was hard. "She died in child-birth later on. She had a tough time giving birth, and Papa knew it, but he kept burdening her with children. So he managed to kill her, too."

"I'm sorry."

"A proud day for him, I'm sure. Once she was out of the way and couldn't protect us, that's when the fun began." By the tone of Ostryg's voice, it clearly had not been fun. "Stop right there," he added as she reached the edge of the alcove where the ladder was. She gladly dropped the piece of cloth she'd been dragging. It was beginning to come apart in her hand.

"How do we get them down?" Dyrfinna imagined climbing down while trying to gently guide the mess of bones, dried skin and flesh, and rotting clothes down the ladder ... she gagged. In order to keep her stomach under control, she took a slow, deep breath – but the smell only made it worse.

"Get out of the way. We're gonna drop them."

"But ... there'll be a mess." She burped again, thinking of bones and who knows what exploded all over the floor below. Odin's *eye*, if she didn't get out of there soon ... "Wait, just wait. I'm going to try and find some kind of cloth to wrap them in."

"We don't have any," Ostryg sighed. "I don't want to be up here all night looking for cloth. Let's just kick the bodies down and then get some dinner."

How he could even think about dinner was beyond her. "We can get some sailcloth out of the ... oh. I guess we can't." She kept forgetting that her ship had gone all up in flames just a short time ago.

She went past Ostryg into the loft, tiptoeing past the

bodies, looking around for something, anything, to wrap them in.

Ostryg huffed. "Leave it, Dyrfinna. Besides, even if we find some cloth, Juni needs it more than these dead bodies to. She doesn't have anything to wrap wounds with. She still has some bandages, but not near enough for tomorrow."

There were a lot of rags lying around the floor – somebody's old clothes, which had been dumped out of the chests long ago and rifled through, probably by the men who killed these people. Most had already fallen apart. But here was a chest that had been shut after it had been searched through. To her relief, inside was a blanket, rolled tightly to keep the fleas out. It was chewed by moths but was mostly intact. She held it up triumphantly.

Wrapping five or six dead people in a blanket didn't sound like much work, but it was as if the skeletons didn't want to be wrapped up, for the dead fought them through the exhausting and horrifying process. They were finally wrapped enough to where they could be lowered to the ground below, Dyrfinna holding on to the corners of the blanket. Thus did she manage to maintain some semblance of dignity for the dead, which was some comfort.

She was certain that, if the dead had been ignobly dumped to the floor as Ostryg had wanted, that would have been followed by her vomiting copiously all over the place. By avoiding the first outcome, they avoided the second outcome, and she was grateful for it.

As soon as they dragged their burden outside into the sweet night air, Dyrfinna breathed deeply of it as if she couldn't get enough, her heart juddering in her chest, feeling as if she'd walked out of a fever nightmare.

The grave had already been dug, she was relieved to see, and Skeggi waved them over. Her whole army was watching from their cookfires and their rocks, making various signs to protect themselves against the dark influences of the dead. Gefjun watched from the great doors, bookended by the carpenters who had stopped in their door-hanging work to watch as well.

Dyrfinna and Ostryg dragged the dead to the grave and laid them in, wrapping them in the blanket. Ostryg asked Gefjun if she wanted to keep the blanket and make bandages out of it. She stared at him as if she wanted to scream at him, and then she'd burst into tears. So they took that as a no.

It was late at night when the grave was filled in, and the rocks stacked on top in a makeshift cairn. Skeggi sang a lament for the people who had died, and the grave was hallowed.

But Gefjun shuddered at the grave. "Wash yourself up," she snapped at Ostryg and Dyrfinna. "I pray that you two have not brought some curse upon yourselves for having done this! If we die here on this island because nobody can find us, then you'll be to blame."

Skeggi came to join them. "Juni, don't talk like that," he said. "Pray to the eternal gods and ask their blessing. I'm sure Rjupa's been trying to find us."

⚜ 17 ⚜
IMPALED

Skeggi was right – Rjupa had actually been searching for them all that day.

But one never really appreciates how enormous the world is until they have been flying for a long time on dragonback, looking for the tiniest trace of their friends' ship, which had been blown off course.

Rjupa had been flying ever since yesterday, after she'd been sent out to find Dyrfinna's ship.

The dragons that were traveling with the Queen's fleet weren't able to leave, of course, for those dragons were for the protection of the ships and the Vikings on them. But since she was a messenger, she volunteered to go.

Rjupa and her silver dragon had set out immediately, worried. Dyrfinna had a crew that was smart enough to know how to stay out of trouble, and the fact that they'd disappear in the terrible storm a day or two ago all but screamed to her that something had gone terribly wrong for Dyrfinna and her friends from the Corae Guard.

So she and her dragon had flown slowly up the coast, as high as they could while being able to see a longship from the air. The pace was too slow for her, in her worries – her sweetheart Skeggi was one of those on Dyrfinna's ship – but the coast curved and twisted so much, and there were so many islands, and she was afraid to miss any of them.

At first, Rjupa didn't notice the smell of burning. Her dragon, Shriken, had the smell of scorch clinging to her at all times, and besides, Rjupa's mind was wrapped up in trying not to miss any little detail on the ground.

It didn't really sink in that something was wrong when Shriken's crests suddenly rose in mid-flight.

"Rjupa," her dragon said in a strange voice, dipping closer to the ground.

Rjupa, broken from her reverie, looked down.

At first, from dragonback, she thought that it was a doll that lay, splayed and abandoned, at the side of the road at the village edge. There were some bundles lying in the road nearby, as if dropped. A pile of black rags lay in the weeds at the side of the road.

But then a ringing in her ears started, growing louder and louder as the dragon swooped lower, and the images suddenly resolved themselves into the truth.

"That's not a doll," she murmured, the awful comprehension rushing over her.

"No," her dragon said, slowing her flight. "No doll bleeds."

That was a toddler lying there, its delicate face and limbs tinged with blue. What she thought were black rags in the weeds was actually its father, crumpled unmoving, arms stretched toward the dead child.

What she thought were bundles in the road was actually a mother's body lying atop the children she'd tried to protect.

All of them lay cold and still upon the ground, blood streaking their horrified, open-eyed faces.

"Freyja, protect us; Freyja, help us," Rjupa whispered, a cold sweat springing out on her brow.

The village was very still in that cold gray morning. The only things moving was a wisp of fog that drifted over the village like a ghost, and the smoke boiling up from a burning house. No sound but the crackle of flames.

Rjupa was sitting upright, unable to stop shivering. With the ringing in her ears came a sense of unreality, muffling her hearing and her feelings.

This was too familiar.

She had lived through this, once.

She had never wanted to think of those days ever again, though in her day-to-day life, a memory would often burst upon her, bringing her a flash of some wretched scene from the past. As it was now – for now she saw the faces of her attackers. She stumbled over the bodies of her mother and sisters. She tasted blood. She stared with deadened eyes over the burning and rape of her village as she was dragged by rough hands into thralldom.

She didn't want to see what had happened to these people. She wanted nothing more than to keep flying, and pretend that the travesties below never existed.

"Take me down there," Rjupa croaked in a voice she did not recognize.

She could not stop shivering.

Shriken banked gently. "I've got you," the dragon said. "I swear I'll keep you safe from whatever is lurking here."

"That's ... that's not what I fear," Rjupa said in a quiet voice.

They drifted down to that scene of horror. Now she could smell the bright copper stink of blood.

They touched down, Rjupa holding a spear that her friend Thora had crafted for her, a symbol of their friendship. The silver dragon turned her head this way and that in the foggy air, looking for enemies.

"Take care," Shriken said softly, as Rjupa, spear in hand, unfastened her strap and slid off her back, her booted feet landing on the cold ground. Rjupa crouched slightly, letting sounds, smells, sensations come to her as she took stock of her surroundings. The blood was rushing too loudly in her ears to allow her to hear. At least she had a dragon at her back to burn any murderers or monsters into ash.

Shriken looked around her. "How many have died here?" she asked. "Are there any survivors? And are the killers still lurking here?"

"I pray they are," Rjupa said, gripping her spear. "I want to pay each of them in blood."

She went to the dead child first. It was a little boy, maybe three years old, whose eyes were still half-open with shock where he'd been thrown. "The poor baby," she whispered again, kneeling at the boy's side, trying to close his eyes with one shaking hand.

A sound, the scrape of a boot on pebbles.

Both Rjupa and Shriken went silent, instantly on alert, staring into the village ahead of them for a long moment. Rjupa pressed against her dragon's hot side, peering into the shadows, trying to be aware of her surroundings the way Dyrfinna always was.

"Might be a survivor," Shriken whispered.

"Might be somebody we need to kill," she whispered back.

They listened for another long moment. Nothing.

"Come," she said.

Shriken usually made a wisecrack about the situation, but not now. She too was alert, and even the fine, skinny feathers on her head drifted upward in her body's heat, making her look even more alert and on edge.

They stepped forward, slipping past a longhouse at the edge of the village, tiptoeing around the great structure of old, marked pine, watching the door as if it might burst open. Nothing else moved.

The smell hit her first from the middle of the village. The stink of hot blood and slaughter, as before a feast when several oxen were killed. Only this blood and flesh had been left to rot.

Rjupa whispered a prayer as they turned past a tidy

longhouse where the door had been smashed in, where a perfect riot of garden flowers still bloomed incongruously. Somebody's bare foot stuck out from under the broken-down door. The noise of buzzing came from inside the house.

"Flies," she whispered.

The buzz ahead was much thicker, as thick and pervasive as the sound of the ocean.

She felt Iron Skull's fingers reach through her thick hair and yank. She nearly cried out from the pain. But Iron Skull wasn't there – he had been dead for years.

He is dead, Rjupa reminded herself; I killed him myself. I watched him die. And yet those memories of his cruel hands felt every bit as tangible as the day it had happened – and every awful sensation from those long-ago days were now being brought back by the filmy eyes of the dead.

"I'm not ready," she said, as her feet bore her, all unwilling, around the corner to the middle of the town.

Here was the middle of town where the dances and processions and bonfires were held.

It was as if all of the people of this village had been dragged here and executed in small groups, or singly. Some had clearly put up a fight, and after death their arms and feet had been hacked off. Some women still lay where they'd been raped. Children lay as if flung here and there.

The blood fled from her face. The world faded. In the next instant, a sudden shock woke her: She had fallen to the ground, and her eyes sprang open.

Shriken was nudging her where she lay on the ground. "Look at me," her dragon said gently. "Look in my eyes."

Rjupa's teeth were chattering. After a moment, she did as the dragon asked her. Shriken's yellow eyes blinked and her pupils grew larger.

Shriken twittered softly, like a bird singing. "I am with you. Be strong. Be strong."

Her dragon was trying to do magic – but now the red

carnelian jewels on the dragon's golden collar sparkled, then began to glow, counteracting her dragon's will. Nothing happened.

Rjupa wished that she could remove the collar, and let Shriken do her magic. However, if the collar were removed, her dragon would only go wild – even kill her where she stood.

"I ... I wish I could just do this one thing..." Shriken said as to herself. She tried again, her wings unconsciously opening with the effort, but once again the red carnelians glowed.

"Don't worry about it." Rjupa gently rubbed her dragon's cheek.

"Pah!" Shriken whispered in a burst of frustration. The gems glowed very brightly for an instant, and she subsided into a gentle, "I can't do it. I'm sorry." She nuzzled Rjupa's face.

"It's okay," Rjupa said, trying to concentrate on her dragon's liquid gaze, and lay her hand on Shriken's cheek. "I love you, my sweet dragon. Don't worry about it."

Shriken gently rubbed her nose against Rjupa's side. After a time, the gleam of the carnelians faded.

"Come," the dragon said patiently. "We must see if there are any survivors among the dead."

"I don't want to." Rjupa's ears were ringing again, and her dragon seemed to be far away – everything was.

"I know. I will walk with you."

Slowly, Rjupa pushed herself to her feet. They walked toward the dead. Everything was so far away. Shriken's wing came out, curled around Rjupa.

There was one survivor. As soon as Rjupa saw him, her heart leaped with hatred. It was a man in full armor lying on his back, his arms out, his shield just out of his reach, a short distance away, as was his gleaming helmet and his sword. The breath rattled in and out of his lungs.

On his armor was an image she'd never seen before, that of a skull. A child's skull. Rjupa gripped her spear.

"Who are you?" she asked, wondering why the man did not get up. Then, in a flash of horror, she saw why – he had been speared, impaled to the ground, fixed in place like an insect. His heels had dug pits in the gravel where he'd tried to fight his way free.

Her breath caught in her throat.

At the sound, the man's eyes rolled over to her. Bloody foam dribbled from the corner of his mouth.

"They wanted me to help them kill," he said in a mere shadow of a voice. "Before she came to lead our band of warriors, we were content to pillage and ruin villages and put their occupants to the sword, and walk away with their gold. But now she's taken the deaths to an inhuman degree. I assure you, I have killed before, in many raids, but they were honorable fights, where my opponents were armed. But today, after what she did ... I put down my sword and refused. So they left me here. Like this. An example."

Rjupa went to him then, took the soldier's hand. "Let me see if I can free you."

He shook his head, though the slight movement pained him. "As much as I want to be rid of this thing, don't do it. She made sure to drive this lance through one of my arteries. Once it comes out, I will bleed to death in an instant."

Shriken was trembling with rage, her silver wings flung open. "Who are these monsters? Are they draugrs, hungry for flesh? Vampyren, who drink blood? Tell me, sir, if you please."

The man's eyes fluttered as if he were on the verge of passing out, but he spoke as if he were unable to stay silent. "They are an accursed army, roaming under many names. They have no hearts, no leader but her. They call themselves the Child-Killers, and a cold bitch leads them."

Rjupa had seen enough of the banality of evil people – how they were all evil in the same ways. Oddly, the understanding helped her master her revulsion, though she still felt it strongly. "And you refused. May Odin grant you a seat at the table at Valhalla." She picked up his sword and placed it in his hand. "If you die, you will die with great honor."

Tears came to his eyes. "Thank you," he said. "The bastards kicked my sword out of reach. When I take my seat at the table among my fellow warriors, I will tell them of your kindness." His breath grew short, his eyes glazing from pain.

Rjupa felt herself blush at his generous words, but at the same time thought of how wrong this was, that he had only death open to him now – even if it was, at the last, a warrior's death. "Sir, please tell me about this so-called leader before you die. Who is she?"

His face darkened, here, even at the end of his life, and his eyes flashed fire. "The accursed whelp, dog-fornicator, shit-eater, whom the gods should split along every vein in her body," he spat. "That blonde bitch has blood on her face and hands, and she laughs at the pitiful dead she's left in her wake. Her name is Nauma, and I pray that —"

But as soon as the name left his lips, Rjupa felt the backflash of a curse that had been placed upon the man, coming off him like a small explosion and blowing her hair back.

His head lolled and fell back before he could finish speaking.

"He is dead," said Shriken in a leaden voice.

She stared in horror for a long moment until a sob burst from her. She leaned her head on the dragon's side and wept.

Finally she looked back upon the bodies of the dead. "We need to find the nearest village and tell them the news," she said softly to Shriken.

Her dragon rested her head upon Rjupa's shoulder.

"And when we return with the others, I will help burn the dead."

In a moment, Rjupa was on Shriken's back and flying to a nearby village they'd noticed from the air.

"Thank Freyja that my friends don't have to see this," she murmured.

Unfortunately, she was wrong.

❦ 18 ❧
THE WOMAN IN MIDNIGHT

BACK AT THE GREAT HALL, DYRFINNA VIGOROUSLY washed herself, then ate cold puffin and the only remaining piece of bread, which was gritty from having fallen into the fire. She attempted to sleep, lying on the floor near the central hearth and staring at the stars through the opening in the roof – for they had managed to open the shutters.

Finally, too keyed up to sleep, Dyrfinna hiked out alone to look around the area from which they were fighting. She wrapped herself in her wolf-trimmed sea cloak against the chilly wind blowing in from the sea and talked with the night watch for a while, looking at Nauma's fighters camped on the shore far below, well out of the reach of rockslides. The night fog was beginning to drift in from the ocean, softening the edges of the ships down below.

Dyrfinna walked around the ruins of the old mead hall, wondering which king had presided over the banquets, wondering what king had fallen here in this hall so long ago. Had the king been among the dead they had just buried? There had been no jewels on any of them – likely they had been taken by the people who had killed them. Without his royal trappings, the king was just like any other person.

A cold mist fell. The fog had rolled in, and tiny snowflakes swirled in the mist. The world softened, vanished around her. She breathed deep of the misty air, smelling pine resin, soil, the salt of the sea.

Something moved in the fog ahead of her.

Dyrfinna stopped, squinting into the darkness. Yes, there was a dark shape, the soft sound of a footfall in the misty leaves on the ground.

Leaves? She looked down. Green ash leaves lay around her feet. But there had been no leafy ash trees up here in the rocks, and certainly no leaves on the ground. There had not been any ash trees growing anywhere near the old mead hall, only the apple and cherry trees – and anyway, all of the trees around the hall had been cut down.

She shook her head and breathed deep, wondering if she'd somehow nodded off while she'd been walking.

No, she was not asleep. A figure stood in the fog before her.

Dyrfinna's hand fell on her hilt, prepared to draw, and she cast around her, checking to be sure nobody else hid in the fog to spring on her.

"Who goes there?" she asked in a low voice.

The fog uncurled from around the dark figure. A tall woman wearing a dark-blue cloak with white armor underneath towered over Dyrfinna. This woman held a spear that stood a cubit taller than she, and it cast a faint glow. A great shield sat on her other side, emblazoned with an enormous eye.

The woman turned. A long, severe face. Dark, unknowable eyes fixed on Dyrfinna.

As if she *knew* her.

And as soon as Dyrfinna met those eyes, her breath caught in her throat.

She choked in terror.

And she jerked awake, heart pounding.

Dyrfinna found herself lying on the ground next to the

dying campfire with the rest of the fighters, wrapped in her sea cloak. She didn't even remember having laid down.

She pushed herself up to her elbows, looking around. But there were no green ash leaves on the ground. No fog, no mist, no snowflakes, and no spectral woman in white armor. Just the wolf light of early dawn in the east, the glowing embers of the fire, and an exhausted soldier snoring.

Who was that woman, and why had she been so afraid of her? Was she a ghost? Was she one of those who had died? Dyrfinna had no idea.

19

THE FIRST DAY OF BATTLE

DYRFINNA PULLED HERSELF TO HER FEET. SHE WAS STILL exhausted, but sleep had fled. She did not want to think about what her dream might mean, but she couldn't get the ghost's eyes out of her head. How those eyes had *known* her. As if they had weighed her worth and found it wanting.

"Enough," she muttered, wrapping the sea cloak tightly around herself. She had worse things to contemplate.

In a few hours, her people would face the enemy in battle. Some of them would fall to their foes. This was simply a fact of war. But as their commander, everything that happened next, good or bad, would be her responsibility – and this is what made her heart rise into her throat.

The truth was, in battle, things could go sideways very quickly. She had fought in battles when one thing went wrong, then another and another, and like the rockslide the previous day. Everything had gone wrong with such breathtaking speed that it was only through the narrowest of chances that Dyrfinna had been able to save herself and survive the battle. It had been a total and cataclysmic failure.

The worst part was, you could be doing everything right – you could be fighting with all your strength to make the right decisions – but one decision at the wrong time, one stroke of bad luck, would be the rolling pebble that triggered a deadly landslide.

You never knew.

And Dyrfinna felt as if that woman she'd seen in her dreams knew this – and now she was watching Dyrfinna to see how well she'd make those difficult choices.

Dyrfinna tiptoed into the great hall to check on her sword-friends. They sprawled, asleep, around the great hearth in the middle of the floor.

Ostryg and Gefjun were cuddled together. Skeggi lay on his back with the back of his hand across his eyes, as if he were an actor who had just performed an overly dramatic scene. His other hand lay touching the ash bucket where the dragon eggs were hidden.

The flames flickered from the dying fire. She gently laid another log on top, propping it on another piece of wood that was nearly to embers. She blew on them and watched them glow, watched the bottom of the log start to smoke from the heat, then it leaped into flame.

All were asleep. Moving slowly so she made no sound, she eased to the ground next to Skeggi and opened the ash bucket where the dragon eggs were buried. Carefully, she dug her fingers into the ashes until she found one of the eggs, and gently lifted it out.

It was grey with the ashes it had been buried in, but when she held it in her hand, it slowly took on the color of the palm of her hand. Camouflage. She could feel the shape of the baby dragon inside against the palm of her hand. It twitched a little, shifted inside the shell, was still again.

What would their future hold? What kind of life would they live, she and her little dragonet? Would she be able to protect it?

Would her father take this dragonet away from her,

the way he'd taken the command of her ship from her? The way he'd taken away her place in the Corae Guard?

Just then, she noticed the glimmer of Ishaq's eyes from where he lay on the opposite side of the fire. When she raised her head, he shut them and rolled onto his other side so his back was to her.

Her heart thudded. The large, stone brazier sat between them, hiding her body and the ash bucket from his view. He couldn't have seen what she held in her hand, or known what brought her to this place.

All the same, she was disquieted.

Anxious, moody, she quietly buried the egg back in the ashes, then walked back outside to the stone fortifications that stood between her fighters and hundreds of the enemy. The east was already brightening, though it was still night. The days were getting much, much longer. Winter was a sky of everlasting stars, while summer was a sky of everlasting sun.

She found some of her crew, the ones who had been chosen for second watch, standing next to the wall and whispering.

"What's happening?" she asked in a low voice as she joined them.

One of the fighters gestured for her to look through a gap that had been made through the rocks, then he pointed at the thin spruce forest that grew farther down the side of the rocky mountain.

Stooping, she looked. For a while she could make out nothing. Then her eye picked up a flicker of movement among the rocks below. Too big to be a bird or pika. She focused on it. Yes. A person with a fur cap, crouched among the stones, trying to hold very still.

"Huh," she said, stepping back into the shelter of the rocks so her words wouldn't travel down the mountain to where the spy was hiding. "Is he the only one who's spying on us?"

"There seem to be five of them altogether," the guard said. "Scouts."

"Too bad they're out of arrow range," Dyrfinna said wistfully.

"We shouldn't waste our arrows on anything that wouldn't be worth shooting," he said pedantically.

It wasn't as if Dyrfinna suggested flinging a quiver of arrows at them just for wasteful fun. She held back her exasperated sigh. "Well, no, of course not. Any sign of more behind them?"

"Nothing we can hear or see."

In the meantime, one of the shieldmaidens approached. "I made some slings," she said. "If any of you are good with these..."

"Pff," said one of the guards. "A child's toy."

"Not if you use it to hurl sharp flint at the enemy's eyes," Dyrfinna said, now intrigued, taking one. "It's got more range than a sword, and, unlike the archers, a slinger will never run out of ammunition."

"We're standing on a mountain *made* of ammunition," one of the guards added gleefully, whirling a sling at his side and launching a sharp-edged stone at the spy, who ducked as the small missile sent a cloud of needles and twigs flying.

"Can we make more of these?" Dyrfinna asked the crowd in general. "How many of you are adept with slings?"

"I hunt birds with them," said one of the warriors, pulling out a well-used sling made of woven hemp.

"Find out how many of our numbers are skilled with using slings," Dyrfinna told the guard. "We'll place you among the lines to hold the enemy back as they're approaching. That will help us to save arrows."

Dyrfinna sat with them as they made a few new slings, eventually dozing off where she sat.

A little while later, Gefjun took her shoulder and

shook her awake. "Good morning ... commander," she said.

Dyrfinna's eyes popped open to a brighter night sky and Gefjun stooping over her. The stars were still out. She nodded, though she felt as if that responsibility suddenly settled upon her shoulders like a cloak of lead.

Gefjun stooped beside Dyrfinna and offered her a sea-biscuit and some puffin soup with a rich-smelling broth. Dyrfinna's stomach grumbled at the savory smell as the steam rose into her face. She hadn't eaten very much last night, so she appreciated it more.

"Thank you," she whispered, accepting the crockery bowl.

She ate, and it tasted glorious, for Gefjun had added herbs and greens to the soup. Dyrfinna ate the hard biscuit by dipping it in the soup, and when she'd finished, she felt strengthened as she looked over the rocks out at the enemy's lines.

"I expect Nauma's army to be moving into battle formation soon," she said. "Wake the others up. Let's get ready for battle."

Her command went out, and the troops started waking up. Several started building up their fires and cooking what little breakfast they could manage, using what they'd managed to catch or find the night before. Dyrfinna could see the enemy troops by the ships begin to move around, and she could hear their quiet talk, even from this distance.

She looked at Gefjun.

Dyrfinna nodded and stood, chewing her last bite of puffin, and drank the last few drops of broth from the bowl. "This was good. Thank you."

Gefjun took the bowl. "I will be carrying water to the fighters along the wall before I get the hall ready for the incoming wounded today. Do you want to come with me?"

"I need to get the battle lines in order first," Dyrfinna said.

"Then I'll hand these water bladders out as you go," Gefjun said.

"Actual warfare is a lot different than those games of King's Table I used to play with Thora," Dyrfinna confessed to Gefjun as they walked. "Especially the part where I constantly want to throw up."

"Why?" she asked.

Dyrfinna and Gefjun distributed water bladders among the fighters who sat among the rocks, sharpening their swords and spears. Some of the warriors, who she'd known since she was a little girl, joked with each other, telling rude stories about other battles that they'd fought in. Others braided back their hair while their battle partners helping them strap on their armor. Now Dyrfinna sent them to their positions behind the rocks, giving some of her fighters slings as well as spears and swords.

"It's hard to order the deaths of all these people," Dyrfinna said quietly when they stepped away. "I'm their commander. I led them into this. At least we're in a better position for survival on this mountain. We've also managed to pull the enemy off the water, so they're here instead of traveling to Skala. But what happens next is going to be ... difficult." She lowered her voice. "For all our advantages, we're still a small force with limited resources and limited supplies, trying to hold off a larger force. I do my best to face this stoically. I want all who will die to earn a place in Valhalla. But, selfishly, I would rather keep everybody alive so we can all go together to revenge Thora. And to raise these baby dragons."

"You still have your priorities straight." Gefjun laid a hand on her shoulder.

Dyrfinna leaned on her. They stood like that for a minute.

Dyrfinna thought of old days at Gefjun's house, making mud pies, trying to tame her rooster, playing warriors around the streets of town. Then, later, learning swords and weapon skills with the sword master that Thora had hired for them. It seemed so long ago.

The fighters were finishing their breakfasts of porridge or leftover puffin. They were all ready for battle in their chainmail or leather armor and were buckling belts, sharpening weapons, or stowing food away in their packs. The Christians had just finished their Mass on the east side of the mountaintop and were coming back to the lines, freshly blessed. Warriors shouted directions back and forth.

"To your positions," Dyrfinna called.

Just then, a great stir came from Nauma's lines – a many-voiced shout, loud as the ocean on the rocks.

"Stay alive, friend," Dyrfinna said to Gefjun.

"You're closer to the fight than I am," Gefjun said. "Don't let them hurt you. We need you."

They kissed each other on the cheek, the way they used to do every evening when their parents called them home.

Gefjun went back to the wounded. Dyrfinna walked toward the gap in the rock piles at the top of the slope. This gap was where Dyrfinna's fighters would stand in ranks to stop the enemy as they came in. She took her shield down from her back, and pulled her sword loose from her scabbard.

"Here we go," she said as Skeggi and Ostryg, who had joined them at the front, set their shields before them in a wall.

Ragnarok yawned and peeked up over his shield. "Where's the fun?"

Thwack went an arrow into his shield. The shield popped back slightly upon the hit.

Everybody ducked behind the rocks, except for Dyrfinna, who laughed.

"Look at you shy kittens," she said, holding her shield at the ready. "That was just the first raindrop. Wait until it starts to pour. Did anybody see that archer, by any chance?"

They all peered into the forest down the mountainside, but no movement gave the archer away. "If you see the sniper, take them out," she called to the archers.

The enemy was moving into formation, a long line of shields with a second line of shields behind that one. And then a third line.

Next to Dyrfinna, the shieldmaidens stepped into line, their rough armor buckled, axes at the ready. They banged their shields together and began chanting. From all around, up and down the line there at the mountain's top, Dyrfinna's soldiers all began chanting.

A sudden wave of arrows crested from downhill. Several slammed into Dyrfinna's shield so hard that their impact would have knocked her off her feet if she hadn't braced herself. The arrows were clustered at the top of the shield. They'd been aiming for her eyes.

A man screamed to her left, a bloodcurdling sound that made Dyrfinna flinch.

Gefjun raced to him. "I hate arrows," she said. "Get back from him, people. Get back. Lie down." Another moan rose into a scream as the man, on the ground, arched his back, an arrow sticking out of his belly. Gutshot. One of the worst, most painful ways to die.

How she wished Hakr was here to guide her.

20

A BOOMING OF SHIELDS

"Archers, return fire!" Dyrfinna shouted. Instead of a wave of arrows, like the attack from Nauma's archers, her archers were sniping at the Vikings on the hillside before, since they had fewer arrows to use.

A shout from below. A second wave of arrows screeched in, but the shout allowed Dyrfinna to duck behind her shield before they started. The other fighters did, too, so the deadly-barbed wave had little effect on her people this time.

"More arrows for our archers," she remarked, standing and rolling her neck. "Those of you on the back lines, gather what arrows you can find and deliver them."

"If you're not already helping with casualties," Gefjun added as she and Arne carried the gutshot man away to get him off the front lines.

As soon as they moved him, two shieldmaidens came to the front with shields and armor, ready to fight. One of them tapped sword hilts with the man next to her, both saying quietly, "Kill 'em all" as they did.

She had some of her warriors lined up along the high ridge out of sight, waiting impatiently to start avalanches on any comers.

And now the enemy cam up the long slope like a rising

tide, holding their red shields in front of them. As they came closer, Nauma's archers stopped firing so they wouldn't hit their own fighters. Dyrfinna's archers kept shooting, though, as they were high up, hidden behind the rock piles.

The red tide rose to the top of the hill, the archers picking off Vikings through the gaps in the shields. But they kept coming.

"Don't let them lure you out," she said to her fellow warriors over the oncoming roar. "Make them come to you."

"The stories aren't as exciting when we wait for the enemy," Ragnarok complained.

"But I need you to *stay alive*."

She prayed that the queen's fleet would arrive soon.

Because by now, the tide of Nauma's red shields had finished rising. Suddenly, all at once, they pulled out their swords in a loud *shing* of metal that was so wide and stretched so far that it made Dyrfinna physically ill.

She had a sudden, wild thought to pull her army back behind the wall and pile up stones before them.

A part of her rose out of the dark depths of her and sneered. *Your grandmama never felt such things, it said, standing there on her pirate ship, trying to defend her husband against the Romans who held the waters. Are you worthy of her heritage? You, who are crying like a kitten in the face of your destiny?*

She breathed deeply and drew her mother's sword.

NONE SHALL PASS THROUGH ME gleamed down the silver blade in runes of black. Her sword was named Signe, Victory, and her own mother had used this sword in battle. Mama had given this sword to her to protect Dyrfinna and keep her safe.

Now Dyrfinna's voice shrilled out.

"We fight to protect our loved ones at home," she cried. "And we fight now to revenge Thora. Do not yield to these bastards. We will hold the high ground, and they will not prevail!"

She shrilled and thrust her sword into the air. An arrow shot past her arm, close enough to cut the skin, and blood ran down. Trilling, she sang a victory song as she ran two fingers through the blood and streaked her face and eyes with it.

She didn't dare infuse her song with magic for fear of it backfiring and killing her fellow soldiers the way it had done with her little brother. But she sang loudly with spirit, and her warriors sang back, a call and response war cry that everybody in Skala knew.

Though she couldn't infuse the song with magic, a few other people were – she could feel them drawing magic into the notes they sang. Everybody in her army sang along, stamping their feet in time, pounding on their shields, until the music echoed and reechoed off the rocks around them.

Dyrfinna thrilled with the music, filled with purpose. She swept her sword through the air, shaking her shield at the enemy.

The enemy army were trying to sing against Dyrfinna's fighters, but they were singing two different songs – the child-killers sang a cruel ditty, while the Moors were singing something grand and glorious that Dyrfinna would have loved to listen to, if the stakes had not been so high.

The songs ended, followed by great cheering on both sides.

"They really are at odds," Skeggi muttered.

"Stand solid and firm before whatever they send at us," Dyrfinna shouted. Ostryg and Skeggi blasted their war horns, and the wild music was taken up all around her.

With a great shout, the enemy came running in. Another rumble and roar on the far left, and a fresh avalanche of rocks came roaring downhill at them. This one, though, was not as deadly as the first one. Though some still were crushed under the incoming rocks, the remains of the first rock fall slowed the second one down and kept it from traveling as far into the enemy's army.

"It's still better than being slaughtered on the water," she muttered, then screamed like a hawk and swung at an oncoming fighter.

Metal clashed against metal as swords met across the fortifications, and the percussive boom of shields striking shields rang up and down the battle line. Slingers shot stones into the enemy's army, occasionally with deadly effect, until the enemy's archers began to target the stone-slingers.

The press of Nauma's army crammed against the gap in the wall. Only a few of Dyrfinna's people were needed to defend the gap, while the rest of her army could act as reserves. Still, the fighters who stood within the gap were stretched just to stay alive, and the pressure of the attackers was intense.

But Nauma was not in the press of fighters, nor was her henchman, Illugi. And those two were who Dyrfinna ached to fight.

The gap in the wall was thick with shields and swords. The enemy fighters attempted to push their way through, the air thick with flying blood, sweat and screams. Dyrfinna soon lost herself in the battle, hewing at the attackers, wielding her sword with deadly effect, but also narrowly escaping death time and again.

After some time had passed – she wasn't sure how long, but now the sun was up – Dyrfinna returned to herself, realized she was exhausted, and also realized that she was too close to the action to direct the battle. She looked over her shoulder at the warriors waiting behind her, and stepped back from the fight.

Two of her fresh fighters sprang into the gap, their swords gleaming, eager to add more bodies to the pile of dying.

Dyrfinna caught her breath. Drops of blood dripped from the hair that had escaped her braids and helm, though she wasn't sure if it was her blood or somebody else's. Her arms were spattered with blood past the elbow. She was bone weary, and longed to fall asleep where she stood, but instead she pulled herself together and went to inspect the line.

Dyrfinna realized that the end of her line was giving way before Nauma's army, falling back before an onslaught of swords and screaming maniacs as the attackers began to find a way over the rock piles.

She grabbed a shieldmaiden behind the front of the line. "Quick," Dyrfinna said. "Run up to the crags above there and throw rocks down at Nauma's fighters."

As the shieldmaiden clambered into the rocks with several of her friends following, Dyrfinna strode into the fight, her bloody sword at the ready. "Push them back! Push them back!" she shrilled, and started hewing at Nauma's army. Her fighters rallied, and pushed Nauma's forces back. Dyrfinna pulled fighters in from the back of the lines, but there were only a few remaining in reserve. Soon there would be none.

The first boulder crashed into the press of Nauma's fighters, striking flesh and bone with a terrible sound. A second, larger boulder did even more damage. The child-killers scrambled back from the fight. But some shouted at their archers, pointing up at the shieldmaidens, who were easy targets.

"Stay out of sight as much as possible!" she called up to them as arrows came flying in. One of the shield-maidens fired back with her sling and stones. She was one of those who was able to hunt birds with her sling, because the rocks she flung would hit their targets very effectively among the enemy. But then an arrow struck her, and a cry she tumbled off the crag.

But now Dyrfinna realized that her own archers were shooting less and less.

"Nobody is bringing us any arrows," one of her archers called down to her as she passed.

Dyrfinna grabbed a wounded man who was limping past. "Gather some arrows for our archers."

"But I was heading to the fight over there," he said, pointing away from the main battle.

"What fight?" she cried. "Look, I'll take care of it. Pick up arrows quickly."

Dyrfinna needed to run, but all she could manage was a trot.

Oh, Freyja. Over here, in the back part of the rocks, her fighters were letting Nauma's army in a few at a time, so they could fight with them in straight-on combat. But their plan had gone sideways, because to her horror, two child-killers was torturing one of Dyrfinna's fighters. One of them was using the knife, chuckling cruelly, while the other one held off her fighters who were trying to put a stop to this.

She strode up and with a great swing of her sword caught one of the enemies unaware and killed them where they stood.

Others of Nauma's army climbed over.

"You fighters, defend the wall," she yelled, turning a few of them and shoving them in that direction. "Earn your glory by defending our people, or I'll have you hung by your thumbs, see if I won't."

Several fighters rushed to the top of the wall and started cutting Nauma's army back.

Her weariness grew.

A huge rumble shook the earth. Everybody looked toward the noise, including one of Nauma's child-killers. Dyrfinna took the opportunity to run him through, then yanked the sword out and kicked his body down the hill.

An avalanche of rocks fell. She gave thanks that some of Nauma's forces were dumb enough to try and come up the opposite side of the hill.

She truly wished all of them would.

The fighting raged on all day. Nauma's army had no end of fresh fighters.

Gefjun and several of the wounded worked as nurses. Her friend's face had aged with weariness, but she pressed on.

At the moment, Gefjun was trying to staunch Arne's bleeding, her exhausted head hanging low as the warrior gritted his teeth and tried not to writhe in agony.

"Arne," Dyrfinna breathed in shock. "What happened to you?"

His face was red and bloody where they had ripped part of his skin off. It hurt Dyrfinna just to look at it. But what was more alarming was the slow spread of dark, shiny red across his shirt.

Arne's words, like his breathing, were slow and ragged. "A group of Nauma's men got hold of me. They made my original wound worse ... and they did this to my face."

"He insisted on going back out into the fight," Gefjun snapped. "The bastard wouldn't listen to me."

Arne, whose shoulder had been neatly stitched up by Gefjun yesterday, had been hacked all bloody again, and was bleeding profusely. Under the blood that painted his arms and face, he was almost white, except for the part of his face that had been flayed. He was bleeding to death.

He patted her hand, his formerly booming voice now down to a mere thread. "Now, now, it was worth it, coming here and killing the King's men," he said, and Dyrfinna had to lean forward to hear him. "Revenge the Queen's daughter for me. I dearly want to, but I can no longer continue the fight."

"Ah, don't say that," Gefjun said, but Dyrfinna could hear how little hope was in her voice.

"Tell my sons I'm sorry," he said, fighting to speak. "Tell them ... tell them I wanted to build that ship for them ...."

He tried to breathe, but his chest rose and fell a little less each time.

Dyrfinna stopped for a moment to put her hands on Gefjun's shoulders and give her a little extra strength while she sang healing magic over Arne. Dyrfinna had little strength to give, but Gefjun didn't have much either.

Despite their efforts, Arne was fading, the luster dying from his eyes.

Quickly, Dyrfinna laid his sword upon Arne's chest and rolled his hand around its hilt, using her hand on his to keep it closed.

"I will tell your sons that you fought valiantly, and that you have passed on to Valhalla," she told him. "And I will give your sons gold, so they can build that ship."

Arne sighed a little. He mouthed the words *thank you*, no longer able to speak. Dyrfinna sat with him, holding his hand on his sword's hilt, as his breathing slowed – stopped – then one last gasp – then no more.

He was traveling to Valhalla.

Dyrfinna exhaled, and allowed his hand on the sword hilt to go slack.

Any other time she and Gefjun would have wept together. But now, here in the crush of war, Gefjun just swore loudly.

"I know," Dyrfinna said.

Gefjun shook her head, gently closed Arne's eyes as best she could, and closed up Arne's shirt to cover the wound that had killed him. Then she went to work on the next patient. There was no time to grieve. No energy for grieving. What little they had left was for survival.

In the meanwhile, outside the barricades, the bodies of the enemies started piling up, a gruesome second wall. Nobody on the enemy's side was dragging the dead out of the way—because anybody who tried ended up being cut down themselves.

The enemy fighters merely climbed over the top of the blood-slippery limbs to get at Dyrfinna's army, while the survivors in the piles of bodies wailed, and cursed, or begged to be killed.

"Please let the Queen's dragons get here soon,"

Dyrfinna prayed into the wind, gazing a moment over the empty sea. "Please."

But gods only answered prayers in their own time – if they ever did.

So she brought her shield down off her back and returned to the fight.

⚜ 21 ⚜

A GREAT-HEARTED
DRAGON

THE SUN FINALLY, MERCIFULLY, SET. NIGHT CAME ON. The sky darkened until the enemy, unable to see, pulled back from the wall and returned to their camps by the inlet.

Dyrfinna's forces stayed where they were. Soldiers lit cook fires behind the wall and cooked what food they had. Some just ate salted fish from their backpacks and fell asleep on the ground right where they sat.

Dyrfinna met Skeggi, who limped toward her. His arms were covered in blood past the elbow, and his brown beard was rust-colored from all the enemy blood that he'd shed, but he was unbowed.

"We held them off," Skeggi said. "Well done, commander."

She didn't feel as if she'd done particularly well. "We've lost five fighters," she said quietly. "Five out of about a hundred Vikings. And twelve fighters are too gravely wounded to fight tomorrow."

"Has anybody seen a sign of the Queen's fleet?" she asked.

He lifted a hand toward the mead hall. "Gefjun has a few of the wounded men out there, watching the seas, but nobody's seen anything but a few dragons out past the horizon, where they can't see us."

Dyrfinna swore quietly. She had been praying constantly for the Queen's fleet to arrive. If her dragon friends had come flying in over the ocean and saw the wild battle raging on the hill, they would have joined the fray in an instant.

Dyrfinna was too weary to feel any anger or sadness at them for not showing up. That aspect was out of her control, anyway. Better to save her energy for the things she *could* control.

Dyrfinna saw to her wounded and exhausted fighters, as a good commander should. She talked to everybody who stood guard next to the wall, to her soldiers who were eating by the fires, to the blacksmith who had returned to the smithy as soon as the battle was over, where he fed the fire and began repairing shields, swords, and spears.

The three sword-friends came back to the mead-hall, where Gefjun had been knee-deep in the wounded, so they set about helping her as well.

But then Ishaq said, "That brooch you wear," pointing at the silver dragon brooch that pinned Skeggi's cloak. "All of your friends wear that same dragon brooch. Tell me, what is its significance?"

Dyrfinna and Skeggi and Gefjun and Ostryg looked at each other.

Skeggi nodded and spoke. "It's a gift from the Queen's daughter. She had them made especially for us after our friend Corae, a garnet dragon, gave her life to help us escape from the invading Danes. They had us surrounded, and we were trying to get Thora back to safety. We were willing to give our lives to save her – but Corae did that for all of us."

Gefjun's mouth tightened as her eyes went red-rimmed, as they did every time the great-hearted dragon was mentioned.

Skeggi gave her a compassionate look. "Afterward, the Queen insisted that Thora appoint a guard for her – so she chose us. Thora had these brooches made and had us trained to fight and defend her. We learned to ride dragonback. This was all out of Thora's gratitude – and because she believed that each one of us were worthy of the position."

"Did the Queen play any part in your selection and appointments?" Ishaq asked.

"No," Skeggi said. "It was all initiated by Thora."

"But we are good friends with the Queen," Ostryg said snarkily, raising his head.

"The queen who thinks nothing of killing King Varinn's child and feeding his heart to him," Ishaq said, his voice shaking. "This is your friend? Your *friend*?"

"Odin's tears, Ostryg." Skeggi put a hand on his face. "Please do not provoke—"

"What, our esteemed and valuable guest?" Ostryg blurted. "Whose esteemed and valuable king killed Thora?"

Ishaq's voice was like steel. "Varinn did not kill her."

Ostryg rolled his eyes. "Well, he certainly hastened the process."

"Why in the name of all that is holy would King Varinn kill his own bride?" Ishaq cried.

"You tell me," Ostryg said, "because whatever he did to her made Thora come back as a draugr."

"You think King Varinn can do something like that?" Ishaq sneered.

"He's got powers we don't know about."

"So does she!" Ishaq flung an arm out at Dyrfinna.

What?

Dyrfinna took a step back. Everybody stopped dead. The whole room went silent, even the wounded people who had been engaged in conversations around them.

"What do you mean?" Dyrfinna's voice was low, tremulous.

Ishaq narrowed his eyes. "You're boiling with chaotic

power. What kinds of magicians do you have, not to be able to see that? To not be trained in that?"

"We're ... not magicians," she said, her breath short. "We are trained in magic, but only up to a point."

"Why not? You're dangerous. You're all dangerous," he added to the rest of her friends. "Letting her run around like this, with only a little ring on her finger to curb her powers. I don't understand why you don't have her out there on the battlefield, bringing cold death to our soldiers with those powers."

Her blood ran cold. That flame leapt to life in her heart – that flame that she never wanted, that ruined all her cherished hopes and dreams.

Dyrfinna blindly turned and left the great hall, not wanting to hear any more. As she did, loud arguing broke out behind her. Let them argue. She wanted no more part of this. She went out in the rain, tamping down the flame so that nobody else would be hurt by it, and ended up sitting on the cliffs, keeping watch over the sea, thinking about her life.

Dyrfinna returned much later, well after midnight. She found Gefjun sleeping in Ostryg's arms near the fire in the great hall, and he too slept. Several of the wounded men were tending the wounded, talking to them as they washed blood from their arms and faces.

"My leg hurts like hell," said a shieldmaiden, lounging on one of the platforms next to the fire. Her left leg had a deep cut in it, to the bone. Gefjun had stitched it up as best she could, but it still looked awful.

Dyrfinna stopped and talked with the shieldmaiden a while, brought her some water, and gave her some of the hardtack out of her pack that she had been saving for later.

Gefjun jerked awake. "Oh, these dreams," she whispered. Ostryg stirred but stayed asleep.

Dyrfinna lay down next to Gefjun and wrapped herself in her sea cloak, which she still hadn't taken off. Soaked in blood and still wet, it slapped her leg, but she was too tired to care.

She laid a hand on Gefjun's arm. "Try and rest."

Gefjun pulled her arm away and turned over, her eyes narrowed. "Are you going to help me by singing your magic?"

Dyrfinna was taken aback. "What?"

"I know you can sing," Gefjun snapped. "Ishaq was just being stupid. You're not dangerous."

"I don't want to talk about it."

"Just because ... just because *that* happened with Eirik doesn't mean you can't do magic. You can unleash all that power on the enemy, anyway, just like he said. Walk over there and kill them all."

At the words "kill them all," Dyrfinna grew cold all over. Her face tingled as if she were going to faint. "Don't make me do it. I can't. Not again."

"Liar." Gefjun pushed herself up on one elbow. Her eyes filled with tears as she swept an arm over her wounded. "There's no way I can save them all alone. You have the power. You can help me. If you want your fighters to stay alive, then go out there and use your magic and kill the enemy!"

Dyrfinna looked at her lifelong friend for a moment, struggling against a web of emotions that she didn't dare name. Slowly, unable to even understand what she was saying, she opened her mouth. "If I did, I'd kill our people, too. Juni, I can't control this power, and if it backlashes, which it has before, then I end up killing our people as well."

"You can get farther away and do it," she snapped.

"I don't trust myself!" Dyrfinna cried, startling several sleepers.

She shook her head, drew a ragged breath, and tried to speak more quietly. "It would be an accident, but they'd be all dead. Then all your work would truly be for nothing."

Gefjun just glared at her, tears streaming down her face.

"Don't make me do this," Dyrfinna pleaded. "I don't know ... I don't know what would come out of me if I sang. I am not. I am not going to ... do that again. Ever."

Gefjun gave a little shake of her head.

"It's not that I ... that I killed my brother," Dyrfinna said. "It's more than that. I'm afraid. Because I made him die. I didn't know that I had ... that kind of power, and we were arguing, and he died because of it. And now that I have these fighters dying, everything is coming back." She meant the guilt, the agony, the pain, the hopelessness that hung over her and squeezed her. Clouding her judgment, making her wonder if death was gentler than this.

Gefjun huffed and patted Dyrfinna's arm in a patronizing way. "You need to get over yourself sometimes," she said, lying down again with her back to her friend.

Dyrfinna shook her head. "It's not just about getting over myself," she said, annoyed. "I'm not Corae. She was a great-hearted dragon. That's not me..."

Gefjun merely lay down her head, and was instantly asleep.

"You're not taking me seriously, are you?" she said quietly to her sleeping friend.

Dyrfinna was such a tangle of emotions that she doubted she'd ever fall asleep.

And yet, as soon as she shut her eyes, she was out.

22

A VISITATION

As Dyrfinna slept, she saw again and again the battle, watching the destruction she wrought against her enemies, the horrifying scenes of the day brought back for her to relive.

Then the scene shifted to the night that Corae, the sweet, great-hearted dragon, died while defending Dyrfinna, her sword-friends, and Thora from the attacking Danes.

With a roar, Corae opened her mouth, her great teeth glimmering, and blasted fire out over the Danes. Screaming, intense heat. Blazes. People on fire screamed and crashed to the ground.

"Have Corae pick up Thora and carry her to the city," Dyrfinna cried, turning her face away from the fierce wall of heat that rolled back to them. *"We need to get you out of here."*

"No. I'm not going anywhere without the rest of you," the queen's daughter said fiercely. *"Corae can't carry all of us, and I am not leaving you to be killed by Danes when we're this close to safety."*

One of the Danes was singing song magic against the dragon, to no effect.

"Arrows! Arrows!" another of the Danes shouted over their shrieks.

"Get behind Corae, quickly!" Dyrfinna said.

"All of you, get back to Skala!" Corae's rider said from atop her dragon. Corae spit flames on the Danes. The red dragon beat her wings to fan the flames and send them blazing into the enemies. "Get Thora back to Skala now! We're here to protect you."

Arrows came zinging past, snapping and tearing through the leaves overhead like a deadly rain.

Dyrfinna grabbed Thora. All the sword-friends, covering her, fled toward the city, just as what sounded like a hundred arrows screamed through the air around them.

And Corae, who stood between them and the arrows, screamed.

Over the shouts of the oncoming Danes, their battle cries high and shrill, the red dragon's scream rang out, and she flung her wings wide.

Dyrfinna, who had never heard Corae scream, felt her knees go liquid. "What was that? What happened to her?"

"They hit her with an arrow!" Thora cried, sounding just as astonished as he was.

Dyrfinna couldn't believe it. Arrows usually bounced off the gemlike scales of the dragons. One must have gotten in between the overlapping layers of the scales.

Now a new roar from the Danes, as when an attacker is on the hunt for prey and sees victory. A furious screaming, a roar for revenge, as the Danes rushed at them.

Corae lit the world on fire, roaring in pain. Dyrfinna glimpsed the arrow sticking out of the side of her face as she ran with Thora, keeping the dragon between her and the full might of the Danes.

"Get the girl who killed Iron Skull!" somebody yelled.

"Kill the queen who is with her!" somebody else shouted.

"Run for the city," the dragonrider shouted.

A spurt of blood from her neck. She reflexively flung a hand up. Then she slumped over on her dragon's seat, dead from an arrow that pierced her neck through.

"No!" cried Skeggi, his voice lost in a chorus of pain from the rest of his friends.

Dyrfinna said, "Go!" in the next breath, chivvying them

away from the dragon. "Those were her last wishes. So carry them out, now!"

Corae screamed again, and more arrows had pierced her. Blind with pain, she sprayed fire at everything.

"Corae, fly! Get out of there!" Gefjun shouted over his shoulder. "You don't have to do this! Please!"

"She won't," Dyrfinna said, tears running down her face as she dragged her friends toward the city. "She won't fly. There are too many Danes for us to fight. Corae's going to guard us from the Danes until she dies, because she loves us so." Her voice broke. "So if she's going to sacrifice herself for us, run faster!"

They ran, all of them crying.

Corae roared with pain. Her serpentine tail struck and flung to bits any Danes that tried to sneak around her. Fire billowed and blazed from before her, silhouetting Corae's wings and the dragonrider's unmoving form on her back.

"Keep running," Dyrfinna cried fiercely through her tears, as they fled like shadows through the night forest toward Skala

When Corae's wings opened, fire gleamed through the holes that had been punched through the wings with arrows.

And then came the last cry from Corae, a broken shriek that sounded like the end of the world.

DYRFINNA WOKE UP WITH A GASP, SITTING UP, HER heart pounding in her chest as if she had actually been at a dead run.

She was back in the great hall. She'd fallen asleep some distance from the fire, wrapped in her sea-cloak, her head pillowed on the wolf hair trim her mother had sewn around its neck.

Other soldiers slept around her. The hall was still, the fire in the center of the hall burning low. Even Gefjun was asleep, curled up in Ostryg's arms. She felt a pang of jealousy.

Out of the corner of her eye, she noticed a movement.

Dyrfinna turned her head – and to her shock, a complete stranger was standing there.

It was the blue-cloaked warrior woman who she'd seen in last night's dream, now in the flesh – as real as her own friends. Except this woman was incredibly tall, standing several heads higher than Dyrfinna, and she was supernaturally beautiful, with dark eyes in a stern face.

Dyrfinna's hand fell on her sword. "How did you get in here, past our guards?"

The woman did not speak. But her cloak began to widen behind her.

This was not a midnight-blue cloak after all. These were black wings with a dark blue iridescence that made them look blue.

The black wings slowly opened behind the woman. The feathers nearly touched the floor, even when opened, and the wings spanned the entire length of the hall.

In the ambient light from the fire, the woman's white armor glowed, and her long spear gleamed. The woman looked down at Dyrfinna with a quizzical expression on her face.

And suddenly, she realized who it was. She had never seen her before, face to face, but all the same, Dyrfinna knew exactly who she was – a knowledge as clear and immediate as if she'd known this woman for her entire life.

Dyrfinna's mouth went suddenly dry. "Skuld," she croaked.

She went down hard on one knee and bowed her head low, trembling in every limb.

Skuld was one of the Norns, the fates who cut and wove the threads of life, who shaped the course of human destiny. But Skuld could unweave fate. She could cut threads that were not supposed to be cut. Sometimes Skuld went against what her sister fates had ordained.

And Skuld was one of the Valkyries who chose which warriors died.

Those black, uncanny eyes that saw the birth of the world scrutinized her.

So which of my warriors are you here to take? Dyrfinna thought, but she caught herself before she could speak, and bowed her head again. You had to be extremely careful when you talked to the gods. You never knew which intentions they'd notice, which ones they'd choose to follow.

Dyrfinna didn't have to look up. She could feel those infinite eyes burning holes into her, who'd never felt so small in her life.

"I welcome you, goddess," she said. "You honor me and the rest of my people with your presence. My people are courageous warriors. I ask you now to spare my people," she pleaded, head still bowed. "Nauma's army calls itself ... I won't go into that." Because saying that they were the child-killers might make the name take on a more terrifying reality. "I have a little sister, and I love her deeply. I can't let those people, any of those people, come to Skala. And we need to survive so we can revenge Thora, our beloved queen-to-be, as we vowed to do before the deathless gods."

Then Dyrfinna met those immortal eyes, though a terrifying fear gripped her when her mortal eyes met them.

She croaked, through a dry throat, "Goddess, spare my people. Show mercy to those who have already died, but don't cut any more threads. I will dedicate my life to your worship, and do great deeds in your name in battle. But let my people live. We must revenge Thora, but we also must keep Nauma's forces from going to Skala. I would prefer to kill them if I can, with your blessing."

Skuld didn't speak.

Suddenly it felt as if somebody had given the entire world a hard shake. The ground yanked out from under her feet, and she fell –

And she jerked awake on the ground, surrounded by

her snoring men and women, the sobs of the injured. From outside she could hear a thin scream from the piles of the dying stacked up along the wall.

No Valkyrie. No Skuld.

The goddess was gone.

Heart pounding from the encounter, Dyrfinna stared up at the stars, truly awake this time.

23

FROM BOREDOM TO
HORROR

DYRFINNA RUBBED HER FACE HARD IN HER SEA CLOAK, getting rid of the sheen of sweat that had popped out on her forehead from the very thought...

Skuld had *looked* at her.

The very thought turned her guts to water.

Dyrfinna felt the shivering start deep within, spreading out into her arms and legs. She drew her sea-cloak tightly around her body.

"She wants something of me," Dyrfinna whispered, her heart failing to think of it. "But I don't know what it is."

She gazed over the sea. She was close enough to the cliffs to see the white tops of the waves in the starlight where they broke around the many barren rocks that stuck up through the water.

Far out on the immense, starry horizon moved a single red star – a garnet dragon flying so far away that nothing of it could be seen but its light.

Her heart leapt with hope.

She instantly looked around. Could they could set a fire, one large enough for the dragon to see and come to their aid? A few camp fires burned low, but nothing large enough to be spotted from that great distance. Then she remembered that firewood was scarce – they had cut down all the trees that had stood around the mead hall. They needed to ration the wood to make it last. Once that wood ran out, they would start taking the great hall apart, piece by piece.

She watched the dragon's light, praying that it was coming toward them, hoping that the light would grow larger – but it did not. It slowly moved from right to left just above the horizon line.

And besides, she thought, watching that distant red spark, *by the time we kindle a fire large enough to be seen from that far away, this dragon is going to be gone.*

Even as she realized this, the spark was growing fainter and fainter. After another moment, it could not be seen at all.

A quiet curse under her breath. The sea was enormous – the world was limitless. Dyrfinna knew that the Queen's forces couldn't be that far away because her ship had been blown off course in a storm. But at the same time, there were so many islands and so many wrinkles in the land that it would be a challenge to find them. There were so many strong currents in the sea that could have carried them off in a direction that it wouldn't occur to the Queen's forces to search.

"Help the Queen's dragons find us," she said to the gods. "Please, have them hurry."

Just then, a thin scream came from the other side of the great heaps of rocks that formed the barricades.

She sat up, brow furrowed, listening hard. That sound, that thin scream. It went silent. Then she heard it again, wobbling in a way that raised the hair on her neck. Gone.

Though it spoke in no words, she knew what it was saying.

"It hurts ... hurts ... I'm so hungry ...."

Silently, she unwrapped her sea cloak and stood up. Her sword was already in her hand, as she kept it with her as she slept, just in case attackers came in the night.

Skeggi, who was one of those who'd been set guard

behind the piles of stones, was using his slingshot to fling rocks as far as he could toward the enemy ships and camp. In the pale light of the stars, the stone could not be seen as it flew out over the mountain. But from far below came a wooden *thunk* as it struck some part of a ship. He grinned and picked up another.

"Bored?" she asked quietly, joining him.

"You could say that. Watch out." She stepped back as he whirled the sling at his side with a whooshing sound, then flung the stone toward the enemy troops. They were both silent, listening, but no sound came in return. Skeggi shrugged and ran his fingers over the stones on the wall to find another that fit his sling. "So how about you? Can't sleep?"

"You could say that. Listen, did you hear an odd noise a moment ago? Like a strange scream?"

He turned a stone over in his fingers, listening to the silence for a moment. He shook his head.

A long moment passed as he loaded his sling and shot another stone at the enemy troops.

"Fuck!" somebody snapped from far below.

"Nice," Dyrfinna said.

The keening noise came again. Skeggi turned instantly toward Dyrfinna, frowning, as if seeking confirmation.

"Yes. That one," she said, keeping her words as quiet as possible.

The sound came from over the wall, somewhere among the dead that the child-killers had left to rot. King Varinn's army had collected their dead, and a pyre burned brightly far down on the rocky beach before the sea. Earlier in the evening, they'd started to pick up the dead of the child-killers, but then Nauma had shrieked something at them. King Varinn's fighters had curled their lips and looked disgusted, but had left the child-killers lying where they'd died.

"There's a survivor out there," Skeggi said.

"No. I don't know. That voice ... it doesn't sound human."

"It's because they're in agony."

Dyrfinna shook her head. "There's something wrong."

Just then she thought she saw movement, there in the dark. She went still, gripping Skeggi's arm.

Something made a strange hissing noise. Involuntary grunts as it seemed to push itself up to its hands and knees, though it was too dark to be certain. Every sound that came from its voice gave her the shivers. Something was wrong with the way it was breathing ...

She signed to Skeggi to move behind the wall, even as every nerve sang with tension. He didn't move, just staring, trying to understand. Dyrfinna pulled him back.

"Do you think they have a hole in their lungs?" Skeggi whispered. "And the air is ... doing *that*." For the strange bleating noise came again from that person, like a dying animal, sharp and sudden.

"Hungry..." That voice again.

Just then, one of the soldiers came to join them from the camp. In the darkness, away from the fires, Dyrfinna thought she recognized the form of that soldier's body, but apparently he'd been wounded in the leg or foot, because his steps were slow and dragging.

A light breeze blew up the dying embers in a nearby campfire, and a small flame caught, flickering. It threw a light upon the man's face: Arne's face, looking haggard and paler than Dyrfinna had ever known. His hair and beard were completely flattened on one side, and his jaw looked almost unhinged, hanging open as if it were broken.

In her shock and confusion, Dyrfinna whispered. "Arne, what's the matter? What happened to you?"

He turned blankly toward her and she was shocked to see filmy eyes. Arne's mouth opened as if to say something, but only a squeak came out, as if he'd forgotten to inhale.

Now Skeggi gripped her arm. "No," he said as if out of breath. "This is impossible. Arne died earlier today. He's dead."

24

"RUN, YOU FOOLS!"

HER EYES WIDENED, AND HER SWORD WAS IN GUARD position.

Habit is stronger than memory, and her shock at seeing Arne had blocked her memory of how he'd bled to death on the previous day.

Now Dyrfinna realized that the sounds his body made came from air being forced out of its lungs, or he would make a bleating sound as it accidentally sucked air in. His voice only sounded when air was forced through it. It wasn't that his breathing was wrong – it was the fact that he wasn't actually breathing at all.

As she stared at him, Arne's glassy eyes kindled with a faint bluish light, soft as the glowing lights that gather over a marsh in the dead of night, caused by the spirits that drift those boggy areas in the haunts of the dead. His fingers curled and clenched as the foglight gathered around his glare, as if some kind of magical power or strength were coming to him.

"Arne, don't do it," Dyrfinna said, her grip tightening on her sword. She remembered then, too late, what the old king said in Queen Saehildr's hall so long ago – that cold iron would not stop a draugr. The dead would have to be fought in hand-to-hand combat before the killing blow could be struck.

And then he exploded into motion at them, moving so unbelievably fast that Dyrfinna felt as if she were back in the dream she'd just had.

The only things that could move this fast were ghosts – and draugrs.

She barely managed to guard herself as Arne crashed into her, his great hands grabbing. She fought desperately to keep them from closing around her, striking them as hard as she could with her sword, but though she was using all her strength against him, his terrible power was overwhelming.

She didn't have a monster's strength and she knew it, for she was straining herself to the limit in her struggles, striking away his hands and arms. She finally managed to wrench herself away before he could pull her back toward him, and she staggered a short distance away, laboring to breathe.

"Why is he a draugr?" Skeggi cried.

"I don't know, maybe you should ask him?"

Arne opened his mouth again, and his hands came out and he lumbered toward them.

"Get away," Skeggi said quickly, getting in front of her, blocking him with his shield, sword at the ready. "Run to the mead hall and—"

Arne was upon him, mouth hanging open, an odd squeaking sound coming out of it at every grab and lunge he made. Skeggi was driven back, valiantly blocking every move Arne made with his sword. But he wasn't fast enough, and, worse, his sword was not cutting Arne in any way, though Skeggi struck skillfully with the blade.

Dyrfinna swung the flat of her blade directly against the side of Arne's head, hard enough that she felt her blade flex in her hands, hard enough to make him stagger to the side. Arne shook his head as if an insect were bothering him.

She smacked Arne on the other side of the head. "I'm not running to the mead hall to hide," she shouted at Skeggi.

"You're the commander – we need you!" Skeggi cried, wild-eyed, just as Arne came at him again. "Hide!"

Dyrfinna glanced off to the left, where her fighters were encamped. She couldn't leave them to be attacked by a draugr – and she wouldn't let Skeggi be killed. She'd been lucky in being able to stop and subdue Thora's draugr when she came slathering into the Queen's mead hall, hungry for blood and flesh. She thought of the soldiers there – but she also thought of the dragon eggs slumbering in the warm ashes.

She looked around, her mind clicking swiftly through ideas to trap Arne's draugr. Could they make a tree fall onto him? No, there were no trees left. What if they somehow pinned him under a boulder? No, he would lift up the boulder and hurl it back at her men. She had a silly thought about setting up Arne as a catapult and somehow training him to hurl giant rocks at the incoming enemy ...

But that stray thought, as ridiculous as it was, sparked an idea. Dyrfinna went to Skeggi's side at once, to help him block the draugr's attacks. "Come with me," she said in a low voice. "We're going to lead him out of our encampment and to the enemy's camp. Now."

Still fighting, they retreated backwards toward the gap between the piles of rocks, moving faster, barely able to keep out of reach of his flailing arms that were strong as wolf traps and more dangerous.

Arne's draugr grabbed a handful of Dyrfinna's hair and hauled her toward him, teeth snapping, and her heart failed. With a desperate sweep of her sword, she slashed her hair off. A flash of red pain from her scalp, for she had cut herself – but the gambit worked, because she was free from his grip. She scrambled out of his reach.

"You're bleeding," Skeggi said in a faint voice as both of them hurried backwards.

"Scalp wound. It'll do that." Besides, there was no time to investigate, because Arne stuffed his fistful of Dyrfinna's hair into his mouth and chewed. Then his mouth opened with a sticky-sounding moan and the hair fell out.

He turned again on Dyrfinna and Skeggi. His nostrils flared, and he snuffled, a sickening parody of a dog catching a scent – and his eyes went wild, fixing on Dyrfinna.

"That blood on your head," Skeggi said, backing up fast. "He smells it."

With an eerie squeal, he raced at them.

There was no time to think. They turned and fled down the slope toward the enemy's camp.

Arne's draugr came after them, a silent terror, moving frighteningly fast, even faster than he ever had when he was alive.

They had been leading Arne's draugr away from their camp before – but now Dyrfinna and Skeggi were running for their lives, straight down the slope toward enemy lines, flying at a speed that Dyrfinna was sure that she'd never touched before in her life.

It was almost exhilarating, except she knew that if she tripped or stumbled, Arne's teeth would rip into her flesh and that would be the last thing she knew.

From the enemy's camp just ahead, an arrow shot through the dark, narrowly missing Dyrfinna. And here they were, running toward the enemy guards. If any of them captured Dyrfinna or Skeggi ...

"Stop! Who goes there!" one of the guards called, and they came running out of the trees that lined the swift-flowing stream, swords drawn.

"Keep running!" Dyrfinna grunted to Skeggi, pulling her sword. "With me!" It was dark enough for them not to see her very well...

Dyrfinna, with Skeggi following, plowed straight

through the enemy guards without stopping, slicing two of them with her sword as she shot past.

"Run, you fools!" she shouted. "Run!"

There was no time for them to run, anyway, because the instant she said that, Arne's draugr crashed into their group, grabbing one of the bleeding guards and crushing him in his arms with an excited groan-squeal. Dyrfinna heard something crack.

Everybody started screaming.

A group of guards blocked her with a wall of shields. Dyrfinna and Skeggi both skidded, she grabbing his arm, as they changed course. One of the guards grabbed her other arm, nearly pulling her off her feet, but she stabbed him with the point of her sword. Skeggi hauled her away, knocking down another attacker as they fled the enemy's lines, staggering back up the long slope toward their camp.

Pray they don't follow us, Dyrfinna thought, too out of breath to say it aloud. But then new, horrified shouts rose from behind them.

They were chased for a short distance, this time by the enemy guards, but Dyrfinna was already swift with terror – Skeggi was too, because he was keeping pace with her – and they were not caught.

Once inside the perimeter of the rock piles, their friends from the encampment grabbed them to drag them to safety. Several people took up slings and fired sharp-edged flint at the pursuers. One of the enemy screamed, "My eye!" and they retreated under a barrage of flying rock chips.

Only now, now that they were safe, Dyrfinna's legs gave out under her and she sat down hard on the ground, gasping for breath.

In the meanwhile, Skeggi collapsed against one of the rock piles, weeping. "Poor Arne," he said in a choked voice, covering his face. "This shouldn't have ever ... why did this happen to him? Of all people?"

"I don't know," Dyrfinna said softly. She couldn't weep – not yet. She was still half-crazed with terror. She looked downhill toward the enemy's camp, where a clash of arms and screams told where Arne's draugr was cutting a swath through the enemy. "But he always loved us. And now, though he's not here, he's striking terror into their hearts in a way that he would rejoice to see if he were still alive."

Skeggi pressed the heel of his hands against his eyes, rubbing out the tears. "Yeah ... but just the way that draugr looked at me just now. When he was trying to kill us. That was Arne's face looking at us with death in his eyes." He looked at Dyrfinna. "Here's what I truly hate: After Thora's draugr tried to kill us, I couldn't think of any memory of her without seeing her draugr's face. And now it's going to be the same with Arne."

"How'd Arne turn into a draugr?" somebody else asked. "He's the last person you'd expect to see ripping people up. Outside of battle, that is."

"It doesn't make sense." Skeggi rubbed his face. "We buried him with the right rituals. He died valiantly, with an axe in hand. He was blessed by the gods."

"Or so we thought," Dyrfinna said, still staring down the hill where the screaming continued.

25

SMOKING HOT

Dawn came too early, too soon. Dyrfinna, who had somehow managed to fall asleep despite the screaming from the enemy lines below, dragged herself awake before the first light of dawn.

Dyrfinna vigorously rubbed her face, got up, and shook out her sea cloak as she looked over the piles of stones at the enemy's camp.

Skeggi yawned, trying to wake himself up. "Is anybody still alive down there?"

"They're up and about," she said, looking around the ships at the bottom of the long slope. "I'm curious if they actually managed to put Arne's draugr to rest, or if he's sated and hiding from the sun."

Indeed, the enemy camp seemed unnaturally quiet this morning, and not as many people were going about their business around the cookfires.

"Perhaps they're demoralized by the draugr attack," Dyrfinna said. She felt a little glow of pride from having led a draugr against the enemy.

But then that deflated when Skeggi said, "But Arne's body is still wandering the world, unhallowed, filled with rage. A warrior like him should be sitting in Valhalla in peace."

"Yes. He should be," Dyrfinna said, her heart low.

Skeggi frowned over the rocks. "If he's a draugr, then his spirit is not in Valhalla, but is likely wandering in the nether regions, lost."

"Ah." This was even worse. "I'll have to talk with one of the Moors about reclaiming his body – if we can find it."

"But if we find him during the day, we could possibly send Arne to his rest while the sun makes him powerless," Skeggi said.

"*If* they'll let us do this. The child-killers would pitch a fit if the Moors helped us out."

Skeggi ran his hands through his thick brown hair. "I can't stop thinking about this. Did I do the ritual wrong? Did he become a draugr because of me?"

"I doubt that," she said, heartbroken at the anguish in his face.

"I thought I did everything correctly." He rubbed his hands over his face, hard. "But I left something out of one of the prayers. Something that tore the spirit from him ... that allowed the body to walk..."

Dyrfinna wanted to put a hand on his shoulder to comfort him – wanted to take him in her arms and kiss the grief from his face.

Instead, she cleared her throat. "It wasn't you. There are dreadful things afoot here, things that will happen in this haunted place, even if you do your best to keep them at bay. First things first, though," she said briskly. "We need to see to the battle lines and our warriors."

She and Skeggi went to talk to the fighters who were preparing breakfast or gathering in their lines of battle. Dyrfinna walked from place to place, making sure her fighters were ready and awake, and that every point of attack against Nauma's army was defended. She talked to her fighters, listened to their thoughts on battle-matters, sent others to find what they needed – if those supplies were available – and went on to the next.

"Ay, Finna, what happened to your hair?" Ostryg said, passing them on his way to the mead hall. "Are you sporting a brand-new battle style?"

Dyrfinna gingerly touched it, and found a mess under her fingertips. The blood from her scalp wound had clotted in what was left of her hair on that side of her head. "I had to cut myself loose from a draugr's grip last night."

"Good thing he didn't grab your arm."

"If he had, I wouldn't be alive now, like Grendel in that old story."

"I was watching you two leading Arne into the enemy's lines last night," Ostryg said, walking with them. "That was pretty exciting."

"You saw us being chased by a draugr but didn't do anything?"

Ostryg shrugged. "I wasn't in the mood to get eaten up by a draugr, to be honest."

"You know what's *really* exciting?" Skeggi asked. "Trying to run fast enough to stay out of a draugr's reach. That'll put hair on your chest."

Ostryg, pretending to be outraged, ripped his shirt open and gestured wildly at his hairy chest. "Do you really think this needs *more?*"

"Did you put a goat under your shirt? Because that's a lot of hair," Dyrfinna joked.

"I should go out there right now and show this luscious chest to that Nauma girl. Make her die of horniness."

"Or laughter," Dyrfinna said.

"Anyway!" Skeggi said. "Could we please go back to talking about Arne's draugr?"

"Did you see if they managed to neutralize his draugr?" Dyrfinna asked Ostryg, who was now trying to arrange his ripped shirt over his chest to better show it off. "I passed out while the screaming was still going on."

"Did you miss that?" Ostryg said grimly. "I think they

must have a magician over there. After you two came running back, there was screaming, screaming, screaming for a long time. It reminded me of the time my family sailed out to that monastery that used to be out past the Point. They got their knives and sneaked into the place just before the bells rang for Lauds. That's what the screaming reminded me of."

Skeggi was just staring at Ostryg. "That took an unexpected turn."

Ostryg just shrugged. "Anyway, I could hear Arne ripping people up. I was squinting in the dark, wishing that we had enough light to see what kind of damage Arne was doing. But then I heard an angry shriek, like a gigantic pissed-off bird. Out of nowhere, there was a flash of blue light, as if lightning struck. I couldn't see anything for a while after that – just darkness and the silence of the dead. I don't know what happened, but it was damned effective. The screaming stopped, anyway, so I assume Arne stopped too. Or *was* stopped."

"By some magician who uses lightning," Skeggi said slowly.

"So Arne's body is over there now, in the enemy's hands."

"We'll have to get it back after the battle," Skeggi said. "Pray that they don't desecrate the corpse."

They continued with their survey of the fighting force, but this did not take much longer. Dyrfinna had no more fighters in reserve. Many of the people who sat on the front lines wore makeshift bandages made from Gefjun's clothes wrapped tightly around the wounds on their hands and arms. Only the worst of the wounded, those who hovered near death, or were incapable of sitting or standing, remained on the back lines.

They went into the mead hall to check on Gefjun, but she was already up and around, seeing to the wounded and assisting with breakfast preparations.

Dyrfinna wandered over to the hearth and sat down

next to the bucket of ashes, warming herself at the fire while stirring through the ashes with one finger, checking the eggs. They each moved under the ashes at her touch – one egg was busy kicking and stirring, one moved when she touched it, and the third was quiet as she ran her finger around it, the dragonet inside barely stirred.

On the other side of the hearth, one of the men, his head and arm wrapped in bandages made from Gefjun's dress, was in charge of breakfast for the rest of the fighters. He gave Dyrfinna, as well as her friends, part of a nicely cooked puffin and a little bit of pan bread to eat in one of the crockery bowls.

"Thank you," Dyrfinna said, devouring it. She'd eaten little since yesterday morning.

Gefjun came over. "I'm running low on bandages and herbs. I counted on having enough until we met up with the rest of the fleet." She held up her arms. She'd left Skala in a long-sleeved shirt, but now her arms were entirely bare. "I've torn up all my sleeves and the bottom of my shirt and skirts for bandages. If you have any clothes you don't mind sacrificing, please send them to me."

Dyrfinna reached under her armor and ripped off her sleeves. "A gift for you," she said, handing them to Gefjun, who grinned.

Ostryg, not to be outdone, ripped off his entire shirt and gave it to her. "It was ripped anyway," he said. "Now the enemy can see me in all my glory."

"And stab you full of holes," Dyrfinna added.

Gefjun wrapped it in her arms. "I'm half tempted to keep this one for myself. But I won't. Duty calls."

"Watch out, Juni," Dyrfinna said. "He says that Nauma's going to look upon his smoking body and die from unrequited horniness."

Gefjun looked Ostryg up and down and nodded. "Do it. I believe in you."

He put his hands on his hips, puffed out his hairy chest, and jutted out his chin.

"You need some red paint," Gefjun said, a slow grin crossing her face. "I actually have some here, in my sea chest."

Ishaq's voice came from the back of the hall. "O merciful God, let me die now, for I cannot bear this talk any longer." Only now did Dyrfinna notice him at his table in the back of the hall, busily eating his breakfast.

"Oh! Are you still here?" Dyrfinna asked, grinning in spite of herself.

Ishaq stopped eating and gave her a long, cold stare. "It would seem that, unfortunately, I have little choice in the matter."

Dyrfinna heard Ostryg laugh behind her. "Paint my body red, honey," Ostryg said to Gefjun. "Oh, *yeah*, baby."

Ishaq grimaced at what he saw, turned a woeful eye upon his breakfast, then slowly pushed the crockery bowl away.

"I'm sorry," she said, and this time she meant it.

A hint of a smile crossed his face, causing his dark-brown eyes to sparkle. "Every day when I awake here, I tell myself, 'It cannot get worse,' and then every day I am proved wrong."

Dyrfinna shrugged. "But that's where you're wrong. It could be a lot worse. You could be me."

He barked with laughter, and she grinned.

Just then, a shout came from outside, turning into the roar of a crowd, swelling louder and louder. It was Nauma's army, cheering over something. And Dyrfinna wasn't sure, but she thought she heard a single scream from among the cheering. She stopped to listen, furrowing her brow, but now she couldn't hear it.

"And here we go," Ostryg said, giving Gefjun a sloppy kiss as she held her red hands in front of her so they weren't touching anything. She hadn't wasted any time: Half of his body had been painted red.

Gefjun then began putting handprints all over the parts of his body that hadn't been painted. "So if that Nauma does die from one look at you, she'll know what you're *mine* while she's dying."

"SPEAKING OF DYING," Ishaq said from the back table.

Skeggi shrugged on his shield. "Come on, you love-birds," he said as Dyrfinna joined him. "Stop showing off. We have a war to fight."

26

THE SECOND DAY OF BATTLE

"OH, WHY COULDN'T ARNE HAVE TAKEN THEM ALL out?" Dyrfinna groaned as Ostryg and Gefjun joined her. They headed out of the mead hall together, Dyrfinna stuffing the rest of the meat into her mouth and chewing as fast as she could. She put the uneaten bread into her pouch at her waist for later.

Dyrfinna went to the front of the lines to see what had happened, joining the other Vikings who were looking over the rocks to the enemy at the bottom of the long slope. Gefjun was coming to the front lines just for a moment, so she could check on her walking wounded and make sure they were still holding up.

"They're forming up into battle lines," one of the fighters said as Dyrfinna and her friends joined them.

They stood for a moment looking over the rocks at the enemy troops striking their shields, blowing war horns, and making a racket. Once again, the child-killers and the Moors stayed slightly apart in two separate groups. The Moors gathered in lines as if they had some sense of strategy, chanting something and occasionally breaking into three-part harmony, while the child-killers were standing around in large groups, screaming and making rude gestures.

"So how did quality troops like King Varinn's forces get matched up with that rabble?" Ostryg asked aloud. "Does anybody know?"

Naturally, Skeggi had the answer. "Ishaq said they allowed Nauma's forces to join them, because they told the Moors that they, too, were out to avenge King Varinn."

Ostryg coughed something that sounded like "Bullshit!"

"As it turns out, you're right," Skeggi told Ostryg. "There was a lot of feeling against letting Nauma and her shiploads of child-killers join their forces, but the commanders knew they needed the extra men. And now here they are," Skeggi concluded. "Ishaq told me that the Moors are ready to get rid of Nauma's forces very soon."

"The Moors at least have standards. Not like Nauma's forces."

"I find that hard to believe," Gefjun said quietly.

"I'll tell you what," Dyrfinna said. "At least King Varinn's troops are much better fighters than Nauma's. Varinn's men are honest fighters. They know how to handle a sword and spear, and you don't have to worry about them trying to rip your skin off for sport."

"Ugh!" Skeggi shuddered.

One of the so-called child-killers was waving his rump at them and pointing at it.

"Too bad he's out of arrow range," Ostryg grumbled.

Just then there came a shout from the child-killer side of the battle lines.

Nauma came walking out of the lines with her henchman and a group of her soldiers.

"Too bad *she's* out of arrow range," Ostryg added.

"She's still wearing Thora's crown," Dyrfinna growled. "Look at her."

All four of the sword-friends went silent – Thora's former guards-of-honor, her dragon-guard. The golden circlet with the gleaming ruby in the front was nestled on top of Nauma's golden, oily locks.

"Desecration," Skeggi whispered.

"She makes me sick." Gefjun spat.

"We are going to rip Thora's crown off her head and make her beg for mercy," Dyrfinna said.

"And we're going to make her tell us how she got Thora's crown," Skeggi asked. "That's the part I don't understand."

"Who cares how she got it?" Ostryg said, annoyed. "That's not what I'm worried about. I'm just pissed she's wearing it."

"She had to have stolen Thora's crown off her burning funeral ship. If that's so, then did she manage to steal anything else that belonged to Thora?" Skeggi asked pointedly.

Now that gave Dyrfinna pause. Thora's funeral ship had been a mass of flames on the ocean. How could anybody have taken anything, much less Thora's crown, out of that inferno?

"Hey! Come here, Nauma," Dyrfinna called. "We have a little present for you."

Nauma turned at once toward them, a sneer on her face.

"Come here," Dyrfinna called. "We only want to talk."

But the child-killer laughed, touched the crown she wore on her head, and walked back into her troops. "Attack!" she shrilled, and the enemy troops roared and raced uphill toward them.

"That *coward*," Dyrfinna spat, getting into guard position as the first attackers came into range.

Dyrfinna's forces sent down another rock fall at the enemy, but now that Nauma's forces knew to expect the rocks, they started sprinting as soon as the telltale rumble started. Then more troops followed in their wake, taking the paths that the others were taking to dodge and survive the rock falls.

As the enemy grew closer, the rock-slingers began firing sharp pieces of flint down at the attackers, spinning their slings until they hummed, and then letting the rocks fly. Some rocks were merely annoyances, but a few well-aimed rocks brought enemy combatants down, wounding some, killing a few. Then arrows came arcing down at the sling-bearers, and they had to scramble down from their places.

Once battle was joined before the rock piles that blocked out most of the enemy, Dyrfinna felt a little better. Battle looks the same wherever one goes, even if the means of killing were different, and she fell into the strenuous rhythm of it.

Before long, however, the second day of battle turned into a slog. The battle sent on and on, and Dyrfinna held on to her sword and cut down as many as she could. Her muscles burned in her arms, back, and legs. Time slowed to a crawl as endless attackers kept coming on. The sun hung motionless in the sky, not bothering to get any closer to the horizon.

Dyrfinna kept looking up from the battle, trying to see if Nauma was in the crowd. She was ready to drop everything and fight her at a moment's notice. But, to Dyrfinna's frustration, she never appeared. Once Nauma made her appearance at the beginning of the battle, she considered that enough of an effort for the day.

"Oh, I'm going to get that crown," she kept muttering to herself every time she scanned the crowd.

They were in the midst of battle when one of the wounded Vikings that Gefjun had patched up called to Dyrfinna.

"Juni said you need to come to the hall at once," he said.

They had just driven off a wave of fighters and she felt guilty leaving her warriors, but the patched-up soldier stepped into the gap she had left and prepared himself for the next onslaught, and Dyrfinna trudged, exhausted to the hall.

As soon as she came in, before her eyes had a chance to adjust to the comparative darkness inside the hall, Gefjun scolded, "Finally you show up. I was sure you were going to miss it."

Dyrfinna blinked and the room swam into focus after the bright sun outside. Skeggi, Ostryg, and Gefjun, as well as the other number of wounded who could sit up or move, were gathered around the brazier or watching from their palettes.

"It's time," Gefjun sang, motioning at the dragon eggs.

⚜ 27 ⚜

SMALL MIRACLES

Dyrfinna joined them at once.

Next to the brazier sat a shallow baking crock with an asbestos cloth laid at the bottom, upon which the three eggs had been set.

"It's to keep them warm as they emerge," Ishaq said as her eye fell upon it.

Dyrfinna stared, aghast, at Ishaq, who was sitting at Skeggi's side. His face was alight with interest, and his hands were still bound, and he leaned forward, watching the eggs.

"Why this prisoner here with us?"

Skeggi was crouched next to the crockery. "It's okay, Finna. He worked with dragon eggs back at his old home in Córdoba. I thought it would be remiss if we didn't have his counsel."

She wasn't so sure about that, but she joined them, sitting in the spot they'd saved for her.

The rest of the wounded were gathered around, watching. One of the wounded swordmaidens fluttered with excitement. "I can't believe we're lucky enough to see this. I wish I had a dragon egg."

Dyrfinna smiled as one of the eggs made a loud peep

and rocked a little. "I hope someday this hatching will become more common."

So far the eggs had struggled in the hot ashes. But now, one of them tore. A rip appeared in the rubbery shell.

Everybody went silent.

In the silence, the noise of battle came to them. Dyrfinna felt torn to be sitting here, waiting for eggs to hatch, when her people were fighting and dying just a short way down the hill.

What if this was going to be a long process? She hadn't even sat with the dying this long. On one hand, an event like this should not be missed, but she thought it was unfair that she got to see this, while the other brave fighters did not.

Then what looked like a small beak peeped through the tear in the eggs, and she instantly forgot all that.

More loud peeping. One of the other eggs struggled more fiercely, and the shell tore as well. Much peeping back and forth. The last egg did not peep, and had been resting longer.

The dragonet inside the second egg struggled. The tear in the shell grew longer, and the color in the rubbery shell became dull.

"Ooh," said Ostryg, like a child receiving a present. Everybody's eyes were as big as the moon.

"Skeggi, Dyrfinna, you should be closest to the eggs. After all, it was through your efforts that we are having this moment now," Ishaq reminded them.

His voice was soft as if to not interrupt the magic.

The first egg struggled harder, quietly peeping. The beak came out further, a little green beak ... an emerald.

In its struggles, the shell ripped a little more.

"Should we help them?" she asked, noting that the third egg was not struggling.

"After a moment," Ishaq said quietly. "They strengthen themselves in their struggles. To assist before they're ready to emerge might mean hurting them. They are very delicate right now."

They lay quiet for a moment, the thin shells moving in time with their breathing, before trying again.

But then through the crack in the first egg, a long, thin head thrust its way out like a snake seeking light, its eyes closed, its scales almost black. Everybody went silent.

The dragonet's eyes opened as it stretched upward, and its throat swelled as it took its first breath.

Dyrfinna and Skeggi leaned forward.

It pulled the rest of its body out of the shell and lay in the hot ashes, ash sticking to its wet scales. After a moment it pulled itself up, wobbly.

The little black-scaled dragon sat up and peeped, looking from Dyrfinna to Skeggi.

"Hello, little one," Dyrfinna breathed. The dragonet chirruped at the both of them.

On its back lay its wings, tightly folded. Now the drag-onet arched its back slightly, and up came its wings, opening – to display a pair of what looked like a pair of withered rags.

From the onlookers came a gasp, or stifled groans. Dyrfinna felt as if she'd been punched in the chest, but tried her best not to show it.

"No, wait," Ishaq urged. "Give it a moment. Just watch."

The dragonet crouched, its eyes closing. Its withered wings spread out flat over its sides. Its body humped, once, twice ... and color suddenly rushed across its black scales in brilliant, fiery waves of emerald green with a gleam of gold. Its body pulsed with each wave of gleaming emerald rolling across it. With each pulse, the wing skins uncrumpled slightly, uncrumpled some more.

"It's like what butterflies do, when they come out of their cocoons," Gefjun breathed. "It's just the same. Look."

With each pulse, the skin of the wings expanded,

smoothed out, elongated. The wings turned from black to emerald, brightening with each new wave of gleaming color. Now the wings were open and curved over the dragonet gracefully, and gleams of light chased each other down the membranes.

"They're beautiful," Skeggi breathed.

Now the second dragonet was emerging. The emerald dragonet swung its head to look at it, and chirruped as if encouraging it. Dyrfinna instantly imitated the chirrup.

The dragonet looked at her, curious, and stretched out its wings. No longer withered, they were gleaming emerald and Dyrfinna marveled that so much wing surface had come out of that little egg.

At the chirrup, its eyes met hers.

She was instantly in love.

She held her hands out to the dragonet. It sniffed her fingers with its long nose, delicately. Then it wobbily rose and placed its front feet on her fingers, staring into her eyes. Its small feet were warm and soft, and one of them wrapped around her finger.

Then the dragonet climbed up on her hand and continued up her arm with small, nimble feet, closing its wings against its back. Its claws, nonretractable, were very sharp, but she barely felt them, because it used its soft feet, not claws, to climb. In a moment it crawled across her shoulders, underneath her hair, its warm scales sliding against the back of her neck. It sniffed her ear, and Dyrfinna squinched her eyes shut, trying not to burst out in maniacal giggling, afraid to scare it.

Then it lay down across her shoulders, letting its legs hang down. It purred.

A quiet flurry of happiness from the others. Dyrfinna couldn't take her eyes off of it.

But now out came the second dragonet, a gleaming yellow as she pulsed yellow as a sunbeam with bits of orange and red like flames dancing across its body, and then its wings as they expanded over its back.

Dyrfinna and the dragonet chirped encouragement. The flame-yellow dragonet wobbled to its feet, then leaped into Skeggi's arms.

The final egg finally tore open. Ostryg and Gefjun leaned forward, worried.

It peeped but a weaker sound. But gradually the small dragonet emerged, and fell on its side, struggling to right itself.

"Give the little one a hand, Ostryg, Gefjun," Ishaq said.

The little one pulled itself up and then clung to Ostryg's hand. His eyes were big as moons, and he looked like he would even cry for a moment. The brought his other hand under the dragonet to support it. The small dragon crouched and pulsed .... And its scales suddenly gleamed blue, a brilliant sky blue. Everyone gasped.

Dyrfinna laughed. "You got the rarest one of all. Good work."

They met eyes. Ostryg's expression was being pulled in two different directions at once, between joy and sudden tears. "It's so ... I've never ..." he whispered as the little one gazed at him. This one looked so small and delicate, its scales gleaming with a blue as vibrant as the open sky.

Gefjun laughed as she put an arm around Ostryg, happy tears in her eyes as well. "We can name you Gledi, Joy," she said softly, and she kissed Ostryg on the cheek.

He wiped his eyes and chuckled, stroking the little Joy, who crawled up on his chest and lay down and went to sleep.

"Now feed them," Ishaq said.

Gefjun took some of the puffin meat that was warming at the edge of the brazier, where the fire was not as hot, and handed out the little drumsticks and breast meat to the three sword-friends.

Dyrfinna's dragonet grabbed the small drumstick with its little sharp teeth, trying to tug it out of her fingers and swallow it whole.

"Oh boy, somebody's hungry," she said, tearing off the meat, which the dragonet devoured, chomping through it with its mouth wide open.

Skeggi's dragonet was gentler, and it rubbed its head against his finger, like a cat, before daintily accepting the meat.

"Oh, you got the polite one," Gefjun said as Dyrfinna's dragonet devoured the drumstick meat as fast as she could shuck it off the bone, and then it grabbed the bone and cracked it in its teeth.

"Who's hungry?" Dyrfinna laughed, pulling more meat off the puffin to give to the hungry dragonet.

Ostryg was coaxing his blue dragonet to eat, gently stroking its side. It raised its head and accepted the meat.

"Give it some of the organ meats," Ishaq suggested. Gefjun picked out the liver and kidneys for the dragonet, who perked up upon eating them.

Dyrfinna's dragonet hopped over to the brazier and sank its claws into the puffin. Its wings beat like crazy as it tried unsuccessfully to lift the whole puffin and fly away with it, but its wings were too young and it tumbled down the side of the roasted bird. Everybody laughed.

Dyrfinna grabbed the dragonet up before it could burn its feet. The emerald dragonet startled, wings wide, eyes astonished and jaws wide open, staring at Dyrfinna as if it could not comprehend what had just happened. Everybody laughed again at the dramatic expression on its face.

Dyrfinna gave it another piece of juicy meat. It gulped down the meat, busily chomping it with jaws open. She gave it a few more pieces. The dragonet wrapped its legs and tail around her arm, looking eagerly from the meat to Dyrfinna's face and back to the meat.

"Yours is a handful," Skeggi said.

"Do you speak?" Dyrfinna asked her dragon. She scratched its head, and it twisted its head around in all directions as if trying to get her to scratch more. She obliged. But it did not speak. It crawled back up on her shoulder again.

Skeggi whistled a note at his dragon. It gazed at him as if trying to understand. He whistled another note. This time she peeped back the same note he'd whistled. Skeggi looked at the others, his eyes wide. "She's going to be a singer. I'm going to call you Mella," he added, gently stroking her flame-yellow scales.

Dyrfinna's dragonet was lying comfortably across her shoulders again, the warm scales of its throat against her bare arm, and she could feel its heartbeat pulsing vigorously. It snuffled at the blood on her arm and busily began licking it off.

"Aye, there's a bloodthirsty one," said one of the older warriors. "Mark my words, that one will love the battle and the sword."

"I hope so," Dyrfinna said softly, meeting her dragonet's adoring eyes before it went back to licking her arm clean of blood. It tickled. "I'm going to call this one Renegade."

She waited until her dragonet fell asleep before running outside to check on the battle. Her heart was soaring. For the first time, the battle held little interest for her – only the dragons.

Everybody who saw her radiant face became excited – the news of the dragon eggs and their hatching had swiftly all over the battlefield, so now everybody wanted to "take a short break" and go back to the hall and see the dragonets.

She allowed those of her fighters who were exhausted to go back first, but she was torn over going back to the hall herself, though she wanted to more than anything in the world.

Little Renegade will be waiting for me when I get back, she reminded herself. *It won't be long now. Duty calls.*

She hurried back to the battlefront, so filled with happiness that she could hardly think of anything else.

28

THE FURY OF AN UNCOLLARED DRAGON

ALL THAT EVENING, AFTER THE BATTLE HAD ENDED AND the sun had gone down, she'd been asked the story of how they'd come to have dragon eggs, and she and Skeggi had told the story, again and again.

The Skalans had seen baby dragons only a few times during their lives, several times when they had been children and they had gone up to the dragon stables at every opportunity to see the baby dragons, then one time when they were older.

That night, Dyrfinna barely slept. She kept waking up to look at the dragonet, who was curled up next to the brazier with its eggmates in a pile of gleaming emerald, beryl, and gold. The three dragonets gleamed like jewels, like the richest treasure. She could hardly believe she'd been able to capture dragonets of her own.

Dyrfinna wasn't the only one who had fallen madly in love. Every time she woke up, different members of her army were gathered around the baby dragons, love in their eyes, exchanging amazed whispers.

"Think of what this means for Skala," said one, with a frown at Ishaq. "Three more dragons for the Queen's forces, to defend ourselves against people like King Varinn's evil forces."

"Let me talk to you about evil," Ishaq replied, butting in, but Dyrfinna was pleased to see that everybody ignored him.

A hard-driving rain began late, a cold wind blasting off the sea and seeking out every crack in the walls of the mead hall.

The morning of the third day dawned dark, with rain pouring straight out of the sky.

Dyrfinna's guards were out in the rough weather, watching across the wall, but Nauma's troops didn't bother showing up to the battlefield.

Dyrfinna's troops, seeing nobody attacking, returned to the great hall, leaving several guards out in the rain to watch the enemy, swapping them out with other guards every couple of hours. Others kept watch around the mead hall. Nobody trusted Nauma – especially now that three newborn baby dragons were exploring the mead hall.

The dragonets were trying to learn how to fly, much to the general amusement of Dyrfinna's forces, who had gathered around to watch the small dragons' antics. They'd rise up on their tiptoes and beat their wings with a tiny bugling sound, then tried to lift off, only to tumble off the table. Sometimes they'd chase each other around the tabletops and floors, growling and wrestling. Joy, Ostryg's sky-blue dragon, always tired quickly and would crawl back under his beard.

Renegade never stopped, and was the first to learn to fly. She went bugling around the rafters for a while until Skeggi's dragonet, Mella, figured out how to get airborne, and they chased each other, swooping just over everybody's heads, an emerald and flame-yellow gleam in the dark reaches of the roof.

Renegade flew down and crash-landed on Dyrfinna's shoulders, then knocked Dyrfinna silly by beating her around the head with her wings while trying to get her footing. She had not realized how powerful those tiny wings were until that moment.

"Ah! That hurts!" Dyrfinna said laughingly.

Immediately Renegade became apologetic, gazing into Dyrfinna's face with her bright golden eyes, then nuzzling up against her neck with the sweetest little trills. She gently stroked her hand across her dragonet's smooth scales and her folded wings. The dragonet looked so fragile, but she was solid muscle. Even though she was not even a full day out of the egg, Renegade had a lot of power in her tiny body.

"How are we going to collar them?" she asked. "If she's this powerful today, imagine how strong she's going to be in a month. She's going to knock down our houses every time she gets excited about supper."

Renegade gave her a long, disdainful look.

"And I also want you to be able to speak, like the collared dragons do," she added.

According to everything Dyrfinna and her friends knew, the dragons would not speak unless the magicked collars were around their necks.

"But the emberdragon could speak," Skeggi pointed out. "It clearly knew what it was saying, and it was not wearing a collar."

"Yeah, but it was also trying to kill us with the scariest flames I've ever experienced."

"I ... don't think we need to collar them," Skeggi's voice was strained as Mella playfully wrestled in mid-flight with Renegade,. They broke apart and chased each other, their wings stirring up decades' worth of dust in the high ceiling.

"But we don't want these dragonets to just fly away," Ostryg said in a loud whisper. Joy had crawled under his warm beard on his chest and was sleeping peacefully there, the end of her sky-blue tail twitching in contentment. "We want them to stay with us, right?" Worry cracked his voice, a worry that Dyrfinna felt, very acutely:

What if their baby dragons took it into their heads to fly away and leave them?

"I don't think you'll have to worry about that with Joy," Dyrfinna said. The dragonet woke slightly at the mention of her name, looked up at Ostryg with sleepy, golden eyes, then nestled back under his beard and fell asleep. Ostryg melted once more as he stroked the beryl dragon's sky-blue scales with one finger.

"Not so much with the other two." Skeggi watched Renegade and Mella racing swiftly around the ceiling of the mead hall.

Dyrfinna scratched her head. She wasn't especially keen on collaring the dragons, but at the same time, she wanted her dragon to speak. And she wanted, more than anything, for her dragon to *stay*.

Skeggi sat down next to the great fire in the middle of the hall. "Finna, come here."

How that simple request made her heart leap. Yes, she knew perfectly well that his heart belonged only to Rjupa – but she couldn't help it.

Ostryg sat back, stroking Joy's sky-blue wing. "To hear his voice is joy indeed," he muttered, looking at her as he made his smart remark. The tiny dragonet raised her head, cocked her head at him, and yawned in his face.

Dyrfinna laughed. Smart dragon!

"What is it?" she asked Skeggi as she walked toward him, the very picture of decorum, until Renegade crash-landed on her shoulders again, nearly knocking her sideways.

"Give me some warning, honey. If you keep flying in like this, you're going to knock off my head."

The dragonet's face was the picture of pure horror.

Untangling the wild little dragon from her hair, she joined him and Ishaq where they sat next to the fire, looking through the small book that Skeggi had found in the room of the dead.

Skeggi lifted the book in his hand, gesturing at it.

"There's something we need to talk about. Ostryg, Gefjun, come listen to this."

Dyrfinna felt her heart slump. She wanted Skeggi all to herself for once.

"I don't exactly have a lot of time here," Gefjun said, stirring a pot of bone broth made from puffin bones and herbs. "We have several dying fighters who need this broth to survive."

Ostryg got up, cradling Joy, who stretched out on his arm. He took Gefjun's hand, and she reluctantly allowed herself to be led from the fire. "Let it simmer," he said. "Sit down for a little while and rest yourself. You'll be better off for it."

"Don't let it scorch."

Ostryg made a rude noise with his lips and waved her away. "You've been on your feet since dawn. Rest. I'll stir the broth and skim off the froth so you don't have to." She sighed and stretched out her legs, leaning back against the wall, closing her eyes.

Ostryg put Joy on his shoulders, and she took great interest in the smell of the broth and the heat of the fire. He scooped up a small spoonful and held it up to her, and she eagerly lapped it up, undaunted by the heat of the soup.

The other two dragonets landed on Ostryg's shoulders and begged for their own ladles of broth, bossily crowding Joy on her perch. She raised her head indignantly and scolded the others with loud, aggrieved chirps.

"Renegade! Come here." Dyrfinna clambered to her feet because Renegade was about to fall headfirst in the broth while grabbing at the ladle, and Ostryg had his hands full trying to keep the dragonet from doing so.

"Mella," Skeggi sang, and whistled his haunting call.

His dragon obediently flew to him, and he fed her. Renegade noticed the food, and immediately flew to Dyrfinna, fluttering around her head and making pathetic begging noises. She got her own handful of puffin meat and settled her hungry dragonet down.

"I'm going to call you Greedygut if you keep this up," Dyrfinna grumbled, sitting down at Skeggi's side because he called her first. Almost close enough for her to lean on him, too, though she abstained. His beard was crisp and curly, his brown hair in long waves falling around his shoulders. His fingers with the bitten-down fingernails held the book.

As soon as she was settled, and Renegade was busily licking her hand clean of any trace of puffin, Skeggi cautiously opened to a page he'd marked with a leaf from one of the apple trees.

Despite her distrust of books and pages with close-set words written across them, Dyrfinna loved the tiny, intricate illuminations that filled the margins of the books that Thora used to read – all those tiny knights and maidens, colorful scrolls and flowers twining through the margins, tiny pictures inside the letters at the beginning of a story, like a tiny man fighting with a loom, or a miniature group of people peering out of the top loop of a letter. Knights riding snails in battle, or rabbits in a tower throwing rocks at people, all drawn in miniature, with the brightest array of brilliant colors and sometimes a bit of gold leaf glinting off the vellum pages.

Though Dyrfinna couldn't read, she could see that the page in this book was written in the rounded letters of Latin instead of the tiny trees of runes. In the top margin was a tree with red flowers, with its branches stretching over two panels. On the left side of the trunk, a tiny, concerned-looking blacksmith labored over a forge, holding a hammer and tongs. On the right side, he lifted a golden collar into the air to a surprised-looking miniature dragon.

On that bottom of the page was a cunning illustration of a dragon. Around the dragon's neck was a collar with red stones exactly matching the collars their dragons wore. The illustration used real gold leaf, and the painted gems nearly seemed to sparkle.

Skeggi looked up from the page. "This book has a story about the collars that our dragons wear." His tone of voice was ... different, though Dyrfinna couldn't pinpoint the emotion behind it.

"I don't know, maybe we shouldn't read this," she said.

"We need to," Skeggi said, sliding a finger over the illustration of the dragon. "Listen to these words, long written down."

He began to read. As much as Dyrfinna distrusted books, she loved, in the same measure, to listen to Skeggi reading. His deep voice was like the wind in the trees, like the soft applause of raindrops on the thatching. She could never get enough of it.

"In the olden days, dragons were wholly wild. In a few rare instances they worked for Man: In these, they were hatched from an egg and were raised up with great care, as one would raise a horse, with feeding and care and diverse training. But peril and woe came to those who dared raise a dragon. The beast grew into an adult, and began longing for a mate; in their efforts to fly free and couple, they turned wild, and showed their teeth, and killed those who had raised them. Many would burn houses, homesteads, villages. Much woe came to those who handled dragons."

In the margin next to these words was an illustration of a tiny, fierce sapphire dragon who had bitten a man in half. The man's upper half shrugged with a surprisingly bored expression on his face.

Renegade leaned in from Dyrfinna's shoulder, listening to Skeggi's reading and sitting perfectly still for once. So were the other two dragonets. All seem to be enthralled by the words and the story, staring at Skeggi, not a flutter in their wings. Renegade, who was generally on a rampage somewhere, wasn't even blinking.

Skeggi continued reading. *"So a blacksmith, also an enchanter, hammered out a collar made of gold and carnelians to appeal to a dragon's vanity, and he placed an enchantment on the carnelians. He showed this gleaming collar to his dragon, and persuaded him to be fitted with this. Lo, once the collar was on, the dragon became wholly obedient to the smith's command, and fawned, and carried him all around the sky without complaint. The blacksmith then taught the making of these collars to diverse other men, and taught them the secret of enchanting the carnelians to demand absolute obedience from the dragons."*

Gefjun clucked her tongue. "We're not demanding anything. It's not *absolute* obedience. Ugh!"

Ignoring her, Skeggi read on. *"The uncollared dragons, coming to realize that their brethren were being treated as in the manner of horses or other livestock, were wroth, and turned wrathful, and became bitter enemies of humanity. The collared dragons, however, became passive and agreeable, and more were captured and collared, and used to keep their aggrieved brethren at bay. The collared dragons' need for mating decreased, and with it, their propensity for destruction."*

Dyrfinna looked over Skeggi's shoulder at the page. "So he's saying that dragons aren't laying eggs because they're *collared*? Is that true?"

"That's not true," Gefjun scoffed. "They still mate sometimes. They still lay eggs sometimes."

"Rarely," Skeggi corrected.

"What! Your dragons don't couple?" Ishaq cried. "What kind of enchantments are you putting on your dragons?"

"It's just to keep them from destroying everything. Besides, your dragons are collared too. What about them?" Ostryg said.

Ishaq's eyes flashed. "Have you seen our dragons from Córdoba? Actually, you have not, for they turn blue and freeze when brought to this horrendous climate. But we have new dragons all the time. We have dragon eggs because our dragons couple."

"How?" Ostryg said.

Ishaq frowned. "I hope I don't have to explain how dragons couple."

Ostryg threw up his hands, then nearly lost the ladle in the broth, catching it just before it sank out of sight.

"To be honest, it's positively indecent at times," Ishaq continued. "Sometimes you're going about your business and you look up and there's another set of dragons flying past in a passionate embrace."

"That's quite enough," Dyrfinna said, folding her arms, feeling her face go red. Renegade noticed the change and investigated her face, snuffling at her cheeks as if concerned, embarrassing her more. Gefjun laughed, but bumped gently against her side.

Ishaq nudged Skeggi with his elbow. "Read the rest. Let them hear the rest of what this scribe wrote."

"I think we're good," Gefjun said, but Skeggi had already started reading.

"The carnelians compel obedience, no matter the cost. These dragons can think for themselves, but only up to a point, for the spell is such that they are unable to speak about the collar they're wearing. Though a wild dragon is capable of subtle and cunning magic, a collared dragon cannot do magic, which is a powerful but unknown ability. The collared dragon, on some level, understands what has been done to him, but this understanding is somehow kept as the quietest of murmurs in their thoughts."

Dyrfinna's eyebrows went up, thinking of Serja. The dragon had done magic on her – healed her arm after it had been mauled by a wolf – but had begged of her not to tell anybody.

Skeggi was still reading. *"It is only when the collar is removed that the dragon, in a sudden flood of realization, in a torrent of buried emotions, suddenly understands what has been done to it. This is why a dragon will erupt in fire and destruction when a collar is removed, and kills their riders, and sets homes ablaze."*

"I've seen that," Dyrfinna said. "I saw a dragon get uncollared in the middle of battle."

"Ooh," Ostryg said, shaking his head. "Oh, yeah, I was there, too. That was bad."

Dyrfinna had been dragonback during an aerial battle against a small band of Scots from northern Alba. She had been fighting in midair, when a clawing dragon had torn a collar off his opponent's dragon.

"That dragon just went wild," Ostryg said, remembering. "It reached over its shoulder and grabbed its rider with its teeth, ripped him straight up out of the leather straps holding him on, and flung him into the air, let him fall to his death. Then it berserked. It was blasting fire at everybody, went biting and clawing at any dragonriders it could reach – our people, the Scot people, didn't matter. It was biting everybody in half and flinging them everywhere! The air was filled with torsos and legs! It was insane."

"You are clearly having too much fun with that memory," Ishaq said, lip curled in disgust.

"Most of them were Scots." Ostryg shrugged.

"Your papa is Scottish," Gefjun scolded.

"Eh. It would do him good to get bitten in half by an uncollared dragon."

As soon as Dyrfinna and her dragon realized what had happened – as soon as they saw that golden collar falling to earth and the dragon going wild – they had turned and winged it as fast as they could, in fear for their lives if that uncollared dragon should see them. She could still remember that awful piercing note of the uncollared dragon's screams behind her. Even now her heart pounded at the narrow escape she'd had.

The dragonets, hearing this story, fluttered wildly. Renegade and Mella went aloft, circling like bats, making strange keening noises. Even Joy went aloft with them for a moment before flying back to the safety of Gefjun's arms, panting.

Ishaq sniffed, breaking the silence. "This writer is correct," he said. "The histories state that these collars were a bane to the dragons when they were created."

"That's taking it a little far, don't you think?" Ostryg

said, skimming the broth, annoyed. "Your people collar dragons, too. You can't sit there and tell me we're doing it wrong if you're participating in this."

"Yes, yes, but the way we collar dragons is different," Ishaq began, but Dyrfinna talked over him.

"Skeggi, do you believe this?" Dyrfinna asked. "Our dragons don't seem unhappy. They're content. We come up and feed them and you read them books, and it's a lovely way to spend an afternoon. Or, it was," she added, since her father had forever exiled her from the dragon stables.

"It's in a book," Skeggi said quietly, looking at the pages. He hated arguments. "This is a history of our dragons, and it talks about great dragons in the past, and their riders. But this section was written many years ago. If this place has been sitting empty for decades, then this book is even older than that." He was scanning pages as he spoke, but then slowed down, looking at a passage.

"Personally, I think it's wolf shit." Gefjun shook her head over the bandages she was folding.

Skeggi looked up from the pages. "Do you want to know how to uncollar a dragon?"

"No," Gefjun said at once.

"Nobody here's going to uncollar a dragon," Ostryg said scornfully, and kissed the top of Gefjun's head. She looked up, smiling, and leaned back against him.

"How?" Dyrfinna asked. "Tell us."

Ostryg glared at her, but Skeggi was reading.

Those who would uncollar a dragon must be of a single mind about the deed, or the spell will not prosper. One must sacrifice a small thread of flesh to the dragon whom one wishes to uncollar—

"Ugh, how barbaric," Gefjun muttered.

"—and the dragon must eat this flesh, and lick the blood from the wound."

Serja had done this to Dyrfinna – had licked her

draugr-torn arm and had healed the wound this way. A thrill passed over her. So this was dragon magic!

"*Then, the human places blood on their hand and touches this blood to each carnelian on the dragon's collar. Thus will the collar's power be broken, and the dragon will know itself for the first time. He who breaks this spell will perish in the dragon's flames when the dragon reverts to its wild nature.*"

Ostryg barked with laughter. "What did they expect?" he said, getting to his feet. "Such is the gratitude of an uncollared dragon."

29

GOLD AND JEWELS

The day indoors highlighted another problem, however. They now had to ration food. The hard crackers were nearly gone, and the flour barrel had only enough to make bread for another meal.

Everybody took the day to sharpen their swords, fletch arrows – there were plenty of puffin and skua feathers for the task – and clean their armor, clothes, and themselves. Dyrfinna went out into the cold rain for a proper bath and came back feeling refreshed and wide awake.

Some of the crew gathered rose petals and rose hips, which were widely available on the rugosa roses that bloomed gloriously all around the great hall. Gefjun stewed the orange rose hips for her wounded to eat, filling the hall with the smell of apples and roses.

She had discovered an old herb garden that had run wild through the years. They gathered many herbs to flavor the food, and to make healing poultices and teas.

"We're doing fine at the moment," Gefjun said as she stirred the rose hips.

"Fine at the moment doesn't mean we're going to be fine in a few days," Dyrfinna said moodily as she gazed out the door at the empty sea. "Seventy-five people can go through an awful lot of food very quickly. Too quickly."

Just then, Renegade, seeing the open door, made a break for the outdoors, but Dyrfinna managed to catch her in mid-flight just in time. "Wait!" she said at the outraged little dragon, who squirmed in her hands. "Don't go outside! It's ... cold out there. And wet. Look at all that rain, you'd freeze."

Dyrfinna was more afraid of the dragonet flying away than anything, but that fear was one she was afraid to mention. The headstrong little dragon could have taken that fear of hers as a challenge.

Cold rain gusted in on them. Renegade shivered and shot back inside. Dyrfinna breathed a sigh of relief and pulled the great doors shut.

"We've still got to collar our dragonets." Dyrfinna joined her friends, stroking Renegade's head while the dragonet gnawed her thumb like an overenthusiastic puppy. "I don't want them to get lost and never come back." Renegade made a sad little chirp in reply.

"We can't collar them without gold and jewels," Ostryg said.

"I have gold." Dyrfinna immediately pulled off a golden ring she'd especially loved, that she had gained in battle against the Danes long ago, and set it on the table. Renegade pounced on it and tried to eat it, and Dyrfinna had to pick her up again.

Gefjun took off the mystical pendant she wore. "I don't want to give this away, but I want my lovely Joy to have the most beautiful collar in the world." She gently stroked the sky-blue dragon's head, and Joy hopped from Ostryg's shoulders to hers, curling around her neck.

Ostryg took off all three of his rings and plunked them down next to Dyrfinna's, looking straight at Skeggi. "Your turn, big boy."

Skeggi donated two of his rings to melt down, as well

as the arm ring that he'd gotten after Rjupa killed Iron Skull.

"Is that enough?" Gefjun asked, looking around at the wounded. "Where's Afi?"

The grey-haired blacksmith clutched his staff and pulled himself to his feet. "I'm here. Wait a moment, impatient one." He joined them and looked over the gold, then gently measured the dragonets' necks with his fingers. "This is not enough gold. Some of the gold will be lost when it's melted down. This will only make two collars."

"What if you melted down those Corae Guard brooches that all of you have?" one of the fighters asked. "That would give you enough gold ...."

The angry glares from all four of them shut him up right away.

"There is another option," Dyrfinna said slowly. As one in a bad dream, she reached to her upper arm and slid off a golden ring that she'd worn as an armband for years.

Gefjun sucked in a breath. "No, Finna. Not that one."

Dyrfinna turned the beautiful armband this way and that. The images of dragons wrought in gold, worn smooth through all those years of wearing, gleamed in the firelight.

"You can't," Skeggi said, low. "That was Thora's gift."

Dyrfinna had never been more proud than she'd been at that banquet. Thora had called her forward, in front of all her esteemed guests, and had given her the golden gift.

"You are to be my second-in-command when I am queen," Thora had told her, gently wrapping Dyrfinna's trembling hands around the gleaming armband. "I give this to you to honor you, Finna. I give this to you to praise you for your courage in battle, to show my complete trust in you, and to show our friendship. I expect great things of you, and I will be honored to have you at my side."

This was one of her few symbols of Thora's regard for her. It was even more beautiful than the arm-ring that her father had given Sinkr —something she had often reminded herself when had seen Sinkr puffing himself up on the deck of her ship.

Now as she held the band, sick at heart, she looked at her dragonet, imagining Thora's gold around her neck in a beautiful collar.

A tendril of hope unwound as an idea came to Dyrfinna.

She held out the golden armband to Renegade, and the dragonet sat up expectantly.

"My dearest friend gave this to me," Dyrfinna said to Renegade. "I love her and miss her very much. Now I want to give this to you, my friend, to adorn you and make you beautiful. I want everybody to see you wearing this pretty golden band, so they can see how much I want to honor you and show our friendship."

Renegade hopped around, excited, scampered up and down her arms. She licked the armband then licked Dyrfinna's face.

Tears glittered in Gefjun's eyes. "Oh, I only wish Thora could have seen this."

Dyrfinna leaned against her friend's side. "Me, too."

"The armband will have to be modified," the black-smith said, handling it reverently. "It needs a carnelian, and eventually it will need a clasp in the back. But I would prefer to wait until we get home to add the clasp, as I fear greatly doing any harm to this arm-ring. But with Finna's gift to her dragon, we'll have enough gold to collar the other two dragons."

He handed the armband back, and Dyrfinna slid it on over her dragonet's head. It was big around her neck, and Dyrfinna realized she might have to wrap a little precious cloth around the arm-ring so it could stay put on Rene-gade's neck without rattling around.

"We have enough gold to make the collars," Skeggi said as Mella sniffed the rings and stared at the sparkling gems as if hypnotized. "But we don't have carnelians."

"You use gems that mean something to you, for the collars," Ishaq told them. "After all, this collar is a gift and an ornament to your dragon to show your love and appreciation of this dragon who will be throwing its lot in with you. Think of it as a pledge to honor and care for them, instead of as a magical way to demand obedience."

Only Ostryg had seen a baby dragon being collared. His assassin father went to see a friend's dragonet get collared and Ostryg had tagged along. He had been about ten years old.

"The blacksmith did it," Ostryg remembered, "though he seldom worked with anything this fine and delicate. He'd learned enough about it so he could work gold, though crudely. He hammered the gold into shape and set the carnelians in it. Hammered it out and added the gems."

"The instructions for collaring the dragons are in this book." Ishaq flipped through the pages.

"Couldn't we hurry up and do this?" Ostryg asked. "Like, now?"

Ishaq, reading over the directions with Skeggi, shook his head. "Some of these directives are too harsh," he said. "We want creatures who stay around but are still free to regulate their own lives as much as possible."

"I don't know," Dyrfinna said. "What if you're just saying all this so we end up placing weak enchantments on our animals?"

The three dragonets looked at Dyrfinna, ears pricked when she said that.

"You're right, I'm sorry," she said to them, realizing what she'd said. "Our *partners*."

"I care for dragons," Ishaq said passionately. "I have worked with dragons back home in Córdoba. I have cared for them as if they were my own children. I have cared for the sick and helped them through difficult times."

"Mmm," Dyrfinna said noncommittally.

"We can collar them, but you need to add certain elements," said Ishaq.

"What kind of elements?" Dyrfinna asked. "Elements to make our newly hatched dragons sicken and die? Elements to make them turn against us while you smile behind your sleeves? I think not."

But Skeggi took his side again. "We're rewriting the incantation." He had turned to a mainly empty page in the book, using a puffin quill and puffin blood as ink to write things in. He used both Latin and the runic language, the symbols of which were distinctive enough for Dyrfinna to tell apart, mostly.

Once the changes had been made to the incantation and ritual, Skeggi read it aloud, Dyrfinna listening suspiciously. Everything he read seemed innocuous enough, but she vowed to listen carefully to the proceedings to make sure Ishaq wasn't going to try anything sneaky. Skeggi had a good heart but he could be gullible.

But she still felt that fear. How hard would it be for Egill to take Renegade away from her, along with Thora's gift, and give the dragonet to somebody else? Namely, Sinkr?

Skeggi, seeing her downcast state, gave her first choice of the gemstones from his rings. She held each ring up against Renegade's scales to see which one went best with her color. The dragonet became excited about a topaz. It had not been Dyrfinna's first choice before, but she immediately said, "Renegade wants this one." The overjoyed dragonet hopped around with her wings open, first rubbing her face against Dyrfinna's arm, then gnawing on the ring, then chewing on Skeggi's arm.

"Stop, dragon, your teeth are sharper than a puppy's." Skeggi rubbed the squirming dragonet's belly.

Mella circled around Renegade's head, taunting her, until she went chasing after her sister, luring her away from Skeggi.

The rings were melted down and the gemstones pried

loose. "Those were spoils of war from Iron Skull himself," Skeggi said, watching the blacksmith at work. "No big loss ... though I loved feeling rich as a king while wearing all those rings."

The smith fired the gold and poured it into molds he made out of some clay he'd dug up. Once they had cooled, he carefully, delicately hammered the gold and fixed the gemstones in.

"This is supposed to be delicate work," he said, "but I'm afraid I don't have the tools for delicate work. We can make larger, better-fitting collars when we return home."

"I'm fine with that," Dyrfinna said. "This is just a stopgap measure."

Soon the collars were finished — simple affairs with a sparkling gemstone on each. The dragonets couldn't get enough of the gold and sparkling gems on their collars. True to form, Renegade tried to eat hers.

Now it was time to start the ritual.

"This will a looser collaring," Ishaq explained as he watched Skeggi set up the area around the hearth. "This is closer to what we do for our dragons."

Skeggi put everybody into their places, the four of them surrounding the open hearth in the center of the floor. He set the three dragonets on the hearth, each facing their ... *well, not owners,* Dyrfinna thought. Renegade sat in front of her on the hearth, her posture unusually serious, though her tail fidgeted and tapped on the stones, as if sitting still were difficult for her.

"We'll each hold these." Skeggi placed the golden armband in Dyrfinna's hand and had Gefjun and Ostryg both hold Joy's collar. Then he took his place in front of Mella, who perked up like a bright student about to be called on.

Skeggi took one last look at the words, then raised his hand in invocation and began the ritual, singing a blessing unto the holy gods. He was a strong singer, with a delicious voice that gave Dyrfinna the shivers.

The sword-friends all held their collars and repeated Skeggi's words. All the while the little dragons, who sat on the hearth in front of them, stared at the collars, rapt. Now and then Ishaq added in things with his gravelly low voice.

The rest of the Skalans watched eagerly as the sword-friends sang their parts, following Skeggi through the ritual. But little Renegade sitting on the small dais with the other two, Mella and Joy, watched them with wide eyes, listening, shivering.

The baby dragons began to hum in high, shivery tones, holding their wings open, Joy's sky-blue scales looking almost pinkish in the glow of the fires.

Then it was time to fasten the collars. Each stepped forward. Ostryg's voice was rough, and his eyes grew red with tears he fought to hold back, clearly fighting to recite the words. Joy stared at him attentively. He gently snapped the collar golden onto her neck, clicking the latch. Then he then he drew his assassin's knife, pricked his finger, and touched his blood to the gem in the front of her collar. Gefjun did the same, adding her blood to the gem on the collar.

A quiet rushing noise, like the wind on the sea. Joy stood up straight, stretching tall, trembling with the effort, her eyes gleaming into Ostryg's and Gefjun's. Then she said, clear as anything, "Cherish me and care for me, as I will care for you for all my days."

A whispered gasp of awe from the onlookers. Gefjun grabbed Dyrfinna's arm, shaking. "She can speak!"

Skeggi did the same for his dragonet, and Mella sat up on her hind legs and sang her reply. Skeggi's song quavered as her tiny voice joined his, perfectly in pitch. And she recited the words back and when he touched the blood to her gemstone.

Dyrfinna turned to Renegade, her heart pounding, and lifted the collar to her beautiful dragon, her friend for life. *I'm going to remember this for the rest of my life,* Dyrfinna thought, and she'd never felt happier. "I swear to treat you with dignity and love," she said, "and I will be with you always." She pricked her finger with a knife and touched the blood to the dragon's gemstone. A tingle went up her arm from the touch, a sizzle of magic. Renegade jumped into her arms, nuzzling up and wrapping her tail around Dyrfinna's arm.

Everybody burst into applause. Mella burbled a quick bit of music from where she was twined around Skeggi's neck.

Renegade's first words were spectacular. "Let me out of here so I can go bite that Nauma's head," the little dragonet pleaded, lashing her tail.

Dyrfinna laughed with delight. "I can't let you do that. You just hatched."

Ostryg said, "You've got a dragon that takes after you best of all." Laughter.

Dyrfinna didn't mind. "Can we let you outside to eat puffins? And you won't fly away and leave us?"

"Why would I ever leave you?" Renegade asked. "I'll come back."

"Do you swear it?"

"Of course I do," Renegade placed her little paws on Dyrfinna's hand. "We're a team now, you and I. I'll never leave you."

Dyrfinna melted.

"So *now* will you let us go outside into the wide world?" the little dragon added, fluttering her wings impatiently.

"It's raining."

"I don't care. I don't like the cold, but I just want to see the big world for a moment."

The sword friends looked at each other with great dread. Dyrfinna pulled her wits together. "We'll take you outside. A promise is a promise."

The thought of Renegade flying away wearing Thora's

golden armband made her heart go cold, but she had to trust her dragonet.

As soon as Dyrfinna carried Renegade to the door, the other two dragonets wanted to go, too.

"If they all leave, I swear I will end you," Ostryg muttered to Dyrfinna as Joy sat up, her sky-blue wings opening as the door opened.

All three dragonets leapt into the cold rain. Several Skalans gasped or clutched their chests to see them fly out.

The dragonets chirped and sang, caught by the strong winds coming in from the ocean, fluttering like scraps of cloth.

A black form came sailing over. "Look out!" Dyrfinna cried.

Renegade shot up and crashed into the thing with a squeak. Both of them went spiraling to the ground, shrieking.

"Renegade!" Dyrfinna cried, running out to the dragonet, expecting to see her dying.

Instead, the dragonet was standing on top of the puffin it had just killed, crowing like a tiny rooster.

"I killed it!" she cried. "Now take me inside, I'm freezing!"

Dyrfinna swooped up both dragonet and puffin, and the other two dragonets landed on her shoulders to come back inside with them.

"Tonight, we eat like drakes!" Mella sang, eyeing the puffin.

"It's all yours," Dyrfinna said, depositing the puffin and the dragonets in front of the hearth. They set to work on their meal, holding their wings open to soak up the radiant heat of the fire as they ate.

"Their first kill," Ostryg said proudly.

"They didn't fly away," Gefjun added, leaning on him.

30

THE FOURTH DAY OF
BATTLE

THE FOURTH DAY OF BATTLE DAWNED CLEAR AND sparkling. The waves were high and the rocks and grasses were drenched, but the morning was beautiful — perfect for battle.

The dragonets begged and pleaded to go to the battle-field as the warriors put on their armor and sharpened their swords. Renegade was especially upset about not being able to go.

"You want me to kill them? I can kill them all," she begged, hanging upside down off Dyrfinna's arm as she pulled on her boots.

"You just hatched yesterday." Dyrfinna looked at her dragonet with love. "You need to get big and strong first before you go out on the battlefield."

"But I'm big and strong now," Renegade complained.

"You're not big. I can put you in my pocket."

"Then let me go to battle in your pocket!"

But saner minds prevailed. "Stay with us," Joy pleaded from Gefjun's shoulders. "I don't want to go to battle."

"Me neither." Mella landed next to them, folding her flame-yellow wings. "Juni will feed us all day, she said."

Renegade looked so alert and interested in this that everybody laughed.

Dyrfinna, Skeggi, and Ostryg went to the battlefield, dragonless — much to their relief.

"Should we tell the dragonets they'd be in danger of being killed or stolen by the enemy if they come out to the battlefield?" Skeggi asked.

"They're still young," Ostryg said. "Maybe later."

The fighting began at first light, and dragged on and on. It went much the same as the other days. There were no more avalanches now, as the piles of stones that had been set up for this purpose had all been used up – the only stones left were those that built the barricades.

The scorching sun beat down on the fighters, making the day's fighting even thirstier work. The wounded Viking that had been carrying water to everybody had been wounded a second time by an errant arrow, and his replacement was lamed and much slower.

"Nauma's warriors are insane," Skeggi grumbled. "We had one come at me in the heat of battle, trying to pin me down. Said he wanted to carve my heart out. Then Ostryg came by and we both made sure that he would never carve anything again. But even King Varinn's fighters are horrified by what those people are doing," he added. "One of them went past and actually stabbed the child-killer, then pretended it was an accident as he went on."

"Even they have more humanity than the child-killers," Dyrfinna said, deeply disturbed by these reports.

Later in the day, Dyrfinna was stabbed through the arm, putting her out of the fighting. She went back to the mead hall where Gefjun bound it up, the dragonets watching with great interest.

"I don't know how much longer I can do this," Juni said, laying her head against Dyrfinna's shoulder. "We've run out of cloth for bandages, so we have to wash old bandages for this work. We're running low on food. The puffins and skuas won't fly up overhead anymore, so we haven't been able to shoot and catch any. We're out of grain and oil, running low on cut wood."

"I know."

"If somebody doesn't come and rescue us soon, people are going to starve."

"Where there's life, there's hope," she said.

"Ugh! I hate when you say that."

Joy, who was wrapped around Gefjun's neck, said, "We can gather puffins for you. You saw what Renney did yesterday."

Renegade, who apparently had a nickname now, lashed her tail. "I can catch them by the dozens!"

Dyrfinna smiled. This from a dragonet who had only caught one puffin in her life — though, to be sure, she'd caught it very quickly. "Wait until after the battle is over to go out. I don't want them to see you flying around in the air and try to shoot you."

"We've been going outside, but we just stay by the doors where it's warm," Mella said. "We've been sunbathing."

Gefjun nodded, looking exhausted.

"Rest for a moment," Dyrfinna urged. "You're going to force yourself beyond your own strength, and we can't afford that."

Gefjun shut her eyes, and Dyrfinna stroked her hair with her good hand. But then the medic roused herself, looking back at her wounded. "I don't have time. I'll rest when I'm dead." And she went back to her work, and Dyrfinna picked up her shield and went back to her battle.

But there came a point when Dyrfinna suddenly realized that the sun was beginning to set, that the shadows from the trees at the bottom of the long slope were beginning to stretch into the enemy fighters, and the light was growing dim. A horn sounded from below, followed by several others, calling the enemy fighters back to camp.

"Oh, thank you, Allfather," one of her fighters breathed, unhooking his helmet and dropping it in the dust. He sat down next to it a moment later, then lay down, catching his breath.

Dyrfinna, breathing heavily, watched the enemy walk back down the long slope as the dust settled around them. The orange rays of sunset cut through the dust, made it luminous, and she stared at it for a while, her mind too exhausted to do more. But she heard somebody calling her name, and forced herself to turn back to the stones, nearly tripping over the tired warrior at her feet.

"Should we close this gap in the wall with more stones?" one of her fighters asked. "Then the enemy will have to work even harder to get at us."

Dyrfinna nodded. "I think we should. Even after we crushed them with several landslides and the best effort of our fighters, they still outnumber us. How many do we still have left?" she asked her fighters in general. "Did we lose anybody today?"

"I don't think so," Ostryg said, taking off a leather cap that somebody had given him. "Gefjun! How many dead do we have now? How many wounded?"

Now that the battle was over, she was walking along the wall, searching for wounded people to patch up. "As far as I know, all my people today are walking wounded. No new casualties."

Dyrfinna let out a sign of relief.

"Juni!" somebody called from the other side of the wall. A wounded man came through the gap in the rocky wall, returning from the enemy side, tottering on the arms of his fellow warriors. Somebody had tried to gouge out his eyes, and they were both bloody and blackened.

"I can still see," he said when Gefjun shouted in outrage. "I managed to wriggle out of their grip, and gave them back worse."

"But these wounds!" Gefjun cried, beside herself. "Look at this, Finna. They're torturing our people! They keep trying to drag our people down and gouge out their eyes! You saw what they did to poor Arne!" She quickly turned to the warrior. "I'm taking you to the mead hall and patch you up. This is horrible. I could just spit."

Gefjun led the warrior to the hall, turning the air red with outrage as she went.

Now remembering her blood-spattered sword, Dyrfinna crouched and wiped it off in the grass as best she could before she sheathed it. She would clean it properly after she got back to the mead hall.

Skeggi took off this helmet and wiped off his face and forehead. "At least we've held them off for another day. Good work," he said to Dyrfinna.

"Thank you," she said, looking along her front lines. Most everybody was watching the enemy go, but others were coming back from their battle lines to start their cook fires. Some got bows and arrows, or their slings, and went toward the cliffs before the great hall to shoot the puffins and skuas that filled the air with a racket. Dyrfinna realized that during the heat of battle, she had not noticed – or been able to hear the birds – over the battle noise.

Her soldiers all walked slowly, almost sleepwalking. The excitement of the battle was beginning to drain away, leaving her feeling low and exhausted.

She went back to the mead hall. Outside of the well house, warriors had stripped and were washing themselves as best as they could, dousing themselves with cold well water, yowling and shivering and laughing at each other. Dyrfinna longed for the privacy of a quiet stream, her body itching with dried blood and dirt, but she kept going to the main hall. Gefjun would have water she could wash with, and food to eat, and a little mead to drink. She had eaten her little piece of bread long ago, and her empty stomach felt as if were gnawing on itself.

She joined her friends in the mead hall and talked with them and fed the young dragons while she helped Gefjun with the wounded. Renegade sat on her shoulder, snapping cooked puffin from out of her fingers before

Dyrfinna could take a bite. Ostryg sat nearby, coaxing Joy to eat as she lay on his chest, purring. Ishaq and Skeggi were reading that little book again, and his small dragon perched lovingly on his shoulder, her tail draped around his neck as if she'd missed him while he had been gone all day. Skeggi was reading the book aloud to Mella, who listened attentively and occasionally commented.

Gefjun was working with a number of wounded warriors. "I don't have any cloth for bandages!" she snapped at Ishaq, who glowered back.

"Stay here, Renny," Dyrfinna told her dragon, and she turned and went straight back out. First of all, she wasn't in the mood to tolerate Gefjun and her temper. Second of all, she immediately knew how to fix this.

A number of the enemy's dead lay outside the wall. She raised her shield and stooped, making herself small behind it, and she sneaked out to them. The enemy had not yet called for a ceasing of hostilities, so nobody had gathered the dead for burial yet. The sun was setting, so at least it was getting dark, so she hoped that nobody in the enemy camp would notice her.

She crouched next to a corpse and used her dagger to cut off their cloaks and shirts, moving as quickly as she could. Only a few...

A shout from the enemy's camp behind her, and a scramble. She'd been spotted. Dyrfinna's heart pounded, and she gathered up everything she could and scrambled back behind the rocks as the arrows began flying in.

A moment later, she was presenting the cloth to a frazzled Gefjun, placating her anger. Gefjun immediately put Dyrfinna to work, cutting bandages from the tunics and cloaks she'd gathered.

Ishaq was sitting a little way from the fire – the wounded had the best places by the hearth. Skeggi beckoned her over, gesturing at an open space on the floor.

So Dyrfinna plunked down next to him with her

armful of stinking clothes. "Greetings," she said in an overly formal voice.

Ishaq wrinkled his nose as if she smelled. Well, she did. "What are you doing here?"

"I'm cutting bandages. Do you want to help?"

Ishaq curled his lip. "You mean you want me, a prince among men, to do your work for my unholy enemy? Certainly not."

"My goodness, how unthoughtful of me." Dyrfinna laid out the first cloak, a beautiful, thick cloth, colored like a summer sunset.

Ishaq sucked in a breath and was silent. It really was that magnificent.

There would have been a time she would have wanted to simply keep that gorgeous cloak for herself. She gazed at it. Now, battle-dulled and exhausted, she merely picked up her knife and began cutting a long strip off the bottom of the cloak.

"Stop! How can you do that!" Ishaq cried. "You shameless woman, stop!"

"We need bandages," she said, now annoyed at his outcry. "Don't call me names."

"Did you steal that cloak?"

Now she was even more annoyed. "I did not. Who do you think I am?"

"A liar."

Her ears reddened. This again!

"I knew the man who wore that cloak," Ishaq snapped. "He is a good man, honest as a thousand sunrises."

"Was," Dyrfinna corrected, and began cutting.

"Put your knife down. That cloak is an heirloom, from the loom of his great-grandmother!"

"I'm afraid the man who owned this cloak no longer cares about heirlooms, or his great-grandmother's loom," Dyrfinna informed him, setting aside the first strip and starting the next one. "And we need bandages for the wounded more than we need beautiful cloaks."

She was trying not to let her hands shake with the anger she felt toward him. Her chapped hands, calloused and blistered from handling swords and pikes during the battles of the last several days, kept snagging on the fine weave of the cloak. *Ishaq didn't have to fight in the battles I've fought in. How dare he judge me!*

An irrational thought, since, admittedly, she was the one who had taken him prisoner in the first place.

Ishaq sputtered. "Who do you think you are, you craven upstart, destroying a beautiful creation of a man who is so much better than you in every way imaginable?"

"Was," Dyrfinna corrected again, refusing to look at Ishaq as she laid aside the second strip. "*Was* so much better. Now he is food for worms."

The prisoner's nostrils flared, and he struggled to speak as she continued cutting the second strip.

"Are you pleased with yourself in your cruelty?" Ishaq finally asked. "Does this somehow make your breakfast taste better in the morning?"

Dyrfinna tightened her lips and said nothing. She set aside the second strip and deliberately picked up the cloak to cut the third.

"Did you sit here just to taunt me by coldly slicing this cloak to ribbons?" Ishaq said.

"No, I was just going to talk—"

He pulled the cloak out of her hands. "No more! This cloak belongs to my closest friend from childhood. Do you understand that? He fought at my side in every battle."

Dyrfinna's eyes went wide. She looked up and met Ishaq's angry eyes, which were glimmering with tears.

"My closest friend," he added, gently wrapping the cloak around his arms, "which, as you just informed me, is now food for worms."

❧ 31 ❧

COLD POISON

Dyrfinna's face reddened. She dropped her knife as if it had turned into a snake.

The room was dead silent.

She picked up the two strips she'd cut from the cloak, her hands fumbling as she folded them. "I'm sorry," she mumbled stupidly. "I didn't know."

Then, after a long, confused moment, she pressed the bandages into Ishaq's hands, not sure how to apologize.

"No. You may keep those hard-won bandages that you needed so very much," Ishaq snapped. "Keep those bandages that you had to cut off in front of my eyes to taunt me."

"I'm sorry, but I wasn't trying to taunt—"

"And may those bandages seep poison into every wound they bind," Ishaq added.

This really was too much. "It would have been more helpful to me if you'd told me in the first place that this was your friend's cloak. I'm sorry I can't read your mind."

Angry again, Dyrfinna scooped up the rest of the cloth and went to a different place to do her work, flinging down her armful of clothes before she sat down, cross-legged, next to them. *With my luck, my next piece of cloth will turn out to be his little brother's tunic, or something just as heinous.*

Renegade landed on Dyrfinna's shoulder, having come from playing with Mella and Joy. "Give me the word, and I will utterly rend him," the dragonet hissed, her emerald tail lashing.

"Ay, Finna, what did you do to Ishaq?" Ostryg laughed as he came in from the well house, his red paint washed off and his hair wet. "He looks like a dunked cat."

Somehow, Ostryg always managed to say the wrong thing at the worst time. She was suddenly in a mood to seize everybody by the scruff of the neck and vigorously shake them.

"None of your business.".

"Oh, Finna just informed Ishaq of his friend's death in possibly the worst possible way," Skeggi said, walking over to Ishaq and taking a small loaf of bread out of the pouch at his waist.

"Oh, not you, too. *Thank* you for your help," Dyrfinna said.

Skeggi sat down next to Ishaq, ignoring her statement. "I have some bread from this morning, and I would be honored if I could share it with you."

It always sounded courtly when Skeggi took up Ishaq's speech patterns. She had noticed that she always fell into that semi-formal way of speaking that Ishaq had, except when it came out of her mouth, all of it sounded like she was mocking him. Skeggi had the power of poetry on his side, so when he spoke in this way, it sounded elegant.

Not that she was admiring anything about Skeggi's ability at the moment. Quite the opposite, in fact.

"I still need bandages!" Gefjun cried, looking up from her patient. She'd been so busy with her patient that she'd missed everything that had just happened.

Dyrfinna sighed and sliced a few quick strips of cloth from the tunic that lay in her lap, then brought them over with the two cloak bandages that Ishaq had cursed – not that she believed his curses would stick.

Gefjun bound up the warrior's wounds briskly, the bandages incongruously clean against the warrior's stained arm and body. "I need more bandages. More, more, more," she told Dyrfinna, snapping her fingers. "What's taking so long?"

"Don't snap at me," Dyrfinna snapped. "I'm the commander. Why am I even doing this?"

"Yes, yes, why would a commander cut bandages?" Ishaq asked sarcastically, smoothing his hand over his friend's cloak. "This army of yours is the strangest place I've ever seen, where the supposed commander of these forces is bossed around by a lowly healer."

"Lowly healer?" Gefjun squawked, jerking her head up from her work.

"And here is the supreme commander cutting bandages – work that she could easily tell a lowly subordinate to do. It makes absolutely no sense."

"Don't," Skeggi muttered as Dyrfinna got suddenly to her feet. "Finna, don't let him goad you."

Oh, she was goaded. "Odin's *balls*, I've heard more than enough out of you," she said, throwing aside the cloth she'd been cutting and sheathing her dagger.

Ishaq crossed his arms. "Believe me, I feel the same way about you and your little friends, each of you constantly clowning around with your foolish antics. Nobody acts with decorum." He waved his hands, which were tied in front of him, from one sword friend to the other. "How have any of you managed to survive this battle? Everybody here is a fool."

"So you don't want to listen to us any more?" Dyrfinna said, striding over to where he sat with Skeggi on the floor. "Here's a solution that will make everybody happy: We'll take you up into the little room where we found the dead bodies, and we'll lock you inside. Then at least we'd be free of your stupid talk."

"Finna, don't," Skeggi said, picking up his bread before Dyrfinna, striding over, could step on it.

"Don't tell me don't."

"Yes, why do you allow him to talk to you like that?" Ishaq asked. "Everybody talks rudely to you, the commander, even when you're in public when others can see and comment. And you simply allow that?"

Dyrfinna's face grew so hot that it felt as if molten rock were pouring out of her ears. Her dragonet hissed at Ishaq.

She began to reply, but Ishaq was quicker. ""You don't have the slightest idea of what your so-called Queen is capable of. Your father is worse," he added to Dyrfinna. "And I see that same cruelty in you, that same pride and imperiousness."

Everybody was staring at her now, and it felt as if Ishaq were saying all the things that her father had been saying to her ever since she'd accidentally killed her brother Eirik. Bringing all her failures up in front of a crowd. Telling her all the ways in which she'd done wrong, in public, to crush her.

"That includes you, Ishaq." Dyrfinna's voice filled the room. "If I ever hear your didactic voice making its damned dry commentary one more time, I'll take cold poison and jump in the sea."

The prisoner's black eyes gleamed. "That sounds more like an incentive than a threat."

"I will *give* you cold poison and throw you in the sea. I don't care about the ransom. The ransom can go to Hel."

"Do you really mean any of that?"

Ugh. Shut up, Finna. "Skeggi, take the prisoner up to the room where the dead were."

"No!" Ishaq sat up straight, clearly wanting to stand though his feet and hands were bound. "No! Give me that cold poison! Upon the heart of the gods, give it to me so that I may drink it!"

In an instant Dyrfinna crouched at his side. She pulled her dagger and pointed it at his throat. "Just try me."

"Don't!" Skeggi said. "Finna, don't."

"Shut your mouth."

Ishaq turned a scornful eye on the blade. Then he lifted his chin, exposing his neck. "Here. Do it. Then you can rip apart all of my clothes, which I paid for in gold, and you can use them for your sad bandages, all the while congratulating yourself at how very *clever* you are for your ingenuity."

His pulses throbbed in his neck under the point of her blade.

Gefjun broke in. "Nobody wants to hear your clever remarks, Ishaq. I need bandages to do my job. Just stab him already, Finna."

"Yes, listen to her. Are you going to do it? Are you?" Ishaq asked, meeting her eye.

A horrible sense of failure drifted down over her as his eye met hers. She had been nettled enough to act without thinking. She could see, again, how her brother's eyes had slowly glazed over, the color fading out of the irises, as his body cooled after she had killed him.

Dyrfinna lowered her dagger. She had never hated anybody quite as much as she did this man at this moment. He had called her bluff, and now his eyes lit, gloating, as he saw that he'd succeeded.

"We must find a real commander for your poor army," Ishaq continued. "If you would be so kind, please send a message back to my men to free your commander and send him back here directly. Sinkr, is that his name?"

Now Dyrfinna regretted lowering the dagger. "I need you to shut the fuck up."

"Perhaps I should. Otherwise I will be threatened yet *again* with fake violence."

"I would be perfectly happy to threaten you with real violence." Dyrfinna could see herself striking Ishaq across the face. The muscles in her arms twitched, wanting to strike the blow.

Ishaq snorted. "I doubt that," he said, turning his eyes front again. "These are simply more lies from the lips of a liar. Perhaps this Sinkr is less of a liar than you are."

"You're wrong." But there was a tremble in her voice, which filled her with new fury.

"Finna." Skeggi stepped forward, looking concerned. "Let it go."

After all this, now she exploded.

"Do *not* tell me what to do." She rose to her feet and jabbed a finger into Skeggi's chest, her voice hard. "You have said enough. Stop trying to always be the only reasonable person in the room. I am your commander, and you will treat me as such. Is that understood?"

"Finna ..."

"Is that understood?" Her eyes turned to flint, and now she turned them from Skeggi, to Gefjun, to Ostryg, trembling with rage, then turned them back on Skeggi again. "I asked you a question. Are you going to answer me?"

She felt Skeggi's will give way before her, and he lowered his eyes. "Yes. That's understood."

She turned on Gefjun, who had gone pale and wide-eyed, and Ostryg, who merely shrugged. They, too, offered no further argument.

She looked at Ishaq. "Skeggi, Ostryg, take the prisoner up to the room of the dead, and lock him in there, and post a guard at the door. I do not want to see this man's face again."

Skeggi looked as if he wanted to say something, but Dyrfinna fixed him with her flint eyes again, angry enough to strike sparks from them.

Skeggi nodded and motioned for Ishaq to get to his feet. But then he paused, looking back at Dyrfinna. "Will the door be permanently locked? Is that what you're asking here?"

Dyrfinna stared at them both for a long moment. Ishaq stared back, raising his chin, not a tremor in his face – calling her bluff once again.

"Yes," she told him. "And to be honest, I don't care. Give him some food and water and leave him. He can live or die. His choice."

"Nicely done," Ishaq said as Skeggi led him out the door. "I will smile and rejoice as I go to the room of the dead, for I will at last have some peace from these fools."

Once they had left, followed by Ostryg, Gefjun whirled on Dyrfinna. "What was that all about?"

Dyrfinna was not having it. "I just made a command. They obeyed. You should do the same, and not question what I've just done."

Gefjun drew back, wrinkling her lip. "Are you really going to leave him to die?"

"Yes."

"I mean, I don't blame you..."

Dyrfinna cut her off. "And you are done questioning me. Ask somebody else to cut your bandages for you." With that, Dyrfinna strode out the doors into the darkness of the night.

32

A LAST RESORT

THE PULSES STILL POUNDED IN HER EARS FROM THE confrontation she'd just had. To make matters worse, the words that Sinkr had thrown into Dyrfinna's face before the battle came back to her.

*"I don't care about your pretty dragon pins, Dyerfinna. I don't care that you're a **demoted** dragon rider. Do you know what I care about? Your brother didn't deserve to die at your hand. Even if you say it was an accident."*

"You say you take care of your troops. I'll bet — in the same way you took care of your own little brother."

Those words weren't true, any more than Ishaq's words were.

The last thing she wanted to do was take any kind of direction from some ship rat squeaking at her about decorum. Even if he had been a little rat in full armor and a tiny sword, sitting in a small longship and peeping at her that she needed to show more decorum, she still would have told him to fuck off.

How dare he say those things to her? How dare he shame her like that in front of her friends and all the wounded? And she'd let herself be led. He'd grabbed her by the bridle as if she were a horse, and he'd led her up and down like a fool.

Dyrfinna turned toward the cook fires to gripe about it to some of the fighters – but to her surprise, the cook fires were burning, but nobody sat around them.

She stopped there in the dark, all her senses immediately on the alert. It was quiet outside, too quiet. Her troops should have been cooking dinner, talking, singing songs, complaining about things that had happened during battle.

All was dead silent – except for a scrabbling sound on the enemy's side of the great rock piles.

Dyrfinna drew her sword, and the runes that spelled NONE SHALL PASS THROUGH ME flashed at her from the unattended fires. As soon as she took up the sword, she felt how tired her wrist and arm were from the day's fighting. No matter.

She was tired of all this shit. She wanted it to be over.

Dyrfinna took two steps forward and peered through the darkness. There was only the light of the stars to see by, the light from the cook fires.

Dark forms crouched next to the wall — her fighters.

She walked toward them, hand on sword. Her stomach growled – in all the chaos earlier, she had forgotten to eat. That only angered her more.

"What is going on?" Her voice came out louder than she'd intended.

A group of fighters frantically waved her over. On the other side of the rocks came a wild scrabbling, and a faint whisper of an inhuman groan. Dyrfinna instantly went quiet.

"Draugrs," one of the warriors said. "On the other side of the rocks. Lots of them."

The hair on the back of her neck stood on end.

Other warriors began whispering. "The dead started rising after sunset, once the light was gone."

"They have a magician, and she is using seith magic to make the dead walk. Can you hear her chanting?"

Dyrfinna craned her neck. A low crooning came from

far beyond the wall, a disturbing dark music that crept down her vertebrae on spider's feet. The sound of the dead on the other side of the rock piles nearly drowned out the woman's singing.

Dyrfinna stood to look over the rocks.

"Be careful," one of the veterans warned. "Don't let them see you."

She eased herself up, slow as a cat. On the other side were bodies with their skulls split, their intestines spilling out, struggling and crawling and slipping on the rocks. Some of the bodies, trampled by the living, struggled to move, a grotesque writhing. Most prowled back and forth below the wall. They reminded her of the wolves that had once attacked her and her little sister, pacing with their eyes on their prey, searching for an opening.

Though she had been silent and unmoving, a dead face flicked toward her, its filmy eyes fixed on hers. Its mouth dropped open and a wet noise came out.

Immediately, other dead faces fixed on her and came crawling straight at her. They redoubled their efforts to climb the rock wall, their feet slipping on the loose scree, their cold eyes never leaving hers.

She slid back to safety, her heart pounding. How was she going to protect her people from this? Eventually the draugrs were going to find a way over the top, and once they started coming in, her people would not be able to defend themselves against the dead. Her stomach turned, but there was no time for that.

"How many draugrs are out there, do you think?" She stood straight and tall, hand on her sword hilt, mind racing.

"We think that the woman has reanimated *all* the dead outside our barricades."

"One of our patrollers realized what was happening before we did," said a shieldmaiden. "He came running in and ordered us to barricade the opening there with stones and logs before they came ... alive." She took a deep breath. "That's the only thing keeping the dead out."

Dyrfinna sent a silent prayer to the gods, thanking them for the patroller's sharp eyes.

"We could hide in the great hall," the shieldmaiden said. "Barricade ourselves in there."

Dyrfinna thought of Nauma's forces following the draugrs in, protected from the undead by the magician. She imagined Nauma's forces throwing torches on the roof of the hall and laughing.

"No," Dyrfinna said. "I've heard too many stories in which valiant soldiers were burned alive in their mead halls. We will not add to them."

She realized that this draugr uprising had started while she'd been arguing with Ishaq, and was even more furious. If she'd only walked away!

She shook her mind back to the present. "I've asked everybody about their magical abilities before, but just in case, if any of you might have some ability that you've had hiding before, something that could possibly counteract what that woman is doing over there, I'd be happy to hear about it."

The shieldmaiden shrugged. "Just Gefjun for the healing stuff ... and you." She fixed Dyrfinna with a keen eye.

A wave of cold rushed over her, leaving her momentarily light-headed. "I'll use it as a last resort. Because ... that's how people get killed."

The shieldmaiden cocked her head. "Well, yes. Because that is precisely what we need at the moment."

🦕 33 🦕

AN UNHOLY WIND

AFTER DYRFINNA HAD LEFT THE GREAT HALL IN A HUFF, Skeggi was in a peculiar state of mind. Finna had clearly been beside herself after being goaded by Ishaq. But Skeggi was angry at her, too. She could have just let it slide, as usual. And she definitely didn't need to take it out on him.

"Ostryg, a little help?" Skeggi asked. His friend got up from next to the fire and came over, his sky-blue dragon still lying across his neck.

Ishaq watched them imperiously. His hands, which were bound, were still clutching his dead friend's cloak. He'd been holding the cloak ever since Finna put it in his arms, and made no move to put it down.

Gefjun was up, too, and shrewish. "What was all up Finna's ass?" she asked, exasperated. "And your ass, too," she said, whirling on Ishaq. "You were over there, all self-satisfied, picking a fight with anybody who talked to you."

"I was merely expressing my opinion," he said.

"Your opinion is like diarrhea," she snapped. "Nobody ever wants it because it stinks and makes a mess."

Ishaq looked affronted. "Impious woman! Watch that language that you—"

She swatted him upside the head. Her sky-blue drag-onet crowed.

"How dare you!" Ishaq would have returned the favor if his hands hadn't been bound.

"Curb your tongue!" Gefjun shouted, drowning him out, her red hair almost electric around her head. "All I've heard out of your mouth are complaints and whining. What kind of commander are *you*, if you complain so much? I've seen small children who are more patient and considerate in the face of adversity than you've ever been. I am doing my best to heal all these people," she said, gesturing widely at her patients, "and every one of these wounded men and women, even when they're in agonizing pain, even when they're dying, have been a thousand more times kind and considerate than you have been. So don't lecture me and call me impious. See to your own house first."

The dragonets popped into the air and went circling in excitement.

Skeggi hid his smile at Ishaq's open-mouthed outrage, quickly rearranging his face to look serious before he touched the prisoner's arm. "We had better go. Come this way." He picked up the small oil lamp off the table where he and Ishaq had been reading from the book earlier. Then, on impulse, he picked up the book as well.

Ostryg planted a big kiss on Gefjun's cheek as he passed, earning a look of annoyance, and joined them as they walked Ishaq, still fuming, out of the grand hall, leading him to the passageway to the living quarters and the upper room where he would be imprisoned.

Behind them, Gefjun fired a parting shot. "And Ishaq, if you get wounded somehow, pray that whatever god you worship is going to show you mercy. After all, I'm just a lowly healer. Maybe I won't want to help you in your hour of need!"

Ishaq's jaw tightened, but he did not turn around.

Skeggi lifted the oil lamp as they entered the passageway, illuminating the series of open doorways to all those mostly empty, dust-filled rooms.

"Come this way." Skeggi squinted into the darkness of the rest of the hall, now wishing he'd brought a second lamp. The night felt full of sharp edges, though that feeling may well have been the result of the bitter argument they'd just witnessed. That fury in Finna's eyes, though, directed at him. He didn't like it.

"But I *am* the most reasonable person in the room," he muttered.

"You most certainly are," Mella whispered into his ear, glowing like yellow flames.

The ladder to the room above was still there, as were all the bits of dried skin and splinters of bone that had sifted to the ground when Ostryg and Dyrfinna had moved the five dead men out of that room. The sight of that dust and debris of the dead made Skeggi queasy, but he pretended to be impassive. Ostryg would have laughed at him, otherwise.

Ishaq, his legs tied together, hands bound, shuffled ahead of him. Though he was a prisoner, he held his head high, looking around the living quarters as if they were merely another portion of his domain. The whole time he'd been a prisoner, he had refused to take off his silver armor, made of overlapping scales like a fish, for fear somebody would steal it. He had even slept in it without a peep of complaint, the metal on the stones clinking like handfuls of coins every time he moved.

Ishaq had been forced to give up his sword, though, with many curses upon anybody who dared to touch it. But after reading with Ishaq, Skeggi had managed to earn the prisoner's grudging trust – which, clearly, Finna had gotten into her head to ruin.

But Ishaq still carried his late friend's cloak in his arms, the one that Finna had been cutting for bandages. He had refused to put it down.

"Do you think she's really planning to lock you in here ... for good?" Skeggi asked aloud.

Ishaq turned back, regarding him. "She won't," he replied. "Did you not see how he hesitated before she refused to give you an answer? I am not concerned."

"That's what I thought," Skeggi said. "I'm sure she'll change her mind. I've known her for years, and I know she'll let you out, even if she despises you. She's not as bloodthirsty as you make her out to be."

"Stop trying to comfort this man," Ostryg grumped. "He's an angry bastard. He doesn't need your comfort." Joy made a hmph noise as if agreeing with him.

"I thought you were the angry bastard," Skeggi said.

Ostryg shrugged. "I won't deny it."

"I am perfectly capable of speaking for myself," Ishaq said, affronted. "And you need not defend that woman's honor to me. Her actions are more than sufficient to give me a clear understanding of how duplicitous and craven she truly is."

Behind Ishaq's back, Ostryg made the face he always made when Skeggi's vocabulary got out of hand.

"Finna is honest and courageous," Skeggi said. "Speak of what you know."

Ostryg's face cleared and he nodded at Skeggi before he climbed up the ladder and looked into the room. "We need to get another light. I can't see shit up here. Stand under here and hold the lamp up to the hole so I can see." He climbed the rest of the way up and vanished. Skeggi did as he said.

The wind outside was streaming over the hall, almost screaming, and a particularly strong gust shook the building. Seabirds called, adding to the melancholy sound.

"Ugh! This fucking wind is blowing dead people dust everywhere! I got dead people shit up my nose!"

Skeggi gagged, and his lamp wavered.

Ostryg's face appeared in the opening above. "Ha ha, I

knew I'd get you." Skeggi swiped at him with his free hand, and Ostryg laughed again and disappeared.

"Give me a lamp while I'm imprisoned there," Ishaq asked. "I can pass the time by reading."

"No lamps," Ostryg said from above, pushing something heavy with a lot of screeching across the floor. "Unlike *some* of these people, I still remember that you're the enemy. You'd just hold the lamp up to the thatching and burn the place down around our heads while we're sleeping. You'd be sitting up here among the flames, happily chanting your curses as you burned to death. I know how you are."

"I'm afraid you do not." Ishaq's face darkened.

"I can read to you while I'm guarding you," Skeggi offered.

"Skeggi, you're too fucking trusting," Ostryg complained from above. "I keep telling you, you can't make friends with these bastards. I don't care if they can read. That alone is suspicious."

"Thora loved to read."

"Yeah, but that was Thora. This man is nothing like her." Ostryg hawked, then blew his nose in his usual way, by closing one nostril and blowing out the other nostril, then repeating on the opposite side.

Ishaq grimaced. "I regret ever having come to this uncivilized land. I regret it to my very marrow."

Ostryg's only response was to rip out one of the loudest farts that Skeggi had ever heard. "Enjoy your uncivilized stay in your uncivilized room!" He laughed maniacally as he came back down the ladder. "It's all yours. Get up there fast before the wind blows out the ambiance!"

And then just as suddenly − and uncharacteristically − the wind died away. A sudden silence fell.

"Oh, good." Ostryg looking up, rubbing his hands together. "Now the smell will linger."

Ishaq was no longer listening. He stood, head cocked

to the side, brow furrowed, as if trying to hear something far away.

Ostryg laughed and elbowed Skeggi in the ribs. "Look at that. I must have brought some of the ambiance down with me. It's broken his mind."

Ishaq shook his head. "What is happening outside?"

"Wind." Ostryg grinned. "*Breaking* wind."

Skeggi sighed, exasperated. "Yes, that's nice, we get it. Could we move on?"

Ishaq was no longer engaged with what either of them was saying. "Shh." He turned his head to the left, then to the right, the furrow in his brow deepening. "Do you feel that?" he said in a quiet voice. "Skeggi. Since you have a sense for this – do you feel something?"

Skeggi, noticing Ishaq's concern, lowered the lamp. He realized all of a sudden that the ocean's winds did not simply come blasting in out of nowhere and then immediately fade away.

"That wind was not from the sea," Skeggi suddenly said. "Come." He went to the side door that looked out over the slope that led down to the enemy and pushed it open, looking out at the night.

Ostryg joined him. "Has it ever occurred to you that our guest might be tricking you?"

"I am not speaking in jest." Ishaq came shuffling up, his legs tied together.

"Odin preserve us." Skeggi covered the lamp's flame with his palm to snuff it, ignoring the momentary pain.

"What are you doing?" Ostryg asked, but when Skeggi pointed at the rock piles and barricades – his voice died.

Under the starlight and the faint glow of the night sky in the west, they saw the shambling creatures.

Ishaq made a noise as if the air had been knocked out of his lungs. "It's happening again," he said in a voice not his own. "It's the unholy magic."

"Oh, stop," Ostryg huffed.

Ishaq did not stop. "I was one of King Varinn's emissaries who met with Nauma when she asked to throw her lot in with ours. She told us she uses this unholy magic. She explained to us how she'd used it against an enemy village to attack them. She told us how she raised the dead in order to make the enemy crazed with fear, until they ran in the streets in terror. Then she turned her men, the child-killers, loose like dogs to slaughter the survivors."

His voice took on an edge. "Anyone can make up a story. Later, after she joined us, those of us who sailed under King Varinn's banner heard of a village, close to where Nauma said she'd been, where everybody had been slaughtered. Not just the enemy. But women. Venerable elders. Children. There was not a single person left alive in that place."

Skeggi couldn't speak. Even Ostryg, assassin that he was, seemed stunned.

"We didn't fully believe it, even when they bragged about it. Rumors are rumors, after all. Anybody can brag about working powerful magic. But now, as you see, the draugrs are here. This is the first step."

Ishaq lifted the cloak that he'd wrapped in his arms. "And, what's more, my oldest friend is among the dead. His body now walks, an affront to everything he was when he was alive."

Skeggi nodded. "We've had that happen with us. First with our queen-to-be, and then again last night, with a friend of ours." He nodded. "It shakes you, to see them used like that."

Ishaq took a breath. "Though we are enemies, I implore you to allow me to help you stop this monstrous thing she is doing. I prefer to meet my enemies honorably in the heat of battle, where we may each do ourselves honor through the strength of arms. But this – what this woman is doing with her unholy magic and the bodies of the dead – this is beyond the pale."

Ostryg scoffed. "Why should we trust you? You just

spent the whole evening squawking about what a bad commander Finna was."

"My opinion of her is unchanged," Ishaq said. "But when you faced your friend yesterday, who was made into a draugr – how did you feel about that? Was it delightful to see his animated body walking and slathering, like a cruelly-made puppet?"

"Like Thora had been," Skeggi said. "In the mead hall."

A long moment. Ostryg curled his hands into fists, mouth tight in anger. "Fine. I'm with you – but only for the moment. What do we need to do?"

❦ 34 ❦
ALONE

In the meantime, Dyrfinna had her hands full.

She knew how fast the draugrs could move after having faced Arne. If she weren't running at full speed as soon as she was past the barricades, they'd be upon her in an instant, pulling her down like wolves pulling down a full-grown elk. But if she was going to use her magic to fight off the draugrs and destroy them, she needed to get far enough away from the barricades and her army so she wouldn't destroy them. Her army needed the barricades to stay standing, and Dyrfinna knew her magic, once unleashed, would blast a gigantic gap into the barricades that would let Nauma's army in. And she needed her army to stay alive – no matter what the cost.

She turned quickly to some of her warriors. "My magic should be a last resort," she said. "Send somebody to the great hall to get the barrel of mead and some torches. We'll use these to burn the draugrs where they stand."

"Not the barrel of mead!" one of the warriors cried as the messenger ran that way.

One of the fighters laughed. "We will sacrifice the mead tonight so we can drink mead later, once we're off this accursed island."

A shout came from the other end of the barricades. "They're breaching the rocks!" somebody yelled.

Dyrfinna and the others hurried toward the shouting.

And at that moment, as it always does in war, everything went sideways.

The shouts turned into screams.

"No," Dyrfinna whispered, now running.

The first draugr tumbled over the barricades, falling down the rocks at her warriors' feet.

Every one of the warriors were armed with long clubs, and they began sledgehammering the draugr with all their might.

"Don't let it get up!" somebody shouted.

"Break its legs!" another warrior cried. "They can't chase you if they can't walk!"

Except now more draugrs were falling down the rocks of the barricades.

"Lead them to the cliffs!" Dyrfinna cried. "Lead them to the edge and find a way to push them off."

Another scream, now from behind Dyrfinna. She spun and saw a second breach, this one at the logs that blocked the barricades. A draugr had squeezed under the logs, the half-burrowing like a mole to get through a gap against the ground. There seemed to be two more draugrs behind him, because two sets of hands were clawing at the soil around the first one as it emerged.

Ragnarok peeled off to tend to this breach. He heaved up a boulder and slammed it on the first draugr's head, then lifted a second rock, waiting for the next draugr to emerge. "Crush them as I'm doing," he called to the warriors around him. "But watch them so they don't grab you by the ankles..."

Just then came a horrifying wail. A draugr had grabbed one of her men who had been clubbing it. Though the draugr didn't have much of a head left to bite him with, its arms still worked, gripping him tight, and every draugr nearby stopped what it was doing and piled upon the warrior in a way that made Dyrfinna sick. His wails were muffled under the draugrs that were starving for the taste of life.

At the terrifying sight, the magic flamed to life within Dyrfinna's body.

Keep your mind clear. Breathe slowly. Don't let the magic wind out of control.

Sudden electricity charged the air around Dyrfinna, making her hands tingle as if they'd fallen asleep.

Terrible dread filled her. She saw, once again, the lifeless eyes of her brother. She took a shuddering breath.

She had no choice. Once the draugrs finished feeding on the poor soldier, they would attack the rest of her people who could not defend themselves. And it would end with everybody barricaded inside the mead hall, fighting off their defenders – until the end, when the final few of her fighters would be cornered inside the small loft and killed, just as the five dead men had been.

Dyrfinna would have failed her Queen, her people, and their families on Skala – and she would have failed Thora, who she'd sworn to revenge.

Skeggi always said that the most audacious acts lead to the best stories, she told herself.

All this flashed through her mind. Now, Dyrfinna pushed aside the eyes of her dead brother, pushed aside her fear. She could not afford to lose one more person.

She pulled off Thora's carnelian ring.

Her heart within her chest felt as if had burst into flames, a hot, radiant sensation that she'd always found difficult to endure. As if in response, ghostly fire oozed from her hands like wisps of glowing fog, moving up her arms and brightening as it did, lighting up her face from below.

In the quietest of voices, she began singing the magic into being, her eyes never leaving the terrible sight of one of her men being torn apart by draugrs.

You can destroy them with just a word.

As the ghostly fire twined around her face, panic rose. She breathed deeply, tried to quell it, even as the fire buzzed in her veins, blurring her vision.

Somebody cried, "Get back! Get back! Finna's doing it again!" There were shouts.

Somebody else added, in a lower voice, "Stay away from her, unless you want to end up dead like her brother."

Dyrfinna's face heated, and not from the fire rising from her arms.

Skeggi's voice rang out from behind her, full of life and unafraid. "Clear a space for Finna, and let her do her work! Warriors, fall back from the barricades and gather around me at the mead hall. Cold iron will not stop these monsters, but Finna's power will."

He has so much faith in me. She wanted desperately to tamp the magic down, thinking of all her people behind her. She could not – did not dare – to make a misstep. She could not live with herself if her magic spun out of control and killed them, too.

All the same, she'd never felt so alone.

The warrior was dead, his body ravaged like so much meat. The draugrs let him drop, their faces and chests red with his blood, and they rose up to hunt new prey. Their slow eyes turned toward her warriors, who were now gathered next to the mead hall in full armor, swords and pikes ready.

Anger flashed in her heart. The magic rising from her arms glowed more brightly in response, like sudden sunlight cutting through the fog.

"If I am to be alone when I die, then so be it," she said. "I can cut down the draugrs where they stand and save my people, and the gods will smile upon my work."

In this way she could finally redeem herself for having killed her brother.

Her heart leapt. That was all she'd ever wanted.

Dyrfinna stepped forward, breathing deeply, and raised

her arms to cross them before her face, glaring at her enemies.

She would destroy them.

But at that moment, a familiar voice cried out in her mind, curling around her like smoke.

Dyrfinna! I've found you!

For a moment, Dyrfinna didn't understand. But then she gasped, tears springing to her eyes.

"Serja! Serja, it's you!" It was the glorious garnet dragon that had bonded with her.

Yes, it's me, the dragon said. *We have been looking everywhere for your ship, but it wasn't until you started doing magic that I was able to sense you through our bond. What are you doing? Do you need my help?*

"Yes," Dyrfinna said, and her intention glowed as brightly as her joyful heart. "Yes, I do."

35

DROWNING IN
WHITE FIRE

Dyrfinna turned upon the draugrs and flung her arms down, scissoring that power at them. White flame leapt from her, slicing through the dead walkers and flinging them back. They lay motionless, fully dead once more.

Breathing deeply, she turned slowly to the next group of draugrs, the magic filling her to the brim like a cup. If she moved suddenly it might spill – backwashing over her people behind her with deadly results.

"Help me, Serja," she whispered.

I see you, they said, their warm voice anchoring her. *I see the undead that you are fighting. Where are all these draugrs coming from?*

"A magician on the enemy side," Dyrfinna whispered. "My people are standing behind me. I hope they're out of range. I don't want to hurt them."

You're doing fine. Breathe, then unleash the flames at your enemies.

A burst of exaltation. *Serja is helping me!* She breathed, then flung the power at the draugrs as they came shambling over the wall. They fell aside, and lay still.

The magic in her trembled as if it would slosh over the

side. She froze, waiting for it to calm – but now more draugrs were clambering over the rocks. She had to act faster. If she stood there and waited after every strike for her magic to calm, the draugrs would simply shuffle past her toward her people.

Stop, Finna, the dragon told her in a resonant voice. *Let your emotions pass, whether they be good or ill. You can brag about me to yourself later.* A hint of humor in Serja's voice. *Breathe again, calm yourself, and unleash.*

"Fair enough," Dyrfinna whispered, and she breathed, and unleashed her powers. She did so, again and again, to the draugrs that came tumbling over the wall, or crawling out through the gap under the logs, or to the ones that came shambling at her like a crab, too quickly. The fighters that had been killed in battle moved in a grotesque imitation of life, half-severed limbs hanging off their bodies, intestines dragging like wet ropes in the dirt. She knew these sights would fuel her nightmares for months, but she could not step away.

From the corner of her eye, the messenger she'd sent came running out of the great hall, rolling the barrel of mead in front of him – but as soon as he noticed Dyrfinna standing there, boiling with power, he spun the barrel around and rolled it, just as swiftly, back into the great hall.

Dyrfinna strode forward, the fire welling up like a molten spring of white water, burning her even as she contained and channeled it. She flung it at every draugr, throwing it harder than before in an effort to get the power out of her before it overwhelmed her. Now each of her hits flung the draugrs back with an explosion.

Calm yourself, Serja said. Dyrfinna heard the worry in her voice. *The explosions are too much.*

"I know. But ..." But it was happening again. The power was growing more and more, and she felt it beginning to wind out of control. She fought to keep it contained, trying to keep it from exploding as it usually did when it got to this point. She wrapped her arms around it, in a manner of speaking, but it was like trying to grasp and contain a whirlpool. The fire crackled in her ears, and her arms and legs quivered as if she carried a weight that was too heavy for her.

I don't care, she thought. *I am going to cut down the draugrs.*

She walked toward the barricades, carrying the burgeoning magic away from her people huddled around the great hall.

"Serja," she whispered. Tears rose in her eyes, only to turn to steam in the fire she was creating. "Serja, help me ."

Two more draugrs came over. She cut them down with a quick slice of her shaking arm, but she overdid the power that burst from her. White light cut down the draugrs and hurtled beyond them to strike a gigantic spruce farther down the mountain. The trunk exploded with a splintering crack, and it slowly, ponderously, leaned inland from the weight of its branches, and came slamming to the ground with a crash she felt through her feet, and a terrible cascading crackle and rush of its branches that sounded like a waterfall. Branches and splinters flew in all directions from the impact.

Dyrfinna. I can't ... I can't help you control it, Serja said. *This ... the shining things ... I wear them ... they won't let me.* The last statement said with a wrench of frustration.

Dyrfinna kept walking, not daring to stop now. She was sure that the carnelian collar that the dragon wore was gleaming brilliantly, blocking Serja from using their magic, keeping them from even referring to it.

The magic was out of control, on the verge of exploding, and she was going to carry it to the enemy. Carry it to the draugrs, and to Nauma herself.

She was almost to the barricades, her heart pounding as if it were too large for her chest. *This isn't far enough away from everybody!* She cried aloud in anguish, because now the white fire was clouding her vision and mind, even drowning out Serja's voice.

She flung her power ahead of her. The resulting explosion shook the ground and bounced her around. She stumbled through the barricades – or at least clambered over rough stones – as she groped her way forward.

Through the blinding glare of the white fire, she glimpsed part of the barricade to her right, jagged stones where her burst of power had blasted them away. Her feet on a downhill path told her she was facing the enemy.

She took several more steps forward when powerful hands seized her, strong as bear traps. A draugr. She gently laid her hands on this draugr's arms and blasted them into ash.

More hands grasped her. Oh yes: the dead were thick on this side of the barricades – and now they had all turned to draugrs.

Other hands tried to grab her, only to be burned to ash in the fires that now devoured her.

She saw, at last, a way out.

"Give every fighter who died here an honorable death," she pleaded with the gods through her overpowering flames. "Give every one of these people their eternal rest, as it pleases the gods. Give them rest." Then she flung her arms to the left and right, throwing sheets of flame that rushed from her like rivers, instantly immolating the rest of the dead who lay before the barricades. *No more draugrs.*

Brilliant orange flared up on both sides, the stink of burning, but then the white fires overwhelmed her senses again – now even brighter than before. It was as if the more she used the powers, the more they grew.

Dyrfinna stumbled forward. If she could just make it to the enemy's camp before the magic spilled out everywhere, she could at least save her people.

The fires were too painful to bear. They devoured her

inside and out. She forced herself toward the enemy. A few stray draugrs laid hands on her and her power immolated them with a flash of light and fog.

The white fire blazed uncontrollably, dropping her to her knees.

"I'm sorry, Aesa," Dyrfinna whispered to her little sister who she'd left behind. "I'm sorry, Aesa. I promised to come home to you, but I have to break my promise. I'm sorry. I love you, Aesa, Momma, Grandmama. I'm sorry, little Renegade. Gefjun will have to raise you now."

Serja called to her, but it was too far away.

The magic was building up to an explosion. The white fire burned through her, devouring her as if she were a leaf in the flames.

She collapsed and tried to ground the magic by touching the earth, but by this time there was too much of it, and it was in a different form – one of fire, not lightning – and did not drain out of her as lightning would have done.

She couldn't tell if she were still too close to her people to unleash her magic, or if she was close enough to the enemy's camp to kill them with it, or close enough to the barricades to blast them apart. For all she knew, she could have been walking in circles. She was not taking the chance, because she could no longer see.

Dyrfinna curled over, pulling the fire into herself, and held the inferno close, trying to dampen the inevitable explosion. She turned her head from the pain.

For everything I've done, please forgive me, she said, or thought she said.

At that moment, a cool hand gripped her shoulder, though the rest of her was in flames.

Don't touch me, she pleaded, sure that it was one of her friends.

But they were not immolated as she expected. The hand still lay upon her shoulder. A voice she didn't recognize suddenly burst out in song next to her ear.

A strange music she didn't recognize, twining magic all around it.

36

NO MORE DRAUGRS

AT THE TOUCH OF THE HAND, THE FLAMES FADED. THEIR loud crackling was gone, replaced by the rushing of silence against her ears. No pain now from the fire, only the blessed relief of cool air touching her arms and face. She still glowed, but the flames had been quelled. What was that person singing? She didn't recognize the music.

The music directed the power to disperse, grounded out the overflowing magic, drained the death from it, then allowed it to drift away like fog in the morning when the sun touches it.

The white fire guttered on her arms as if a breeze blew on it. The flames dwindled, then went out.

Dyrfinna took deep gasps of the air, shivering from cold and weakness – the magic she had cast had strained her body to the utmost.

The blinding white blaze cleared from her sight as if a cool breeze carried it away. A white afterimage was still burned into her eyes from the flames, but beyond it, she caught a glimpse of the beautiful darkness of the night. *Still there,* she thought. The cool air touched her face and arms, and she could not stop shivering.

Serja's voice bloomed in her mind. *Dyrfinna! Are you still alive? Are you safe?*

A wave of relief. She could barely move her lips. "Yes," she whispered.

The voice was still singing – a man's voice, gloriously dark and sweet. She felt as if she could wrap it around herself like a soft, warm cloak, easing away her pain, giving her comfort.

Who was singing? Still in pain, she slowly raised her head.

Ishaq crouched at her side, singing, his deep brown eyes fixed on hers, singing as if to a friend. She was surprised by how long his eyelashes were. A sky-blue glow came off him, but he had drawn the power out of her dangerous magic as if she were not prepared to deal death upon everybody in range. He did have a sky-blue shield up to protect his people from her power, though. Well, that made sense.

Now that her eyes were open, he got to his feet and changed his song. He was singing to the dead, those who had been turned into draugrs, those whom Dyrfinna had immolated, whose fires still burned along the barricades. He sang peace to them, committing them to the earth, where they belonged. All of this done in a brilliant voice, where every note was a jewel. Enemy though he was, she couldn't help but admire his voice.

At last he finished, and knelt next to her again. She was too addled with exhaustion to comprehend what was happening, and shivering too hard to control her muscles, but she needed to get back to the great hall. She wanted nothing more than to lie down next to the great fire and rest.

"Thank you," she managed to say despite her shivering. She attempted to stand, but the world tipped sideways. The ground pitched up into her face.

A few moments later, she realized Ishaq was carrying her in his arms – had been carrying her, because they were already past the barricades and almost to the great hall, where her warriors cheered.

"Let me down. I can walk." She raised her head, embarrassed by all the people watching her. She was still shivering.

"I assure you, you're wrong," he said. "There is not a drop of blood in your face."

"It's not that bad."

"A mere moment ago, you were warning me to watch out for the invading mushroom men."

"Mushroom men? I did not say any such thing," she said, outraged.

"Ha! Yes, you did," Ostryg said, joining them. "I heard you saying they were on their way right now." He laughed in a way she found particularly annoying.

"Well, I certainly don't remember any of that," she muttered. In truth, she felt as if she were spinning. She wanted desperately to lay her head on something, except the only surface available was Ishaq's chest, so she abstained. "Didn't I just save your asses a moment ago? Didn't I just take out those draugrs just now? Where were you? Show some respect."

"Yes, show some respect," Ishaq broke in.

Oh, don't you start, she thought.

"She did a courageous thing in facing those draugrs ... and her own fears," Ishaq told Ostryg. "I saw what she was doing. She's using a complex magic of two parts. Once the right balance is struck, the antagonistic parts of the magic combine in a way that causes them to spin out of control very quickly. Despite that, she walked willingly out there to kill the draugrs. In doing so, she saved, as she so eloquently called it, 'your ass.'"

There was a long silence. Ostryg simply turned on his heel and walked away.

"Huh. I thought you hated my little white guts," Dyrfinna said, her voice weak as a kitten's.

"Where do you come up with those expressions?" Ishaq asked with a quirk of his eyebrow. "And yes, I most assuredly cannot be called your friend. Make no mistake about that. But I respect courage when I see it, and what you did took courage."

"So ... how does my magic work, again?" Dyrfinna was confused by the way he'd spoken about it, but some of it made sense.

But before Ishaq could reply, here was the great hall, and Gefjun was running to them, visibly fretting. "What the hell was that, Finna!" she cried.

"I saved everybody's asses," she said through chattering teeth. Now she felt worse, much worse. She rested her head against her enemy's cold iron armor, no longer able to hold it up.

"She drowned the draugrs in fire to cleanse them so they won't come back again," Ishaq said, carrying her into the great hall. "Now they can pass on to their final rest or reward, as was ordained."

The dragonets flew over to Dyrfinna, twittering in concern,

"Put Finna down by the fire," Gefjun said roughly. "Then go back to your corner. You're still a prisoner here, like it or not."

Dyrfinna tried to speak, but only a faint hissing came out. Ishaq set her unceremoniously by the hearth, followed by all three dragonets.

Gefjun fussed over her. "You're out of strength," she scolded. "I can't believe you were doing that to yourself."

It needed to be done, she wanted to say, but she was too exhausted to speak. She merely rolled over and blacked out.

37

"WE CAN DECIDE THIS NOW."

DYRFINNA WOKE UP EARLY, THE MORNING LIGHT coming in through the holes in the thatched roof overhead. The first thing she did when she awoke was look wildly around, convinced that Skuld was looming nearby with her watchful eyes.

Dyrfinna wished she could go back to sleep. She had a blinding headache, and she blinked like an owl in daylight. The inside of her mouth tasted sick and wrong, and her body throbbed. She sat up, and immediately lay back down again.

Ishaq and Skeggi shared breakfast as they talked and Skeggi sharpened his spear. Ostryg and Gefjun were necking, but when one of the patients in her field hospital groaned, she broke away to tend to them.

Dyrfinna felt groggy but she wasn't about to let the enemy prisoner notice it.

Ishaq was talking with Skeggi about a dragon he'd known – his own personal dragon, she realized with another pang of jealousy, thinking of Serja. She missed Serja. Her heart-deep bond, the one thing she longed for the most, had been stolen from her by her own father.

"Back in Córdoba, I had the smartest, most intelligent diamond dragon," he told Skeggi.

"Was she collared?" Skeggi asked.

Ishaq frowned. "Our version of this magic is much different than yours," he said. "With our collars, our dragons can roam and satisfy themselves. You see, our collars only subvert a dragon's destructive nature so they won't ravage villages and eat people or cattle. But it also intensifies the bond with their humans so they don't feel the need to roam. They follow the rules of our society. It's still a spell, but not as draconian, if you will, as your collars."

Just then Skeggi noticed Dyrfinna. "Ah, so you're awake."

"Barely." Her voice sounded like she'd been gargling gravel. "Ishaq, may I ask you a question?"

He frowned again. "You may," he said, though his tone of voice sounded more like *if you must*.

"Last night, when you ran to me and then saved my life ... thank you. I have a little sister, a mama, and a grandmama I want to return to. And I want to stay alive for, and friends I want to support," she added, looking at Skeggi. "Thank you for saving my life. I owe you a debt. But why did you do it? Why didn't you simply walk past me and escape back to your people?"

Ishaq crossed his arms. "I told your friends that I wouldn't, and I'm a man of my word. Unlike your other friends."

Dyrfinna tried not to roll her eyes.

Skeggi leaned forward. "May I remind you that these are my friends, too, and I would trust them in any situation, whatever happens."

Ishaq, seeing this, spoke again. "Duly noted. In truth, the real reason is because many of those draugrs before the wall were my friends. They had died honorably in glorious battle, but then their dead bodies were bound up against all the directives of God in an unholy desecration. And ..." Here he cleared his throat. "And I heard what you said out there, when you gave my friends fire and eternal peace."

"What exactly did I say out there?" Dyrfinna asked. She tried to cast her mind back and remember what had happened last night. All that came to her was a confused, jumbled memory of various draugrs in the dark, blazing white fire boiling around her, and a terrifying moment when it went spinning out of control ... then Ishaq's hand on her shoulder, and coolness, peace, calming her fear.

Ishaq merely shook his head. "Let that stay between you and your gods."

Which only frustrated her more, because it wasn't her gods who had spoken, but Dyrfinna. She had every right to know what words were coming out of her own mouth!

Skeggi, who had gotten up while they were talking, came back with two bowls of stewed puffin and skuas with herbs, which he gave to Ishaq and Dyrfinna before fetching one of his own.

Dyrfinna turned to the bowl, ravenous, eating greedily. She noticed that Ishaq's eating style was much more refined than hers, which annoyed her for no reason. Then Renegade flew in from where she'd been hassling Mella and crashed into Dyrfinna's shoulder. It was only her lightning-quick warrior's reflexes that kept her from spilling her delicious stew all over the floor.

Then a new realization struck her, and she forgot her annoyance.

"Ishaq, it turns out that we have an enemy in common," Dyrfinna said between bites.

"Indeed? And who is that?"

"Nauma."

Ishaq raised an eyebrow. "I can't argue with that."

"Well, that's a first," Ostryg grumbled from across the room.

Ishaq's eyes narrowed, but he ignored the jibe. "Nauma has been a bane to our lives ever since she was allowed to join my King's ships, after we got blown off course in the storm."

Dyrfinna nodded. "Last night, I wanted to carry my magic into the enemy camp, kill the child-killers, strike Nauma down, and steal back my friend's crown," Her stomach roiled. She'd been spilling over with power, yet she'd failed to carry it to Nauma and utterly defeat her. "How can I rid that army of her?" She asked Ishaq. "As much as I hate the thought of doing anything to aid you, I feel that it would be better for both you and for me, if Nauma were gone from this world."

Ishaq smiled slightly. "You couch your request in such unappealing terms. Would it not be better if you said, 'She plagues the both of us, so how do you propose I get rid of her?'"

Dyrfinna's eyebrows went up. "If you want to put it like that, I'm fine with it. So do you want to do this?"

"No. I was speaking from your viewpoint. From your perspective. When I say I, I mean *you*."

Dyrfinna frowned. "Well, that's a confusing way of putting it."

"It's not confusing. I was speaking as you."

"Still confusing."

He sighed again. "I would greatly prefer to leave this job in your hands, since the accursed Nauma is technically on my team."

Skeggi looked concerned. "Finna, you're in no shape to be doing anything, much less going after Nauma in combat."

"This is war, and I'm the commander," Dyrfinna said. "What I feel has no relevance here. I need to keep all of you alive and utterly vanquish Nauma."

"You shouldn't be fighting at all today," Gefjun said from across the room, where she tended a patient. "Not after you were blasting fire everyplace last night. Put this work in the lap of your underlings."

"This is my work." Dyrfinna turned again to Ishaq. "If

I can stop Nauma herself, then our armies can stand against each other in an honest fight. If she has no qualms about turning our honorable dead into draugrs, then I have to wonder what other tricks she would not hesitate to pull on your dead in the future ... or on your living men."

Ishaq's face darkened. "I, too, have thought about that."

"I want to fight her myself," Dyrfinna said. "How can I persuade her to come out, alone, for single combat?"

Ishaq hesitated. "In your condition?"

"I don't care," Dyrfinna said stubbornly. "I only want to fight her. I don't plan to die in the attempt."

"Nobody ever *plans* to die unless they're going to end their lives," Ishaq said pedantically.

"Well, thank you for that nugget of information, but I already understood that."

"What are you saying, Finna? You look close to death now," Ostryg said.

Nauma had laughed when Dyrfinna had called herself Egilsdóttir. "And how does Nauma know me?" she mused. "Do you remember, on the ships, when we were introducing ourselves, she suddenly laughed and said that she knew me? As if she was delighted that I fell into her lap. That was strange. I've never seen her in my life."

But then she shook her head. Too much talk. Dyrfinna stood up and rolled her shoulders.

"What are you doing?"

"I'm going to challenge that bitch in single combat."

"Are you crazy?" Gefjun squawked from across the room, looking up from the patient she'd been working with.

"We're in dire straits," Dyrfinna said. "We're running out of food and losing too many people. If I can end this early, I'm going to do it."

Dyrfinna searched her mind for any connection to Serja, but found nothing. Her link to the dragon was gone.

It was possible that the link had only occurred because Dyrfinna had been doing magic – but she shuddered at the idea of using her magic again. She was still depleted from last night's attack.

"Renegade, stay here," she said, setting down her mostly-empty bowl. The dragonet tumbled headfirst into it and began eating up the scraps. "I'm finished with this. I'm going to fight Nauma. I'm going to go challenge her now."

Dyrfinna set off, with Gefjun half-running by her side.

"This is too risky and you're in no shape for fighting, especially with Nauma."

"Don't undercut me."

"I'll undercut you if I think you're acting foolhardy."

"Will Nauma fight you, though?" Skeggi asked. "She was nowhere to be seen during the last several days of battle."

"She was hiding," Gefjun sneered.

"I would have taken Thora's crown back if I had seen her," Ostryg growled.

Ishaq cleared his throat. "Nauma does not like affronts to her bravery. She likes making a spectacle of herself, especially if everybody can see her being cruel."

"I can challenge her in single combat. I just want to rip Thora's crown off her head. And of course, see her dead."

"That is one thing we both agree on. We want her and her rabble gone, just as much as you do. Kill Nauma in single combat. Make her an offer she cannot refuse."

Dyrfinna took a look around the great hall, now with many more suffering warriors than they'd started out with – about half their force. Their bread was low, Gefjun was overwhelmed and overworked, even despite all those who were helping her.

"I would be happy to," she said, and took a final, long drink of water.

"So ..." Ishaq ventured. "Am I still to be shut away in the tiny room where the dead men lay?"

Dyrfinna snorted. "No. By some miracle you have redeemed yourself by helping me in a difficult moment, and offering good counsel."

"I wouldn't go as far as to call that good counsel. For all you know, I could be out to simply see you slaughtered by Nauma, and I might cheer her on as she cuts you down."

"For all that, you are still as annoying as a gadfly. And I don't care a whit about what you just said. I only want to fight her. That is all."

"Fight her and *win*," Skeggi added.

"Well, yes," Dyrfinna said. "That was a given."

※ 38 ※
THE GOLDEN SNAKE

The eastern sky glowed orange. Though Dyrfinna was still exhausted, she pulled her sword and sharpened it.

Renegade came flying over, acting very interested in her work with the sword, landing on her arm that held the sword steady to investigate, peering at her work with first one eye, then the other. "Who do I need to kill?"

"I wish you were full-sized." Dyrfinna paused in her work to gently stroke her small dragon on the side of her face. Renegade's golden eyes closed, like a contented cat. "But you need to stay here. Nauma would kill you or steal you if she could. Can you do that for me? Stay here and protect your brother and sister. Keep them safe from enemies."

Renegade's wings went up as she looked over at Joy and Melle. She launched herself up to the ceiling where she perched in the rafters, pacing back and forth, glaring around as if daring enemies to come on.

"Thank you. I'm so happy I got such a strong dragon," Dyrfinna said. Renegade puffed up with pride.

"She's not hurling herself into anybody now," Ostryg said.

"She had a job to do. That's why," Dyrfinna said, realizing the reason as she spoke. She would have to remember that in the future.

Then she strode out of the great hall to meet the day and, if it were the will of the gods, to cut down her enemy.

Skeggi, Ostryg, and Gefjun followed her. "Are you insane?" Gefjun complained, keeping pace with Dyrfinna. "Do you think you're up to fighting anybody in the shape you're in?"

"Look at our forces," Dyrfinna said, sweeping her hand across what was left of their army at the wall – a depleted, diminished force. "How much longer do you think we'll be able to hold Nauma's little bastards back? Are we going to fight to the last man?"

"That's how I expected it to happen," Gefjun said. "Our Queen's forces have got to find us eventually."

"Unless they're engaged elsewhere in battle with King Varinn's army," Dyrfinna reminded her. "If that's the case, it's going to be a while until they find us."

They were close to the wall. Ahead, one of the shield-maidens was kicking at a pile of ashes that had once been a draugr that Dyrfinna had immolated in magical fire. The shieldmaiden suddenly stooped and swept away the ashes, and she picked up something that gleamed.

"Come over here. Look!" she cried, holding it up.

"What is that?" Ostryg asked at once as they gathered around.

"I saw this glimmering," the shieldmaiden said, and blew away the ash.

Immediately everybody cried out, because the glint of gold met their eyes.

But Gefjun cried out even louder, a hand on her forehead as she pointed at the golden thing. "It's Thora's ring! It's her snake ring! The one she got for her twelfth birthday!"

Gefjun was right. It was a delicate golden ring in the shape of a snake that once twined around Thora's finger.

"One of the rings that Thora was wearing on the

funeral ship," Dyrfinna said, staring in complete astonishment.

The shieldmaiden rubbed off the ashes with a shaking hand, and they all gazed in wonder and disbelief at it.

Other soldiers came running, and gazed sorrowfully at the small golden snake.

"How did the ring get here?"

"The draugr was wearing it – he was originally one of the dead child-killers on the other side of the barricades before Finna turned him into dust."

"How did Nauma's rabble get this ring?" Ostryg demanded. "I'll kill them where they stand."

The shieldmaiden gave the ring to Gefjun. "Here. This belongs to Thora. You can wear it until we return back home, and you can give it back to the Queen."

Gefjun shook her head as she accepted the ring. "I can't wear this on my fingers. There's no way that I'm covering Thora's ring with the blood of the wounded." She added Thora's ring to a chain se wore around her neck, and tucked it inside her shirt. "I'll keep it safe until we get it back to the Queen," Gefjun promised.

"What kind of enchantment would allow somebody to walk onto the deck of a blazing ship to steal Thora's gold?" Dyrfinna mused.

She remembered again how the ship blazed upon the sea, spurts of flame rising up into the sunset sky. The sail had completely burned into tatters, and the mast collapsed with a crash that could be heard on shore, sending a whirlwind of sparks high into the sky. Even from her high seat on Serja's back, as the dragons flew one last circle around the burning ship, Dyrfinna had been able to feel the intense heat from the flames.

"Search the other immolation sites," Dyrfinna said. "Every place where a draugr was burned. See if we can find any more of Thora's things."

They searched through the ashes, and found some gold coins that might have come from Thora's ship, as well as a ring with a carnelian on it that had been broken by the vicious heat of the fire.

Dyrfinna ran a finger over the broken carnelian. It had glowed in a rich, beautiful red when Thora had worn it on her finger. Now the stone was dull and blackened.

Seeing it made her think again of the dragon collars. She wanted to shove it into her pocket and think no more about it. Instead, she gave it to Ostryg, who was standing next to her. "Keep it safe for the Queen," she said. He looked surprised, but nodded.

"I don't know how they've taken Thora's things off her funeral ship," Dyrfinna said. "These gold coins, these rings, her crown ... to be honest, I don't care how they did it. I only care about one thing." She pulled her sword. "Cutting down the bitch who stole them, and putting an end to her child-killers bullshit once and for all."

A LATRINE RAT DESERVES
BETTER

"Nauma," Dyrfinna cried, striding to the logs and stones that had been hastily piled across the gap in the barricades. "Nauma, come here! I have something to say to you."

Jeering came from the enemy's camp. "Come closer so we can cut your throat," somebody called.

"Oh, yeah, I have something to say to her," somebody else said.

Dyrfinna stepped into a gap that had been hewed between the logs that barricaded the larger gap. Piles of ash lay all around where she had immolated the draugrs, and she saw yet another soft, golden gleam in one of the piles of ashes. She stooped and picked up a delicate brooch of beech leaves made of gold. This one had melted enough in the magical fires to destroy the delicate veins of the leaves.

Dyrfinna's hand convulsively closed around the beech leaves as she got back to her feet.

"I thought Nauma was a warrior," Dyrfinna cried, "But clearly I was mistaken. A coward would hide during battle. A coward never shows her face on the battlefield." An arrow came arcing down from the other side, and she brought her shield up and batted it aside. "I have been wanting to fight her for the last few days but she never has shown her face since she left the ships. Where is she?"

Jeering rose from the enemy, but Dyrfinna laughed in their faces, looking up and down the ragged ranks of the child-killers. "I thought Nauma might be a leader of account, but now it's clear that I was wrong. She is no better than the poor women who have come from some conquered village somewhere, forced into thralldom, weeping bitter tears. She's a thieving magpie who is jealous of her betters. A rat that lives in a latrine, swimming in piss. But I shouldn't say that," Dyrfinna added. "A latrine rat deserves better than to be compared to Nauma."

Now the child-killers were shouting rude things. Dyrfinna laughed again, her heart beating fast, and drew her sword. When the inevitable arrows came arcing in, she swung her sword and cut them into splinters before they could strike her.

"We can decide this now, once and for all," Dyrfinna called, sword in hand. "Come up and fight me in single combat. We can settle this battle right now!"

"Oh, shut up. I get tired of your stupid babbling." Nauma came through the ranks in full barbarian queen attire, with a gigantic caribou fur around her shoulders, braids in decorative patterns on her head, and a dangerous-looking axe in her hand. Black ash from the fire pit was smeared around her eyes and half her face, as if she started smearing it and just couldn't get enough. Thora's crown gleamed in the hateful woman's hair.

Dyrfinna rested her sword on her shoulder, completely annoyed with this sad excuse for a woman. "Where were you yesterday?" she shouted. "I would have fought you myself if you'd been in the battle in the first place. Were you scared? Were you crying in the back lines? Were you afraid to face real warriors?"

Dyrfinna knew she looked exhausted and bloody.

Nauma was fresh and looked fine with only a little spatter of blood across her kirtle, very pretty-like.

"I was busy," Nauma said. "I wouldn't have come out at all if I hadn't wanted to show you what I did."

Dyrfinna's heart veered in a different direction. Nauma was waiting eagerly for an answer, as if hoping she would be curious. Indeed, she was, but the last time she'd been surprised, dreadful things had happened. So she held her tongue.

"Oh, you ..." Nauma muttered, and turned to her troops. "Bring her out! Let this bitch see what cruelty we're capable of! We are the child-killers, after all."

"I don't know if that's something you should really brag about ... Odin's *eye*, what have you done with her?"

Because Nauma's henchmen dragged a bloody-faced woman out of their ranks.

Helga, the shieldmaiden who had vanished during battle yesterday, who had been thought dead, came staggering forward, dragged by Illugi, Nauma's henchman. With one broad hand, he shoved Helga forward so she fell to her knees and screamed in pain. She shook through her whole body, to the ends of her hair, because her eyes had been gouged out, leaving bloody pits in her head. Even worse, her arms and legs had the skin torn from them.

Nauma's forces jeered and laughed as Helga staggered to her feet, still shuddering. She was clearly in shock and pain, but now the shieldmaiden clammed shut in that determined way she had, and she didn't make a peep.

A cry of outrage rose from Dyrfinna's troops.

Gefjun's outrage was even louder. "How can they do this?"

"Are they going to do this again to our people in Skala? I think not!"

Dyrfinna, filled with disgust, wanted to shake her head, but abstained and looked back at her friends—at Skeggi, Gefjun, and Ostryg, standing next to her behind the rock fortifications.

"I've got to kill Nauma," Dyrfinna said. "She's not going to do this anymore."

"If you lose this duel, we all die," Ostryg said.

"If I don't fight this duel, we're all going to die anyway. And they'll do shit like this to all of you while you die," she said, gesturing toward Helga. "She doesn't deserve this. We've got to get her back, now."

Dyrfinna looked back at her opponent. Nauma watched her hungrily, leering, as if assessing how distressed Helga's appearance made her.

Dyrfinna couldn't help it. She felt the magic leap to life inside of her. Yet she closed her eyes and breathed until she was able to let it drain away. *No magic.* No uncontrollable fire, no exploding magic, no magic that would lash back at the warriors around her. All she really wanted to do was fight Nauma, face to face, and cut her down with her own sword.

"That's bullshit," Dyrfinna said, opening her eyes. "Are you making a point about how bloodthirsty you are?"

"You don't want this girl back, I take it," Nauma said.

Dyrfinna knew she had to tread carefully. She didn't want sweet Helga to be hurt any further, and Nauma knew it.

"I just want to be sure that you're not going to use my people, who you tortured, to weasel your way out of fighting me."

"I'm calling the conditions," Nauma said.

"Oh really? It's easy for you to torture innocent people, but a little sword fight scares you."

"If you fight me, you don't get this girl back. And we'll carve her up some more, and you can watch."

"So you *are* trying to weasel your way out," Dyrfinna said. "Look how low you are, torturing a girl just so you can take the coward's way out."

"I'll fight you." Nauma grinned, swinging her sword. "But if you lose, we get to take you as our prisoner and do whatever we like to you. "

"That doesn't sound creepy at all," said Dyrfinna, "but I don't think I'll let it get that far. If I win, the siege ends."

Nauma sneered. "Do you think you can negotiate with me? You can't."

"That's true," said the Moorish leader for King Varinn's army. "You can't negotiate with her. But you can negotiate with *me,* because you have taken one of my able commanders as your prisoner – and I am very eager to work through terms with you."

The child-killers hissed and jeered.

"You damned fools!" Dyrfinna told the child-killers. "Did you forget these Moors are your allies? Be careful how you speak to them, or we'll align with them for a brief time, simply in order to take out your wretched, bloody selves."

"You can't do that," Nauma said.

Dyrfinna, staring at her, tipped her head to the left and to the right, cracking her neck. Then Dyrfinna turned aside and bowed gracefully to the Moorish leader. "Though we are at war, you are an honorable man. Unlike *some* people I could name," she said. "As you might have seen last night, your commander has done me a great service, and also may have saved your lives last night. I propose that we exchange prisoners, giving Ishaq for Helga here."

The commander pursed his lips in surprise. "Does she rank that high?"

"No, but she is still valuable to all of us."

"You won't give Ishaq to us, free and clear?" the Moorish leader said.

"Only if you do the same for Helga. Which is what I'm proposing anyway."

"What about your commander that we've captured?"

"Oh, you go ahead and keep Sinkr. We've been doing fine without his interference."

The other man roared with laughter, then stopped abruptly. "No, we will not keep that man of yours," he said. "Upon my soul, but these are the strangest negotiations I've ever participated in."

They agreed to exchange Ishaq with the Moors, while Nauma's people would return Helga to Dyrfinna's army.

"Tell them to hurry up," Gefjun said, shaking with anger. "At least I have a little bit of willow bark left to help soothe her pain. But that flayed skin will keep her in agony for weeks."

"We will exchange our prisoners once the duel is over – *if* the conditions are met." Skeggi said when they'd finished talking.

But Dyrfinna turned away, shaking her head, feeling the exhaustion seeping into her bones despite her eagerness to face Nauma. She wiped the sweat from her brow. "Give me some strength, friends. Not so much you, Gefjun. You need your strength for your patients."

Gefjun huffed loudly and put her hand on Dyrfinna's at once. "Hands in," she told Ostryg and Skeggi, though Skeggi already had his on Dyrfinna's arm.

Several years ago, Gefjun had learned a spell from Thora that allowed her to give some of her strength to her patients, which helped to bring them back if they were failing. It was an easy spell, one that truly helped the weak. But it helped them to heal from their wounds. The spell also allowed Gefjun to pull strength from other people who were willing, if they had their hands on her.

Ragnarok came over to join the group, resembling a kindly mountain with blackened eyes. He'd had his nose broken during a particularly fierce altercation with one of the child-killers. Ragnarok lay his hand on her other arm. "Take all the strength from me that you want." Gefjun flashed him a grateful smile.

"Sing quietly." Dyrfinna unwound a bandage on her hand and tightened it. "I don't want them throwing any stray notes in on you," she added as they put their hands together. "Make it look like we are conferring."

But one of the magic-doers in Nauma's army, seeming

to realize what was happening, started singing against them. Even from this distance, over the crowd noise, Dyrfinna felt her magical intent working on them.

The shieldmaiden's song pulled the air askew. Dyrfinna kept having to catch her breath as the song magic pulled the air from her mouth.

Gefjun met Dyrfinna's eyes. "Please. You sing, too. Help me."

Dyrfinna took a deep breath and exhaled. "I can't."

"You mean you won't," Gefjun snapped.

"I won't," Dyrfinna said, so Gefjun could hold to that angry energy. "Just ... sing to me. Look in my eyes, and sing to me."

Gefjun narrowed her eyes at Dyrfinna, like a cat. But then she softened. "I wish...."

"No," Dyrfinna said. "Not now. Just sing me strength." Her last word was cut off as another errant note from Nauma's army snatched the breath out of her mouth.

Ostryg hummed a note. Skeggi joined in, making a musical bulwark against the army behind them. Ragnarok, who did not sing, gently squeezed her arm.

Gefjun quietly sang, meeting Dyrfinna's eyes the whole time. The razzing and jeering from the Viking army grew louder, and little bits of notes came in to trip up Gefjun's music.

But under the hubbub, where nobody could hear, Dyrfinna was humming with Gefjun's music, building it stronger. The whole time they gazed in each other's eyes, supporting each other.

Gefjun made it to the end of her song.

"Thank you," Dyrfinna said.

"Whoo," said Ostryg, shaking his head. "I didn't think Gefjun's song was that strong."

Gefjun opened her mouth to reply ... and promptly collapsed.

"Honey!" Ostryg cried, stooping at her side.

Dyrfinna whirled on Nauma's army. "You cretins!" she shouted. "You made her magic go wrong!"

They jeered and laughed.

Dyrfinna turned back to Gefjun as she blinked, confused, and tried to sit up. "Are you okay?"

"Yeah. I just gave you a little too much. But what ... what do you mean, the magic went wrong?" she asked. "I did everything right."

Dyrfinna knelt at her side and brushed her hair away from her forehead. "They don't need to know that. I want them to believe the spell didn't work so they think I'm weak. I love you. Thank you."

They kissed, and she hugged Skeggi. Ostryg was too busy seeing to his Gefjun.

"Wait for me," Gefjun said, trying to get up. Dyrfinna waited until Ostryg helped her to her feet, and she leaned on him. Together, the sword-friends stepped to the wall.

Nauma called her army back and had them sit down. Dyrfinna's army sat up on the rocks above to watch the fun.

Dyrfinna turned to her archers. "Archers," she said quietly. "Take your positions. If Nauma's army goes back on their word, I need you to take out as many of the leaders as you can."

"Understood," said the head archer, and they stole away to their positions.

Dyrfinna cleaned her sword and drank some water. Even with the gift of energy from her friends, her head swam and her body ached all over.

But that didn't matter. She was going to fight Nauma at last, and her heart sang with delight of battle. It was all she wanted.

She swung her shield up on her back and came down the hill. Skeggi and Ragnarok followed.

"Are you all right?"

"Oh, yes. I'm looking forward to this," she said.

❧ 40 ❧

HELGA'S BLOOD

Nauma's warriors sat on the ground as they were bidden, leaving a large ring around the place where Nauma stood, leaning on her sword and leering at Dyrfinna as she and her three guards came down the long slope.

"You pathetic bitch. Do you really think you're going to win over me?" Nauma said in a deep voice.

Dyrfinna did not reply. She was keeping an eye out for surprise attacks from Nauma's child-killers.

King Varinn's army of Moors formed over half of the large ring, and though most were watching her, the fighters who stood closest to the child-killers kept turning their eyes to them, watching suspiciously, and their hands hovered near their sword hilts, ready to draw. Though they were Dyrfinna's enemy, they were also more interested in an honorable outcome than the child-killers.

Nobody in Dyrfinna's entourage spoke. While Nauma waited impatiently, Gefjun checked Dyrfinna's battle armor and secured it. Dyrfinna ignored Nauma's glare as she retied the small strips of cloth around her palms to protect her blistered hands.

The field of battle was small, but level and covered with grass, which at least would be good for fighting.

There were a number of stones sticking out of the ground that she'd have to watch out for.

Nauma stood there with her sword on her shoulder. Her dirty blonde hair had been braided back out of her face, and Thora's golden crown, which had been nestled among those oily locks, looked tarnished – a further insult. Nauma stared at Dyrfinna with ice-blue eyes and a slight smile, as if the thought of killing her gave her much pleasure. She had drawn two lines across her cheekbones with blood, and some had run down her face. Dyrfinna doubted very much that the blood was Nauma's own.

Her magic, noting her anger, flickered into life. Dyrfinna breathed deeply and tamped it down, twisting Thora's ring on her finger. As much as she wanted to speak a few words and call up that power to destroy Nauma, there were too many people nearby that would die if she did.

Skeggi had sent a runner back to the hall for a small cup of mead, which he brought to Dyrfinna.

She poured a libation to Thor and Odin and Freyja with a practiced flourish, praying to them for strength and the ability to strike her enemy down. Then she drained the cup. Nauma merely laughed and drank hers, and flung away the cup.

Dyrfinna rolled her neck and shoulders, and stretched her weary arms and legs. *They call themselves the child-killers,* she thought. It was possible that these so-called child killers would go back on their word and attack her while she was separated from her army. She thought of her archers and prayed their aim would be true.

And of course, if Nauma's army did go back upon their word, Dyrfinna was prepared to run through as many fighters as she could.

Dyrfinna drew her sword and nodded to Skeggi. He stepped up with her extra shield, as Nauma's second.

Skeggi looked at Nauma, who sneered and pulled her

sword. She swung it in a slow circle, then tightened her hand on her shield.

Dyrfinna thought of Skuld, the Valkyrie, looking down at this scene. What would she have thought? Were her shears prepared to cut somebody's thread of life today?

Dyrfinna set her shield at the ready and held her sword in guard position, tensed like a spring.

Nauma's eyes never left Dyrfinna. "Are you scared, bitch?" she asked, her cold smile widening.

"I was in the front lines for every battle we fought against your people. I never shirked a battle, and cut down many of your people for the ravens to pick at and the wolves to feed upon. But I never saw you," Dyrfinna replied. "Where were you? Were you huddled in the back of the lines, crying? Are you afraid of a little blood?"

The hateful smile never left Nauma's face, but her hands tightened on the sword's hilt. "You'll never understand."

"You're right. I have never understood cowards." She smiled.

Skeggi stepped back and cried, "Begin!"

Dyrfinna feinted with her sword to bait Nauma into making the first move. Her adversary was not fooled that easily, though. Nauma took a step forward and Dyrfinna took one back, then waited, tense, for Nauma to strike. The moment stretched longer and longer. Dyrfinna breathed slowly, staying relaxed.

With an impatient lift of her head, Nauma stepped to the left, looking Dyrfinna over as if she were a piece of wood and Nauma was deciding what would be the best place to start hewing. Dyrfinna stepped to the right, always keeping her in front of her.

Dyrfinna lazily struck at her sword, testing Nauma. She struck back; every blow from her sword sent a stinging sensation through Dyrfinna's arms.

A lunge from Nauma, and Dyrfinna sprang back, the sword cutting close to her belly. Dyrfinna allowed her to push her back, assessing the strength of her attacks, parrying each strike. Thora's crown gleamed in her hair, but Dyrfinna ignored it ... for now.

Nauma swung her sword at Dyrfinna, leaving her side wide open. Dyrfinna blocked the blow with her shield, while her own sword sprang out and cut Nauma on her exposed arm. Then she took a quick step forward to slam her shield against Nauma's, bullying her back. Shields thudded, the metal bosses in the center ringing.

Nauma's shield had a sharp boss on it, which she tried to shove though Dyrfinna's defenses. Dyrfinna ground her teeth. Every time Nauma tried that little maneuver, Dyrfinna stabbed her sword past her shield. The chain metal that the woman wore turned aside Dyrfinna's hits, but with each attack, Nauma would pull back, furious.

"Where are you from, daughter of Egill?" Nauma asked Dyrfinna as they broke apart and prepared to attack again.

"The bitch is from Skala," one of Nauma's soldiers said. "Just like all the rest of that fucking crew."

"I knew that," Nauma snapped over her shoulder at him, annoyed. "Stick to telling me things I don't already know, Olav. Can you do that?"

Dyrfinna took advantage of her lapse to dart in. She grabbed a handful of Nauma's tangled blonde hair and yanked hard, some of her hair ripping off in her hand.

Thora's crown went flying, a gleaming golden spark.

Nauma yelped in disbelief and pain as Dyrfinna hauled her down by her hair – but she dropped her sword, pulled a knife, and stabbed it into Dyrfinna's side.

Dyrfinna instantly shoved her away, the knife still standing in her side.

But she didn't even feel the knife, because her eyes were on one thing only. As soon as she shoved Nauma away, she dashed forward and lunged at the ground ... and scooped up the golden circlet that she had ripped off Nauma's head.

"Finally!" Dyrfinna crowed, immediately turning her shield toward Nauma as she stared at her treasure. "Thank you, Freyja!"

A cheer broke from Dyrfinna's warriors as she held Thora's crown aloft.

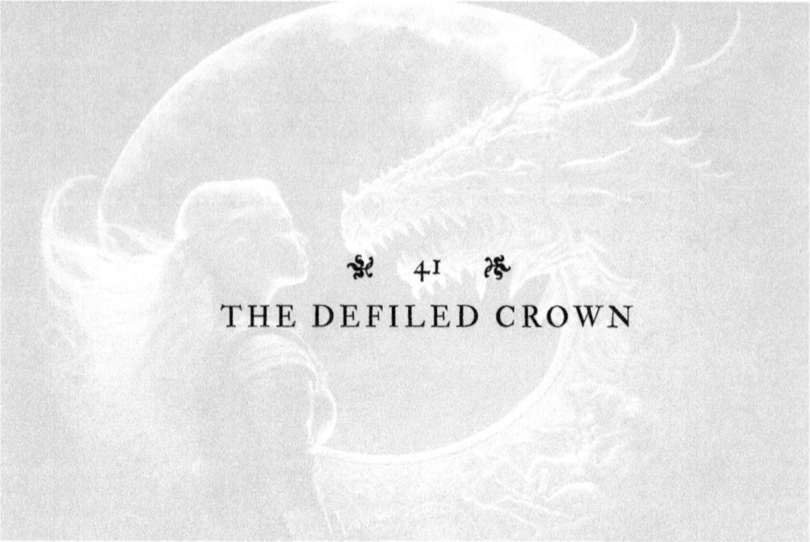

41
THE DEFILED CROWN

DYRFINNA'S EXCITEMENT AT SNAGGING THORA'S CROWN was so great that she felt as if a spark of lightning jumped into her fingers when she touched it. She gripped it tightly, her heart beating high in her chest, and even kissed it out of sheer joy.

It was Thora's crown, all right. It was even slightly bent from that time that it had fallen off Thora's head.

Several years ago, Thora had been climbing up on Serja's back to go flying, and the dragon had accidentally stepped on it.

"Your crown!" Dyrfinna had cried.

"Oh, I'm sorry," Serja said, moving their foot. "I didn't even feel it."

"Don't worry." Thora had jumped down to move the dragon's foot and pick up the crown. "No harm done."

"It's bent," Rjupa had said.

Thora shrugged. She rubbed the crown on her tunic to clean the dirt off, then plunked it back on her head, adjusting it. "Not badly. It still fits fine. I can get it fixed later."

True to form, Thora had put off that task, the way she always had with tasks that were unrelated to her work in taking care of the people of Skala.

As Nauma went staggering, Dyrfinna turned the crown from side to side in her hand. No sign that it had lost its shape on the burning funeral ship – but her thumb ran over a rough patch on the inside of the crown that should not have been there. This part seemed to have melted slightly in the fires. Her eyes widened. Several strands of somebody's hair had been melted into the gold from the intense heat.

Thora's hair.

"Odin's eye," Dyrfinna whispered. "It's really hers."

In this short space of time, while this was going on, Nauma regained her feet. Seeing the circlet in Dyrfinna's hand, Nauma reached up to her hair and felt through her greasy locks – and her eyes popped.

"You ... bitch!" Nauma shrieked, and she lunged with a scream, her sword blazing against Dyrfinna. "That fucking crown is mine! Mine!"

Desperation and fury lent power to her attack, and for a moment she burst through Dyrfinna's defenses. Dyrfinna flung up her shield against Nauma's attack and, behind its protection, transferred the crown into her left hand, which held the shield, even as Nauma hacked at its light wooden frame, shock after shock shaking her arm, splinters and the occasional chunk of wood flying off its top and sides.

"That crown never belonged to you," Dyrfinna cried. "You are never going to defile it again, I swear it!"

Then Dyrfinna yanked the knife out of her side, where she'd left it all this time. It came out with a sharp pain. At least it had been slowed by her leather armor before it had pierced her. She plunged the knife at Nauma's sword hand, but missed. Nauma thrust back, nearly skewering her.

Dyrfinna leapt aside, flung the knife at Nauma's face, and pulled her sword again with her free hand.

Nauma dodged the flying knife. "Give that crown

back!" She was coming undone, her eyes wide, spit flying from her lips. "You had no right to steal it!"

"Bullshit." Dyrfinna leapt forward, and her sword struck a divot out of Nauma's shield. "This is Thora's crown. How did you get your dirty hands on this?"

"That is not Thora's crown, it's mine!"

"You robbed the dead! On a burning ship! I don't know how you did it, but these are her things, bitch!"

Nauma sneered as their swords clashed. "You rotting whore. You think I'd dirty my fingers with the trinkets of the dead?"

"Well, yes, since you were flouncing around with the trinkets of the dead on your nasty oily head." For some reason the inadvertent rhyme she'd made only added to her annoyance with Nauma.

They clashed again, slicing at each other, then Dyrfinna broke away. Her fury about the crown was adversely affecting her fighting, and she knew it.

Though Dyrfinna's arms felt like they were on fire, she went back on the attack, swinging her sword hard at Nauma, right and left. "I don't know why I even talk to you, because everything that comes out of your mouth is a damned lie. But tell me now, how did you walk upon the deck of a burning funeral ship and steal these priceless items off a queen who far surpasses you in worth? How?"

Nauma gaped at her. "What? I never walked on a burning funeral ship. Nobody does that. Are you out of your mind or just stupid?"

"No. That was the last place I saw this crown," she said, holding up the crown, which was still behind her badly-cut shield. "This crown lay on the forehead of my friend as her burning funeral ship sailed away from us." Grief fell over Dyrfinna's heart when she said those words.

Nauma laughed. "Look at that sad face of yours, it's so funny. Do you know what? Fuck your friend. You're just saying shit."

Dyrfinna's face flamed. "Never talk like that about Thora."

"Yeah? I'll say whatever I please about that bitch. And that crown isn't hers. It's mine! It was given to me."

They clashed again, but now Nauma was even more vicious than before, to Dyrfinna's astonishment. Her sword was everywhere, and it was all Dyrfinna could do to deflect it with sword and shield.

"Given to you? How?" she scuffed out between gritted teeth. "Who gave it to you?"

Nauma stepped back. "Do you really want to know?"

Dyrfinna's sword stilled. "Yes."

"Your ass gave it to me." Nauma laughed at the disdain on Dyrfinna's face, then leapt forward in a powerful attack

Dyrfinna flung up what was left of her shield against her, but Nauma broke through her defenses, this time getting a hard hit in on her other arm and cutting through her leather armor again.

"Look at you," Nauma sneered as her rabble screamed and cheered. "Look how tired you are. You can't hold us off forever. There are too many of us, too few of you." And while Dyrfinna's sword hand was high, Nauma whirled and struck her shield with her sword with a muttered exclamation under her breath, and Dyrfinna felt the magic behind it — too late.

Dyrfinna's shield shattered. She twisted out of the path of Nauma's sword – and Thora's crown leapt out of her grip, rolling across the ground.

42

TO THE BOTTOM OF THE WORLD

Dyrfinna swore as she and Nauma dove for the crown at the same time. Their bodies collided and their skulls cracked with a sound that probably could have been heard back in Skala. Dyrfinna reeled from the pain but she swiped the circlet out of the dirt. Nauma grabbed for it an instant too late, clawing the back of her hand.

A terrible shriek. "Give it back, bitch!" Nauma drew back and slammed the metal boss of her shield against Dyrfinna's head, once, twice, three times, rattling her teeth together.

The shield boss was wet and red as Nauma raised it again, and hot blood dripped into Dyrfinna's eyes as she struggled to hold it back.

Dyrfinna pulled the sword up against her head just as the shield came down again – but this time the shield struck the point of her sword, whose hilt was braced against the ground. Nauma's shield glanced off the sword's point, the blade slicing her arm.

Nauma swore. Dyrfinna, addled from the blows, crept back. Nauma was too fast. She crawled over her like a spider, knife in hand, and stabbed it straight through Dyrfinna's arm that held the crown, pinning it into the ground.

Dyrfinna whooped in pain. Nauma grabbed the crown in her hand, but Dyrfinna refused to release it.

"I'll make you let go," she hissed, and shoved her knee into the space under Dyrfinna's rib cage, pushing all the air out of Dyrfinna's lungs. She fought to pull anything into her lungs, but Nauma merely smiled and dug her knee deeper. "Look at you, gasping like a fish. You're funny."

Nauma pulled her axe out of her belt with one swift motion. "Now let's fix your head so you will never wear a crown," she said, and swung the axe up to cut her skull in two. Her crew shouted in anguish.

Grimacing, Dyrfinna grabbed her sword with her free hand and stabbed the point into her enemy's exposed armpit.

It was a very poorly executed stab, but it threw the axe's blade off.

When Nauma swung the axe, her knee lifted slightly off Dyrfinna's diaphragm. Air rattled into her lungs. She turned her head, and the axe thudded into the dirt next to her right ear with a sharp pain like a flash of light. Ignoring the pain in her ear and in her arm where Nauma's knife still pinned it, Dyrfinna took advantage of this new-found freedom of movement to roll over her side toward her pinned arm to throw Nauma off. The knife came out of the ground, though it still pierced her arm. In the same instant, Dyrfinna rolled over and tried to clamber to her feet – but her arms crumpled, unable to support her weight. Blood dripped off her face where Nauma had banged the shield into her head, splashing on the thirsty ground.

Gefjun shouted, "Come on, Finna, what's the matter with you? Get up! Kill her!"

Dyrfinna pulled the knife out of her arm. That should have hurt more than it had, though a huge, thick numbness had taken over her wounded arm.

The crown, at least, was still in her hand. She couldn't

stow it under her armor, and she couldn't defend herself while holding it. Her brain was working so slowly.

Dyrfinna did something she never would have done if she'd had her wits around her.

She placed Thora's crown on her head, as if she were putting on a hat.

In that instant, *everything went black.*

Confused, Dyrfinna scrambled back, thinking she might have gone blind, perhaps from being struck by the shield. In that same instant, she realized that the sounds of the crowd around her had also been silenced. She couldn't have passed out, because she was still moving. Without thinking, she clambered to her feet.

Wait, how did I manage to stand? I couldn't even push myself up off the ground a moment ago. She placed a hand on her head, which had been battered by Nauma's shield. It was still wet with blood and ached ferociously, but seemed otherwise intact. And her wounded arm wasn't hurting. How?

The black faded, or her eyes adjusted, and faint figures appeared – the crowd that surrounded her and Nauma. But what she saw only confused her more. She squinted.

The crowd and Nauma ... Nobody was moving.

Faces were frozen in mid-expression, mouths open in howls or shouts, arms stilled in mid-gesture. Nauma was frozen where she was getting to her feet, entirely off balance. In that position, she should have fallen on her back – but she hung unmoving in the air, her face twisted in a snarl, her arms thrown wide. Skeggi was frozen in holding an outraged Gefjun back. Juni seemed about to burst from his grasp, her hair flying, but even her hair hung impossibly in the air, unmoving.

Dyrfinna turned in the partial darkness, trying to understand what was happening. Everybody stood frozen in mid-moment as if time had stopped.

Curious, Dyrfinna hooked a foot around Nauma's leg to yank it off the ground and make her fall, but to her surprise, Nauma was as immovable as a stone pillar. Kicking Nauma in the shins hurt, as if she'd kicked a solid wall.

What's more, every move she made felt as if she were pushing through thick, wet mud. She had barely moved her feet, but she felt as if she had strained her legs.

Now she became aware of a vibration so deep that it pervaded everything, so low that, when she noticed it, she realized that it had already been going on for a while. The earth, the air, her own body, was overcome with menace. Her skin crawled.

She placed her sword into guard position and watched the immobile people around her for any flicker of movement, looking farther out for any hint of danger. With a thrill of horror, she realized that not even the ocean was moving. Every whitecap hung poised, ready to fall, but nothing broke.

The low vibration had grown into a low groan, such as a mountain might make before it collapses on your city, crushing alive you and everybody you've ever loved.

From out of the depths groaned a voice that spoke without words, as if the stones deep in the earth were giving voice. *Who are you?* it said in a voice that vibrated her very bones.

She spun, but nobody was there.

"I'm Dyrfinna of Skala, daughter of Egill ... unfortunately," she said out of sheer force of habit.

A long silence, except for something stirring far below the earth. Then came the voice like the grit of ash. *Leave her alone,* it said, painfully loud. *Give Nauma back the crown, and go. It does not belong to you.*

Despite the otherworldliness of the voice, Dyrfinna snorted. "It doesn't belong to her, either." She tried stepping on Nauma, but the very act of raising her foot was incredibly difficult.

Stop this, the voice roared. *You cannot affect her in any way. You are outside time.*

"Outside of time?" Dyrfinna was forced to put her leg down, gasping. The only way she could completely catch her breath was to step back into the space she had occupied a moment ago. "Whoo. None of this is making any sense. How can you be outside of time?"

The voice began to say something, then stopped. *I am not going to explain of this to you,* it said at a normal volume.

Dyrfinna huffed. "I'm stuck here in this weird semi-blackness with everybody frozen around me and this disembodied voice yelling at me, so you *should* explain. And who are you, anyway? And why are you so interested in Nauma? She's a real bitch, if you haven't noticed." She turned around again, looking for the speaker, wondering if it was going to burst out of the earth. How was she going to fight this unknown enemy?

That is none of your concern. Give the crown back to Nauma or I will force you to give it up.

Though the voice was beginning to make her sick at her stomach, she couldn't help but laugh at its demand. "No. I already told you, she stole it." Dyrfinna's hands went to her bloodied head, making sure that Thora's golden circlet was still in her hair. "Wait, are you some kind of sightless spirit who is in league with the powers of darkness, sent to occupy Thora's crown to yell at everybody with a, let's face it, very loud and annoying voice?"

A hissing rose around her, and Dyrfinna instantly regretted her bold talk.

Come and see, the voice said.

The ground crumbled. Her feet were pulled out from under her, and suddenly she was tumbling backward into blackness.

Her stomach swooped as she scrabbled at the air, but there was nothing to stop her fall.

43

MALICE-STRIKER

FRANTIC, SHE PULLED OFF THE CARNELIAN RING THAT Thora had given her. "Catch me! Catch me! Don't let me fall!" she cried desperately.

Light burst out of her. In her desperation, all alone in the air, she boiled over with magic that banished the darkness.

But her voice stopped in her throat at what the light revealed.

She was falling through what seemed to the upper canopy of a forest of ash trees. If this had been an actual forest canopy, at the rate she was plummeting, she would have been through it in a flash before hitting the ground.

Instead, an endless series of ash leaves and branches went flying past her. Sometimes they thinned out as if they were about to end, but then the canopy became thick and green again, filled with that spicy scent of sun-warmed leaves. Huge branches, wide enough to build houses upon, flashed between the leaves and were gone. A few times — and she couldn't believe her eyes — through the leaves she glimpsed entire cities bustling with houses and people, and the spicy scent of wood smoke from all those chimneys hit her nostrils. These cities were much larger than any she'd ever seen, even in her travels with

Thora back in their happy days together. Other times she saw what appeared to be strange lands through the ash leaves. One place was teeming with mountains and waterfalls and strange monsters roamed the land. One place was an endless ocean where a gigantic shining ship rode upon the angry waves. But as soon as she glimpsed the worlds, they were gone.

She grabbed wildly at the ash leaves and branches as she fell. The cool surfaces of the ash leaves struck her with soft smacks, yet she slipped through them as if she were made of water.

Just then, out of nowhere. Serja's panicked voice burst into Dyrfinna's mind. *Finna! What is happening to you?*

Relief rushed through Dyrfinna. Their bond had returned once Thora's ring was off. "Serja, Serja, I don't know! I got Thora's crown back from Nauma and I put it on, and this gravelly voice yelled at me, and all of a sudden I'm falling through this endless ash tree ..."

Slow down, Finna. I'm confused. I can see that you are falling, and—

But in that instant, Dyrfinna broke through the bottom of the leafy canopy, and she shouted in terror.

She was falling through empty space.

Far away to her left stood a gigantic, endless cliff of some dark brown, grey stone that matched the color of the ash branches she'd fallen through. Here and there, huge trees, larger than any she'd ever seen, grew out of the cliff's side. Below, obscured by the mist of great distance, gleamed a wide body of what looked like brackish water. Though she was still falling fast, these immense trees and the cliff barely seemed to move.

"*Serja, what is this?*" she cried.

Serja's voice was awed. *Finna, don't you know what you're seeing?*

"No! And I'm kind of freaking out here!"

This is Yggdrasil, the World-Ash.

"That's a *tree?*" Though as soon as she spoke, she knew

it was true. She'd never imagined anything of this size and scale could have existed, in this world or any other.

Below, among the gnarled roots of the ash tree, which stretched on forever, something moved and uncoiled like an endless serpent.

Finna, you can stop falling, Serja said. *Your ring is off. Make yourself stop falling.*

"What?" But as she spoke, she understood. After all, she had so much magic coming out of her that she was lighting up an entire mystical ash tree.

She stretched her arms wide and willed herself to stop ... and to her astonishment, her plummet slowed. Now she was drifting in a controlled fall, as if she were a bit of dandelion fluff.

Awed, she looked back up into the upper branches of the world-ash. So whole worlds were held in those gigantic limbs! She looked around for the limb that Odin sacrificed himself upon, hanging there for nine days, staring down into the dark waters of Hel in order to gain secret knowledge.

The dark waters of Hel ... Dyrfinna's gaze dropped to the roots of the world tree, to where a dark ocean washed at its foot. In the water, something that looked like a gnarled root was sitting up and stretching from the tree.

Finna, no. Stop. Serja sounded terrified. *Go no closer.*

She stared hard at the root ... then realized with a cold wash of horror that this was no root.

This rough gnarled thing was covered in what looked like thorns, and it twined slowly through the roots, diving now and then into the fierce ocean, then re-emerging elsewhere. Large plates of armor covered its sinuous body, clicking like bones as it slid through the branching roots. It was either a gigantic serpent or a dragon, though she had never seen anything like it. It was much, much larger than any earthly dragon she'd ever seen. Even at this great distance, it was gigantic, otherworldly.

Then it stopped moving. Dyrfinna stared at it, not

sure which end was in the front. Then her vision resolved itself, and with a sudden shock she realized that what she thought was an odd, jutting-out part of the serpent was actually its face, bristling with a dangerous ruff of thorns and horns, staring at her with malevolent orange eyes like twin flames. There was no dragon in Midgard that would have matched it in size.

This is Nidhoggr, Serja said, *and I need you to come away from here right now.*

Nidhoggr. The ancient dragon, Malice-Striker, who flew over the fields of battle gathering corpses in its wings. The dragon that gnawed the root of the World-Ash, trying to fell the tree, trying to hasten the onset of Ragnarok.

Serja whispered, *Finna! Come with me, now!* Dyrfinna felt an odd sensation, as if a ghost dragon gingerly tried to pick her up with its mouth, like a dog picking up a stick.

Serja, what are you doing? Is that you? Dyrfinna asked silently, looking down at her waist where the

Yes! Now come with me, now! But when Serja tried to pull her out of that world, Dyrfinna didn't move.

The dragon looked at her now and said in that voice of ash and desolation, *Well met, Dyrfinna. I've been waiting for you, and I see Nauma has brought you to me.*

Dyrfinna's heart sickened and died at its words. *Waiting for … me?*

It uncoiled from the root of the tree, rising out of the foaming water and the tempest. *Oh, yes. Don't you know what you're supposed to do? You are going to be instrumental in holding Ragnarok at bay.*

For a moment she thought Nidhoggr was talking about the friendly soldier on her ship, whose real name was Thorvald. But then the meaning sank in — and she immediately pushed it away. "I'm sorry, but I think you have me confused with somebody else."

Nidhoggr unfurled a set of enormous black wings. Its mouth opened, exposing rows and rows of teeth. "You think I have you confused with someone *else*? Do you think I am that old? A doddering old fool?"

"Well, I mean, you're not exactly young," Dyrfinna said.

Serja was beside herself. *Stop! That dragon has the ability to turn all our worlds to dust and ashes!*

The ocean boiled around Nidhoggr, turning a sickening brown as the gigantic worm began to rise out of its depths. Its armor clicked upon itself, and the wings on its back expanded in unholy blackness like the end of time, preparing to blot out everything she'd ever known.

Out of the wings leapt a plague of tiny stinging insects that swarmed up toward her, converging on her and stinging her. Hot pain like electric shocks struck her from every sting, and a cloud of them surrounded her. She tried to knock them away, but she could barely move — her arms and legs felt as if she had to push them through thick, wet mud.

Finna, come to me now! Serja cried with anguish. Dyrfinna did not hesitate but mentally reached out to the dragon.

The only sound outside of the overwhelming buzz of the insects was Nidhoggr's cruel laugh as the dragon blocked Serja from Dyrfinna's mind. Her grasp closed around empty air where her friend had been.

Nidhoggr laughed as Dyrfinna writhed under the insect attack. *You short-lifers are so courageous until you actually feel our wrath,* they said. *We aren't even doing that much to hurt you, and yet here you are. It takes no effort on our part to destroy you, and yet you come in here with your shiny needles and think you can destroy us.*

Dyrfinna remembered her magic — she used it so seldom that it had completely slipped her mind — and swept heat out of herself to push the insects away.

Oh, you are not getting free of me that easily. Its voice sunk low.

The voice suddenly struck Dyrfinna with a terrible

sound that rattled through her body – a noise of utmost desolation and despair, like the voices of all the dead. Its eyes gleamed with malice.

Dyrfinna pressed her hands over her ears, but the awful sound was inside her, like the rattle of fluid in the lungs of a dying mother, or the weak cry of a child giving its last breath, or the shrieks of a warrior bleeding out on the battlefield. All these sounds were multiplied in a heartbreaking cacophony – but then came the sound of her brother Eirik's final gasping breaths.

She heard them, just as clear as if she were kneeling over him once again, crying, watching that faint smoke drift out of his gaping mouth after her magic had spun out of control and brought down the lightning. He took a short breath, his jaw slack, his blue eyes half-open. A long moment. Another gasping inhalation. And then ... nothing. No more breaths. She clutched Eirik's hands as they slowly went cold and stiff in hers.

"No, please, no, stop," she whispered.

No, please, no, stop, Nidhoggr said mockingly. *You earth-dwellers always think you are better than I am, until I hurt you in the most basic ways. But enough of this. You will come to me now.*

As if a string holding her aloft had broken, she plummeted toward Nidhoggr's gaping mouth, unable to stop.

Enjoy eternity among my teeth, the old dragon sneered, opening its jaws wider.

❧ 44 ❧

A BRUTAL DUEL

TAKE OFF THE CROWN, SHE TOLD HERSELF. *TAKE IT OFF!*

Dyrfinna reached up and tore Thora's crown off her head.

Darkness was replaced by light.

Silence was replaced by the yells and screams of her friends and enemies all around her — the sweetest sound she'd ever known.

She was back in the duel circle, back in the mundane world. But now that she was not falling through empty space, she couldn't get her feet under her. She stumbled over the rough, rocky soil and tumbled to the ground, crown in hand.

Nauma was getting to her feet but staggering backwards, off balance.

Everything was just as it was before she'd put on the crown. Praise Odin, that awful sound – that terrible memory – was gone.

But Eirik's half-open eyes stayed in her head. She had tried to close them, frantically, with a shaking hand, because she could not stand to see him looking that way. But they would not stay closed.

And the next moment, Egill had screamed and scooped up his son, and had ceased to be her father.

Her sword-friends whooped, as did the rest of her crew, shaking her out of that awful memory. "Finna's up! She's up!"

Dyrfinna swiftly handed the crown to Skeggi and took the shield he was offering her. "Stow that in your shirt," she said of the crown. "Do *not* put it on your head. And do not let anybody take this from you. Upon her bones!"

"Upon her bones," Skeggi said fiercely, hiding the crown under his armor while Dyrfinna whirled back to face the enemy.

Not quickly enough. Nauma was rushing in, axe swinging down, and she struck Dyrfinna's shoulder through her leather armor. It burned with pain as she yanked back.

Nauma's forces exploded with cheers and laughed with cruel glee.

"Did that hurt?" Nauma sneered. "Poor baby, are you going to cry to Mama?"

Dyrfinna's eyes narrowed. How was this woman the avatar, if that's what it was, for the ancient dragon? "What are you, seven?"

"Oh?" Nauma's eyes lit with malice. "No. But do you know any seven-year-olds – like a little sister, for instance?"

Dyrfinna went cold.

"You have a little sister who is close to that age," Nauma purred. "A little sister that you really, really love. A little sister named ... Aesa."

Dyrfinna landed a hit with her sword that Nauma blocked with her shield pitch back, and she slashed at Nauma's face, but she dodged back too quickly. Nauma laughed, and their swords clashed.

She had to take this bitch down. Swift as a striking snake, Dyrfinna levered her shield under Nauma's and forced it up. Into the gap her sword leapt, piercing Nauma's leg.

Nauma shrieked.

Dyrfinna yanked it free and held her bloody sword high so all could see it.

Nauma shrieked and cursed. An outraged shout went up from Nauma's army.

Dyrfinna's soldiers cheered as she brandished the sword, still circling Nauma. Dyrfinna kept her shield at the ready, her eyes never leaving her adversary's. "Who's crying like a bitch baby now?"

Nidhoggr speaking through the crown had helped her fight, some disinterested part of Dyrfinna speculated as she blocked her enemy's blows. *Maybe it gave her extra powers and strength – which, may I add, she doesn't have now.*

Dyrfinna pushed Nauma's sword out of the way with her shield and slammed her sword's point against Nauma's ribs. Her sword couldn't pierce the armor, but Dyrfinna knew from experience that this kind of hit would leave Nauma with a huge, painful bruise for weeks. She prayed that she'd broken a rib.

Nauma gasped and pulled back, her shield arm pressed close against her ribs. Her teeth showed in hatred. She leapt forward, slicing at Dyrfinna, but now, due to her pain – or the lack of crown on her head – she no longer had any power behind her strikes.

Dyrfinna stopped Nauma's sword on hers, forcing it back. She pushed her shield against Nauma's, holding it in place so she couldn't rip it away.

With Nauma immobilized, Dyrfinna leaned in, fury in her eyes. "Guess what? You are not going to hurt innocent people any more, whether they're children or adults. I don't care how many soldiers you have. We are few but we are going to utterly vanquish you."

Dyrfinna's sword ripped down the side of Nauma's sword and cut her face, a hard slice on the cheek.

"There's my kiss," Dyrfinna said, "and now you're going to die." And she leaned in and her sword struck Nauma's shield aside.

Dyrfinna no longer saw Nauma, no. Instead she saw

the wolves that tried to kill her and her sister. And the red came down over her vision as she raised her shield, thrust back Nauma's parry, and swung at her exposed neck with her sword.

Suddenly from the heavens there came a thundering roar.

Dyrfinna's killing thrust went wide, and Nauma went scrabbling out of Dyrfinna's reach.

Cheering went up from Nauma's forces.

A black dragon was flying across the sea toward them – one of King Varinn's onyx dragons, its scales gleaming with hidden fires like embers in the flames. Its outspread black wings were wide enough to cover a ship, and its tail curled behind it. She could hear the rider's cold laugh.

"Oh, really? *Now* you show up?" Dyrfinna cried, furious enough to spit fire. "That's great timing, thanks a lot."

Nauma shrilled in victory, and her troops joined her.

"That's enough of that." Dyrfinna sprang after Nauma, but she went scampering away – just as the black dragon swooped in, jaws open, claws out, directly at Dyrfinna.

All her sass vanished. Dyrfinna was faintly aware of all the troops fleeing for their lives, but she was not going to be able to outrun this dragon.

She pulled her shield and sword into a defensive stance and prepared herself, unafraid, still in the heat of battle.

Jam the shield between its teeth, she thought. *Then stab your sword into its eye. Pray to the deathless gods that it doesn't breathe fire.*

Suddenly, a red dragon popped up over the top of the mountain.

"There you are, you bastard!" the dragon jeered. With two hard wing strokes it hurtled in and plowed into the black dragon's side with a smack of scales and muscle that blew Dyrfinna back from she stood wide-eyed on the ground. The black dragon went tumbling from the blow, its rider holding on for dear life.

"You shitty excuse for a fighter!" the red dragon jeered as it rose into the air for a second attack, his rider clinging to his back. "You mewling piece of crap! I'm a hundred and fifty years old, and you still can't slow my roll, no sir!"

For a dizzying moment Dyrfinna couldn't wrap her mind around what she was seeing.

Then Serja rose up over the mountain, their garnet wings flashing in the morning sun. The dragon trumpeted until the surrounding mountains rang with their voice. The dragonrider on their back was singing.

"We've arrived!" Serja cried. "Finna, when you cast that spell, we were able to follow the trail of your magic here. Now we've found you!"

"Yes!" Dyrfinna was almost ready to dance with joy. "The Queen's dragons! We're saved!"

45

"DON'T LET THEM ESCAPE!"

OLD RED DASHED AFTER THE KING'S BLACK DRAGON AS it tried to regain its balance before it fell out of the sky. "I'll tell you, I've fought tougher dragons – in your *grandfather's* time." His roar shook the very rocks under Dyrfinna's feet.

The dragons screeched and clawed. The black dragon blasted fire at Old Red.

"Oh, piss," Old Red called, bursting through the fire. "I can shoot more fire from my asshole." He let loose with a blast of flame – from his mouth – that passed over the heads of Nauma's troops, close enough to set the hair on several heads on fire.

"To the ships! To the ships!" somebody shouted. Dyrfinna's troops began chasing the enemy down the long slope, cheering and laughing.

Overhead, King Varinn's dragon struggled to gain altitude, wings beating, spitting out a blast of fire that nearly curled Dyrfinna's hair.

Old Red met it with its own fire and gave chase, and Serja joined the pursuit with a happy cry. "Swift wind and delight of battle," their dragonrider sang, a poem that Skeggi had written and set to music. The dragons shot past overhead, the hot gusts of winds from their wings pushing her this way and that.

Cool air rushed back as the dragons flew over the ocean, continuing their pursuit over the waves.

Far out over the waters, Dyrfinna saw, barely visible in the distance, the Queen's fleet following the dragons in.

"Look!" she shouted, pointing, and her soldiers cheered.

"We're saved! We're saved!"

"I hope they have an extra barrel of mead for us."

"Oof!" Dyrfinna spun at the sound. Skeggi fell to the ground, an axe sticking out of his chest. Nauma's henchman Illugi bent over him, shoving his hand under his armor and pulling out Thora's crown, though Skeggi held on to his arm.

"Skeggi!" Dyrfinna shrieked, running to him.

Illugi pulled his knife to cut Skeggi's throat, but Skeggi, despite being downed by an axe, punched him in the jaw and sent him reeling. Illugi went running, crown in hand.

Dyrfinna ran to him. "Skeggi!" His whole soul was in his dark eyes, his curls hanging in his face and lifting in the ocean's winds. Odin's tears, if he were dying ...

"No, Finna," Skeggi coughed, pulling out the axe. "I have a metal plate there under my armor. Don't worry about me, just get the crown!"

Blazing with fury, Dyrfinna pursued Illugi into the maddened crowd, sword raised, racing after him toward the ships of the enemy. An arrow shot past her, so close that she heard the wind sing in its fletching. The sun flashed off Thora's crown, gripped in Illugi's grimy fist.

"You're not getting away," she grunted. "And I'm not letting you and your stinking army go to Skala. This ... ends ... here!"

"Finna, no!" somebody shouted from behind, and strong arms grabbed her. Their old friend Ragnarok.

"Let me go! He's got Thora's crown!" She wrenched free.

"You need to get back to safety before some rogue fighter decides to kill you. You're our commander, and we need you to stay alive."

She broke away. "Archers! Magicians! Find a way to take Nauma down. She's escaping with Thora's crown, and she is going to Skala next to kill our children. If *any* of you can hit her at this distance, I'll give you a shitload of gold. I am not joking."

Everybody who had a bow started shooting, and several people who did not have a bow ran to find one. Arrows rained down on the enemy, but Nauma waved an arm behind her as she fled, raising a magical dark-red shield behind her.

The dragons, locked in combat, rose above the ocean, wings laboring, clawing at each other and unleashing fire. Old Red was right on the black dragon's tail, chasing it down with great blasts of flame that Dyrfinna could feel even at this distance.

Serja wheeled around over the island, preparing to get another strike in on the escaping enemy ships.

"Serja!" Dyrfinna cried. "I'll give you gold if you can take out Nauma!"

I don't want gold. I want freedom, Serja said. *But I would be happy to kill Nauma for you, after seeing her connection to Nidhoggr.*

The garnet dragon's shadow rushed overhead, the sun shining scarlet through the webs of their gigantic wings. Then they were gone, and the hot winds of her passage blew over them.

But King Varinn's black dragon came blazing in to protect Nauma and Serja was forced to turn aside and fight it instead.

Dyrfinna shouted in frustration. There was Nauma and Illugi running with her henchman to the remaining ship. The crown gleamed in her hair again.

Up to this point, Dyrfinna had held back because Ragnarok was right: She needed to stay alive and be a commander to her crew. They needed her. She was honored to lead such a courageous and resourceful crew.

But now the Queen's dragons were here, and soon the Queen's ships would be here — along with Egill. That familiar shadow had fallen over her spirits. She realized she no longer had any faith that merit would win out in the Queen's army — because that faith had been taken from her, just as everything else had been.

She ran toward the enemy.

And as she did so, she removed Thora's ring.

Raw magic boiled out of her, illuminating the trees with a stark white light. Her crew shouted warnings behind her. Gefjun shouted, "Finna, no!"

Dyrfinna grimly kept going, running into the enemy, who scattered before her as she pursued Nauma. *I swore I'd get Thora's crown. And this is one thing that will **not** be taken from me.*

She ran inside a whirlwind of power that grew and grew. Out of the corner of her eye she glimpsed a mage preparing to stand against her, but a ripple of her power flung them aside.

Nauma and Illugi were still too far ahead.

Carry me there faster, she thought to the magic, remembering how it had acted as as she was falling past Yggdrasil.

She hurtled across the ground like a shooting star, and the people who were unlucky enough to be in her path went flying in all directions.

Nauma turned around in the instant before Dyrfinna crashed into her and sent her sprawling.

She was on top of Nauma in an instant, blazing brighter than ever, grappling with her with supernatural strength.

Nauma laughed. "There's nothing you can do to me. The crown is mine."

With a supernatural roar, she flung Dyrfinna aside. Dyrfinna, unable to keep her magic balanced at this sudden movement, fell on her back. Her magic responded with an uncontrolled explosion that rattled every bone in her body.

A moment later, when she groggily raised her head from the ground, she saw that some of the trees had their closest limbs blown off, and several of Nauma's people had been knocked over, bleeding from the ears. They did not rise again.

But Nauma, who had been in the center of the explosion, got to her feet, and she laughed again, unscathed.

"How?" Dyrfinna whispered.

Nauma hauled Illugi to his feet. He staggered, bleeding from one ear. She shoved him ahead of her, and began to walk away, looking over her shoulder to laugh at Dyrfinna.

She reeled, feeling as if the ground pitched and rolled under her feet. The powerful magic that had not been spent in the explosion had drained completely into the ground, leaving her with nothing.

Dyrfinna used her last scrap of strength to crawl after Nauma. "I have to get that crown," she whispered. "Odin, Freyja, help me now."

But Nauma was running farther and farther away, and she was nearly to the ships.

Out of nowhere, a green spark shot past her. At first she thought it was her imagination.

But then she whispered, "No!" and reached helplessly after it.

It was Renegade, her precious dragonet, and she shot straight toward Nauma's head. A million imaginings struck her ... all of them ending in the brash dragonet's demise.

Dyrfinna held her breath.

Renegade held her wings in a glide, sliding down the back of the wind, and lifted her tail slightly so it wouldn't drag. One paw hung low, the small black claws relaxed, like a cat poised to snag a fish out of a pond.

The dragonet skimmed right over Nauma's head, and with the dangling paw snatched the golden circlet out of her oily blonde hair.

Then Renegade banked hard to the left and into the branches of a spruce tree. She flattened herself on top of a wide limb above Nauma, the crown tucked under her body, hidden by the dangling evergreen branches. And her scales turned brown to match the bark of the tree.

Her mouth opened. She'd never seen a dragon do that before.

Nauma, who had been running, paused and looked around. She glanced up as if she'd felt something.

"Piss off, bitch!" Dyrfinna screamed to throw her out of her train of thought.

Nauma shot a snarky smile back at Dyrfinna's outraged face and laughed. She shoved Illugi ahead of her and kept running.

Dyrfinna continued playacting, telling Nauma what she could do to herself ... but the whole time, though she never looked at the spruce tree, she was acutely aware of her little dragon holding utterly still on top of that branch.

If Nauma knew that two of the things I treasure most — no, three — were on that branch ...

Renegade stayed put, watching the woman carefully, until she had climbed aboard her ship. Then the dragonet put the crown in her mouth and shot back to Dyrfinna, flying swiftly as an arrow through the thick branches of the spruces for cover.

She caught the dragonet in her arms and hugged her. "You did it! You saved her crown! And you did it in such a strategic way where she didn't even see you! My amazing friend!"

Renegade deposited the crown in her hand.

"I know she was your friend," the dragonet said

formally, curling her tail around her arm. "And you gave me a gift, your most precious possession, the arm band she gave you. But now I give you her crown. This is my gift to you."

Dyrfinna couldn't help her tears as she rested her head against the dragonet's. "Ah, my friend."

"Also she was doing bad things with it, and we can't allow that," the dragonet added in a very serious tone, and Dyrfinna laughed.

"Your dragonet is very wise," said a man's voice.

Dyrfinna sat up, completely on the alert.

Out of the chaos of retreating soldiers walked Mundir, the Moorish leader. Head high, calm and self-possessed, he gently led the sightless Helga, from whose ruined eyes tears still ran, through the chaos and over the rough ground.

"I think this means you won the duel," Mundir said, guiding her to Dyrfinna. "Here is our prisoner, as promised."

46

COURAGE SHOULD
ALWAYS BE REWARDED

DYRFINNA SNAPPED TO ATTENTION AS RENEGADE LEAPT to her shoulder. "The prisoner exchange," she said. "Gefjun, come here, Helga needs help."

"I'm already here." Gefjun ran to Helga and gently embraced her, both women weeping. Gefjun took her aside and began to look over her terrible wounds, making scandalized sounds of protest as she glanced now and then at Mundir, who pretended not to notice.

"Could somebody bring the prisoner down?" Dyrfinna called.

"Already on it." Ostryg was walking down the slope with Ishaq slightly in front of him. The prisoner had been freed of his bonds, and he once again carried his sword and gigantic shield with the roses painted on it.

Skeggi clasped hands with Ishaq. "Though we are enemies, I still found it a pleasure to talk to you. Perhaps someday we can sit and talk again about poetry and history."

A broad smile broke across Ishaq's face. "Perhaps there is hope for your people after all, if there are souls such as yourself among them."

Dyrfinna rose unsteadily to her feet. "Is he always this

free with the backhanded compliments?" she asked Mundir in an undertone.

Mundir remained impassive – though his mouth quirked with mirth.

Now Ishaq and Dyrfinna gazed flatly at each other. "Are you always this free with the offhand remarks?"

"Only when I have reason to make them."

Skeggi singsonged under his breath, "It's not the ti-ime, Finna."

Mundir lay a hand on Ishaq's shoulder, and Ishaq started slightly. "I must explain," the older Moor said. "We have a code of conduct in our King's court that our people have brought from Córdoba. One of courtly speech and noble acts that all of us are expected to follow," he added.

Ishaq wore a long-suffering look. "We should depart." He gazed at the ships, where their people were frantically waving at them to come on.

"Gladly," Mundir said. "One more thing. We are no longer affiliated with Nauma's group. We will have nothing to do with such a dishonorable and cruel people."

With that, he bowed and left with Ishaq as the first of Varinn's ships sailed away.

Dyrfinna took her helmet off and knelt, sending a prayer of gratitude to Freyja – and Skuld – for the lives of the crew she'd been gifted. She stood, rubbed her eyes with the back of her bloody hand, then looked for the next thing she had to do.

Serja and Old Red landed behind Dyrfinna, roaring at the departing ships. Little Renegade roared with them from where she sat on the nearby stone.

"Who is this little one?" Serja cried, sniffing Renegade, who went up on her hind legs and stretched out her wings threateningly.

"Why, don't you have eyes?" Old Red cried. "This is a young-un! Looks like one of Patiliel's offspring from down the coast. Got the same snout, see?"

Renegade dropped to all four feet, now curious. "You know my mama?"

"Oh, yes. She's a fierce one! I'm surprised she let Finna here have you, to be honest. I was sure she would have burned her to a crisp if she set foot on her island."

Dyrfinna's face burned. The emberdragon had certainly tried to kill her for taking the eggs. Renegade swiveled, catching her guilty look.

"Are you the only one?" Old Red asked.

Renegade perked up. "No! I have sisters!" She whistled, and her sisters came flying, much to Serja's delight. Both dragons cried out in joy to see the three of the dragonets.

"Oh! Look at you!" Serja cried, and flopped to the ground to play with the dragonets.

Just then, Dyrfinna's crew called, "There she is!"

Skeggi called to her crew, "Soldiers! Vikings! Warriors! We've managed to survive, and now we've won the battle – all thanks to Dyrfinna." He raised her arm as if she were a boxer that had won a match, and her fighters cheered.

Dyrfinna laughed in surprise. "You don't need to do that. This victory was due to your good counsel, my friend, and to all of you – all of your demanding work and sacrifice."

Then she saw something that took her breath away. "Everybody, look!"

More dragons were flying in – their old friends from the Queen's keep. Serja trumpeted to greet them.

And among them was a silver dragon that came gliding in, singing sweetly.

"Shriken!" Skeggi leaped into the air and waved. "Rjupa! Over here!"

The silver dragon's rider laughed as Shriken glided over the rock wall, wings trembling against the force of the wind, long tail curving behind her. She hung in the air for a moment, then landed neatly in front of the mead hall, folding her wings.

Rjupa slid off the dragon, and Skeggi grabbed her in her arms and spun her around.

"Skeggi!" the dragonrider said, "Put me down, you big galoot!" He did, and then they shared such a long kiss that everybody started hooting.

Shriken, who was watching with an inscrutable look, unfolded a wing to bump the two lovebirds off their feet. They stumbled, and everybody laughed. Skeggi had tears all over his face, and Rjupa wiped them off with her thumb. "Now, now, honeybee, I'm back," and they kissed again.

Ostryg bumped Dyrfinna. "Stop. You look like a starving dog watching somebody else eat."

Dyrfinna was about to snap at him when Gefjun grasped her shoulders.

"Don't pester Finna," she told him. "She has every right to have these complicated and conflicting feelings. Now come on, let's see Rjupa. I've missed her so." Gefjun grabbed Dyrfinna's hand as Ostryg went ahead. "See, we're all together now, the Corae Guard. And we're in it to the end."

"On her bones," Dyrfinna swore.

"On her bones," Gefjun replied.

Well, there was that – their friendship, their bond, which wrapped around all five of them from their time in Thora's service. And it always would.

"There you are!" Rjupa cried with her radiant smile, throwing her arms around Ostryg and Gefjun and Dyrfinna.

Rjupa took a wide-eyed joy from the world and her friends, and had an honest, generous heart. "Oh, Finna, it's so good to see you again." She gave Dyrfinna an extra squeeze. "Look at you! You have been through the wars!"

"I have indeed," she said. "I'm sorry you missed all the fun."

"Some of those ships I recognized as King Varinn's,"

Rjupa continued, "but I saw some ships leaving that weren't Varinn's. Was that your esteemed enemy?"

"Yes. They threw their fortunes in with King Varinn's army – called themselves the Child-Killers." Seeing Rjupa's surprise, she added, "They're led by a truly awful piece of humanity – actually, I can't call her human – someone called Nauma."

At the name, Rjupa went white. "You faced her?"

"Yes." Dyrfinna was surprised by her reaction. "You know Nauma?"

Rjupa had to stop speaking. Shriken, her silver dragon, nuzzled up against her side like a cat, and Rjupa put an arm around her.

The silver dragon's voice was low as she replied. "We have seen her handiwork, Rjupa and I. It was a village of innocent people. One of her soldiers had been left alive, but dying, and told us. Nauma and her child-killers had murdered everybody in that village. Babies, chicklets were lying dead in the streets. People of all ages had been slaughtered."

Gefjun put her hand over her mouth, then put her arm around Helga.

"This terrible woman," Dyrfinna breathed, "may be the source of all our agonies and woes if she keeps walking on this earth. She's gotten away, but if we move fast, maybe we can catch her."

"Yes!" cried Rjupa and Shriken at the same time.

But just then, a great shout came from the troops.

"The fleet is here! They've arrived! We're saved!"

The ocean was filled with ships. Queen Saehildr's fleet had arrived at last.

Seeing the carved wooden dragons on the helms of those ships, those familiar ships from home, made Dyrfinna's heart bound.

A great cheer rose up from her forces at the top of the mountain. Dyrfinna nearly cried, listening to that glorious sound.

The queen's fighters climbed over the sides of the ships, swords in hands, grabbing their shields. They gathered around the bows of their ships, cheering and shouting and blowing horns to their comrades at the top of the mountain.

"Hop aboard," Rjupa said to Dyrfinna, jumping on Shriken's back. "We'll coast down the mountain to the troops. Technically, it's not flying, right?"

Dyrfinna laughed and climbed up, holding onto Rjupa. Her silver dragon leapt into the fierce winds blowing in off the ocean, gliding down to the bottom where the ships were. It felt so right to be airborne again, even for that short moment.

Shriken landed at the bottom of the slope, and Dyrfinna slid off her back. "We welcome you here," she called. "We give thanks to the Allfather today that you have arrived. But we must have healers, medics, anybody who can help our wounded. We have one woman doing all the work on her own. She needs help. Bring supplies for the wounded, as well."

Dyrfinna was filled with relief ... and dread. She had more than proven herself in battle.

Courage should always be rewarded, her father had always said.

Now, she had to wonder.

Skeggi was squinting at the bottom of the slope, where King Varinn's ships had been only a short while before. "Why! There's somebody already down there."

"There is?" But now Dyrfinna noticed him, strutting along the pebbly shore toward the Queen's ships as if he were the owner of the island going to greet his petty followers.

She clapped her hand to her head. "No! Are you serious?"

For whom should it be, looking as fresh and pretty as a daisy blooming in a pile of shit, but Sinkr.

47

A BLOOD-STAINED ARM, A
CLEAN ARM

AND NOW SINKR CAME SWANNING IN. "I'M IN CHARGE now," he said, looking around as if he owned the place.

"Why, Sinkr!" Dyrfinna cried. "I guess the enemy finally got tired of you and let you go. Did you have fun while you were in captivity? You look fresh as a daisy."

Sinkr had gotten about half a million fancy braids put into his beard. That kind of braid-work took hours upon hours. Nice to know that he'd had a little leisure time while he'd been cooling his heels in captivity.

"Nauma has escaped," she said. "Now that the field is secure, I need a group of strong fighters to pursue her before she gets entirely away."

Sinkr looked down his nose at her. "You let Nauma get away? Why?"

All voices went utterly silent.

Skeggi pushed his way to the front of the crowd. "Because I told her to," he said. "Finna had just fought Nauma in single combat and was about to drive home the killing stroke when the red and black dragons joined in battle. She wanted to pursue the enemy, but I forced her to run to safety."

"I need a force," Dyrfinna said, "and we need to hurry before she gets away."

Sinkr waved her away like a gnat, wrinkling his lip. "Your request is denied," he snapped. "You've done enough damage to the queen's fleet and to her mission. You fled the enemy from the fight on the sea, and then you fled them again when you could have ended this whole conflict at one stroke. You've killed thirty-five of your own fighters because you didn't have enough sense to stay on the water the way you were supposed to."

"Where did you get those numbers?" she said through clenched teeth, feeling as if lava were coming out of her ears. "You've been cooling your heels in the enemy's camp during our whole battle. At last count, we have nineteen fighters dead, which is not bad against four hundred fighters."

"Four hundred?" somebody in the crowd said.

"That's an estimate," Dyrfinna replied. "Sinkr should have a better estimate, since he spent the last four days with them in their camp, eating their food and enjoying their hospitality."

He cut her off with a wave of his hand. "Enough. Your conduct is unfitting for a good soldier. You're still getting those twenty lashes you earned through your insubordination at the beginning of the battle. I don't care what you've done since then."

Dyrfinna, her heart pounding, shook her head. "I object! My people have fought gallantly and with distinction against an enemy three times our size."

Sinkr thrust a finger into her face. "You're in way over your head, little missy."

Though she would not have let that ridiculous taunt stand, this time she ignored it, staring at his arm. "Huh. Wait," she said, taking his hand. "Look at this."

Confused by her sudden soft words, Sinkr stopped and let her take his hand.

She stretched his arm in front of him, then held hers up next to it.

His arm was pale and clean. Next to his arm, her hand

was sticky and red with blood and broken blisters; her arm was black with dried blood, dirt, cuts, and huge, colorful bruises from sword hits. She also had an ugly slash that she didn't remember getting, now black and crusted.

Sinkr's face darkened with anger. But she didn't release him. Not yet. *Let everybody take a look.*

"My fighters have been doing some intense fighting over the last several days with precious little food, water, or rest," she said in a quiet voice that carried. "We have scores of dead to bury, and prisoners to process. You might not realize this, since you've been a prisoner of the enemy for the last four or five days, but we need a good meal and some rest. If you could tell the Queen's forces to pitch in with this work, you would be doing *my* fighters a great service."

Only now did she release his arm. He yanked it back. "You are not the commander. I am," he spat.

"Yeah, you were the commander until King Varinn's men grabbed you at the beginning of the sea battle and hauled you into their ship as their prisoner."

Sinkr flushed. "You burned my ship!"

"It was my ship, Sinkr, not yours." Her voice was hard. "And we had to burn it so the enemy wouldn't take our supplies and goods. It's a fact of war. How many battles have you fought in, anyway?"

"Never talk to me in that tone of voice," he snarled, shaking a finger under her nose. "This is why women should never command! You always overreact!" he said, overreacting. "You always get too emotional!" he added emotionally.

Dyrfinna projected her voice so that the hushed troops around them could hear. "We fought draugrs, Sinkr, without your help, and we immolated them in fire without any assistance from you. I fought the commander of the child-killers in single combat, without your help. I commanded some mighty warriors while you, Sinkr, were lying back at your leisure in the enemy's camp, getting your beard braided. I only ask that you treat these fighters with the honor they have earned. Give us food and provisions. Help us bury our dead."

Sinkr looked at the tiny, intricate braids in his blonde beard, rolling them between his fingers. Then he glared at Dyrfinna with raw hate in his eyes. "I told you when this battle began, that you earned twenty lashes for your insolent behavior. Nothing has changed. Once we are settled in here, I will see to it that you will be chastened. Your punishment *will* be carried out."

✖ 48 ✖
WHIPPING POST

THE NEXT MORNING, DYRFINNA WOKE UP TO FIND that, sometime during the night, somebody had tied her hands together, and they'd relieved her of sword and shield. They must have knocked her out with magic, for she was a light sleeper and she should have wakened as soon as somebody had touched her.

Just then she heard the loud *crack* of a whip being plied.

Dear Allfather, no, she thought.

The bottom of the slope, where the enemy ships had congregated, was now lined with the Queen's ships. Near them, where the enemy had been, stood Sinkr next to a great pine tree, brushing up on his whip-cracking skills.

"Watch this," Sinkr said gleefully to his friends. He cracked the whip and an explosion of chips and splinters sprayed from the side of the pine tree. "You see that? You see? Oh, I'm going to put that insolent bitch through so much pain today." A louder crack, and splinters flew from the pine tree's side. He and his friends laughed so hard that they choked.

She wanted to vomit. If the whip was turning the tree's bark into splinters, imagine what it would do to her back.

Her sword friends joined her at the fire, quiet and angry.

"I don't want to eat," Dyrfinna said, too sick to even look at the delicious breakfast.

"Don't worry. I'm not cooking for anybody while they're doing this to you," Gefjun snapped. "Those bastards can get their own breakfast."

"Do you want me to fly you out of here?" Rjupa asked in a scared little voice.

Dyrfinna immediately looked up. "Yes."

Rjupa hesitated again. "I mean ... I want to. I'd be in so much trouble. And I'm afraid that they'd punish you more once they found you."

"And the dragons would tell on her," Skeggi said. "As soon as they knew you were gone, they'd ask the dragons where they took you, and they don't lie."

But those points were moot, because here came one of the commanders now, who Dyrfinna knew as Helga's father.

"Dyrfinna," he said. "It's time. Come with me now."

A scrim of horror fell over everything.

"This is wrong," Dyrfinna said as he dragged her to her feet. "Should I have let all my people die?"

"I'm sorry, Finna, but these are the rules."

"These rules are wrong," Skeggi said.

"This is the way it's always been done, and it's his word against yours."

"What about my word?" she snapped. "Why does his word matter more than mine?"

"I'm sorry, but if you were a commander, it would be different."

"I *am* a commander." Dyrfinna could hardly see straight. "I have my own ship. I chose my own men."

"Somebody higher than me deemed you unworthy of command."

"You mean my father," Dyrfinna said coldly. "And he

made that choice to retaliate against me, because I had accidentally killed my own brother."

"There's no help for that, I'm afraid. Come along."

Her knees were water and she could barely stand. She would be tied to this post and forced to undo her tunic and bare her back to Sinkr's whip – and he was just standing there smiling as he watched her walking toward him, enjoying every moment of her agony.

But then her friends came running, surrounding her, walking at her side after watching her whole conversation with the commander.

"You can't do this," Gefjun choked.

"I'm sorry, but this is a matter of military discipline. Come, Dyrfinna."

Dyrfinna pulled herself together. She would go to her humiliation like one of the old heroes of legend. She would show no dismay. So she stepped out with her head high, thinking of Skuld in her bare feet and midnight-blue cloak, the gigantic black wings of the Valkyries opening behind her. She walked with the easy confidence of a goddess, unperturbed by the shocks and arrows of the mortal world.

A whipping post had been made using a large pine tree near the ships. A large crowd already gathered, watching her wide-eyed as she was led toward them.

Most of the Queen's crew were clean and wearing fine linens and furs and gold. But her crew still wore the stinking, bloodstained clothes they'd worn over the long days of the siege. Their tunics had been torn by swords. Their gauntlets and boots were red with blood, their backs and sides dirty from having slept on the ground or fallen during the battle.

She thought of how she'd put her battle-bloodied arm next to Sinkr's arm, and laughed.

Her crew stood together, arms crossed, wearing the proof of their hard fighting, showing the rest of the Vikings how much they'd gone through.

And as Dyrfinna passed, there came a shout. Her crew drew their swords and axes, and then with a great, many-voiced shout, held them high to Dyrfinna – their weapons battle-dented, scarred, even broken.

"We do this to honor you," a deep-voiced Viking called from the midst of the crowd. "Dyrfinna, wolf-snuffer, cleaver of skulls, dueler of the wicked. You drowned the draugr army in fire, you brought back our blinded shield-maiden. For this, we honor you and ask Odin to look upon you in approval."

Her crew cheered, shaking their weapons, while the new arrivals murmured in astonishment.

Dyrfinna stopped, her heart overflowing. Their eyes met hers, fierce and battle-hardened.

"I'm proud of all of you," she said. "You fought with gallantry and courage against incredible odds."

Sinkr rounded on them. "That's enough," he snapped at her fighters. "Not another word out of you."

Absolute silence fell – and then somebody hissed him.

"They shouldn't be doing this to you," somebody muttered as Dyrfinna was prodded past.

A roar of assent from her crew.

"We'll always remember how they treated you," somebody else cried.

"*You're* our commander – not that dog Sinkr."

A louder roar of assent from them, which stopped as soon as Sinkr looked at them.

"Who said that?" he asked.

Dyrfinna's survivors glared at him, but none of them said a word – though somebody in the back of the crowd laughed under his breath.

Sinkr's face reddened as he shoved her forward. "That's enough of that," he said. "Trying to make us feel sorry for you? It's not going to work. We know how you really are."

"No, we know how *you* are," muttered one of her

shieldmaidens, but when Sinkr quickly turned back, her whole crew were looking innocent.

Her crew was watching – her crew, of whom she was so proud. Dyrfinna would show no fear or pain, whatever Sinkr did to her, however undeserved it was.

But as she was led to the post, to her shock, Skeggi ran in front of her and flung his arms around the tree.

"Here! You let go of that whipping post at once," the commander said.

Skeggi's face blotched, but he said, "If you're going to whip anybody, it should be me. I allowed Nauma to escape. I should have gone with Dyrfinna to finish the job."

Their eyes met, both of them looking half-crazed with dread, but Dyrfinna had never loved him more than at that moment, as he stood there with his arms around the tree, his beard mashed against the bark, his proud brown eyes staring at her.

"You don't have to do this," she said, her heart about to burst for his sake. She was willing to sacrifice herself for him. "Go. I'll be fine."

Sinkr sputtered. "Now, Skeggi, that's enough out of you. Let go of that tree so we can get this troublesome episode out of the way and set sail."

"No, thank you." Skeggi tightened his arms around the tree. "If you're going to punish her, then I should be punished as well."

And now Rjupa came to join them. "Put that whip down, Sinkr. You're not proving how strong you are. Quite the opposite." She put her arm around Dyrfinna.

"You're amazing," Dyrfinna said, leaning on her.

Sinkr shrugged. "Well then, we'll be happy to accommodate you. Get in line behind Dyrfinna. Unless you'd rather go first."

But at that moment, Gefjun joined Skeggi with her arms around the tree. "Piss off. I want to go first." Her voice was louder than usual.

"Unhand that tree at once," the commander said.

Gefjun shook her head. "You should whip me. I tried to stay the dying of nineteen of our warriors, and I could not save them." Tears stood in her eyes. "I failed this army, and now I need to pay the punishment."

"Oh, Juni. Don't," Dyrfinna said. She went to the tree and put her arms around her as well.

"I'm doing it," Gefjun said, meeting her eyes with a steely gaze despite her tears. "I don't want to be standing here *at all*. But do you know what I hate more? The thought that you're being forced to do this."

"Get those three away from the post!"

"Now, you're not at fault here," somebody told Gefjun, who made a rude noise in reply.

Impatiently, Sinkr ran the whip through his fingers. "This stupid talk is stupid. If these idiots want to be whipped, let them be whipped. I don't care who it is."

Just then, Ostryg came up and embraced the tree right next to Gefjun, standing between her and the whip. He cast a seductive look over his shoulder at Sinkr. "Oh, big boy," he said in a seductive purr. "I want to be whipped."

Sinkr's face went from satisfaction to horror in an eyeblink.

Ostryg opened his mouth and gave Sinkr the biggest wink. "Come on, honey, whip my ass right now," he said in a mincing voice, and with one practiced move he shucked down his pants and kicked them aside. True to form, he wore nothing underneath.

The rest of the Vikings roared.

"Don't let him whip that!" Gefjun shouted, alarmed. "Do you want to have children someday, or not?"

Ostryg turned around and wriggled his butt at Sinkr, dancing in a fake-seductive way.

"Can I have some of that?" Dyrfinna jokingly asked Gefjun.

"NO YOU CANNOT."

Just then, the rest of Dyrfinna's crew came running up in a large group to surround her in their battle garb.

"You're going to have to whip us to get to Finna," one of the shieldmaidens taunted.

"She's our commander, not you."

Several of Dyrfinna's Vikings began to strip and dance around with Ostryg, a scene that would have struck terror into any sane person.

One of the Queen's commanders said, "Sinkr, get your troops under control. That's an order!"

Alarm leapt into Sinkr's face. He cracked his whip over the heads of Dyrfinna's troops. "You people, get away from that tree. Now! That's an order!"

"Why don't you get me yourself? You know you want this." Ostryg put his hands behind his head, busily thrusting in every direction.

"That's enough," Sinkr cried, and raised the whip. "I'm going to start with your ass, since it's already exposed."

Dyrfinna's troops started chanting, "Whip us, whip us, we don't care."

"Sinkr," cried one of the commanders, "Get these troops under control!"

Dyrfinna came out of the crowd, meeting that commander's eye. Then she turned to her troops. "Hellions! Attention!"

They immediately stood tall with a single "HA!" and were silent, their eyes fierce and fixed on Dyrfinna.

She turned to Sinkr.

"Respect ... must ... be ... earned."

Sinkr snorted. "All you've done is lost my respect even more. You and your stinking troops."

And it was then that the three young dragonets came flying in, circling over the crowd and screeching at everybody.

"Renegade! No!" Dyrfinna cried.

Her dragonet heard her voice over the chaos and flew to her.

"I wanted you to stay at the mead hall," she whispered to her dragonet, who merely crept under her hair and hissed at everybody.

"They're not going to hurt you," the dragonet said. "I won't let them."

She saw the change flash over Sinkr's face — could see the naked want in his eyes when it sank in that the dragonet belonged to her.

The rest of the commanders and their people went dead silent at seeing the baby dragonets. Joy landed on Ostryg's chest, as usual, while Missa went circling around and around Skeggi.

Everybody started shouting in excitement. "Are those baby dragons?? Are those yours??"

"Put away the whip!" several of the commanders said to Sinkr, but his eyes were full on Dyrfinna's little dragon. His eyes a threat to her.

Anything I have, they can take away. Even now.

Just then a new voice broke in.

"Enough. That's quite enough." Rjupa came out of the crowd, leading the blinded shieldmaiden, Helga. "Commanders, I need you to listen to us now."

49

THE BLINDED
SHIELDMAIDEN

RJUPA CAME TO THE PINE TREE, GUIDING THE SIGHTLESS Helga, her destroyed eyes looking even more bloody in the morning light. The baby dragonets settled down and the crowd went suddenly silent.

"I protest," Rjupa continued, looking at the crowd. "Dyrfinna should not undergo this punishment, especially at your hands." She skewered Sinkr with her eyes.

"You shouldn't be up here at all, dragonrider," Sinkr sneered.

Rjupa merely stared at Sinkr for a long moment, then continued. "Helga wanted to speak to the commanders, and she has a perfect right to address them."

"What, her? A girl who was stupid enough to be blinded by the enemy?" Sinkr sneered.

Everyone went deadly silent.

"Which way are the commanders?" Helga asked in a quiet voice, turning her face with its sightless eyes to the left and right.

Rjupa showed her where to face the people. "Commanders, with your permission, this young shieldmaiden would like to have a word with you."

The others went silent as Helga turned her bloody eyes toward them.

Her face had been cleaned, her eyelids were sunken and closed, and blood still crusted them, and tears kept sliding down her cheeks from her eyes. The parts of her face and arms where her skin had been painfully peeled off were now black. The sight was distressing. Dyrfinna felt a flash of pain in sympathy.

"Rjupa is right," Helga said, turning toward the crowds of people. "Dyrfinna did her utmost to save us when we were surrounded by the enemy, both on the water and on land. She made tough decisions to keep us safe, and she was willing to risk her own life to do so. Please, don't punish her after everything that she did for us."

"Helga, my daughter!" One of the commanders came forward in the crowd, his eyes stricken. He commanded six ships that he'd raised from among the farmers that lived outside of Skala, a hard-bitten crew.

He came swiftly through the crowd and seized the blind shieldmaiden's hands, startling her. "Helga, it's me, your papa. Oh, my sweet girl, what did they do to you?"

"They tortured me, Papa," she said, raising a hand toward her bloody, blinded eyes without touching them. "Nauma and her child-killers did this to me and laughed at my pain. But Finna got so angry about this that she came out yelling at Nauma and challenged her to a duel, one on one. Finna said that if she won, they had to give me back. That's how she rescued me. Otherwise they would have killed me. I swear it on the gods, papa. That's why I'm pleading with you to show her some mercy."

Stricken, he swayed, and he clutched Helga's hands, gently stroking her cheek. Tears were in his voice as he spoke. "Put down that whip immediately, Sinkr. Dyrfinna has brought my daughter back to me, alive. My brave daughter, my strong fighter."

"Sir, what are you saying?" Sinkr asked, astonished.

"I'm commanding you to let Dyrfinna go."

"But ... the punishment!" Sinkr was shaking with fury.

"What about military discipline? You've got to keep the troops in order."

Helga's father straightened up, gazing at the people who were all clustered around Dyrfinna on the pine tree's trunk. "If I allow this punishment to go forward, I'll have a wholesale mutiny on my hands."

"But ... I commanded it. I refuse to remand my command."

Helga's father just sighed and turned away from Sinkr. "You chose this crew?" he asked Dyrfinna.

Dyrfinna just shrugged. "To be honest, they've worked out pretty well. I couldn't have found a better crew."

"We're with her until the end," Helga said. The other crew members who had gathered around Dyrfinna grunted in agreement and patted her on the shoulder.

"That will be satisfactory," Helga's father said. The other commanders approved, bowing to him and going on their way. Sinkr merely scowled, spat on the ground, and stormed away.

Helga's father smiled slightly under his beard. "Thank you for your work, Dyrfinna," he told her quietly. "Thank you for sparing my daughter and rescuing the rest of your soldiers."

50

THE CORAE GUARD

LATER, AS THE REST OF THE COMMANDERS ARGUED OVER who would take Dyrfinna's crew – since they were shipless – Dyrfinna went to pay tribute to the burned ruins of her ship, and to Hakr and her other two soldiers whose ashes rested within it.

The blackened, charred ribs of Saebrandur jutted from a heap of ashes on the bank of the river. She rested her hand on one of the ribs and patted it, as if to comfort it. Her little dragonet flew up around the ship, looping wildly around the exposed ribs, returning to Dyrfinna every time.

Dyrfinna thought back to when she'd left Skala, having been freshly snubbed by her father and her command taken away, and how it had hurt her deeply. But she'd still managed to keep her people alive. What would Hakr have thought of her work? Did she do this right? Was he watching her with approval from Valhalla?

Just then, Helga's father came across the rocks toward them. "I'm sorry about the Saebrandur. She was a good vessel. I've seen her many a time at harbor in the old days, and she'd slip through the waves, light as a seal."

Dyrfinna patted the burned ship's rib again. "We were forced to leave her behind. We took everything we could up to the top of the hill and torched the rest so the enemy couldn't use it for themselves."

"A regrettable part of war," Helga's father said, squinting at the charred timbers.

"Indeed."

An awkward silence. Dyrfinna didn't look at him. After having all the commanders knife her in the back over Sinkr, she wasn't sure if he could be trusted.

"Listen," he said. "Helga told me about what happened on this island."

She thought of Hakr and how the old commander would have responded. Odin's *tears*, how she wished he were still alive. She pushed aside her distrust. "Your daughter's been through horrors, but her spirit never flagged. She's a true warrior."

"That goes for your crew as well – and to you."

Dyrfinna nodded, looking out over the ocean. "We rely on each other. We saved each other."

"We should have listened to you before rushing to judgment on Sinkr's word."

Now she turned to him. "Yes. You should have."

He actually had the decency to look embarrassed. "I accept responsibility for my actions. I want to make it up to you. My crew is small. I would be honored if your crew joined mine as we sail on to our next battle site, wherever that may be."

"Will Sinkr be on this ship with us?" she immediately asked.

He colored again. "Yes, unless he chooses to go elsewhere."

"Will Sinkr be the commander of this ship, then?"

He smiled. "No. I will be."

"Unless my papa decides to make him your commander, too."

Helga's father laughed. "He wouldn't do that to me."

Are you sure? Dyrfinna wanted to ask. Instead, she thought of Hakr and curbed her reply. "I appreciate your offer, but after that episode at the whipping post, I would prefer to not have him near me or my crew. I hope you understand. He shared no part of our privations. He did not see my people suffering and dying on that battlefield."

Now Gefjun broke in. "Sinkr was sitting at leisure in the enemy camp, eating and drinking and having his beard braided, while I was struggling to heal the wounded and stay the dying of many warriors who were far better people than he," she snapped. "He did no fighting, left no dead for the eagles to tear and the ravens to eat."

"He didn't fight draugrs the way that we had to," Skeggi added, wandering up with Rjupa.

"And he doesn't understand how bad this woman Nauma is," Rjupa said, her eyes suddenly glittering with unshed tears. "Begging your pardon, but I'm afraid that you and the other commanders don't understand the magnitude of the threat our home now faces because you allowed her to get away – and refused to allow us to pursue her to kill."

"You really shouldn't talk to me like that," he said.

"Sir, I am speaking to you now in the capacity of the Queen's dragonrider," Rjupa said. "And this goes for the rest of us." She swept her hand over Ostryg, Skeggi, Gefjun, and Dyrfinna, her arm lingering on her.

"She's not a dragonrider," Helga's father said.

"Yes, she is," Rjupa said. "She's part of us, the Corae Guard, Thora's personal guard. If Thora were still alive right now, you would not dare to say those words. I guarantee it. And even now that she's ... gone, that changes nothing between us. Dyrfinna's still one of us. We'll do everything we can to protect her."

Dyrfinna stood straighter, surrounded by her sword-friends.

"It doesn't matter what you or anybody else says," Rjupa continued. "Finna's still a dragonrider. Now, before we leave this island, I'm begging you to help us. If we can pursue Nauma and find her, we might be able to stop her before she reaches Skala. At the very least, we need to fly home and urge our people to defend themselves. But time is of the essence. It is imperative that we start as quickly as possible." Rjupa told Helga's father about what she'd seen, what Nauma was capable of against unarmed people.

And now Dyrfinna noticed Serja sitting on the cliff overhead, a gleaming garnet dragon, watching the whole scene.

Rjupa's right, Serja said. *You're still a dragonrider. And after everything that you've been through – after every sacrifice you made for your people – I need you at my side for the upcoming war.*

"The upcoming war?" Dyrfinna said, low.

Yes, Serja said. *The time is nigh. You heard what Nidhoggr said. And you are going to be one of our most important fighters.*

THUS ENDETH BOOK TWO.
LOOKETH THOU FOR BOOK THREE:
<u>A GLORY OF SPARKS</u>

A GLORY OF SPARKS WILL BE OUT IN 2023. YOU CAN preorder it anywhere EXCEPT for a certain gigantic book conglomerate, which I will not name here, that has monopolized the entire book industry. Sorry about that!

THE PRECARIOUS BOND BETWEEN A WARRIOR AND A dragon.

Dyrfinna and the rest of her Viking crew have been left reeling after a stunning defeat. But that night, she experiences a vision that shows her home village being burned, her little sister brutally killed. To get back there, she has to break her society's biggest taboo – uncollaring a bound dragon – and flee her own army in a doomed attempt to save the lives of the people she loves most of all.

Little does Dyrfinna know that this series of events that she's set in motion is going to lead to her banishment – and certain death.

A GLORY OF SPARKS, the third book of the Dragonriders of Skala series, is going to be a hell of a ride, I promise.

AUTHOR'S NOTE

Author's Note

January 2023 — I went to the 20Booksto50K conference in November, and I came back all pumped up and ready to do a lot of things to re-up my writing career. I started a side gig of editing books for LMBPN Publishing, which I've been learning a lot from. I started the new job at the local TV station. I was ready to jump to the next level, do a backflip, and then kick ass left and right.

But then, boom, the very next week my husband ended up in the hospital. December was all hospital stuff. I revised this story in various hospital rooms. Just when we thought we were out of the woods, we discovered we were not, and January has been filled with more hospital stuff.

There's an old story that my husband tells now and then about his great-grandparents, John and Sophie Schneider. Let's see if I can tell this right.

They were moving from Texas to open an implement company, but they had to choose whether to go to St. Louis or to Maryville. They deliberated for a while but couldn't decide, so finally they decided to flip a coin to choose.

Brad says that there's a moment when the coin's up in

the air, and all the choices there are suspended in that moment. But then the coin lands, and that choice is manifest, and your whole future crystalizes and branches out before you. It's that classic conundrum you see in every time-travel movie, where every choice you make is going to change your future -- but sometimes that coin is up in the air, and it's all up to chance, and you don't get to make that choice.

Sometimes you hit a point in your life and you're just watching that coin turning in the air, and you don't know how it's going to land.

Sometimes it's just a little choice you need to make, like do I want to make a waffle or a bowl of cereal. Sometimes that coin is in the air and you don't know if it's going to come down on life or on death, and it's out of your hands in that brief instant -- but that instant changes everything.

Just kind of an interesting concept that I've been thinking about in the last two months, and it might make for a good story at some point. We've been lucky so far, in those metaphorical coin flips. I just hope our luck lasts.

Anyway, we are in a better place now — a great relief. And my in-laws have come over to help clean up and organize the house, which went all to hell over the last year. They're awesome folks. I hope you have folks in your corner who are just as great.

Now that things are straightening up at last, I'm putting myself back on that track that I wanted to get on after the 20Booksto50K conference. I've finally finished my Indoor Gardening book that I had been working on for wayyyyy too long, and I'm starting on the next book in the Hungry Garden series, which is under my Rosefiend name.

But I'm also writing the outline for A GLORY OF SPARKS. I have a bunch of scenes already written for it, but after editing the LMBPN books, I'm adding in more of the tropes that fantasy readers love, while sticking to my unique vision and sense of humor and adventure. I hope you love it.

P.S. John and Sophie ended up going to Maryville on that coin flip, which I think was a solid choice all these years later.

All best,
Melinda R. Cordell
Nodaway, Mo.

ACKNOWLEDGMENTS

Every writer works from within a community, even if the writer happens to be a complete hermit who, at least inwardly, is quietly sidling away from any human contact whatsoever, if not galloping outright.

Big thanks to C. Dennis Moore, who got me into self-publishing in the first place, but who was also my accountability buddy for this novel and kept me writing when I was wandering off doing everything else BUT writing. If he hadn't showed up in my email back in 2016 and told me all about the fabulous world of self-publishing, I would be the most miserable gal in the world right now. But I'm happy as a lark. I no longer make myself miserable by sending queries out to agents and editors. Now I'm publishing my own damn books, and I have fans who are some seriously nice people. A total win!

Anyway, now we send our daily word counts back and forth, which is our accountability thing, and it's been extremely helpful for keeping me on task. Thanks a million, Dennis. If you like horror, go buy his books.

Hats off to Ky Bateman, for his excellent critiques and all his help on these stories. Check out his book here: My Book, and if you need some insanely thorough editing done, give him a holler at selfpubedlisheditor@gmail.com.

I had a contest to name Dyrfinna's sword, and my newsletter folks voted and chose Signe, which means Victory, as its name. Many thanks to Tina Lonergan, who came up with this name!

And of course Brad, Sophie, and Stevie. You guys are my entire world.

ABOUT THE AUTHOR

*This was me back in 1995 when I was just starting my writing career and I was a real writing hotshot.
To tell the truth, I still am.*

Melinda R. Cordell has written a truckload of YA novels, including the <u>Dragonriders of Fiorenza</u> series (like *Game of Thrones*, with Vikings).

A former city horticulturist and a long-time garden writer, Melinda has also written twelve books in <u>the Easy-Growing Gardening series</u> under the name Rosefiend Cordell.

Melinda lives in northwest Missouri with her husband and two kids, the best little family to walk the earth, and is writing about 24 books at once, fueled by passion and caffeine.

If you want to keep up with her, <u>subscribe to her newsletter</u>, to get YA dragon adventure called *A Whisper of Smoke*, set in Viking times. Or drop her a friendly note at <u>rosefiend@gmail.com</u>.

Follow her on <u>Patreon</u> to get a behind-the-scenes look at this author's world. See new book covers, read excerpts of upcoming stories before anybody else does, help her name characters, and superfans get to show up in her novels! Buy Melinda a cup of tea every month <u>here</u>.

Don't forget to leave a book review on your favorite retailer, or on BookBub or Goodreads!

Thanks for reading!

ALSO BY
MELINDA R. CORDELL

A FINISHED DRAGON SERIES

THE DRAGONRIDERS OF FIORENZA

Well, I am writing my way through this whole Skala series and trying to get this series finished in a timely fashion. Ha ha! As if I do anything in a timely fashion!

At any rate, while you're waiting for my next book (I *really* hope you're waiting for my next book), why not splurge on my completed six-book series about a young dragonrider in 1200s Florence, and her fiercely loyal dragon Ryelleth. They love each other with all their hearts and they are ready to set the world on fire to keep from begin separated.

The Dragonriders of Fiorenza series

Assassin's Blade

Dragon's Inferno

Guardian's Race

Witch's Plight

Warrior's Doom

Traitor's Oath